THINKS *out* LOUD A BLOG *at* FIRST

MARTIN PERLMAN

MARROW BOOKS

Portland, Oregon

LOYAL READERS,

This is a work of fiction. All of the characters, organizations, and events protrayed in this novel are either products of the author's imagination or are used fictitiously. Any resemblance to actual persons, living or dead, events, or locales is entirely coincidental.

www.marrowbooks.com
www.facebook.com/marrowbooks

Book design by Catherine Renee Dimalla

The Library of Congress has cataloged the Marrow Books edition as follows:

Perlman, Martin
Thinks Out Loud, a blog at first / Martin Perlman.—1st ed.
ISBN 978-0-9975039-0-6
2016906104

Marrow Books ISBN 978-0-9975039-0-6

Marrow Books titles may be purchased for educational, business, or promotional use. For information on bulk purchases, please contact Marrow Books Sales Department at sales@marrowbooks.com

First published in the United States by Marrow Books
Second Marrow Books Edition: 2017

Thinks Out Loud is more than it could have ever been thanks to the support and perceptive feedback of my wife, Lane, and my daughter, Lila. My editor Erik Fenner put the overweight manuscript on a diet to make it a leaner yet more muscular creation. Designer Renee Dimalla used her artistic prowess to convey the itness of the book in an inviting and captivating way.

As far as a dedication, this one's for Max, my late son, who inspired me in ways that go far beyond putting words on paper, with his love of life and ability to persevere in the face of major challenges.

Night Warrior

Entry No. 499 - POSTED JULY 18, 2011

In the heavy mist, Gwel sensed guarded movement. Holding his position behind a massive fir, he peered around the edge of the deeply etched bark to observe the approaching cloaked intruder, a dull metallic object held loosely in the gauntlet of his right hand. Wait, just wait, the defender cautioned himself. Shifting weight and pulling back, he tested the balance of his sword. Patience. Let him come to you. There! At the moment his foe's shadow crossed the tree's axis, Gwel howled, hurtled forward and

And? What the fuck?? The rest of my post just disappeared into the Ethernet! And of course this was the first time I didn't do a backup. Damn. Was going to be a great satire of fantasy/gothic with a nod to Rings, Potter, and every other classic in the genre I could think of. Well forget that.

Bear with me...I've got a fun surprise for tomorrow.

[During the interim, loyal followers, check out some earlier posts at Earlier Posts, although I'll probably lose some of you to your favorite artistic nudes site.]

-Isaac

LABELS: BLOGGING CHALLENGES, OOPS, BACK IT UP

VIEW COMMENTS (21)

2Spacer JULY 18, 2011 AT 8:22 AM
Time to move to the cloud?

HindSite JULY 18, 2011 AT 8:48 AM
Hemingway lost a suitcase filled with early short stories. Actually his wife left the suitcase unguarded at a train station.

Ringside JULY 18, 2011 AT 9:23 AM
Probably for the best that we'll never be able to read Isaac's lost posting.

SHOW MORE COMMENTS

HUMOR ME

Hey, look who reached magic 500!!!!

Entry No. 500 - POSTED JULY 19, 2011

LOYAL READERS,

Sorry about yesterday. My bad. Anyway, it's a special occasion for Thinks Out Loud! Who could have guessed 499 postings ago (5 years ago!), I would make it to this day? Little did I know when I started out with the original concept (Indo-European word roots in modern English—*gror, tark, ven*), this humble blog would evolve into a potent satirical take on current events, politics, and vitamin supplement recommendations. Or that I would have bunches of hits a day. [Note to self: Start limiting checking of analytics to twice a day.]

Remember Posting #227 where I'd gone off coffee cold turkey—goodbye lattes!—and all those misspellings, overuse of italics, and wrong application of the subjunctive—until I succumbed yet again to my caffeine habit?

Or what about that anonymous commentator back in the early 300s who suggested I quit and become a roofer? I think not! (And it's not because I'm afraid of slipping off a pitched A-frame.)

Or Phillipa who accused me of ripping off her blog, as if I'd ever heard of Engage! (Is it even still around?)

Then there was that unexpected threat of a lawsuit by a large technology firm whose name I can't mention per the settlement.

Ah, the memories, and the challenges, of writing words worth reading. Stamina helps. Plus having a good supply of refined carbs by your side. Lots of competing blogs have gone by the wayside, including MindGames, JustForFun and IslandHopping. (Why are people so fascinated by islands?) They tried, but they lacked what I call true Blogismo, an inner commitment to put blogging first and foremost on your to-do-list.

The question, naturally, is, what comes next? Fortunately, there are always celebrities going off course, politicians lost in their verbiage, and corporations pretending they're people.

Stay tuned.

–Isaac

LABELS: BLOG ACHIEVEMENTS, NEXT ADVENTURES, BRAGGING RIGHTS

VIEW COMMENTS (31)

Enabler JULY 19, 2011 AT 8:01 AM

I liked his early stuff. Funnier.

Gobbler JULY 19, 2011 AT 8:18 AM

Thinks Out Loud may have peaked. You can always check out my blog, Catching Up.

Etruscan JULY 19, 2011 AT 9:15 AM

That's a hell of a lot of blogging. When do you have time for anything else? On another note, is it necessary to devote so much of your blog to satirizing bold startups and dynamic high-tech firms (including their CEOs)? Aren't those the pinnacles of today's creativity, insight, and progress?

SHOW MORE COMMENTS

○ ○ ○ **THINKS OUT LOUD** ✕

HUMOR ME

Breaking News

Entry No. 501 - POSTED JULY 21, 2011

LOYAL READERS:

I can't help it. I've been addicted to science fiction since age 11, and my favorite movie is 2001: A Space Odyssey.

Shuttle changes course to Mars

The Shuttle Atlantis, due to land at Kennedy Space Center Thursday, 5:30 am EDT, is apparently on a new trajectory to Mars. In a series of unanticipated communications to Mission Control, Commander Chris Ferguson informed NASA he and his crew were extending the final shuttle mission "for the good of the country, our posterity, and the book rights."

"Let me explain," cut in Pilot Doug Hurley. "Houston, you may have noticed a deviation in our course at 0100 hours. We are about to begin a burn that will increase our speed to escape velocity."

"My turn!" exclaimed Mission Specialist Sandy Magnus. "Surprised? We began planning for this mission extension last year when we heard the shuttle program was being terminated. With the help of the ISS crew, we modified Atlantis by adding a 468 Big Block Chevy, 871 Blower with Electronic Fuel Injection."

"And some pinstriping detail during the last spacewalk," added Mission Specialist Rex Walheim. "The right front of the orbiter now reads *Mars or bust!*"

"Roger that," answered Mission Control. "However our computer simulation down here indicates you won't make it much beyond the Moon. You don't have enough fuel, enough supplies."

"Negative, Houston," answered Ferguson. "We fueled up at the space station. Plus we've got a 3D printer! We're good to go."

Alerted to the situation, President Obama told Mission Control "to offer them medals, lots of medals," if the wayward astronauts would return to Earth.

"Looks like they've got the right stuff," said Neil Armstrong, barely able to contain a giggle.

LABELS: LAST SHUTTLE MISSION, GOODBYE SHUTTLE ATLANTIS, SPACE SHUTTLE DISCOVERY LANDS IN WASHINGTON DC

VIEW COMMENTS (28)

Anonymous JULY 21, 2011 AT 11:50 AM
If that's the case, what did we see landing at the Kennedy Space Center today? Believe me, I do not trust anything the government is involved with, because every word that comes out of the white house are lies....

JustSayin JULY 21, 2011 AT 12:10 PM
Huh?

tallboy JULY 21, 2011 AT 2:00 PM
Heard a report that a stolen shuttle took the royal newlyweds William and Kate up to the International Space Station. Two upset furloughed NASA engineers hid inside the shuttle's EVA spacesuits and bided their time until the crew's focus was on deciding which board game to play before retiring for the periodic sleep cycle. Once in control, the hijackers coasted back to Earth, dropped off the crew, picked up the royal couple, and extended their stateside tour into space.

Said the prince in a garbled broadcast, "We are in a zero gravity environment. We fully understand the challenge of bowing and curtsying under such conditions."

"Jolly good!" reportedly exclaimed William's father, Prince Charles.

"We are not amused," admonished William's grandmother, Queen Elizabeth. "Come back to Earth at once."

SHOW MORE COMMENTS

Caution

Entry No. 502 - POSTED JULY 22, 2011

LOYAL READERS,

I asked them, the brothers, if they would send a message back one last time for a first time. I had to cajole and wheedle and offer a box of the finest dark chocolates (with absolutely no hard candy shell), and finally they agreed to one last/first time.

This gives me the chance to speak to you directly and to offer not exactly a warning but at least a cautionary note as you venture deeper into this blog: Keep all your senses on alert, maintain a healthy skepticism mixed with a touch of faith, and be willing to open your mind and your heart to what may seem like unrealities beyond our "normal" world.

That's more than enough for now, or as Teva would say, "The fish do not wait."

Back to business.

Sorry for the delay in putting out a new posting this week. I had a project due, updating web bios for trapeze instructors at a "new circus arts" school, and, as you know, my freelance work actually pays as opposed to a labor-of-love blog.

Today's post takes a poke at an admittedly easy target. Maybe I'm just getting lazy. Even did some thematic borrowing from that recent Tallboy royal couple riff. Not bad, Tallboy.

The Other British Royal Couple Tours the States (SEATTLE TIMES HEADLINE, SUNDAY, JULY 10, 2011)

William and Kate Visit California: From Polo Match to Celebs to Skid Row

Lesterville, WY—Prince William and his new wife, Kate, may have wowed the gentry at the Santa Barbara Polo and Racket Club, toasted the town with Hollywood's own royalty, and made a statement that "they care" by watching a dance group in the Skid Row section of LA, but another British royal couple is experiencing a different kind of reception as they tour the United States during their first weeks of marriage.

Geoffrey Bainbridge and his new wife, Vicky Mainard, formerly of Las Vegas, NV, are traveling the States in somewhat different fashion from the Prince William contingent. Bainbridge, a second cousin twice removed from William, is listed as being 22nd in line to inherit the British Crown.

Highlights of the Bainbridge excursion have included enjoying an all-you-can-eat buffet in Pittsburgh, crashing a bowling tournament in Toledo ("I got three strikes in a row," exclaimed Vicky, a one-time cocktail waitress), and touring a meat packing plant in Omaha. ("Very efficient operation," said the Duke, who works in a London haberdashery.)

This other royal couple is now headed to California. ("Disneyland, that's a must," said the Duchess. "I want my husband to see the real America.") Needless to say Mickey and Minnie will not be inclined to bow or curtsy when Geoffrey and Vicky are standing in line at the ticket booth.

LABELS: DUKE AND DUCHESS OF CAMBRIDGE, PRINCE WILLIAM AND KATE, ROYAL U.S. TOUR, ART OF HABERDASHERY

VIEW COMMENTS (30)

Enabler JULY 22, 2011 AT 9:31 AM
Send a message back one last time for first time? I don't get it.

tallboy JULY 22, 2011 AT 10:51 AM
Isaac, it's 'tallboy.' No cap.

Sleeper JULY 22, 2011 AT 11:21 AM
Americans seems more impressed by royalty than the English. (Didn't we have a Revolution to make a break from all that?)

SHOW MORE COMMENTS

Excuses Excuses

Entry No. 503 - POSTED JULY 24, 2011

LOYAL READERS,

This one was supposed to come out yesterday, but my computer's battery died and didn't want to recharge. I did this posting from my local public library. (A bedrock of our society.) For that matter, do you folks have any idea what it takes to blog on a regular basis? of the personal sacrifices bloggers make to keep the posts coming? of the pressure to produce?

Okay, I'm taking a deep breath, focusing on a memory of a warm beach, lifting my eyes from the computer screen to gaze toward the library's paneled walls near the non-fiction section. Apparently, I shouted a moment ago, and a reference librarian (they still have them) came over and asked if I were all right. I tried to smile politely and said, "Sorry."

All better. Here's the posting: An offer you shouldn't resist.

–Isaac

CloudCover Computer Storage

Welcome to CloudCover™, the latest way to store your computer content—no more cranky hard drives, no more frustrating "sorry full" popups on your screen. CloudCover gives you convenience, flexibility, and a godlike feeling of omnipotence.

We offer only the finest vapor storage units. All clouds are pretested using a rigorous 10-point quality control system. No fog, no mist, only pure fluffy clouds are selected by our experienced Cloudies.

CloudCover is designed to fit your budgetary considerations and storage needs: Choose from Basic Cumulus, Extended Nimbo-stratus, and Premium Cirrus.

For those of you with concerns about cloud dissipation, relax. Our CloudCover Remain™ technology guarantees the cloud for your storage will stay puffy and intact for years to come.

What are you waiting for? It's time to take to the clouds.
(Offer not available in the high desert.)

VIEW COMMENTS (29)

Anonymous JULY 24, 2011 AT 10:30 AM

Is this supposed to be joke or have they really learned how to store information in water particles, cause maybe with hydrogen you could link data in the form of electrons?

EscapeGoat JULY 24, 2011 AT 11:11 AM

It's not as far-fetched as it seems. There are alarm clocks that are powered by the ions in water. Just think about how our brains store info.

HindSite JULY 24, 2011 AT 12:32 PM

Is there a start up? Where do I invest?

SHOW MORE COMMENTS

○ ○ ○   **THINKS OUT LOUD**   ✕

HUMOR ME

Yoga Plus

Entry No. 504 - POSTED JULY 26, 2011

LOYAL READERS,

Feeling a little off my game. A stomach virus? I was actually required to do some research for this one. I also discovered most yoga teachers don't share my sense of humor. Take a deep breath and hold it, you guys.
–Isaac

> Forget Ashtanga (power), Anusara (spiritual) or Bikram (hot) styles of yoga. The latest version is Upakarana (machine) in which traditional poses based on animal and other nature forms are replaced by elements of modern technology.
>
> Popular positions include khanitra (back-hoe), yantra (turbine), and marutnaukaa (space shuttle).
>
> "What I find satisfying about these poses," says Upakarana instructor Aspen Leaf, "is that while we live in a modern, technological age, these positions humanize the mechanical objects we now depend upon. We also hope these positions might be more appealing to potential male students. Oops, have I fallen into a gender stereotype pose?"

VIEW COMMENTS (24)

Anonymous JULY 26, 2011 AT 11:21 AM

Oofasana!

Krishnaman JULY 26, 2011 AT 12:20 PM

Hey, funny boy, I do yoga on a regular basis and it keeps me calm and centered! So back off.

VincentFrederick JULY 26, 2011 AT 2:30 PM

Is it just me or are TOL's followers getting grouchy? Maybe cause the economy is rebounding so slowly. Or perhaps due to the drought gripping a large part of the country. Could be something they ate.

SHOW MORE COMMENTS

○ ○ ○   **THINKS OUT LOUD**   X

HUMORE ME

Lost Hippy Commune Discovered

Entry No. 505 - POSTED: JULY 28, 2011

LOYAL READERS,

Is this posting really so far-fetched? Aren't tribal peoples who've had no contact with modern civilization discovered from time to time? Could I really make up something like this? (Plus a shout out to the Santa Barbara Review where I had my first news internship.)

–Isaac

Santa Barbara County, California

Deep in the canyons of the Santa Ynez Mountains behind Santa Barbara, California, a counterculture commune has been found that has had no contact with the rest of the world since the group's founding in 1969.

The alternative lifestyle group, Sun Days, has lived totally outside the bounds of civilization for more than 45 years. Their tilled fields, domesticated animals and simple dwellings were discovered when an AT&T cell tower installation team came across the commune during what turned out to be a mid-summer greening festival.

"As far as we can determine, this was one of the last social groups on the planet that had no knowledge of modern technology: smart phones, tablet computers, reality TV," said Yi Chan, a doctoral student in cultural anthropology at the University of California, Santa Barbara.

"Their way of life is similar to that of what once were called pre-literate tribal societies, which are extremely rare in these days of the post-modern social media environment," noted Chan.

Numbering 45 adults and 17 children, the Sun Days commune members were initially wary of any interaction with outsiders ("Layin' a bad trip on us," was the phrase used). The elders met and decided the commune should remain, as it has always been, an alternative to the "greedy capitalistic pig plastic world." A Be Here Wow celebration was declared to purify the group. However, on the second afternoon, two of the ten-year-olds were caught texting with a phone the tower installers had accidentally left behind.

LABELS: PRE-LITERATE CULTURES, COMMUNES, LAST OF THE HIPPIES

VIEW COMMENTS (23)

MasterMind JULY 28, 2011 AT 8:37 AM

I, for one, see certain advantages in being pre-literate and free from the modern, fragmented world we inhabit.

WayOut JULY 28, 2011 AT 9:32 AM

I googled Sun Days and they came up. Looks like they have a line of hand-knitted scarves and hats made from yarn from their own sheep.

DiJester JULY 28, 2011 AT 11:54 AM

Thinks Out Loud is becoming formulaic. Take this attempt to get some laughs out of a forced faux news report.

SHOW MORE COMMENTS

○ ○ ○   **THINKS OUT LOUD**   ✕

HUMOR ME

Newest Facebook Settings Options

Entry No. 506 - POSTED: JULY 31, 2011

Formulaic? So you think I'm getting too predictable? Hold on a second, I don't have to give excuses. And you don't have to read my posts! (Which is a road more and more of you seem to be taking.)

Loyal Readers, I apologize. Don't seem to be myself lately. Have some non-blog matters vying for my attention. Bills upon bills. I think my bank account has been compromised. Sprained my finger trying to open a pickle jar. Car needs a new radiator, and an alignment. She said no to a second date. And I've been wondering about my relationship to blogging.

(Is that a heretical thought?) I do well enough in the satire vein, but is there something more, an alternative approach, another way?

Wait, don't go. Hey, no big deal. Here, read this…
–Isaac

A Warning

For a hoot, scroll to the bottom of your FB page where it says in little blue letters, "Do not, REPEAT, do not go here." Click on it anyway. A page shows up that says "Warning, do NOT go any further!" Ignore the text and press the small green button on bottom right. A final page comes up with the words, "Too late, sorry." You'll discover your home page has been permanently translated into binary code. What fu01101110 00100000 01110100 01101000 01100001 01110100 00100000 01110111 01101001 01101100 01101100 00100000 01100010 01100101 00101110

* * *

Three new relationship categories:
F+   "Friends who owe me money"
F-   "Friends I owe money to" (not used much), and
X--   "Ex-spouses living within 300 miles"
* * *

Do any of us really know what others think of us?

Here's how to find out. Go to the HyperSettings page, select the Ostensible Compliments button and voilà the seemingly nice things people have been posting about you ("like") will be translated into what your "friends" are really thinking ("boring!"). Caution: This setting is not for the thin-skinned.

LABELS: FACEBOOK TIPS, FACEBOOK SETTINGS, GEEK HUMOR

VIEW COMMENTS (17)

Aladden JULY 31, 2011 AT 10:01 AM
01010011 01101000 01101001 01110100 00101100 00100000 01001001 00100000 01110000 01110010 01100101 01110011 01110011 01100101 01100100 00100000 01110100 01101000 01100001 01110100 00100000 01100111 01110010 01100101 01100101 01101110 00100000 01100010 01110101 01110100 01110100 01101111 01101110 00101110

tallboy JULY 31, 2011 AT 10:18 AM
How 'bout this? The latest competitor to emerge in the social media world is AboutFaceBook. Designed for the artist/introvert, the cowboy out on the range, and those who are so frustrated with the latest FB changes, they can't stand it anymore.

At AboutFaceBook, there are no actual postings, no way to friend anyone (except in person). Even the web address is kept under wraps. "Brilliant," writes A-One, a blogger for DoReMedia.com, "I tried to sign up but couldn't!"

Explica JULY 31, 2011 AT 12:44 PM

Isaac, you weren't funny at all during our marriage. Is someone ghostwriting your material?

SHOW MORE COMMENTS

○ ○ ○   **THINKS OUT LOUD**   ✕

HUMOR ME

Latest Harry Potter Products

Entry No. 507 - POSTED: AUG. 2, 2011

Feeling an intense personal and professional pressure to produce. Stayed up too late last night catching up on Mad Men, season 2. (They sure make the early '60s seem like a distant dream. Oh, they are a distant dream—when everyone smoked at every opportunity and drank before breakfast. Have the Puritans won?) Now: Staring with tired eyes at a blank screen: the writer's nightmare. Too soon (two days) to satirize Facebook again. When drawing a blank, turn to the tried and true and make fun of Potter. Harry Potter. (Did you know there are websites dedicated to Potterdom that claim the series is non-fiction? That beings with special powers actually exist? They make astrology believers look like amateurs.) Back to Harry.

–Isaac

1. Hogwarts Blend Gourmet Coffee
Conjured to order in Hogwart's state-of-the-art roasting dungeon. Fair trade, shade grown, curse-free beans. Choose from sporty Quidditch Blend, medium Gryffindor Roast, and Bellatrix Bold. Sourced from dragon-patrolled coffee fields.

2. Hermione Body Potion-Lotion
Hermione's gentle moisturizing body potion contains Chinese Chomping Cabbage, Mandrake Root, and Horn of Dragon. Leaves your skin feeling soft and clean without that soulless Dementor-dry look. No muggles harmed (very much) during testing.

3. Lucius Malfoy Dark Arts Chocolates
Devilishly rich and sinfully delicious, these handcrafted sweets are

to die for. 72% cocoa with cranberries and eye of newt. Give in to temptation: There is no defense against dark arts chocolates. Just ask chocolatier, Tom Riddle.

4. Harry Potter Potty Paper

A roll of papier de toilette featuring the mugs of Harry or his comrades-in-magic on every sheet. Two-ply bathroom tissue made of 100% recycled parchment. Come up with the right spell and the roll never runs out!

Owlmail orders 24 hours a day. Overpriced but worth it.

LABELS: HARRY POTTER COLLECTIBLES, THE DEATHLY HALLOWS PART 2, THE DARK MERCHANDISING ARTS

VIEW COMMENTS (14)

DiJester AUG. 2, 2011 AT 11:32 AM

See formulaic. Pick something easy to satirize (Pottermania), combine with another easy target, i.e. catalogs, throw in some recognizable references to the said target, and presto, you have a posting. I rest my case.

Jeannie AUG. 2, 2011 AT 1:10 PM

All artists have their highs and lows. Maybe TOL is in a lull right now. At least he's trying. I say give bloggers the space to fail. Gotta go! Late for a flash mob at Westlake Center.

Anonymous AUG. 2, 2011 AT 2:01 PM

Hey, Isaac, don't mess with Potter.

SHOW MORE COMMENTS

○ ○ ○   **THINKS OUT LOUD**   ✕

HUMOR ME

To réks éh₁est

Entry No. 508 - POSTED: AUG. 4, 2011

RESTLESS READERS,

Listen: Not once upon a time, but some 6,000 years ago, the peoples of the steppeland of what would someday be called Eastern Europe spoke a language that would become the original common core of English, German, the Romance Languages, Russian, and even Punjabi and Urdu. It took several hundred years for linguists to figure out that all these languages sprang from this one proto-language. That's why today, you can order soup (seu-⁴, TO TAKE LIQUID), salad (sal-¹, SALT), and meat (mad-,

QUALITY OF FOOD). Yes, your order would be quite different if Proto-Indo-European hadn't been around, "on round," (ret-, TO RUN, ROLL).

Why do I care about this, you ask? Well, in our post-modernist age where words basically mean whatever you want them to mean, where ideas float around lacking any tether to reality, these roots of our languages point to a common connection, an original seed that grew and developed over centuries into the flowers of the languages we use today.

Long live Proto-Indo-European!

But that's not what I want to blog about today.

For kicks, I took the Human Evaluation Quiz, the one going around the Internet that supposedly grades you on your contributions to humanity. So I took it. And. I. Got. A. 7. Out of a possible 100. (Almost a negative score.) I was shocked. I mean, I'm not bully, car jacker, or embezzler. But if you want to get a better score, you have to have brought some sunlight into the world in some way. Apparently I haven't. According to the scoring, I'm "more a hindrance to, rather than a source for, improving life on the planet."

LABELS: PREHISTORIC LANGUAGES, ABLAUT, ZERO-GRADE, DIATRIBES, WORTHLESS QUIZZES

VIEW COMMENTS (97)

Slice AUG. 4, 2011 AT 9:01 AM

You must have done something good along the way? Any door-to-door political canvassing? Volunteering at a food bank kitchen? Taken in a lost puppy?

Carrotty AUG. 4, 2011 AT 9:32 AM

Actually, he sounds lost. And off on a tangent in the form of that Indo-European lecture.

DaggerOtype AUG. 4, 2011 AT 9:54 AM

Not much humor any more on this so-called humor blog.

Jeannie AUG. 4, 2011 AT 10:28 AM

I, for one, enjoy reading about our glorious Indo-European past. Did you know IE's word for man was wiros meaning VIRILE? It's fascinating! (To réks éh₁est means "There once was a king.")

SHOW MORE COMMENTS

Break Time

Entry No. 509 - POSTED: AUG. 6, 2011

LOYAL READERS,

Not sure what bled out of me yesterday. But it's given me pause. There have been something like 97 comments on yesterday's post, the majority of them wondering about my psychological state.

Listen, blogging can be taxing! It's like climbing a mountain yet never reaching the peak. These past couple of months, I tried to be upbeat and can do. It was cool to hit #500. Still, I feel like I need a major retooling. Some time off to re-charge the batteries.

That's why today I am announcing my taking of a sabbatical to pursue non-electronic forms of entertainment, relaxation, and procrastination. And discovery, both inner and outer. Truth be told, I need to figure out why page views have plateaued and are now beginning to decline. Not to mention most of my visitors seem to be from unincorporated towns in the Texas hill country, escort service sites and former republics of the Soviet Union.

Have I in some way leveled off in my own life as I approach the Big 4-0? In a larger sense, if I were to really stop blogging, what would become of me? And what about that dopamine hit I get every time someone likes one of my postings?

On a more immediate front, to keep the pages fresh, a bevy of Guest Blogger Interns who've shown some promise in the comments section have signed on to keep you in the know. I've subleased the studio apartment, the one on the western slope of Queen Anne Hill with the sweeping views of Magnolia and a cut of the Sound, to a post-doc physics student from China, sold my comic book collection for a tidy profit, and drew down my meager savings.

Stay tuned.

–Isaac

Thinks Out Loud *is not responsible for the views, language, or staleness of Guest Blogger remarks. All Guest Blogger entries are the sole responsibility* *of said blogger and do not necessarily reflect the views, opinions or wishful thinking of* **Thinks Out Loud.**

VIEW COMMENTS (41)

Anonymous AUG. 6, 2011 AT 9:07 AM

Good luck, man.

Closer AUG. 6, 2011 AT 9:22 AM

Quitter.

DiJester AUG. 6, 2011 AT 10:12 AM

My theory? Isaac thought he'd break through and make it big as a blogger. No such luck.

Blue Baby AUG. 6, 2011 AT 10:37 AM

While I enjoy Isaac's postings (except when he satirizes Harry Potter), I support his decision to deplug. Wish I had the willpower to power down.

Adventuress AUG. 6, 2011 AT 11:10 AM

Question: Is Isaac showing an ounce of courage here or taking the coward's way out? Or both?

SHOW MORE COMMENTS

○ ○ ○   **THINKS OUT LOUD**   ✕

HUMOR ME

Jeannie's guest blog!

Entry No. 510 - POSTED: AUG. 8, 2011

Willkommen, bienvenue, aloha!

Hi, I'm Jeannie, the first guest blogger (I'm honored!) to sub for Thinks Out Loud, one of my favorite blogs that I've just recently started reading. I came upon Thinks Out Loud by mistake 'cause I was actually trying to find another blog, Thinks Outside the Box, but auto correct diverted me to TOL. From what I can determine, based on my take of his earlier postings, we share an interest in Thai cuisine, sunset kite flying and, yes, Indo-European root words. "To réḱs éh₁est." Anyway, this is so exciting, I can't contain myself. I mean this posting is going up on the Internet where it can be read by people all over the world and beyond. Words that will last forever (or as long as there is a web or its successors—what will they be?).

Last I heard, Isaac was en route to *an Indo-European Roots Seminar*

(*Advanced*) *at the renowned Krenskvi Institute in the Ukraine.* Wish I could be there!

But I'm not, so I'll just have to content myself with doing this posting.

Now, what should I write about? Me? Grew up in a small town that was outside Atlanta until Atlanta kept expanding and took it over. (Ever see the move, *The Blob?* A young Steve McQueen is in it.) Goodbye pastures and farmland. Hello indoor malls, chain restaurants, and oversized houses on small lots. Got my BA in Film Studies with a minor in Linguistics. I could do a meta-analysis of animal imagery in Bergman's oeuvre.

Maybe later.

I can see the challenge bloggers have each time they begin typing. Catching up on fantasy books I've read? (Maybe) Politics? (Scary) Commentary on modern times? (Yawn) Fashion? (Tempting, if I apply a dialectical approach.)

I notice the tagline for Thinks Out Loud is "Humor Me." Does that mean I have to be funny? I don't like forced humor. Funny is best when spontaneous.

Hmmm. I think I have a good sense of humor, but I don't know if I can be funny on command. I could do jokes. I like word-play jokes, but I forget them as soon as someone tells them to me. Let's see if something funny happened to me yesterday…got up, went to work at the non-profit [Shout out to HighHopes], had lunch with my office mates at a food truck, the taqueria one. Hey, that's pretty new—food trucks—What could be funny about food trucks? Where would be a new, good place to locate a food truck?

[Jeannie, your time is up.]

What? I was just getting started.

[Sorry. Time to hit "Publish Post."]

Awe gee and I was having a really good time!

[Hit "Publish," Jeannie.]

Oh, all right. Here goes. Thanks for letting me expre___

JustPlainHank AUG. 8, 2011 AT 11:32AM

Is this for real or is Isaac pretending to be Jeannie? It can't be real.

WatchYourBack AUG. 8, 2011 AT 1:50 PM

Jeannie must be real. You couldn't make her up.

Anonymous AUG. 8, 2011 AT 3:07 PM

You could make her up, but it would be better to spend your time doing something constructive, like making fresh pasta.

SHOW MORE COMMENTS

○ ○ ○   **THINKS OUT LOUD**   ✕

HUMOR ME

Guest blogger: My turn!

Entry No. 511 - POSTED: AUG. 10, 2011

I'm tallboy, your other new guest blogger. Seattle born and bred. Before I get going, I just wanted to offer yesterday's blogger, Jeannie, some advice: Don't quit your day job at the nonprofit! (Either she was writing the most subtle blog satire I've ever come across, or she's totally unsuited for the blogosphere. I think she broke just about every blogging rule. On behalf of all real bloggers, I apologize for her ineptitude.)

According to what I've heard, Isaac is actually *on a walking tour of the watering holes of the Duchy of Grand Fenwick, but I can't confirm that because he has taken a kind of vow not to use modern means of communication to stay in touch with us. Hey, he could at least send us a postcard.*

Now for some bonafide blogging...

Deciding to stick with hosting The Apprentice rather than running for president in the 2012 election, Donald Trump is still running after the president to bite his trousers.

Trump is now demanding to see Obama's third-grade transcript, the president's dental records, and a full listing of his iTunes downloads. ("I'll bet there isn't a country and western song among them.")

"Does he have something to hide?" questions Trump. "Do I hide anything, except parts of my upper forehead?"

Additionally, Trump is curious to know Obama's favorite color, how many sugar cubes he takes in his tea, and his favorite Seinfeld episode.

"It's time," says the real-estate-developer-turned-reality-TV-host, "for Obama to come clean and stop seeking safety behind that so-called presidential podium. The ball is in his court."

The president could not be reached for comment. An aide said Obama was downloading and enjoying new iTunes from "a variety of musical genres and styles."

(See, Jeannie. That's real blogging!)

LABELS: GUEST BLOGGER, POLITICAL SATIRE, OBAMA'S BIRTH CERTIFICATE BREW HA HA

VIEW COMMENTS (22)

RepoMan AUG. 10, 2011 AT 10:28AM
Better than Jeannie. More bite. (Hah!) And actually, it's 'brouhaha.'

EveningMist AUG. 10, 2011 AT 2:43 PM
Give 'em both a chance. Do wonder what Isaac is really up to.

JoeCurr AUG. 10, 2011 AT 3:22 PM
I was going to be a blogger, but I had to keep post-poning it.

SHOW MORE COMMENTS

○ ○ ○   **THINKS OUT LOUD**   ✕

HUMOR ME

Look, I'm Blogging!

Entry No. 512 - POSTED: AUG. 13, 2011

Admittedly, I'm still getting used to this blogging game. It's a great time-filler instead of looking for work. Could never have predicted at age 19 that I, deep into 29, would be so lost. Or am I exploring options? Okay, here's today's posting. Tell me if it's too corny. Or not corny enough.

–tallboy

Goodbye, Gutenberg

May 23, 2018 —"It's the end of the printed book as we have known it," said a teary-eyed Janet Bernstein, editor in chief of Random Dutton Norton and Knopf. The last hard copy book, titled Men

Are Actually From the Asteroid Belt, had just rolled off what the publisher's staff affectionately calls the assembly line. A half dozen solemn employees had gathered round the bound volume.

Unfortunately the world's last book was marred by an error, a section of out-of-order pages apparently the result of the quality control staffer texting rather than paying attention. "I'd fire him," said Bernstein with a smile conveying irony, "but he's getting laid off this afternoon anyway." A sharp-eyed reporter noticed a KindleExtreme peaking out of Bernstein's purse. "Oh, that," she said sheepishly. "If you can't beat 'em, you know the rest."

LABELS: ELECTRONIC BOOKS TRIUMPH, LAST OF ITS KIND, GALLEY HUMOR

VIEW COMMENTS (31)

Anonymous AUG. 13, 2011 AT 10:58 AM
It's corny enough. A good B effort.

TS AUG. 13, 2011 AT 1:34 PM
I feel so guilty about the end of physical books because I haven't bought one in three years. It's my fault isn't it?

Aladden AUG. 13, 2011 AT 1:52 PM
Someone probably said the same thing when scrolls replaced stone tablets. And, hey, now we're back to Tablets!

SHOW MORE COMMENTS

○ ○ ○   **THINKS OUT LOUD**   ✕

HUMOR ME

Jeannie's guest blog, redux

Entry No. 513 - POSTED: AUG. 16, 2011

Hello, again, Fair Readers! (Or is it Fare or Faire?)

I'm back. Rumor has it Isaac is *really bicycling on a Western China stretch of the Silk Road.* Wish he'd check in with us.

Before today's post, let me take care of a little business.

Tallboy, thanks for the critique. Coming from someone so obviously experienced in the art of communicating, your words were filled with wisdom and keen insight into human nature. If we all just followed your helpful advice, the world would be a much better place. Oh, and I happen to like my day job at HighHopes where we're helping people in need to explore their options. (Need some help in this area? Sorry, we're booked up for the next two months!)

By the way, I don't know what your day job is, oh, you don't have one— but you might consider adding a night time position as a stand up comic specializing in arcane references to classical culture. I'm sure you'd be a big hit with the Cambridge and Harvard crowds. Just keep your nas out of my werǵ.

Now then, back to the posting.

[Thank you, Jeannie.]

Oh come on. Not again! I was just getting started.

[You had your chance. You are done for today.]

It was just a little throat clearing.

[You might want to go directly to your posting message next time, without the asides.]

Not fair. Not fu___

LABELS: ART OF BLOGGING, GUEST BLOGGER, BLOGGING MISSTEPS

VIEW COMMENTS (39)

JustPlainHank AUG. 16, 2011 AT 9:30AM
Isaac is having fun with us, I hope.

WatchYourBack AUG. 16, 2011 AT 11:01 AM
I'm sticking with my theory: she is too lame not to be real.

DaggerOtype AUG. 16, 2011 AT 1:23 PM
Who's the site's Moderator?

SHOW MORE COMMENTS

○ ○ ○   THINKS OUT LOUD   ✕
HUMOR ME

Entry No. 514 - POSTED: AUG 18, 2011

Hey, Jeannie, it's tallboy. No cap. Like e.e. cummings. Got the knickname when I grew six inches in three months when I was 16. Just grew. Didn't gain a pound. (I did a lot of pushups in college and managed to add some heft by late junior year.)

Still no official word from Isaac. He had mentioned something about looking for anti-oxidant rich plants on Bora Bora.

Now, I don't want readers to think I'm into dolls (well, what if I were?), but I can't pass up Barbie's 52nd anniversary!

Newest Barbie(s) and Ken(s)

To commemorate Barbie and Ken's life after 50 (the new 45), Mattel is introducing an overdue, updated line. "With Barbie and Ken together again after a mutually agreed upon seven-year separation, we thought we could do both some back story as well as bring them up to and beyond their chronological ages," said Mike Urstein, Director of Doll Enhancement and Accessorizing.

Urstein ticked off the re-branded versions of these classic characters:

Mama Grizzly Barbie - "It's a natural evolution of the line. Some critics who've seen a pre-release version of the pregnant Barbie have complained that her 'with child' proportions are totally unrealistic if she were to be blown up to true human size. We've been through this before with Barbie's, um, rack. Chill! She's a doll, for God's sake! And, yes, the dad is Ken."

Offspring - "Lots of room to expand here. We're starting off with Ella and Max, but we can easily nurture the line if there's the demand. And we think the kidlinks are going to be a big, big dynamic."

Cubicle Ken - "Let's not forget the Man. He's Mr. IT these days. There's even room for a surfboard, less often used, alas, over in the cubicle's corner."

CEO Barbie - "It's high time to get Barbie into the Boardroom. She can fend off a hostile takeover like the best of them. And watch her negotiate for increased stock options."

Downsized Ken - "A tough decision, but we want to reflect, to some degree, the challenges real people are facing these days. He'll bounce back, I promise you."

Urstein emphasized these latest iterations of Barbie and Ken, while breaking new ground, are still true to the basic Barbie (and Ken) philosophy. "I can't quite express it in words," said Urstein as he began to choke up. "These dolls mean more to me than my own family. Um, that's off the record, okay?"

LABELS: 50TH ANNIVERSARIY BARBIE, BARBIE MAKEOVER, DROLL DOLL HUMOR, WHAT ABOUT KEN?

VIEW COMMENTS (33)

Aladden AUG. 18, 2011 AT 9:58 AM

What about Retirement Community Barbie and Ken? Barbie tells Ken he should no longer drive and takes away his keys. Ken tries to watch TV on his microwave. Ken pours his Ensure down the drain.

Anonymous AUG. 18, 2011 AT 11:38 AM

Is nothing sacred?

SHOW MORE COMMENTS

○ ○ ○   THINKS OUT LOUD   ✕

HUMOR ME

Jeannie's guest blog; third time's the charm

Entry No. 515 - POSTED: AUG. 20, 2011

Isaac, was that you? Are you the one who keeps cutting me off? Show yourself! Look, I have as much right as the next blogger to express myself.

Grrrrrowl.

I'll bet you are not anywhere! You're probably still in Seattle or maybe holding out at a llama farm on Vashon Island. Well, I'm typing this from a Starbucks right in Belltown. Why don't we have a little showdown, just you and me?

I thought so. No reaction. Coward.

You remind me of this bully I had in fourth grade. After a while I couldn't take it anymore, so at recess I punched him in the stomach. He let out a huge whoosh of air and stared at me, wide-eyed, but I held my ground. Didn't bother me after that. Actually became a friend. Haven't seen him since high school. He's not on Facebook. Phil, if you are reading this: A big shout out!

[Jeannie, say goodbye.]

Oh, no, you're not getting rid of me that easily. I got a friend to add a firewall. I'm safe. See I'm still typing.

[Jeannie, you just do not get it.]

No, you don't get it! I have rights! Freedom of expression. Are you doing to this to me 'cause I'm female?

[Your internship is hereby terminated.]

You can't terminate me! I'm terminating you. You can take your blog and sh

---

LABELS: GEEK HUMOR, BLOGGING, CHOKE POINTS, CLUELESS

VIEW COMMENTS (38)

Anonymous AUG. 20, 2011 AT 9:24 AM
Wow! Very theatrical.

PrimeMary AUG. 20, 2011 AT 10:57 AM
Does somebody have an anger-management problem?

Explica AUG. 20, 2011 AT 12:04 PM
I dunno, I kind of enjoy her rants. There's power in her voice.

SHOW MORE COMMENTS

○ ○ ○   **THINKS OUT LOUD**   ✕

HUMOR ME

Got...blogger?

Entry No. 516 - POSTED: AUG. 23, 2011

GOT WHAT IT TAKES TO BE A BLOGGER?

Whew, I don't want to get in the middle of the Jeannie firing thing, although her situation did get me thinking about the art and science of blogging.

Blogging is not for everyone, especially someone we all know.

To help determine if you have the mental and physical constitution to be a blogger, here's a revealing questionnaire based on a draft of Isaac's I found in his Thinks Out Loud working file. (See, Isaac, I am giving you credit where credit is due.)

Choose the answer for each question closest to your personal version of the Truth. (Remember, cheaters never win, though they do sometimes come in second.)

–tallboy

I like to blog because
1. Why is this even a question? Blogging simply Is.
2. I think I have something to say.
3. I got laid off from The Daily and this is my only outlet for investigative reporting and the detailing of public health warnings.

Readers of my blog
1. Are important, no vital, to me, my raison d'être.
2. Are certainly welcome to visit. We're all in this together. I love comments, even weird ones.
3. Consist of my second cousin in Spokane, my roommate, and an adolescent hacker from somewhere in the Midwest.

My level of blogging activity:
1. Every couple of minutes, pretty much nonstop, alternating with Twitter.
2. Two or three times a week or as the muse moves me.
3. I most recently posted during Obama's first year in office.

When someone flames one of my postings
1. It runs right off my back like Evian.
2. I try and understand the flamer's point of view.
3. It hurts, it really hurts.

Scoring
For every 1 you answered give yourself 3 points.
Every 2 gets you 2 points.
And a 3 equals 1 point.

Now, add up your score.

4-6: You are an anti-blogger. I'll bet you didn't even finish the quiz or add up your points. In fact, you probably didn't even read this posting.

7-9: You are a bloggette, a wee little one afraid to even stick that baby toe into the big cold lake.

10-11: You are a demi-blogger, and I mean that in a nice way. Is that a new typeface? It looks good, really.

12: You are a blogging fanatic who lives for the next posting. Some might call it an addiction. You call it a calling. But don't forget to take out the compost and recycling.

So, there you have it. To blog or not to blog? Let's hope we've answered that question.

LABELS: GEEK HUMOR, BLOGGING QUIZ, TIME SINK

VIEW COMMENTS (42)

StrongArm AUG. 23, 2011 AT 9:29 AM
Hey, I got an 11 and I'm not even a blogger. Maybe I should be.

BlueRibbon AUG. 23, 2011 AT 12:50 PM
Don't believe in tests and scores. Visit my blog, Destiny's Pile.

Heiress AUG. 23, 2011 AT 2:31 PM
HA! A perfect high score for a perfect lady, assholes!

SHOW MORE COMMENTS

○ ○ ○   THINKS OUT LOUD   ✕

HUMOR ME

Not a Quiz

Entry No. 517 - POSTED: AUG. 26, 2011

Okay, got several requests to veer away from quizzes for a while. Something else is on my mind anyway.
–tallboy

Space Needle retired

Seattle —The iconic 605-foot-high Space Needle is being retired from service. "Launched" during the 1962 World's Fair as a symbol of America's space ambitions, the George Jetsonesque tower will be consigned to a role more reflective of the country's current mood and desires. The change occurs just weeks after the Shuttle program sputtered to a stop, and, according to many former astronauts, as the U.S. makes a u-turn from its very being and destiny.

Kevin Barrow, Director of the Space Needle's parent company, Puget Soundings Inc., sees the change in different terms. "Now that we are passing the space baton to China and India, it's time to redirect the direction of this country," said Barrow. "The reposturing for the Space Needle is a reflection of our post-modern sense of who and what we are as a people." Barrow said the plan calls for bringing the "Needle back down to earth. No more of this attempt at soaring to new heights. Think horizontal and you have what will become a multi-use facility in keeping with Seattle's downtown urban lifestyle. It will snake its way through the Seattle Center (site of the futuristic 1962 Worlds Fair)."

Last chance to see Seattle from the top of the Space Needle will be next week. Barrow did admit, "It was a fun ride while it lasted."

LABELS: CHINESE SPACE PROGRAM, MIXED-USE FACILITIES, GOODBYE EXCEPTIONALISM

VIEW COMMENTS (44)

Adventuress AUG. 26, 2011 AT 9:29 AM
The observatory view at sunset on a clear night is to die for.

JoeCurr AUG. 26, 2011 AT 12:30 PM
I was going to be a Space Needle elevator operator but I realized the job had too many ups and downs.

SpecMan AUG. 26, 2011 AT 1:45 PM
I want more quizzes!

SHOW MORE COMMENTS

○ ○ ○   **THINKS OUT LOUD**   ✕

HUMOR ME

Breaking news: tallboy assumes control of Thinks Out Loud

Entry No. 518 - POSTED: AUG. 28,, 2011

tallboy: We haven't heard from Isaac since he took off, and since it looks like that Jeannie girl is history, by the authority vested in me, I do hereby announce my intention to assume control of the blog Thinks Out Loud. (I mean no matter where the guy is, he could've at least sent ONE email, text message, or Tweet—if he were really interested in the fate of his blog.)

Hey, Isaac did a great job, as far as that goes. Admit it, he had a limited range. I stand on his shoulders as we look to the future of this blog. By the way, what's so good about the tagline "Humor Me"? What does that mean? Why don't we try something a little different, something with more gravitas. Most of my posts are pretty substantial and perceptive, thank you very much. So, let's see…a new tagline… "The truth, even if it hurts" or "The site for insight." Maybe I should have a tagline contest. I'll get back to you.

LABELS: CLEAN BREAK, PROACTIVE, COUP D'ETAT

VIEW COMMENTS (37)

FactSeeker AUG. 28, 2011 AT 9:24 AM
Wow, Mr. Can Do!

VincentFrederick AUG. 28, 2011 AT 1:34 PM
Uh, excuse me, but can tallboy take over the blog this way? What is the protocol for dealing with a blog that's lost its blogger?

SHOW MORE COMMENTS

○ ○ ○   **THINKS OUT LOUD**   ✕

HUMOR ME

Needed: New tagline for Thinks Out Loud

Entry No. 519 - POSTED: AUG. 31, 2011

This week, I did some SEO, joined 14 online chatrooms, and sent out a barrage of tweets to drive users to the blog, which I hope include some of you. If this is your first time at the site, please feel free to browse. If you are a returning visitor, um, feel free to browse.
–tallboy

Now to this week's business.

Taglines define one's enterprise creatively, concisely, and in a way that reverberates throughout the known universe.

No tagline, no consumer arousal, no marketing thrust or penetration.

Some classic taglines:
Alka-Seltzer – I can't believe I ate the whole thing
Bic – Flick my Bic
Wheaties – The breakfast of champions
Be careful to not overstate your case:

George W. Bush – Mission accomplished

So, with the above in mind, let's re-tag Thinks Out Loud.

Here are the current contenders. Please vote for your favorite or submit your own. (The decision of the judges is final, unless a really good tag ((with legs)) comes in after the Sept. 7 deadline.)

Thinks Out Loud

Where horse sense meets nonsense

Humor without the extra calories

We've got mirth

Whimsy without regret

Where words come to play

Or?

LABELS: BLOG HUMOR, FAMOUS TAGLINES, THE BLOGGING LIFE, ESOTERIC CONTESTS

VIEW COMMENTS (60)

JohnsBrain AUG. 31, 2011 AT 10:25 AM

"All my random thoughts in one convenient location."

DexTerra AUG. 31, 2011 AT 11:49 AM

I let anagrams influence all my important decisions! For example, and selecting an entry at random…"Whimsy without regret" produced these choice morsels:

Humorist, He Grew Witty.

Mush Wiry Wit Together.

Tight Wee Wry Humorist.

Uh, Got Merriest Wit, Why?

Why Greet Humorist Wit?

Why Register Mouth Wit?

Weightier Worthy Smut.

—Take your pick (not an anagram).

Aladden AUG. 31, 2011 AT 1:00 PM

"No tagline, no consumer arousal, no marketing thrust or penetration." Based on that statement, your tagline needs more sexual innuendo: Where words come to (fore)play.

Heiress AUG. 31, 2011 AT 1:43 PM

Doesn't matter which tagline you go with, the blog is beyond saving.

SHOW MORE COMMENTS

International No Blogging Day

Entry No. 520 - POSTED: SEPT. 2, 2011

I'm excited to be taking part in International No Blogging Day, an annual event in which bloggers of all faiths, creeds, and biases refrain from doing a posting and instead spend their time meditating, cooking a real meal, or migrating over to Twitter.

In my case, I'm going to take a long walk on the top side Discovery Park with the sweeping views of Puget Sound and try not to think about my next posting. (That's like saying "Don't think about a pink elephant dancing around a keyboard.")

–tallboy

LABELS: UNPLUG, DO AS I SAY NOT AS I DO, BLOGLESS IN SEATTLE

VIEW COMMENTS (54)

StucKey SEPT. 2, 2011 AT 8:50 PM

tallboy, if it's No Blogging Day, what are you doing blogging?

CheckIn SEPT 2, 2011 AT 8:58 PM

Maybe he wrote the blog last night and had the posting go live today.

SpecMan SEPT 2, 2011 AT 9:15 PM

But even if he wrote it previously, having it go live today still defeats the purpose of the day. (Does that mean we shouldn't be making comments as well?)

SHOW MORE COMMENTS

Consider the Yawn

Entry No. 521 - POSTED: SEPT. 5, 2011

If you see somebody else yawn, do you find yourself doing the same? (It's called a sympathetic yawn.) If I just mention the word yawn, do you begin to feel one welling up inside? (Just yawned myself.) So, where am I going with this? Let's expand the concept to include a greater range of behaviors and thought patterns. I'm thinking (Out Loud!) you can explain a lot of our groupthink via the way our brain synchronizes itself when another (brain) yawns. Why couldn't the same thing happen when individuals are introduced to ideas, philosophies, and the latest fads?

There's this sympathetic element within us that can't resist mimicking and copying others. You may not have the slightest interest in, say, NASCAR stock car racing. But suppose a couple of buddies start talking up Dale Earnhardt Jr., pole positions, and pit passes. Before you can say, "Darlington stripe," you're into draftin', engine cubic inch displacement, and lots of beer. Or you might be a traditional conservative Republican, and suddenly there's all this talk about something called the Tea Party, and before you know it, you're out on the street corner with a poster advocating for states' rights, repeal of most of the amendments of the U.S. Constitution, and a return to the practice of indentured servitude. And it's all because of our tendency to follow another's yawn with one of our own. Think about that.

–tallboy

LABELS: DAYTONA 500, SIMON SAYS, YAWNING GULF

VIEW COMMENTS (22)

FactSeeker SEPT. 5, 2011 AT 9:24 AM
Wow, it worked. You made me yawn!

CletistheStumper SEPT. 5, 2011 AT 10:21 AM
Yawning and have intense craving for a cup of tea.

SHOW MORE COMMENTS

○ ○ ○   **THINKS OUT LOUD**   ✕

~~HUMOR ME~~

And the new tagline is...

Entry No. 522 - POSTED: SEPT. 8, 2011

Emcee: "Hello and welcome to Decision Night at the Thinks Out Loud USA Tagline Contest. After a week of deep thought, a no-holds-barred exchange of opinions and ideas, and sleep deprivation, the judges have apparently reached a decision for the new Thinks Out Loud tagline."

[Fanfare and medium shot and pan of five distinguished judges and a polite looking German Shepherd sitting behind a long table.]

Emcee: "The tagline finalists include:

[Applause after each contender is named.]

Where horse sense meets nonsense
Humor without the extra calories
We've got mirth
Whimsy without regret
Where words come to play

[Another fanfare and general applause.]

Emcee continues: "We've now seen the finalists undergo a number of rigorous tests, including, Rhythm and Rhyme, Clever by Far, and Remember Me."

[Fanfare and applause.]

Emcee: "Before we announce the winner, we first need to let you know who the runner up is...for should tonight's winner be unable to fulfill the obligations and responsibilities of serving as the Thinks Out Loud tagline, the title will revert to this tagline...first runner-up...*We've got mirth!*"

[Applause and close up of Mirth gasping and smiling and being hugged by the other taglines. Quick cut to German Shepherd wagging tail.]

Emcee: "Thank you, thank you. Congratulations, Mirth! And now, the moment we've all been waiting for...the new tagline for Thinks Out Loud. Giving out the TagCrown tonight will be none other than the reigning Thinks Out Loud tagline, the delightful and talented *Humor Me*. This will be Humor's final act as the current tagline."

[Warm applause. Humor Me acknowledges recognition with broad smile and practiced handwave.]

[Fanfare.]

Emcee: "Now, on to business. Oops, sorry, I dropped the envelope. Yes, I'm nervous as well. I'll try to hold onto it this time. Okay, here we go... Did I ever tell you about the time a blogger came up to me and said he hadn't had a page view in three days, so I had him paged?"

[Much groaning from the audience. Ba-de-bump from the orchestra's drummer.]

Emcee continues: "Okay, you'd rather learn who the winner is, and I can't blame you."

[Emcee pulls out piece of paper from envelope, stares at it, coughs. The hall is silent.]

Emcee finally continues: "And the winner is...the new tagline...is... *Whimsy without regret!*"

[Big, big applause. Zoom in to close up of Whimsy mouthing "Oh, my God!" Other tagline finalists circling around, hugging *Whimsy* who is brought to front of stage, given a bouquet of red roses and pointed toward the runway. German Shepard's excited bark is heard above the audience applause.]

Emcee sings: "Tag you're it, yes, you've won the crown. Tag you're it, such a deal..."

[A positively glowing *Whimsy* wipes away a tear and waves to the cheering audience.]

Emcee: "What a night. What a tagline. 'Course tomorrow the real work of being an active tagline begins. *Whimsy* will be responsible for representing Thinks Out Loud at the blog's many media, community, and social events throughout the year. Best of luck, *Whimsy!* Take care everyone and be sure to visit Thinks Out Loud!"

LABELS: BEAUTY CONTEST PAGEANT, BLOG TAGLINE, AND THE WINNER IS

VIEW COMMENTS (63)

Gregorian SEPT. 8, 2011 AT 8:19 AM
Good luck, Whimsy!

Heiress SEPT. 8, 2011 AT 10:58 AM
Notice how the tagline I submitted didn't even make it to the semi-finals: What's so funny

MasterMind SEPT. 8, 2011 AT 11:15 AM
Sounds fixed to me.

SHOW MORE COMMENTS

SkyHigh Mall must-haves

Entry No. 523 - POSTED: SEPT. 10, 2011

Has anyone ever actually bought anything from the quaint in-flight catalogs? Hey, those are disappearing too!

–tallboy

> **NEW: The MultiMate combo microwave/tablet** Finally, you can warm up last night's pizza while checking the latest gossipy musings on TemperTantrum.com. A great way to reheat old sitcoms. [SHM-234009] $199.95.

> **Wee-Wii, the next generation** Just when you thought electronics couldn't get any smaller, here comes Wee-Wii, just a silly millimeter long. Carry it in your pocket and when you feel the urge, fish out the rice-sized Wee-Wii and accompanying fingernail-sized screen and have at it! Can't find that Wee-Wii somewhere deep in your pocket? Just grab a Digital Tortilla Chip and click on its Sensor App. The louder the beep, the closer you are to your Wee-Wii. [SHM-56955654] $149.95.

Wait! Stop the presses! Can't do the bright commentary mocking aspects of contemporary society today. This Job Hunt 2011 is getting to me. I've sent out resumes and cover letters to high-tech and low-tech places looking for communicators, social media experts, etc. And what do I have to show for it? Nada. Most places never even acknowledge my application. (Whatever happened to business manners?) Shouldn't my current blogging role boost my chances for consideration? Don't I deserve at least an interview? Will I be putting back on my barista apron next week? I'm gonna go check Thinks Out Loud's analytics, again.

LABELS: DOSE OF REALITY, JUST RESUMES, MIND YOUR MANNERS

VIEW COMMENTS (22)

VincentFrederick SEPT. 10, 2011 AT 10:50 AM
Tough luck, kid.

BlueRibbon SEPT. 10, 2011 AT 11:40 AM
Persevere. Did Thomas Edison give up? No. Did Secretariat give up? No. Did my Uncle Phil give up? Well, yes, but he had low blood sugar.

Etruscan SEPT. 10, 2011 AT 11:55 AM

Don't give up, tallboy. I predict a place for you in the high-tech universe.

SHOW MORE COMMENTS

○ ○ ○   **THINKS OUT LOUD**   ✕

HUMOR ME ~~WHIMSY WITHOUT REGRET~~

Reclaiming Thinks Out Loud

Entry No. 524 - POSTED: SEPT. 13, 2011

Dear Loyal Readers,

I write to you on an iPad belonging to my new friend Jawa. We are deep in the jungle of Borneo and are comfortably ensconced at what Jawa says is the original Java Hut (Great coffee!). A satellite linkup provides Internet access. My circuitous journey to this location has involved a smattering of luck, a dose of perseverance, and a pound of hope. But I have survived and am doing better, again, thanks to the ministrations of Jawa who found me feverish and babbling about "time to post" as I tried to leap into a raging river.

Needless to say, I was shocked when I went online and discovered my blog, Thinks Out Loud, had been abducted by my protege, tallboy, whom I thought I could trust and hold in the closest confidence. I was nearly hyperventilating. Jawa urged me to calm down, saying something like, "Often the waters underneath the surface tell a different story."

"Jawa, he is taking advantage of me," I countered. "Looks like he even changed my tagline!"

"Are you not all part of the same tribe?" Jawa asked as he sipped his latte. He added: "The coconut does not fall far from the tree."

I didn't say so out loud, but Jawa had no idea what he was talking about. Through his poor judgment and ill-conceived action, tallboy was certainly no part of my family. Well, maybe on my mother's side.

Anyway, did tallboy have to denigrate my writings in the process of stealing my blog?

"Ah," continued Jawa, "at some point the young yellow-breasted flower pecker must leave the nest." He offered me more coffee, which I didn't need. My body was shaking as if I were stuck jacketless on a Rocky

35

Mountain snowfield. Jawa noticed and replaced the coffee with an aromatic smelling tea. In a gentle voice he advised me to "walk a slower route to your next valley's stream." I slept.

*   *   *

Calmer, now, calmer...

tallboy: I thank you for your efforts to keep Thinks Out Loud alive. If you are willing to behave, you may continue to periodically post. But that new tagline has got to go! Know that I am returning. Within a few days, I hope to reach the coast to board a steamer bound for America. Now about that upstart tagline...Just what do you think you are—

Pause. Jawa has me taking deep breaths again...slow, deep breaths... gentle sighs...as I drift toward the verdant valley...

Dear readers, thank you for your patience and understanding.
–Isaac, originator of Thinks Out Loud

LABELS: BORNEO TOURISM BOARD, SHADE GROWN JAVA COFFEE, UPPITY GUEST BLOGGERS

VIEW COMMENTS (53)

BlueBaby SEPT. 13, 2011 AT 8:25 AM
Finally, he's back! Didn't doubt for a minute Isaac would resurface.

AdamsRibEye SEPT. 13, 2011 AT 8:45 AM
Having to take a few deep breaths myself. Love the Java Hut discovery.

2Spacer SEPT. 13, 2011 AT 8:58 AM
Great to see the old tagline!

Ringside SEPT. 13, 2011 AT 9:22 AM
If he's posting again, is Isaac back from sabbatical? I mean, he's still away physically but not electronically.

BlueRibbon SEPT. 13, 2011 AT 9:35 AM
Finding all this too good to be true? Visit my blog, Destiny's Pile.

SHOW MORE COMMENTS

Don't believe everything you read on a blog

Entry No. 525 - POSTED: SEPT. 15, 2011

Readers, it's not that I don't believe Isaac is really blogging from Borneo. I'm just a tad skeptical. We don't hear from him for weeks, and suddenly he's with this shaman who has an iPad in the jungle. UNlikely. I'm going to need more proof that this really is Isaac and that he's really way over there in the Pacific.

Also, sorry for the gap since my previous blog…have been checking Monster every two hours for blogging jobs.

In the meantime, let's continue. Let there be consciousness.
–tallboy

Puddle's Lament

Water—just a liquid or much more? Many researchers are convinced water is capable of "memory" by storing information and retrieving it. The possible applications are innumerable: limitless retention and storage capacity and the key to discovering the origins of life on our planet. Research into water is just beginning. —http://oasishd.ca

Sure, I'm a shallow puddle, now, though I was once a deep pond. Then came the dry spell. But, hey, I have my pride and my memories. Not too long ago, I hosted frogs, lizards, even small fish. Dragonflies? I loved those guys, the way they skimmed over my mirrored surface. Life was good. Now the only visitors I get are, well, here they come now, the little giants I call them. Booted up and giggly as they stomp and skip and hop in me. In me! Hey, watch what you're doing!

Listen, in my day I was an active part of an ecosystem. I contributed to the great cycle of life. I was a player. Look at me now, a mere shadow of my former self, good for nothing but some boot kicking. I just want to evaporate.

Wait, hold on, did I feel a drop? I thought I did. It sure felt like a drop. And another. Yes. Yes! And another. Hello my moist friends. I can sense you. You are of the clouds. And now you join with me. I celebrate your arrival. Oh, please touch me—I'm talking downpour

and runoff—and, yes, keep coming down, down to me and let me
grow with you. We join together, we are ponding. Peace.

VIEW COMMENTS (44)

StucKey SEPT.15, 2011 AT 9:21 AM
Cool tale. Ponding. I like that

Anonymous SEPT. 15, 2013 AT 10:34 AM
We water droplets should stick together.

SpecMan SEPT. 15, 2013 AT 10:52 AM
Did tallboy write this? Kind of a departure of theme for him.

SHOW MORE COMMENTS

○ ○ ○   **THINKS OUT LOUD**   ✕

WHIMSY WITHOUT REGRET

Posting from the Steamer Bogsworth

Entry No. 526 - POSTED: SEPT. 18, 2011

Ahoy, this is Hank, second mate of the steamer Bogsworth. Isaac,
who's below deck, asked if I could fill in for him today. I said, sure,
no problem. (Full disclosure, I have my own blog, Ports O' Call, which
you are welcome to visit, where we explore maritime issues, steamer
maintenance tips and seafood recipes.)

During my break, I took a read of the blog. Don't have a lot to add,
except to offer a polite critique: Isaac and friends, don't try so hard to be
funny, mates. It's like trying to sail directly into the wind. Let the humor
rise like baking bread until the crust is browned but not burnt. (Isaac,
you have been trying to be funny, yes? Same goes for you, tallboy.
Actually, that deposed Jeannie was showing some promise in a post-
ironic kind of way.)

Thanks for reading. I've got to check the cargo manifest. A second mate's
work is never done. Hmmm, some dark, heavy clouds beginning to mass
on the horizon.

VIEW COMMENTS (35)

I crewed once on a slow boat to Perth, Australia. I was young. I was naïve. Turned out our captain was making more money from drug smuggling than legitimate cargo.

Ringside SEPT. 18, 2011 AT 10:04 AM
Isaac might profit from reading Conrad. Recommend "The Shadow Line," where a young inexperienced captain on his first command runs into every conceivable problem.

SHOW MORE COMMENTS

○ ○ ○   **THINKS OUT LOUD**   ✕

WHIMSY WITHOUT REGRET

Look who's using Facebook

Entry No. 527 - POSTED: SEPT. 19, 2011

Need to keep this blog moving forward. Posts from "Isaac" are unreliable, repeat unreliable. Hank, if you are real, see if this one tickles your funny bone.
—tallboy

A recent HowsThatAgain.com study titled "90 Is the New 81 ½" found some interesting nuggets of information. Turns out the fastest growing demographic on Facebook is the nonagenarian crowd, specifically left-handed 90-year-old cat owners partial to Agatha Christie mysteries.

"Facebook reminds me a lot of talking over the backyard fence with Edna. Gossip. Mostly gossip. And the weather," said Edith Mills of Valdosta, Georgia. "Really juicy gossip, sometimes. Did you know Edna's nephew, the one who can't hold a job was seen...Oh, wait, I just got tagged."

Typhoon Slams Steamer

I INTERRUPT THIS POSTING TO BRING YOU BREAKING NEWS: 2nd mate Hank here, and I need to type fast! Typhoon Fitow decided to change course and is upon us. Taking water aft. Pursuing all measures to ensure the safety of the crew and to keep the ship from floundering. Haven't seen Isaac. Thought I heard some of the crew suggesting we throw our guest overboard to appease the sea gods, but of course we would never do that. Still, haven't seen him during the past hour. Look at the size of that wave coursing our way! Brace yourselves, mates!

LABELS: TEASING FACEBOOK, SWEPT AWAY, JONAH COMPLEX

Sleeper SEPT. 19, 2011 AT 8:28 AM

Damn.

Freezone SEPT. 19, 2011 AT 11:31 AM

Hell, that ain't nothing. Back in '83 I was on the schooner Amber that got caught by Monsoon Mitag. Dragged us 200 leagues off course. Drifted another 20 days until a cruise ship happened by. Ended up training stewards and emceeing their nightly talent shows.

Hummer SEPT. 19, 2011 AT 12:23 PM

Typhoons are in the eye of the beholder. Or maybe they're in the beholder of the eye.

Jive SEPT. 19, 2011 AT 12:44 PM

Hummer, you've obviously never been in a typhoon. I fear for Isaac.

SHOW MORE COMMENTS

○ ○ ○   **THINKS OUT LOUD**   ✕

WHIMSY WITHOUT REGRET

Is there an interim host blogger in the house?

Entry No. 528 - POSTED: SEPT. 20, 2011

Hello devoted readers of Thinks Out Loud. Once again, we know not the whereabouts of the blog's founder. As 2nd mate Hank of the typhoon-embattled tanker noted, Isaac may or may not have been thrown overboard in a sacrificial rite. In addition, we have lost contact with the tanker or cargo ship or whatever kind of boat it is and do not know its fate.

With Isaac's condition also unknown, I see no alternative but to humbly re-re-assume the hosting position for Thinks Out Loud. I will to the best of my abilities continue the blog in a manner Isaac would condone. Despite the minimal chances of a positive outcome, let us hope he has survived the storm and will someday be able to return to the blogging fold. [Isaac, did I get the supplicantal tone right here?]
—tallboy

What to write about? The economic scene is so depressing (ahem—Depression?), I don't want to go there. Everyone and their second cousin has weighed in on the Republican horse race and the president's fix-it-all speeches. What could I offer that hasn't been said already? Global warming? (I mean Climate Change.) Endangered species? My unweekend? Sigh. Maybe I shouldn't be a blogger—yet someone has to keep TOL going. I owe it to Isaac. I'd be in a better mood if I were gainfully employed or had a girlfriend. Or both.

I think I'll go take a nap. Maybe I'll have a dream worth reporting.

LABELS: ASSUMING COMMAND, LOST AT SEA, GENERAL BEMOANING

VIEW COMMENTS (41)

Slice SEPT. 20, 2011 AT 8:38 AM
Isaac, did you turn up in Borneo only to be lost at sea? That would be so unfair.

Dexterra SEPT. 20, 2011 AT 9:08 AM
Don't count Isaac out, yet.

Dolfan SEPT. 20, 2011 AT 10:00 AM
tallboy, if you're moving on, I'm happy to succeed you. Oh, wait, I'm late for a casting call.

SeenIt SEPT. 20, 2011 AT 11:09 AM
I feel for you tb. Try some positive imaging.

SHOW MORE COMMENTS

○ ○ ○   **THINKS OUT LOUD**   ✕
WHIMSY WITHOUT REGRET

Why I'm depressed

Entry No. 529 - POSTED: SEPT. 21, 2011

A lot of you seem concerned about the whereabouts of Isaac. **Hey, can we forget about Isaac** for just five minutes and let me talk about me? Is that too much to ask? If I hear from the guy, I'll let you know. Anyway, he's probably swimming with the sea bass.

So, I admit it. I was depressed. All because of a birthday—number 30. The big one. 3-0. There was supposed to be a party, except everything went wrong. I thought I had Tweeted the right date. I was off by a day. I thought I had gotten the right restaurant off Yelp, but I mixed up cities and sent friends a heads up for La Playa Azul—in Santa Barbara. I should have known something was wrong when Andy text messaged me asking if he had the right directions to the restaurant some 1,350 miles away! I assumed he was joking (it's hard to tell tone when all you have is pure text). And to top it all off, little did I know Ellie was inviting the whole world to celebrate my b-day on Twitter, not that any of them showed.

Course I didn't show either—to my OWN birthday party. I knew I had an hour till party time so I thought I'd check FB to see how many friends had wished me a happy day. Six! Out of 448! I was so bummed, I spent the next hour reading Huff 'n' Puff stories and commenting on them. (I'm now rated as a Level One SuperDuperUser!) Next thing I knew it was 10:30—two hours past party time. You would have thought my so-called friends would have texted me. Turns out my cell battery was dead! So, I fell asleep with a silent phone in my pocket and an empty feeling in my stomach. When I woke at 4 a.m., I somehow put it all together and realized I had blown it!

So, that's why I was depressed. Andy says we can do the dinner later this week. But it's hard to get everyone together on the same night. Some are doing heat seeking yoga, others are in a synth-band or practicing standup or doing an art walk or sleeping.

Great! I just got an email notice that my unemployment insurance is about to expire. (Wish I could make some bucks from this blog.) And I have vowed not to take any more "loans" from los parientes, an idea they quickly seconded.
—tallboy

LABELS: 30TH BIRTHDAY PARTY, MY OWN FAULT, SOCIAL MEDIA OVERLOAD

VIEW COMMENTS (43)

Jive SEPT. 21, 2011 AT 9:08 AM
Repeat, tallboy, if you don't want to blog, then don't.

Ringside SEPT. 21, 2011 AT 9:12 AM
tallboy, I'm not a fan of them, but you should pitch your life for a reality TV show: The Lost Bloggers.

SeenIt SEPT. 21, 2011 AT 10:04 AM
Seriously, turning inward, going down into your psychic basement, using your diaphragm—just try it.

SHOW MORE COMMENTS

Castaway Isaac

Entry No. 530 - POSTED: SEPT. 23, 2011

I'm alive. I don't know how or why, but I'm still breathing. The storm almost did me in. My recollections are hazy: I think the crew were arguing about whether to keep or toss me overboard as some kind of Jonah-and-whale-style sacrifice to calm the seas. Couldn't hear everything being said because the wind was so strong. The ship was rising and falling like a cork in a bathtub. Didn't seem to matter if they threw me overboard or not—the result would be the same. Then the freighter went practically vertical, and I was sliding toward the rail. Can't remember if I lost my balance or was given an unhelping hand, though in an instant I was plunging toward the raging waters. "Take this!" shouted a voice (Hank's?). An inflatable life raft bounced off me and, as I hit the water, I flailed about to find it.

I grabbed a wet rubber handle and even though I couldn't squirm into the raft, I could at least hold onto it as I roller coastered to the stormy rhythm of the waves. In the darkness, I heard a groaning of battered twisting metal and distant shouts: the ship going down? Then a wave actually rolled me into the raft. Pounding rain, walls of waves. A wind far harsher than a torrent of negative comments on a blogger's post. Totally soaked and drained of energy, I tried to pump water out of the raft with my hands. This was not a Wild Waves amusement park ride. To keep from panicking, I rewrote past postings in my mind. Just before dawn, the storm began abating. Nothing had ever felt better. I was happily surprised to find a protected container of food rations and water. Over the next two days I drifted with the currents. Saw no other ships. Planes high in the sky occasionally passed over, unaware of my presence. I fantasized about grande lattes with extra foam, cinnamon, and caramel.

I was running low on food and water when I saw a long shape low on the horizon. A paddle was also included in the supplies, and I finally had a reason to use it. As I slowly closed in on the shape, it grew into an island. Straining, muscles sore, a bit dizzy, I scanned for a landing spot. Rocks dominated, an uninviting welcome. Rounding a cove I spotted a stretch of beach, adjusted course, and fought with the current to avoid being pulled back toward the rocks. My muscles on fire, I paddled as if I were on an Olympic rowing team approaching the finish line and tied for first place.

With one last full thrust, I caught a wave and eased onto the sands like a gliding, though tired, seabird.

Pulling in gallons of air, I remained slumped over in the raft. A voice inside me said, "Move." I felt like I weighed a ton but pulled myself up and out of the raft as it bobbed between shore and surf. Even in my half-conscious state, I started noticing my surroundings. The sand was dark and soft. Beyond the beach, palms and ferns extended inland. Heard some distant bird chants but detected no signs of human activity. This was not a Club Med.

Was I fated to become a modern Robinson Crusoe? I didn't think I had Crusoe's wherewithal. And I hadn't submitted a request for a Man Friday. Then I giggled. "Hey," I said to myself, "Didn't you turn 40 last week? Or was it the week before?"

To be continued...

[*Message sent via DrumBeat, island-to-island communications.]

LABELS: SURVIVOR, AGAINST ALL ODDS, DRIFTER

VIEW COMMENTS (44)

Spirit SEPT. 23, 2011 AT 7:28 AM
What? How? Why? When?

Etruscan SEPT. 23, 2011 AT 8:15 AM
How is Isaac able to blog all this? Did he find WiFi on the island?

Dolfan SEPT. 23, 2011 AT 8:04 AM
Didn't get the part. Maybe I should be island hopping.

EscapeGoat SEPT. 23, 2011 AT 8:23 AM
Isaac, you are probably in a state of shock. Try and breathe slowly, deeply. Remain calm.

SHOW MORE COMMENTS

Caution: Not the real Isaac

Entry No. 531 - POSTED: SEPT. 23, 2011

tallboy: I'm sorry. I read Isaac's supposed blog from a tropical island after he purportedly survived a monsoon. C'mon, in this age of identity theft, how do we know that's the real Isaac?

It's so improbable that 1) he was ever even in the South Pacific; that 2) he was thrown overboard from that cruise ship or steamer or whatever to calm the seas; that 3) he drifted in a life raft until he came across some island; and that 4) he somehow got a message out to the blog world.

The last posting is by an obvious impersonator from a call center in Mumbai, a 12-year-old hacker who inhabits a basement, or The Government trying to take over this blog as part of a plan to control the Internet. Unscrupulous carrion!

Well, I for one am not going to let Thinks Out Loud be hijacked. Face it, Isaac is gone. Only I remain to keep his memory alive and to continue Thinks Out Loud in a way that would make him proud. (Course if he is making all this up, then I am but a pawn in his game plan.)

LABELS: FALSE BLOGGERS, IDENTITY THEFT, GETTING METAPHYSICAL

VIEW COMMENTS (36)

Anonymous SEPT. 23, 2011 AT 12:19 PM
So, tallboy, how do we know if you are real?

Ringside SEPT. 23, 2011 AT 1:13 PM
So, Anonymous, how do we know if you are real?

Anonymous SEPT. 23, 2011 AT 2:35 PM
I'm as real as you are, Ringster.

The Good Doctor SEPT. 23 AT 2:55 PM
At this point, we don't know through verification, if Isaac is alive or not. tallboy is premature in his rush to judgment.

SHOW MORE COMMENTS

○ ○ ○   THINKS OUT LOUD   ✕

HUMOR ME ~~WHIMSY WITHOUT REGRET~~

Message from a castaway, continued

Entry No. 532 - POSTED: SEPT. 24, 2011

Weary from my struggles at sea, forlorn about my prospects on a deserted island's beach, I collapsed onto the warm sands and fell into a deep sleep. At some point I dreamt I was blogging. It felt so real. I could sense the concave shapes of the keyboard under my fingertips, could see the words I was writing popping up on the screen. It felt good to be back.

Then I awoke with a handful of sand in one hand, grains sticking in my mouth, and a sun-baked feeling. It took me a minute to realize I was still on the island. I had a funny thought, like you do when you are half awake. Since I've been out of contact with digital media (except back at Jawa's hut, when I discovered my blog had been kidnapped), I was trying to imagine what I had missed:

A reality TV show about the making of reality TV shows had revealed that they're story boarded and scripted.

In a brilliant and unexpected move, Facebook adopted a new philosophy: Simplify, Simplify, Simplify, which was reflected in the latest makeover of the site.

Likewise, Netflix earned the love and loyalty of a growing customer base by lowering prices and making its DVD by mail and online streaming seamless and easy to use.

A screeching seagull interrupted my reverie. It circled overhead like, gasp, a vulture. I needed to make a plan, and I needed to do it fast...

To be continued...

[*Message sent via DrumBeat, island-to-island communications.]

LABELS: CURRENT EVENTS, ECONOMIC RECOVERY, FUN WITH FACEBOOK AND NETFLIX

VIEW COMMENTS (39)

Rookie SEPT. 24, 2011 AT 9:18 AM
Anything is possible if you are making it up, right tallboy?

Explica SEPT. SEPT. 24 AT 9:34 AM
Damn you, Isaac. Just because we are no longer married doesn't mean I'm not worried about you, up to a point.

Sleeper SEPT. 24, 2011 AT 11:05 AM
Seems like we could track him down using Google Earth or a spy satellite aimed at or near Tahiti.

JoeCurr SEPT. 24, 2011 AT 11:45 AM
I was going to be a beachcomber, but they didn't have any current openings.

SHOW MORE COMMENTS

ALL of Facebook

Entry No. 533 - POSTED: SEPT. 24, 2011

tallboy: I need to counterbalance Isaac's ostensible beach blanket bingo romp and return to the original purpose of Thinks Out Loud: astute commentary on contemporary issues…such as providing an example of the latest Facebook tracking option.

It's called ALL (Algorithmic Latitude Listing), where your every moment is digitally recorded:

10:50:09: Breathed in.
10:50:14: Breathed out.
10:50:24: Noticed cat sleeping on chair.
10:50:32: Wind stirring leaves outside house. Temp 71° F/22° C
10:51:02: Sun came out from behind cloud.
10:51:24: Had funny thought.
10:51:34: Cleared throat. Cat's right ear twitched.
10:51:45: Rear section of Upper Atmosphere Research Satellite (UARS) crashed through living room.
10:51:54: Cat now fully awake.
10:52:17: Thirsty.

LABELS: FACEBOOK HUMOR, LATEST FACEBOOK STRATEGY, DECAYING ORBITS

VIEW COMMENTS (31)

Fate SEPT. 24, 2011 AT 12:30 PM
9:09:14 I think it would be a great option.

Ringside SEPT. 24, 2011 AT 12:50 PM
To be fair, we should know what Facebook is doing.

DiJester SEPT. 24, 2011 AT 1:14 PM
You're still on Facebook?

SHOW MORE COMMENTS

Castaway like in Cast Away

Entry No. 534 - POSTED: SEPT. 25, 2011

Isaac: Since I had no idea when or if I might be rescued from this remote tropical island, I focused on Survival 101. I now regretted only staying in the Boy Scouts (actually the Cub Scouts) for one year. Based on movies I'd seen (Tom Hanks in *Cast Away*), I knew I needed to make a spear from a downed tree limb and go target some fish. (Not my forte.) Luckily the raft's provisions included a Swiss Army Knife. Since I was out of bottled (Fiji!) water, the fresh variety was also a high, high priority, so I had to find a spring. And I wanted to figure out how to befriend those coconuts tempting me from high in their trees. Periodically I scanned the horizon for any signs of a boat. All I saw was the endless ocean.

I walked inland, the sound of the waves growing quieter. Palms dominated the low grass and smaller trees. The land began to slope uphill, and I soon reached a rise that again gave me a view of the beach beyond the trees. As I grew more tired and thirstier, my determined hiking became more like aimless wandering. I thought, "On the whole, I'd rather be blogging about the presidential candidates' latest gaffes." I could feel the massage of the breeze and smell the island's sweet scents, but such niceties seemed unimportant compared to my need for water.

I stumbled on. Walking took effort. It was like hiking the Rockies. Except the elevation was 10,000 feet lower. And this was more humid, the air thicker. But there were also similarities. Like not knowing where you were going. There was the day I drove up from Denver and chose a trail on a ridge just outside the boundary of Rocky Mountain National Park. It was a weekday with fewer hikers. Actually no other hikers. The ridge was not particularly steep, the forest of lodgepole pine. As I walked I slid into reverie that was interrupted when I realized I wasn't on the trail. I was heading slightly downhill and couldn't remember when or where I'd veered off course. I stopped and took a breath and looked in all four directions. Forest all around. Best not to go further down. Better to turn around. Should I head straight up the incline or bear slightly to the left. Which choice would most likely bring me back to the trail? How could it be this easy to get lost? I imagined the headlines in the Post: Unprepared Hiker Found Dead 10 Feet from Trail.

A faint bubbly sound brought me back to the island. I tried to place the source, walked this way and that, stubbed my toe on a rock, scraped my arm on a bush, started crying, and finally fell right into the stream. Cool, clear water playing over the rocks. Rocks that hurt my chest and bottom, but so what? Lying in the stream, I let water drift around me and flow into my mouth. Now I was laughing and coughing and shouting, "Eureka!"

Following the stream on its dancing course toward the beach, I was surprised to see it reached the ocean just a half mile from where I had come ashore. I'd made a great circle on what seemed to be an uninhabited island. I had a few provisions (mixed nuts, 70% dark-chocolate bars, organic corn chips, grass fed beef jerky, dried pineapple—packaged, ironically by Trader Joe's—left in the raft's survival kit, so I held off on my next challenge: spear fishing. The sun was setting, and I realized I should collect some palm fronds and bed down for the night. So far, other than the seagull and a few colorful birds, I hadn't seen any animal life. Would I be visited in the night by the island's greeting committee?

For those wondering about my being lost in the Rockies…I chose to go left and take the midpoint angle uphill. I watched the forest floor and hoped to see something familiar, maybe a larger tree or boulder. How had it gotten to be so late in the afternoon? Why hadn't I brought matches and more snack food? Was it clouding up? The woods turned darker. Surrounded by trees, I felt enclosed even though I was outside. The quiet was deafening. Then, like a gift, as I made one more blind step, the trail appeared. When it had gone left, I'd ventured off right. I mouthed, "Thank you" and took the direction that led back to the parking lot. At the most an hour had elapsed since I'd lost my way. In this case, a long hour. Attention, attention, I said to myself.

To be continued…

[*Message sent via DrumBeat, island-to-island communications.]

LABELS: WILSON, WELCOME TO OUR WORLD, FEDEX, THE 10 HIKING ESSENTIALS

VIEW COMMENTS (46)

Topper SEPT. 25, 2011 AT 8:21 AM
Who hasn't fantasized about being a castaway on a tropical isle? It's a form of escape from Modern Life.

AdamsRibeye SEPT. 25, 2011 AT 8:52 AM
Wonder what I would do in a similar situation, like being lost in the mountains?

(Follow the creek or river downstream, I remember that part.)

HandyMan SEPT. 25, 2011 AT 9:39 AM
Isaac, if you can read this, do you have any duct tape? If so, you will be able to construct a sturdy, comfortable and clean lean-to using fresh palm fronds, feathery shore grasses and a host of tapered ferns.

SHOW MORE COMMENTS

○ ○ ○   **THINKS OUT LOUD**   ✕

WHIMSY WITHOUT REGRET

Blogger tallboy diatribes about the Internet

Entry No. 535 - POSTED:SEPT. 26, 2011

The Castaway routine. Trite. Trite and boring. Gilligan's Island redux. So predictable. And I suppose Isaac wants me to send a rescue party. Right. Sorry, busy. He probably never left the Java Hut.

Did I ever post about the time *I* got lost in the woods? Trite. Boring.

Or how I got sick on this topsy turvy ride at an amusement park when I was 12. Very trite and very boring.

Much better to offer an intriguing theory about the Internet. I've been thinking about this for the past week. Here's my idea: The Internet is an information leveler. Good old newspapers (wish I still read one) let you know immediately what the top news of the day is. On an Internet site, there's little indication of priority. It's all monotone. Huff 'n' Puff tries to promote one story each day IN REAL BIG LETTERS. But it's a pale version of the classic press. Then there are all the non-news opinion sites vying for attention—how can you tell which ones are bonafide and which are mere reflections of some 12-year-old's imagination? (Not that some 12-year-olds don't have great imaginations.)

So, the Internet, diminishes the Big Story. This new medium has another unanticipated affect: It raises the trivial and the tedious to the level of news. This non-news is now threatening to take over. Think Facebook, which should really be called Fakebook or Twitter (better known as Twiddle). Do I sound angry? Good.

(Hey, I'm guilty of these sins as well. I can't help promoting myself as a caring, insightful, slightly offbeat kind of guest blogger. Even today's posting, probably my most penetrating ever, comes across as just another blogging item. And ultimately, who's going to want to read all this verbal compost in a generation or two except for some sociology or anthropology grad students?)

Isaac, let's suppose tonight you are out there in the vast South Pacific. At least you're free from all this background noise permeating our culture. (And ironically, here I am adding to it.)

Cheers,
tallboy

LABELS: TELLING MEDIA ANALYSIS, OLD MEDIA, POST-MEDIA

VIEW COMMENTS (37)

Dolfan SEPT. 26, 2011 AT 8:31 AM
tallboy, I have a feeling similar comments were made when hieroglyphics first appeared, when Gutenberg started pushing out printed books, when paperbacks went into mass production. At first the change seems overwhelming, but we adapt to it. Announcement: May have a role in local production of *Hairspray*.

PrimeMary SEPT. 26, 2011 AT 9:10 AM
Um, okay. Whatever.

EveningMist SEPT. 26, 2011 AT 9:22 AM
I think tallboy is acting out his frustration about not finding a paying job.

SHOW MORE COMMENTS

○ ○ ○   **THINKS OUT LOUD**   ✕

HUMOR ME ~~WHIMSY WITHOUT REGRET~~

Castaway blogger's diary

Entry No. 536 - POSTED: SEPT. 28, 2011

Isaac: This is an uninhabited tropical island.
I'm writing this "posting" in a small notebook I found in my lifeboat's survival kit. Perhaps it will be uncovered some years hence and serve as a record of my experiences. Much of my day revolves around the basics. Spear fishing, trying, unsuccessfully, to snag coconuts, efforts to keep a fire going. We're talking the struggle to survive. I grow leaner. I grow bronzed. I grow facial hair. My initial shock and awe about my condition has gradually morphed into an exhilarating feeling I can't fully explain. Well, I do have one thought: Things matter. Like whether I catch some dinner. What I do here matters.

Part of that has to do with what I'm not doing. For the first three or four days I was frantic. Here I stood in this incredible place but—no emails, no text messaging, no Tweets, no Facebook updates. I felt cut off and alone. I was having the adventure of a lifetime, and I couldn't announce it on my FB page! I was feverish, dizzy. But like a receding tide, I gradually let it all go. And I began to live a life in the present— uninterrupted, direct, and visceral.

My spear fishing and sea harvesting are improving. I'm now averaging two small fish and a smattering of shellfish daily. At first I was clumsy and inaccurate in my jabbing as I stood on a low outcropping of rock that jutted into a lagoon I discovered where fish like to congregate. Luckily, the hunger drive bettered my aim. I have some waterproof matches, allowing the gift of fire, so I'm not eating sushi. My trout-fisherman father would be happy to see I can now prepare a fish without getting nauseated. Necessity is the mother of a stronger stomach.

To be continued...

[*Message sent via DrumBeat, island-to-island communications.]

LABELS: BEYOND BLOGGING, SOCIAL MEDIA WITHDRAWAL, POLYNESIA CALLING

VIEW COMMENTS (55)

Anonymous SEPT. 28, 2011 AT 11:15 AM
How's the weather? I'm serious.

SpecMan SEPT. 28, 2011 AT 1:43 PM
I've never been to Tahiti (I did lose my luggage on my honeymoon on Maui), but according to WeatherPro, Octobers in the South Pacific (south of the Equator and thus opposite our Northern Hemisphere seasons) are very comfortable, with highs in the low-to-mid 80s. And the rain season is still a month away. Enjoy!

Enabler SEPT. 28, 2011 AT 1:43 PM
I have questions. How is Isaac able to blog from a deserted island? What is the "DrumBeat island to island communications thing" about?

SHOW MORE COMMENTS

What's up with the universe?

Entry No. 537 - POSTED: SEPT. 29, 2011

tallboy here (wherever that is).

Guest blogging as the cosmos' waistline continues to expand. (Aside: Am still withholding judgment about the veracity of Isaac's island life.)

Am I the only sentient human being in the universe who's depressed about the Nobel Prize for Physics going to some astronomers who supposedly proved the universe that got its start from the Big Bang may expand and expand and expand until everything chills?

There used to be a competing theory that the universe would expand, slow down, stop and then contract back to a single point only to be reborn with a new Big Bang. I kind of liked that view because, even if I wasn't going to be around in my present form, at least there was the cycle of Big Boom, expansion, contraction, and rebirth. Now, thanks to the perseverance of Saul Perlmutter, Brian Schmidt and Adam Riess, there's nothing, I mean Nothing to look forward to.

I get dizzy when I think about the universe and our place in it. And if the whole shebang is expanding, what is it expanding into? Also, what's all this Dark Matter and why does it matter? And where's God in all this? When you get down to it: Why does anything exist anyway? (That question makes me beyond dizzy.)

Sounds like the ultimate disaster movie to me. Enjoy that Polynesian paradise, Isaac—while it lasts.

LABELS: NOBEL PRIZE IN PHYSICS, BIG BANG, DARK MATTER, EXPANDING UNIVERSE, EXPANDING WAISTLINE

VIEW COMMENTS (40)

Topper SEPT. 29, 2011 AT 9:24 AM
Expansion is today's fave theory. Let's see what astrophysicists are saying in 20 years.

SeenIt SEPT. 29, 2011 AT 10:52 AM
The Buddhists will have the last word (if there were a last word) on this one.

Friendo'Kierkegaard SEPT. 29, 2011 AT 11:26 AM
"Why oh why are there essents rather than nothingness. Details at 11."

SHOW MORE COMMENTS

Survival 101

Entry No. 538 - POSTED: OCT. 2, 2011

Isaac: A surprise. I was storing my personal-sized life raft away from the surf the other day, so I turned the craft over to examine the underside. When I flipped it back, I noticed a small brown object had fallen out. A water-protected book. How had I missed that? Apparently it was lodged in a pocket with a flap. The book: *La Livre de la Survivance (The Book of Survival)* by Antoine Cabriolet. Granted it was in French, but there were some useful line drawings as well.

Although my French consists of two years of college-level coursework, many years ago, I gave it a try. The "make a spear" section ("Faire une lance") was pretty rudimentary. The book contained some good ideas. Like "Ne pas panique!" Also, based on a drawing, one afternoon I made a gigantic 'HELP' sign in the sand, each letter fifty feet long—in case a plane flew overhead. I also included, to be fair, in slightly smaller letters underneath: "Aidez!" This is funny: I drew the huge letters on the wrong side of the high tide marker, and they were washed away by the next morning.

There was also a section on harvesting coconuts, something I'd been unable to do. Again, the drawing helped. I'd tried throwing rocks to dislodge the fruit, but even when I hit the coconut, nothing happened. Now I learned how to shimmy up the tree, grab a coconut, turn it until its stem broke and then let it fall to Earth. Back home, coconut tree climbing would be promoted as the latest exercise craze: work the whole body!

Question: Do I want to be rescued?

To be continued...

　　[*Message sent via DrumBeat, island-to-island communications.]

LABELS: VAGABOND, CREATIVE SURVIVAL, ISLAND LIVING

VIEW COMMENTS (43)

Mipper OCT. 2, 2011 AT 9:19 AM

What does the survival book suggest you do if aliens land on the island?

Guest guest blogger

Entry No. 539 - POSTED: OCT. 3, 2011

tallboy: Greetings. Sorry about the tardy posting, but I was just finishing up some busy work. Guess I was feeling a little guilty, which can be a positive thing. So, the BIG news: I've got an interview with a startup day after tomorrow. I'm not at liberty to offer a lot of details, but tech chat rooms are saying this place could be the next Google. What's cool is that I got contacted because a headhunter came across my guest blogging on Thinks Out Loud. She said they're looking for fresh, insightful thinking, and she liked my philosophical thrusts and my ability to embrace the deep questions.

Question: Should I show up in my one navy blue blazer and my one Seahawks blue and grey tie or go with the standard Seattle fleece?

To keep you entertained as I prepare for the most important day in my life, I've asked my kid brother, Eddie, to come on board as guest-guest blogger. Eddie's majoring in Environmental Studies with a minor in History of Technology at the U-Dub.

Wish me luck!

Eddie: Thanks, tb, and break a leg. (Who was he Skyping with when I came to the table just now? He said something like *thank you for any assistance you can provide. Good hunting!*)

Anyway, greetings.

Let's get right to the point. In reviewing what's being discussed on this blog, I only found one posting that had anything to do with sustainability, Carbon Offset Upset, and that one was a failed attempt at satire:

A recent study by the venerable Engstroam Institute shows that carbon footprint offsetting to reduce greenhouse emissions is subject to a secondary effect. Whether the offsetting involves such options as wind farms, tree plantings or reducing your breathing by 15 percent, the actual act of facilitating the carbon offset induces an additional greenhouse emission.

For example, the electronic transfer of monetary funds to offset one's air travel footprint for your Caribbean bachelor or bachelorette party does in fact add to the greenhouse effect, albeit at a much smaller quantity than the original energy usage and is often referred to as your carbon toeprint. However, the Institute has developed a formula for this additional offset-offset based on inverse proportional parameters. For more information, go to Engstroaminstitutecarboncarbonoffset.con. Bear in mind that going to the site will entail further use of energy and enlargement of your footprint.

I call that forced humor.

And someone tell me what's funny about a food truck linking up to the space station:

The latest food trend is coming to the International Space Station. The orbiting astronauts appealed to NASA to add one more shuttle flight to bring up a last-minute addition, a pre-fabricated food truck (in NASA lingo, a calorie-enhancer module).

NASA hopes the new dining option, Heavenly Treats, will prove popular with the station's crew. A revolving menu will include Mexican, Thai and American comfort foods. "Quite frankly people don't come to ISS for the cuisine," said Carl Berger, an astrophysicist and space dust collector. "We have a joke up here. Restaurants do terribly in outer space—even if the food's great, there's no atmosphere."

—Jeannie, thanks for the idea,
Isaac

Well, it's mildly funny. Wonder if they'll offer takeout for return trips to Earth. Hmmm, Isaac acknowledged Jeannie for floating the idea. That's weird. She wasn't aware of the blog back then. (How did Isaac write it last year and thank her before she suggested it?)

Really, this blog should be devoted to what's important: Sustainability, Zerofootprinting, and the Vegan lifestyle, with spaghetti and meatballs the lone exception. (I hope tb gets that job so I can come over here permanently.) Did you know all these products are now compostable: drinking straws, soft drink cups and dog leashes? Did you know Americans spend more on bottled water in one afternoon than Europe spent from 1500 to 1725 outfitting ships to explore the so-called "New World?"

Oh, hey, gotta go. Late for a glee flash mob.

LABELS: CARBON FOOTPRINT, COMPOSTING 101, MILLENNIALS RISING

VIEW COMMENTS (49)

Topaz OCT. 3, 2011 AT 9:33 AM
Young man, you are going to have to prove yourself before you can be considered a serious blogger.

WatchYourBack OCT. 3, 2011 AT 10:24 AM
Actually, he sounds super-serious. Or at least he wants to be considered as serious. This signifies a change in the direction of the blog from satire to self-righteousness. Don't know if we need more of that.

SeaSalt OCT. 3, 2011 AT 10:55 AM
First Isaac takes off. Obnoxious Jeannie gets kicked off. Then tb calls it quits. Best of luck, Eddie.

SHOW MORE COMMENTS

○ ○ ○   **THINKS OUT LOUD**   ✕

~~HUMOR ME WHIMSY WITHOUT REGRET~~
(Actually, neither tagline appeals to me these days.)

Castaway Diary: My Spa

Entry No. 540 - POSTED: OCT. 6, 2011

I've taken to calling the ocean my spa. For fun, I body surf, or, if I feel like a swim, I just ease out beyond the breaking waves and do a casual crawl parallel to the beach. Around the curve of shore is the cove, almost like a retreat, with calm waters walled on three sides by rock sculpture.

The nights here are without compare. I'm getting to know the Southern Sky. No Big Dipper, though there is the Southern Cross, and thousands upon thousands of points of light offering me a glimpse of eternity at no charge. Looking into the heavens puts me in my place—halfway between atoms and galaxies.

I've begun talking to myself to keep myself company. It's a form of insane sanity. Have been having some decent conversations about uses of coconuts, both the shell and innards, varieties of sand, including dark beaches (the predominant color here), and favorite sunset color combinations. What happens if I get bored with me?

My sleep is deep and refreshing. In a kind of evening ritual, I make a bed of large enfolding leaves, enwrap myself like a furry creature seeking comfort and protection, and fall asleep to the rhythmic sound of the surf. And when it rains, it feels more like a warm outdoor shower. Actually, it is a warm outdoor shower.

To be continued...

[*Message sent via DrumBeat, island-to-island communications.]

LABELS: ADAPTING TO PARADISE, LOST OR FOUND, BEACHCOMING 101

VIEW COMMENTS (40)

Dolfan OCT. 6, 2011 AT 8:54 AM
Plus, you are getting your vitamin D. (Vitamin supplements, especially Bs, are a necessity for the high-pressure world of auditioning.)

HighFive OCT. 6, 2011 AT 9:14 AM
What if your island is the same one Amelia Earhart crashed on!

Anonymous OCT. 6, 2011 AT 10:22 AM
My sister is making $2,000 week selling authentic Polynesian carvings. More at PolyPlace.com.

SHOW MORE COMMENTS

○ ○ ○   **THINKS OUT LOUD**   ✕

WHIMSY WITHOUT REGRET

Job on the horizon for tallboy?

Entry No. 541 - POSTED: OCT. 6, 2011

tallboy: You never know for sure how an interview went. I think I did okay, or maybe I flubbed it. Their company is located in Pioneer Square, the old part of downtown Seattle, where a lot of cool startups have set up shop. Lots of old bricks. Historical feel. And some homeless people. The Personnel Dept. interviewer identified herself as the company's Link-to-Life person. She said, "We envision work here as a nested option aggregate, a part of the whole, a whole of the part."

She asked me if I were willing to work hard and have fun. I said, "Yes, work can be rewarding and fun, sure."

She asked me where I thought I'd like to be in five years. "Here, if I'm still being challenged," I answered. Thought that was a good answer.

She asked me if I looked good in white or khaki. I think my head was doing a subtle 'no' shake, but I forced a "Yes, very good." She wore a long white dress that reached her ankles. It wasn't tight, it wasn't loose. I knew she was in there somewhere. She looked young yet not too young. (Near my age?) She was businesslike while also relaxed. Maybe she did yoga. Her voice was so neutral, I couldn't tell if I was moving forward as a candidate or not.

She typed something I couldn't see onto her iPad and thanked me for coming, and I thanked her for her interest in me. She said candidates who make it to the next selection level would be interviewed by Prime Mover (?) in a week or so.

Just got a text from Eddie over at Café Ladro. Time for a mocha. Later.

LABELS: WEIRD INTERVIEW QUESTIONS, COMING UP WITH ANSWERS TO WEIRD QUES-TIONS

VIEW COMMENTS (29)

Dolfan OCT. 6, 2011 AT 9:28 AM

Interviews are like a dance, some are like a waltz, others more a tango. Same goes for auditions.

Ringside OCT. 6, 2011 AT 9:44 AM

Stay positive. Not overly positive. Just positive enough.

JourneyMan OCT. 6, 2011 AT 9:58 AM

Don't you just hate it when they ask you what you worst fault is? Like, what are you supposed to answer? I'm a serial killer, but I'm in remission, or, I don't brush my teeth after breakfast, do you?

SHOW MORE COMMENTS

Guest guest blogger: Where I'm at

Entry No. 542 - POSTED: OCT. 8, 2011

Eddie: With Isaac floating around in the South Pacific and tallboy deep into job hunting, this seems like a good time to check in with me and see where I'm at, lifewise. Twenty. Almost twenty-one. In school. Yes, parents are covering the tuition. (Am supposed to work part time and summers to help with food and housing.) My History of High-tech seminar is actually interesting. We do meet physically in one location twice a week and sit around a big table. It feels very retro. Our thirtyish professor says he wants real face time with us.

This blogging gig is fun 'cause I haven't done it before. It also seems retro when compared to tweets and texting. You have to write so much. Like this. It's a challenge to see if I can stick with it. On the plus side, my professor says I can get extra credit if I do a paper on my posting experiences. And, no, I don't have a girlfriend. (Should I keep or shave the wispy beard?)

My parents told me college should be a time for exploration. I don't think they really meant it. If I were to show up Thanksgiving with a tongue piercing and a "transgendered boyfriend," how do you think they'd react? Still, I get what they are saying. This is my chance, before career, marriage, whatever, to scan my horizons, unfurl my sails and cast off, even if I don't have a destination in sight. Hey, isn't that sort of what Isaac has done? Except he waited until he was in decline.

An aside: Ever since I was a little kid, I've always wanted my life to be like a movie. Or put another way, I'd like my life to make a good movie. Maybe this marks the beginning of a scene or two.

LABELS: INTRODUCTIONS, MILLENIALS RULE, AH YOUTH

VIEW COMMENTS (39)

Gym OCT. 8, 2011 AT 9:04 AM
Eddie, stay in school. It's a scary place out here in the workaday work world.

FreeZone OCT. 8, 2011 AT 10:10 AM
This is guy is so Millennial! I predict he doesn't have the attention span to keep up a blog. Call me a confirmed Gen Xer.

Okay, you're a confirmed Gen Xer. Sorry.

SHOW MORE COMMENTS

○ ○ ○   **THINKS OUT LOUD**   X

BEYOND JESTING* ~~WHIMSY WITHOUT REGRET~~

Castaway Diary: The Body's Revolt

Entry No. 543 - POSTED: OCT. 10, 2011

Several weird days. Maybe I ate some bad seafood or drank some spoiled coconut milk. Yesterday, my body went on strike. At least no one else was around to have to be near me. Stomach cramps. Some throwing up. Loose bowels. I left my camp and wandered inland. Colors seemed too bright, sounds too loud. I tripped over vines and bumped into coconut trees. Finally, I collapsed into a tight ball and ricocheted in and out of sleep. When I awoke, it was night. The moon was right behind the only cloud in the sky. Way in the distance I could hear the soothing sound of waves coming on shore. That gave me an aural beacon to make my way back to the sea.

It's interesting that even in the dark with only the dome of stars overhead, I could find my way over the shadowy terrain. As I neared a tree trunk, I swear I felt a kind of energy push alerting me to its location. Just before coming down on a rock, I got a feeling not in words, more a kind of mental image that signaled "rock below." I became giddy and picked up my pace. The sounds of ocean washing onto shore increased. When I reached the edge of the trees and touched sand, I enjoyed another treat: a bioluminescent sea, waves sparkling as they curved onto the shore. A light show for the Returned. Not feeling tired, rather pulsating with a raw energy, I took a seat on the sands and let the ocean entertain me until sunrise.

To be continued...

*Beyond jesting is now the Think Out Loud tagline.

[MESSAGE SENT VIA DRUMBEAT, ISLAND-TO-ISLAND COMMUNICATIONS.]

LABELS: ISLAND LIVING, INTUITION, THAT VIRUS GOING AROUND

VIEW COMMENTS (42)

Toddler OCT. 10, 2011 AT 9:04 AM

Well, at least you didn't catch it from the coughing guy whose workstation is behind mine. I'm doomed.

SeenIt OCT. 10, 2011 AT 10:52 AM

Isaac, if you have digestive problems, you probably want to avoid all coconut-related items. Actually, with all the coconut you are eating and drinking, you would have been getting sick before this. And since you aren't drinking canned coconut milk, you don't have to worry about guar gum. Blame it on the fish.

SHOW MORE COMMENTS

○ ○ ○   **THINKS OUT LOUD**   ✕

Follow-up interview

Entry No. 544 - POSTED: OCT. 13, 2011

tallboy: In search of employment, I had my second interview (third if you count an initial lengthy email exchange with their Jobsmith) at AltaSystemics. This time it was with the company's Prime Mover, who said he had read my blogging. In fact, that's why I was sitting in a chair shaped like a big palm in a room with the walls painted different distinctive colors: stop sign red, sea foam green, burnt almond. The place was like a beehive, literally. From the first floor where I checked in, a vast open area spread above me with six floors on the right half of what looked like honeycomb rooms. Very sci-fi.

I was led by a young man, a Connector, he called himself, who was dressed in khakis and an apricot colored polo shirt. He took me to Prime Mover's Actualization Space at the top of the honeycombed floors. Prime Mover stood and greeted me warmly when I entered his honeycomb. Short, an inch or two over five feet, and broad-shouldered, he looked to be in his late-thirties or early forties. (I'm not great with ages.) As is the fashion here in Seattle, he sported a goatee. High forehead. Dark deep set eyes that kept glancing into the distance and then returning to scan me.

We chatted more than did a direct interview, and in the course of our conversation, he let me know the position "had crystallized." They needed an energetic "BlogaMight," someone to grow the company's blogging voice. Was I interested? How do you spell D-R-E-A-M J-O-B? Of course I still didn't quite understand what service or product they provided. Their mission statement talked about "reaching new zeniths in the beyond-cloud environment."

"Sounds great!" I practically shouted.

"Good to hear," said Prime Mover. Though shrimpy in height, he spoke with a deep, resonant broadcaster's voice. "This is a fast-track-to-hire position. All we need to finish the process is an email from a reference, say a response from your blog's founder—Isaac. That's been quite entertaining what he's writing—about being lost in the South Pacific."

I tried to keep calm as I nodded. Did my drumming fingers give me away?

"Course that's all a fiction, and he's easily reachable, right?" asked Prime Mover. He raised his thick eyebrows.

I cleared my throat to gain time before answering. I myself had had plenty of doubts about Isaac's escapades and had made lots of jokes at his expense. A couple of days ago, I realized he couldn't be making it all up. He wasn't that creative. It was too detailed. And it wasn't just me who was coming around to believing Isaac's adventure. Most of his readers were also accepting the reality of his situation. It was beyond fiction. With an outward smile toward Prime Mover, I was mentally calculating the steps and time necessary to contact Isaac even though he was currently as unreachable as a seeker on an aboriginal quest.

Can we all say: Dream job dissipating into Seattle mist.

*Tagline: By the decision of the judges, it's Whimsy...

LABELS: HIGH-TECH HIRING TECHNIQUES, CLOSE BUT NO CIGAR

VIEW COMMENTS (38)

BlueRibbon OCT. 13, 2011 AT 9:08 AM
To find out about the real truth about Tahitian customs see my last year's entry in Destiny's Pile.

FactSeeker OCT. 13, 2011 AT 10:33 AM
Again, how is Isaac able to blog from there without a computer or power? Just askin'. Also, I googled 'DrumBeat' and nothing Polynesian came up (although there is a Native American music label that carries authentic recordings). . .

SHOW MORE COMMENTS

BEYOND JESTING ~~WHIMSY WITHOUT REGRET~~

Castaway Diary: Visited

Entry No. 545 - POSTED: OCT. 14, 2011

On an early afternoon I am swimming, diving underwater and skimming along the clear sandy bottom. Rainbow-hued fish keep me company. Like a porpoise I breach the surface, and in the first second of water-filled eyes, see a blur heading directly at me. Time becomes scalloped. With a shake of my head, I clearly discern an outrigger canoe bearing down on me. Forceful paddles cut the water. I shout and dive at the same time. A shadow glides over me. Resurfacing I see the wooden canoe turning. And men. A dozen or so all pointing and shouting. Invaders! I submerge and swim as fast as I can just above the sea's bottom. My heart heaving, I sense the craft gliding above me. I double back and try and get behind them. They seem to anticipate my every move. My lungs bursting, I'm forced to surface, the boat mere feet away. Sputtering "Go away," I begin flailing my way toward shore. A wave carries me in like a toy. Exhausted, I try and run onto the beach as the canoe rides in on the surf with a majesty and poetry I can admire but not duplicate.

Still breathing hard, I stand on the shore. Retreat would be pointless since there is really nowhere to hide. Better to put forward a brave face and let fate carry me along.

Having pulled their craft ashore, the paddlers nimbly jump out of their outrigger and stare at me as if I am an alien from an unknown land. I guess I am. Decorated with tattoos, some in straw hats and grass necklaces, they wear shorts with flowery patterns. They are muscular and sturdy. As they study me, I stare back, my jaw slack. My breath returning, I quickly invent a rudimentary kind of sign language. I try to convey how I had been lost at sea, reached the island on a raft, and survived by fishing and climbing coconut trees. When I begin to illustrate my climbing method—crouching and pulling up—the men start laughing uproariously. Gasping for breath, two fall to the ground.

"Enough!" thunders a solid, broad-shouldered man, his feet planted solidly in the sand. "We seek Isaac, the lost blogger." His unblinking eyes penetrate deep into my soul, while his raised eyebrows make a warmer connection.

"What…how…I mean…"

"Are you he?"

"Yes," I stammer.

The leader's wide smile is like an invitation. "Then we have found you." His men murmur approval.

"How did you know I was here?"

The leader weighs my question before answering. He is in no hurry. "We did not know for sure. This is the third island we have landed at this week. You have kept us busy."

But how did they know about me, my situation? I am confused.

"Ah," says the leader as he begins approaching me. He is just a touch grey haired at the temples and has a broad noble face. The straw hat fits him more like a caesar's crown. "Our search for you began when we received a message from your brother, tallboy."

I think my mouth fell open wider than for a teeth cleaning.

To be continued…

Repeat, the tagline is Beyond Jesting.

[*Message sent via DrumBeat, island-to-island communications.]

LABELS: RESCUES, BEATING THE ODDS, MEET THE NEIGHBORS

VIEW COMMENTS (31)

BlueBaby OCT. 14, 2011 AT 8:24 AM
Pretty much in the nick of time.

Gym OCT. 14, 2011 AT 9:13 AM
This episode is actually raising true metaphysical questions. What is reality? What is Isaac's reality? What is my reality?

SpecMan OCT. 14, 2011 AT 9:52 AM
This is cool. I can see this as a movie. Kind of a Robinson Crusoe meets Nim's Island meets The Lost World, maybe, if the plot turns a certain way.

SHOW MORE COMMENTS

tallboy in motion

Entry No. 546 - POSTED: OCT. 14, 2011

Eddie (tallboy's brother) and the blog's token authentic Millennial here. We're at laid back Café Divertimento where tallboy is attempting to contact Isaac while I try and get to the next level of Tiny Wings. tallboy has commandeered a table and has his laptop, an iPad and his smart phone spread before him as if he is at an electronic version of an operating table. Like a techie on deadline, he is focused, intent and a bit wild eyed. A group of curious onlookers has gathered around him. (Ironically, tallboy is so busy trying to win the blogging job he doesn't have time for Thinks Out Loud, so he asked me to fill in again.)

When asked by AltaSystemic's Prime Mover at the end of the interview if Isaac could send in a reference the next day, tallboy didn't know what to say, especially after the company's head honcho said he had been enjoying the *fictional* account of the blogger being lost in the South Pacific.

tallboy related to me that the brightly-colored walls of the office closed in on him. "I tried to remain calm," he told me, "but was this going to be the end of my chance at the job?" For some reason, my brother opted for full disclosure. He said he doubted he could get that reference by the next day. tallboy told Prime Mover he had become 90 percent convinced Isaac's seemingly fictional story about being lost in the South Pacific was really true. If so, it might take some time to get that reference.

tallboy said Prime Mover began to seem distant, looking more at the room's one wall-sized plate glass window and beyond than at him. The company's leader thanked tallboy for coming in, said they'd be in touch, and finished with "good luck."

Stumbling out of the office, tallboy barely noticed when he'd left the honeycomb building and ended up staring into a gray day of light drizzle. "I was thinking about going back into the barrista trade and losing myself in eight-part espresso orders, and then I figured, why not give it one last try."

My brother doesn't want to go into this, but I think it needs to be said. The reason the Polynesian rescue party showed up on Isaac's island was because of tallboy. He admitted he's the one who used a number of communication systems to contact the islanders, actually people who could contact them—the islanders don't make use of the Internet or other modern technologies—to explain the situation and asking for help to search some of the area's islands for the lost blogger. After more back and forth, the Polynesians agreed to send out an outrigger.

Actually, I played a part, or more accurately our dad helped out. He's retired NOAA. I told him I had a school project for a geography class. Could he help me track down the last known location of a freighter caught in a South Seas typhoon and pinpoint potential landfalls for a drifting life raft? (Our dad was not known for his social skills, but he loved to solve scientific challenges.) I added that this was all hypothetical. He said he'd jump right on it. "School going okay?" he asked at the end of my call. The next day dad sent me an email filled with data about the typhoon's path before, during and after it hit the ship. He said he churned a few sea current logarithms and produced a guesstimate of the potential landfalls a life raft could have made over several hundred square miles of ocean. Apparently this gave the Polynesian rescuers sufficient info to actually find the lost blogger.

"It worked! It worked!" shouted tallboy to the room. "And it can work again, maybe."

So now tallboy is trying to contact them about the reference thing. But tallboy is not taking the time element into consideration. To succeed would require that Isaac return to the home island with his rescuers, that tallboy's message about the reference make it to their island, that Isaac receive the message, that he agree to write a reference, and that he be able to transmit the info back to tallboy. (What if it's only a so-so reference?) All that could take days.

tallboy admits there's a greater chance the Mariners could win next year's world series than he'll get that reference.

I can't believe I'm becoming involved in this. Gotta go. I'm late for a seminar in the metaphysics of urban legends.

LABELS: ARE REFERENCES REALLY NECESSARY, TRACKING APPS, LOST AND FOUND

VIEW COMMENTS (38)

Airborn OCT. 14, 2011 AT 10:18 AM
What happened to the social and political commentary? Am I on the right blog?

Topper OCT. 14, 2011 AT 11:12 AM

The winds blow, the clouds part, the time is now. Get that reference!

PhDer OCT. 14, 2011 AT 11:31 AM

Since I have some time on my hands while I wait for a response from a university, any university, I'm compiling a compendium of words and phrases in this and other travel blogs that reflect neo-colonial descriptors and their sublimation to modern capitalistic power relationships between the colonizer and the other.

SHOW MORE COMMENTS

○ ○ ○   **THINKS OUT LOUD**   ✕

WHIMSY WITHOUT REGRET

The job reference

Entry No. 547 - POSTED: OCT. 14, 2011

Eddie: tallboy says he needs to take a long walk, so I'm going to continue the guest blogging.

So, what happened earlier? tallboy was using all the electronic devices within his reach to try and contact Isaac somewhere in the South Pacific. I'll try to do my best to recreate what happened. tallboy was working non-stop in the coffee house. He had other customers watching him. His challenge was to reach an island that didn't use the Internet, to reach an unreachable Isaac, to get an answer—the reference—before he lost the blogging job that was almost his…if only he could supply a reference from Isaac.

tallboy was on his fourth caffeinated beverage, his eyes wide, his shoulders stooped. Sometimes he cursed under his breath, sometimes he let out a whine or an "Oh, oh." I was getting worried about him. This was worse than the time he played Super Mario Bros. for 14 hours straight. He rubbed his eyes, sighed, mumbled something. Then he froze. Like a statue: Man with iPad. He began moving, shaking his head, saying, "This isn't possible. No way. What the…"

I approached and looked over his shoulder. On the screen I saw: Reference from Isaac, originator of Thinks Out Loud. Then the following words:

To Whom It May Concern:

tallboy has been a guest blogger and interim blogger manager for

Thinks Out Loud during the time the blog's originator was experiencing a host of travel-related activities that precluded his standard blogging schedule. tallboy's blogs, for the most part, are interesting, incisive and impactful. In his early postings, he tended toward bombast and simplification of complex issues. In addition, he had an inclination to denigrate the original blogger of Thinks Out Loud. He has since acquired a more welcoming tone and has produced engaging, thoughtful content. During the extended time Isaac was out of communication, tallboy showed initiative in maintaining the blog. When he thought Isaac was deceased, he had to make a major decision and actually assumed control of the entire Thinks Out Loud concern, slightly jumping the gun perhaps. Upon learning of Isaac's (my) survival and continued existence, tallboy returned to the role of interim manager with grace and enthusiasm.

As important as assuming these blogging duties has been, tallboy distinguished himself even further by helping to organize a search party for Thinks Out Loud, I mean Isaac (me), who was lost at sea. At first a disbeliever of a castaway's dilemma, tallboy reconsidered his conclusions, and applied a true dedication, perseverance and creativity to find help and save him (me). Given all the above, tallboy is highly recommended for employment at your company.

"I don't believe it," I said. tallboy had that look of disbelief people get when they learn they've won the lottery. "How could Isaac get this back to you so soon?" I nudged my brother. "Aren't you still trying to contact him?"

tallboy stood, a mystified statue gazing at the enormity of an unseen something. "I dunno. But there it is. I guess I'll forward it to the company and see what happens."

With a few quick keystrokes, he'd sent the reference to its destination. "I need to take a long walk," he said as he drifted out the door. I was left to gather his gadgets. Before closing out the email with the reference, I hit *return* and wrote, "Thanks!" and then hit *send*. But where was I sending it to? The return line said, Morse Brother the Younger.

LABELS: HINT OF MYSTERY, DAB OF LUCK

VIEW COMMENTS (44)

Aladden OCT. 14, 2011 AT 11:33 AM
It's all done with mirrors.

Good luck, tallboy. Am impressed you submitted a reference that was not 100% glowing with praise. That company will be lucky to have you. Let me know if there are any more job openings. Especially for a seasoned ad rep.

SHOW MORE COMMENTS

○ ○ ○   **THINKS OUT LOUD**   ✕

BEYOND JESTING / WHIMSY WITHOUT REGRET / WHATEVER

Castaway entertains

Entry No. 548 - POSTED: OCT. 14, 2011

Isaac: Trying to be a good host, I offered my visitors a tour of my living area. Vaea, the leader, looked at my makeshift cooking fire. "Very rudimentary, Isaac," he said without sounding pejorative. "Tonight we will build a celebration fire and enjoy a *tamaaraa*, a feast, to honor your survival here and your departure in the morning to our home island."

I felt my mouth open, again, and close as I determined how to respond to his offer. Assumptions were being made without my input. "Thanks, but you really don't have to go to all that trouble," I finally said. "I'm happy to keep things simple. Something light."

Vaea (whose name I later learned meant King of the Ocean) stood up, chest out, eyebrows low. "A fire and celebration. It is our way." Two of his tribe came around from behind their leader and took one thumping step toward me.

I shifted into agreeable. "Hey, I could eat. A banquet sounds fine. I'll show you guys my favorite fishing spot. The crab is to die for."

They stared at me. "Isaac, we know where the fish swim," said Vaea at last.

"Oh, so you've been here before." How was I to know their past experiences on the island?

"This space is sacred for us. We come to perform rites and also for the fish, although we do not die for them. They die for us."

Did that make me an unintentional trespasser? The leader looked into me again. Peeking into my soul? "Perhaps you were brought here for a reason, Isaac." I felt naked around these people, even though everyone else was almost naked.

Without a word being said or an apparent signal given, the crew rose as one, divided into smaller groups, and began their activities. They didn't seem busy or rushed, and within an hour, we had a smorgasbord of fish and crab and shrimp cooking away on a side fire and a truly astonishing bonfire creating a light that could probably be seen from the International Space Station.

We ate and ate and everyone lightened up. I didn't understand the actual words of their language, but I got the drift. Vaea would translate every now and then; good feelings were being shared by all. Then the dancing began. I watched at first as the men created their own percussion music with sticks on coconut shells. Holding their oars like spears, their knees gyrating in and out, and stylistically shaking, the dancers moved as one. Very rhythmic, almost hypnotic, backlit by the bonfire for what seemed like hours. Time took a vacation. Finally I was urged to try the steps. I protested only to be politely lifted into position. I gave it my best, but their laughter was carried up into the night air like the fire's embers.

To be continued...

[*Message sent via DrumBeat, island-to-island communications.]

LABELS: FEASTS, BONFIRES, POLYNESIAN MALE DANCING, CULTURAL FOOT IN MOUTH

VIEW COMMENTS (34)

Freezone OCT. 14, 2011 AT 9:08 PM
Those Polynesians know how to shake it. Actually, I did some instructing myself at a resort on Maui.

PourQuoi OCT. 14, 2011 AT 9:18 PM
Former war dances. Makes aerobic dancing look like sleep walking.

Topper OCT. 14, 2011 AT 9:32 PM
Isaac, I think they are here to save you, not just pay a friendly visit.

SHOW MORE COMMENTS

○ ○ ○   **THINKS OUT LOUD**   ✕

WHIMSY WITHOUT REGRET

tallboy: To blog or not to blog professionally
Entry No. 549 - POSTED: OCT. 15, 2011

Eddie: I guess the reference letter was more a formality than a deal breaker because tallboy got the job offer (via a text message)

and immediately started having qualms about taking the position. From what I could tell of his spoutings, he didn't think he should be paid for blogging, that blogging should be an altruistic, no-monetary-compensation, pure experience. Very idealistic of him. He hasn't given his answer yet to AltaSystemics. (Am I allowed to name the company?)

He was in his room—iPad off, iPhone off. Profoundly quiet. I knocked at the door. "tb, I can understand your feelings."

No response.

"You want blogging to be an intimate and unmediated connection between you and your readers. We talked about that in Social Media 101 last week."

No answer.

"However, this is a blogging job where you are designated to talk about what the company is doing and invite reader participation. And it seems like a good company."

I heard a muffled snort.

"Not to mention you are out of work and about to lose your room in the apartment. And you are out of unemployment benefits. I can't believe this. I'm starting to sound like a parent. Don't make me continue."

The knob on the other side of the door turned slowly. A disheveled brother poked his head out. "Good points," he managed to say.

"Plus you'll get paid and probably have health insurance. Look, give it a try. If you don't like it, tell them it's not a good fit, and go back and be a barista."

He opened the door wider. The room was stuffy with windows closed, shades drawn. tallboy walked like a despondent mule into the IKEA-toned living room. He raised his head and put out a hand, palm upward as if he were addressing an audience. "I, I can do this."

"Yes," I chorused.

His hand went higher. "And I could always write my own non-work blog."

"Yes," I affirmed.

"Okay, Eddie." He turned toward me for the first time that afternoon. "I'll email them my acceptance." He paused. Brushing his chestnut hair away from his face, he now looked more like a three-year-old thoroughbred, readying for a run at Churchill Downs. "And thanks."

"Hey, what are younger brothers for?" I gave him a tap on the shoulder. This for a guy who used to tease me to no end when I was a six year old.

So, it looks like tb is back on track. But I'm still wondering how that job reference from Isaac got to us as tb was in the process of sending the request.

LABELS: SECOND THOUGHTS, GAINFUL EMPLOYMENT, LIMITS OF IDEALISM

VIEW COMMENTS (38)

SpecMan OCT. 13, 2011 AT 8:18 AM
Way to go, Eddie! You are your brother's keeper.

Aladden OCT. 13, 2011 AT 8:30 AM
Job reference turnaround time is a bit mystifying. It's all done with mirrors, really.

SHOW MORE COMMENTS

○ ○ ○   THINKS OUT LOUD   ✕

BEYOND JESTING / WHIMSY WITHOUT REGRET

After the feast

Entry No. 550 - POSTED: OCT. 15, 2011

The next morning, it was unnaturally quiet; even the waves seemed asleep. The first stirrings of dawn teased me awake. With half-opened eyes, I saw the crew members were already busy down near their canoe.

I stumbled over and joined them at the water's edge. "Isaac, we have seat for you. And a *hoe*," said Arenui, The Big Wave, second in command, as he held up a single-sided paddle. Young and energetic, he moved to an inner drumbeat's rhythm.

"Thank you, all," I said slowly. "This has been a terrific visit. And it is an honor to have met you." I nodded toward the group. "Still I can't help thinking maybe I could stay here, be a kind of host when you have your special events. A caretaker of sorts."

Vaea said a few words to his men. They looked as if I had rejected a gift.

"You do not wish to come to our island." Vaea's words were a statement rather than a question.

"I would love to see your home island some day," I said, my hands opening outward. "This is unexpected, but I've adapted to this island. I don't think it's time for me to leave yet."

"Walk with me," said Vaea. It was not a request.

We followed the curve of the shoreline. "Isaac," he said, "I went to university in Hawaii. I took a degree in political science. The elders thought at least one of us should see the Other in their world, much the way you keep tabs on your ___." He didn't say enemy, but I knew what he meant. "At first I was lost and sad, yet over time I made friends, improved my ability to speak English, a very funny language, and even developed a mild appreciation of and limited respect for the haole from the mainland. I knew that some of them had served in the War in the Pacific years before. They had fought bravely and had prevailed against a determined enemy. I respected that. I also knew that their ancestors had conquered the proud Hawaiian peoples."

Vaea was an inch or so shorter than me but seemed taller. Maybe it was the way he carried himself. He cast his eyes seaward as if he could visualize the Hawaiian Islands just beyond the horizon beneath a cloudless azure sky. "The mainlanders were quite friendly in a patronizing kind of way," he continued. "Although on vacation, most of them could not relax, even though they tried. I detected a separation between their inner thoughts and their actions. But they also were moderns. They were continuously using the new machines they surround themselves with. They had an appetite for food and drink and sun. Some of them brought children who were more fun to be around. They had not yet lost a sense of play."

Vaea would be a pretty good blogger, I was thinking. "This is interesting, Vaea," I said, "but why are you telling me this?"

"When it came time, I returned to my home island and reported my observations and experiences. If you come with us today, you will be able to see the results of how that report was received."

To be continued...

[*Message sent via DrumBeat, island-to-island communications.]

LABELS: HAWAIIAN TOURISM, MODERN LIFE, BENEFITS OF COCONUT OIL

Ringside OCT. 15, 2011 AT 9:52 AM

What was that book about the experimental recreation of the Polynesian's South Pacific voyages?

Sleeper OCT. 15, 2011 AT 10:16 AM

Seems to me Isaac has everything to gain and nothing to lose but his life if he stays solo on that island.

2Spacer OCT. 15, 2011 AT 10:33 AM

Isaac failed to mention gamelan music when he was in Bali. Is this an oversight on his part? He certainly seems to be leaning toward the more raw percussive sounds of Polynesia rather than the subtleties of gamelan which builds in speed and volume as the piece progresses.

HighFive OCT. 15, 2011 AT11:02 AM

The book: *Kon-Tiki*. Looked it up on Wikipedia. Thor Heyerdahl and his crew rafted across the Pacific, but he launched from South America to prove that inhabitants from there could have reached the South Seas.

SHOW MORE COMMENTS

○ ○ ○   **THINKS OUT LOUD**   ✕

BEYOND JESTING / WHIMSY WITHOUT REGRET

Decisions, decisions for castaway

Entry No. 551 - POSTED: OCT. 15, 2011

Isaac: A castaway on an admittely beautiful uninhabited Polynesian island, hadn't I still hoped for eventual rescue? Well, it had come in the form of a dozen men in their sturdy canoe paddling directly at me. Over the weeks, though, I'd found a kind of contentment I'd never known before.

As I weighed my options of staying on the island or traveling to Vaea's, once again he stood and watched me. I felt as if I were in a job interview, one not going very well.

"Listen, Vaea, I feel like you are always looking inside me."

He seemed puzzled. "Do you find that unusual, Isaac?"

"Well, yes, I do. Nowadays, back where I'm from, most of the conversations and communications I have are through smart phones or an electronic tablet."

"In your other life, you no longer face the people you are talking with? You do not look into their eyes?"

"Right," I avoided what felt like downright staring. "There's little eye contact or watching what we call body language."

"Ah, I read a book when in Hawaii that said most communication is not of the mouth but through the changes and holdings of the face and body." He stood before me relaxed and open.

"Probably true," I said, trying to return his gaze. "I'm not used to having someone look so deeply into my eyes. I feel as if you can read my inner road map."

"Your what?" Vaea was unbelievably patient with me.

"My soul, my being." I watched a seagull dance above the waves.

"How else can I know you, Isaac? You are a result of how your outer actions connect to your inner self."

"Umm, by reading my blog?"

He didn't laugh. "It is time for you to decide whether to come home with us."

I tried to plant my feet firmly in the wet sand, and my toes began to slowly drift this way and that. I turned away from the beach and regarded the mix of coconut trees and ferns backed by a steep series of rising cliffs. Picture perfect.

"If I go with you, do I have the option to return here?"

"I'd have to discuss it with our elders," he said. "This island is sacred, although it did serve you during your time of survival and growth. And please do not take this the wrong way, if you really examine your situation here, you are surviving but not thriving. How would you do during a tropical storm or typhoon? What if you became ill? What about the touch of another person?"

I admitted those were excellent points. The perfume-scented air caressed me like a full-body massage. The palms had become my friends, the lagoon my living room.

Vaea was being polite with me, I knew. Time to let go. I stroked my beard, my first facial growth since the goatee thing ten years before. "I need to gather a couple of items. And say goodbye."

Vaea nodded. "I shall meet you back at the outrigger. We need to launch soon, Isaac."

I let out the biggest sigh of my life and turned toward my simple encampment, my lean-to of palm branches and long grasses now looking way more makeshift than your basic Swiss Family Robinson treehouse. My diary was really the only item I desired to bring along.

On the other hand, if I took off running while they were busy with the canoe, could I escape and hide in a cave I'd discovered on the far side of the lagoon?

To be continued...

[*Message sent via DrumBeat, island-to-island communications.]

LABELS: INNER GROWTH, INNER STUBBORNISM, SWISS FAMILY ROBINSON

VIEW COMMENTS (35)

AdamsRibeye OCT. 15, 2011 AT 12:01 PM
Run, hide, open up a Polynesian Party Hut.

Seasalt OCT. 15, 2011 AT 12:45 PM
Isaac, it's only a matter of time before a criminal element lands on the island, captures you and. . .

CletistheStumper OCT. 15, 2011 AT 1:15 PM
The individual vs. the group, or more accurately here, the loner vs society.

SHOW MORE COMMENTS

○ ○ ○   **THINKS OUT LOUD**   ✕

WHIMSY WITHOUT REGRET

What a diff a job makes
Entry No. 552 - POSTED: OCT. 16, 2011

tallboy here [before I start my new job]: While Castaway Isaac is deciding whether to hop in the outrigger, let's take a pause from his adventures and bring things up to date in Seattle.

I begin my "BlogaMight" job tomorrow at AltaSystemics. (How should I dress?) Feel like I'm about to start first grade: nervous and excited. So, before I open the next chapter in my career, here's one more posting, for the fun of it:

Headlines we'd prefer not to see

Hugh Hefner Engaged to Great-granddaughter's BFF

China Celebrates 10th Anniversary of Heavenly City Moon Base

Trump Exploring Run for Kingship of Duchy of Grand Fenwick

IBM's Watson 6.2 to Replace Alex Trebek as Host of "Jeopardy"

Palin Vegas Show Extended

Google to buy Twitter, Facebook and Victoria's Secret

And one we wouldn't mind seeing:

Trump Accidentally Fires Self From "The Apprentice"

LABELS: NEWSMAKERS, FAUX HEADLINES, SATIRE BY ANY OTHER NAME

VIEW COMMENTS (35)

Creature OCT. 16, 2011 AT 8:45 AM
tallboy, just remember, the first day at a new job is the longest and most draining. Pace yourself.

Porgy OCT. 16, 2011 AT 9:15 AM
Could you see if their food services could use an upgrade?

FactSeeker OCT. 16, 2011 AT 9:35 AM
Here's another headline: Disco's Revival Stuns Music World!

SHOW MORE COMMENTS

○ ○ ○   **THINKS OUT LOUD**   ✕

BEYOND JESTING / WHIMSY WITHOUT REGRET

Departure into open sea?

Entry No. 553 - POSTED: OCT. 16, 2011

My decision had been made for me.

What was I thinking? With their intimate knowledge of this island, I could not evade the islanders. There was no place I could hide from them for more than fifteen minutes. A stranded sea turtle would have a better chance at escape.

Worn diary in hand, I left my leaning lean-to behind.

As I approached the wide beach, the men were waiting beside their outrigger. "Gentlemen," I said, "it is an honor to travel to your island." Second mate Arenui translated and a deep cheer went up, except for a glum younger member standing toward the back. Pro-football material, he held his head high and evenly took in a breath.

"It is our honor," said Arenui, who always nodded as he spoke. "And it would be an additional honor if you would accept these clothes from us as a gift." I nodded back. And didn't say aloud, "An honor and a way to get me out what was left of my only shirt and shorts."

"Thank you, Arenui. Thank you all," I said solemnly. "By the way, I would like to do my part and lend a hand on the return trip." I accepted their finely balanced paddle, a practical art object compared to the smaller metal version I had left at my camp.

"Of course, of course," said Vaea. "Now, it is time to go. Isaac, we shall position the canoe while you change."

It required only a moment to part with my torn, dirty clothing. I put on the gifts: a flowery patterned cotton shirt and knee length shorts. All too big. Then I realized: not too big except that I had grown smaller during my stay here.

I joined Vaea a few feet from the boat and said in a low voice. "Your crew is great. You know, I was wondering why that tall fellow at the back of the group seems kind of reserved."

"Teva, meaning 'Rain,' yes. He is like a bird that prefers to fly not with the flock. He was against going out in search of you. And now that we have found you, he prefers you stay here and experience a slow death."

That took me aback. "But did I do anything to insult or anger Teha?

Vaea simultaneously looked amused and shocked. "You just called him Sex," he said drily. "It's Teva not Teha."

Tightening my lips, I tried again. "Sorry. So, besides that mispronunciation, have I given him any reason to dislike me?"

"No, nothing except for being an outsider who might bring unwanted attention to us," said Vaea. "I will explain later."

I was confused, even as the waves beckoned. "One last question before we depart. Vaea, what is the name of this island?"

"Fénua Tapu."

"Tapu? Does that mean taboo?"

"Yes, 'Forbidden Land.' Remember, I told you the isle is sacred to us. If this had been 150 years ago and had we discovered you here, your fate would have been quite different from today." He slapped my back. "Come, let us board."

The men were wading into the foamy water and taking turns hopping like gymnasts into the boat. They were athletic without all the strutting and showiness of gym guys.

I wanted to ask more questions, but their focus had turned to slicing past the breaking waves.

"Where should I sit?"

"Next to Teva," said Vaea evenly. "You two need to get to know each other better."

To be continued...

[*Message sent via DrumBeat, island-to-island communications.]

LABELS: CASTAWAY, POLYNESIA, ROBINSON CRUSOE II

VIEW COMMENTS (31)

Flirt OCT. 16, 2011 AT 10:01 AM
Bon voyage! Don't forget your sunscreen. (Am a little bit jealous.)

Mipper OCT.16, 2011 AT 10:18 AM
Isaac, beware Teva! Guess I don't have to tell you that.

The Good Doctor OCT. 16, 2011 AT 10:49 AM
No, Mipper, this is an opportunity to experience and learn another culture for the benefit of both Isaac and Teva, unless, well, they don't get along.

SHOW MORE COMMENTS

Deep waters

Entry No. 554 - POSTED: OCT. 16, 2011

My island home slowly diminished as we journeyed out to sea. After a while, I could no longer make out its individual features—the palms, the grotto, the beach. No land masses on the horizon, all was open water before me. How did this crew know which way to head?

Wanting to do my part, I was great at paddling, for about ten minutes. Then my arms started to ache, and I was breathing out of my mouth. The others, who oared as a team to thrust the boat forward, didn't seem to require rest. One of the boatsmen chanted, like a caller to the waves, and the others answered with a grunting chorus as they sliced their paddles through the glassy water.

We sat on wooden benches layered with thatched straw. Their leader Vaea, one row ahead, told me, as he paddled, to pace myself, row when I could, rest when I needed to. "You are our guest, Isaac," he called back to me. I wanted to tell him I'd run cross country in high school, at an elevation of 5,000 feet, but I didn't think that would mean much to these folks.

Here I was—a blogger being carried along on an authentic outrigger canoe, surrounded by men capable of crossing deep waters—who would have thought this possible?

I took in the salt spray, the cobalt blue sky, the long wooden boat, probably hand-crafted. I tried to nod toward my row mate, the sullen Teva, performing his rowing task without acknowledging my existence and probably hoping I would fall into the ocean blue. (Why does that desire keep surfacing when mariners meet me?)

"Vaea, how do you know which way to go to reach your home island?" I called up to him. I could have sworn I heard Teva make a sarcastic guttural sound. He was defiantly facing away from me.

"Anapa, the Sparkling Sea, knows the ways of the ocean's currents, the mind of the wind, the messages from the clouds," said Vaea. "He follows the courses of birds, the floatings from the land. At night, he examines the starry sky map. To a lesser extent, we all grasp the ways of travel, though Anapa is the True Watcher and Knower."

The navigator sat three rows from the bow. A strategic position? He also paddled, but you could tell he was one big antenna, constantly taking in information. As if he knew I was watching him, the lean yet muscled Anapa looked back and seemed to evaluate me with dark piercing eyes, eyebrows upraised, Vaea-style. Then he turned his head to observe some puffy clouds on the far horizon.

"Vaea, how long until we reach your home?" How could they keep up this pace?

"About a day and night and morning of travel. You see, we are closer than you might have thought. By the way," asked Vaea speaking over his shoulder, "how are Teva and you getting along?"

"We're not." I again regarded my row mate who stayed absorbed in his paddling. "It's hard to start a conversation with him when I don't really know your language."

"Then use yours," said Vaea. "Teva spent half a year with the Amish in a cultural exchange program."

"The Amish?" Once again I was meeting the unexpected. "Why would you have anything to do with them? They live in the 19th century."

"Ah," said Vaea. "Ask Teva."

To be continued...

[*Message sent via DrumBeat, island-to-island communications.]

LABELS: SOUTH PACIFIC MARINERS, TAHITIAN CUSTOMS, TOGETHERNESS

VIEW COMMENTS (43)

JourneyMan OCT. 16, 2011 AT 2:15 PM
The Polynesians were expert sea navigators and capable of traveling hundreds of miles between islands by using sophisticated navigational techniques and perceptive observation of their environment.

Fester OCT. 16, 2011 AT 2:40 PM
Hey, check me out. I'm being paddled! Hope I don't get seasick. This is all pretty funny.

Snark OCT. 16, 2011 AT 3:12 PM
Excuse me, Fester, but if you want to display your immaturity could you do so on another site?

SHOW MORE COMMENTS

Dear Diary: In Search of the Author's Blog

Entry No. 555 - POSTED: OCT. 16, 2011

Eddie, tallboy's brother, back again. As Isaac rides the currents to his rescuers' home island, it falls once more to me to keep the blog going. And ironically, I'm taking that class, Social Media 101, and for this semester's project, I'm supposed to analyze the authorial tone and content of a blog! Perfect. I've got this one. (Full disclosure: I have been a guest blogger for Thinks Out Loud. Is that a conflict of interest?)

So, Thinks Out Loud: I'm looking into how much we learn about the author as we read the postings from this past year. Not much. This is no Dear Diary. His blog aims for a satirical take on contemporary politics and societal and technological developments. There is little about the author himself. Clearly, he is striving for an editorial and authoritative voice rather than the egotistical "this-is-what-I-had-for-lunch" mode. Aside from a quick reference to turning 40, it's almost as if the author goes out of his way to avoid any personal references. Is he married? (An ex-wife made a comment a ways back.) Got kids? What are his political leanings? (He seems to make fun of all political persuasions.) What does he like for breakfast even if he's not going to Tweet about it? Or is there some deep dark secret he's trying to hide? Bigamy? Drug trafficking? Cheating on his SAT?

After reading more than 150 postings at Thinks Out Loud, I can safely say that I have no idea who the author is. In fact, what is his previous writing experience? A PR flack? Who knows. Perhaps he's the figment of some other author's imagination. And I have to wonder who that might be.

LABELS: ANALYZING BLOGS, BLOGGER'S HIDDEN PAST, BLOG AS DEAR DIARY

VIEW COMMENTS (33)

Heiress OCT. 16, 2011 AT 4:52 PM
Eddie, your comments are making me dizzy. I'm surprised you haven't been blocked from the site.

Gobbler OCT. 16, 2011 AT 5:16 PM
Blogs are like fingerprints—no two are alike. Mine, *Catching Up*, is certainly unique. I carefully research the lives of the once famous who are now in eclipse.

Lots of child stars, almost anyone from '70s sitcoms, and some of the Star Wars cast. Kind of a depressing blog.

SHOW MORE COMMENTS

BEYOND BANTER* / WHIMSY WITHOUT REGRET

Teva finally speaks

Entry No. 556 - POSTED: OCT. 17, 2011

As the men continued to paddle at a constant and even pace, the day drifted into late afternoon. Dried fish and what looked like dried kelp were passed fore to aft. I had a nibble and at Vaea's urging took another bite. Periodically two men, one from starboard, one from port would stop their work, do some careful stretching and then exchange places.

I made one more attempt to gain my seatmate's attention. Turning his way, I said, "Teva, you are a fine paddler." I thought I saw him raise his head slightly as he continued to row. I persevered: "May I ask why you went to live with the Amish?"

"All right, all right," he said in a near whisper. "It seems I shall have no peace until you are answered. Please do not interrupt." He paddled, his words issuing slowly. "Our people have lived the Tiarian way for generation after generation. When tall boats came, their strong forces conquered our islands. My ancestors had been fierce warriors if they needed to be, but they could not prevail."

Teva glanced at me, his bushy eyebrows low, his eyes hard. "Tribes conquer tribes. It seems to be the way of the world. So, the elders of our island decided these new men would not conquer our spirit. To maintain our identity, we chose to reject the ways of the intruders. We continued to fish as we always had, to make our clothes and shelter as we had been taught by our parents and they by theirs. Change came slowly to us. Our needs were met. Family and friends were all important. We helped each other in time of need, celebrated and feasted, mourned our loved ones' passings, and enjoyed the company of our lovely wahiné."

I couldn't help but interrupt. "So, how do the Amish fit in all this?"

Teva let out one of what I would learn was one of his many sighs.

Anapa the navigator interrupted our conversation. Speaking rapidly

in his native tongue and pointing off the bow, he quickly gained
the attention of the crew. There was no mistaking the buildup of
thunderclouds on the horizon. Immediately, the men did a course
change, away from the approaching clouds. Although they doubled the
speed of their paddling, the dark mass was gaining on us.

"Please don't throw me overboard," I whispered.

To be continued...

*Beyond Banter has a nice alliterative ring to it.

[*Message sent via DrumBeat, island-to-island communications.]

LABELS: POLYNESIAN HISTORY, NON-MOTORIZED OCEAN TRAVEL, READING NATURE

VIEW COMMENTS (37)

OverDone OCT. 17, 2011 AT 8:42 AM
They are great ocean goers. The sea lives within them.

Mipper OCT. 17, 2011 AT 9:01 AM
Here comes a test for the outrigger. Speaking of paddling, I once won a canoeing
race at camp, although the guy who came in second said I got off to a false start.

SHOW MORE COMMENTS

○ ○ ○   **THINKS OUT LOUD**   ✕

BEYOND BANTER / WHIMSY WITHOUT REGRET

The outrigger and the storm
Entry No. 557 - POSTED: OCT. 17, 2011

The storm clouds were winning. Even though we were paddling as if we
were in the Olympic 2,000 meter finals, the rain enveloped us. Large
fat drops quickly turned to a sharper, meaner downpour. And the wind
picked up. And the waves got bigger. And my stomach felt it all. But the
crew was good, very good. They kept the outrigger positioned so that the
churning waves met our stern not our sides. We were heave-ho-ing but,
so far, not listing, managing to ride with the storm, not against it.

Then came the thunder and lighting. It was as if we were being used for
target practice. A simultaneous blast of thunder and burst of lightning
shoved our craft like it was a play toy. For a moment we were vertical,
poised to enter the raging sea, saved only by a clifflike wave catching
our bottom, straightening us out and letting us surf its crest. The men

shouted in unison, a combination of war cry and utter astonishment. If we made it to their island, this would stand for a great chapter in their ocean sagas. I was practically hyperventilating.

As quickly as it had arrived, the storm abated, the water calmed. Clouds dissipated, and we took in the plenty of the Southern Sky. For a few minutes no one spoke. Our navigator was registering our position relative to the sun and other factors I couldn't figure out. Someone up front said something I couldn't understand that was followed by another's comment and hearty group laughter.

Turning toward me for the first time, his face registering my presence as closer to insect than human, Teva spoke to me. "Rahiti, whose name means Sunrise, said that perhaps we were supposed to have thrown you overboard to appease the gods of wind and rain. But Vetea, Open Sky, added, actually it looks like we were supposed to keep you." Teva returned his attention to paddling.

My paddle over my lap, I was too tired to answer. Beautiful as it was, the South Pacific had a power and majesty to it I could never have imagined. As day eased into dusk, I tried to take in all of my surroundings—ocean, sky, boat, men. My life as a blogger seemed ephemeral. Had it been a way to pass the time or a true calling? Course even now, I checked my pocket to make sure my journal was still there. Though I tried to stay awake as the sky darkened, exhaustion won out, and I slipped into a sleep buffeted by the gentler waves that had replaced the storm's poundings.

To be continued...

[*Message sent via DrumBeat, island-to-island communications.]

LABELS: FAMOUS PACIFIC STORMS, FORMER POLYNESIAN SACRIFICIAL RITES, MODERN BLOGGING RITES

VIEW COMMENTS (33)

FactSeeker OCT. 17, 2011 AT 9:28 AM
Exhaustion can lead to realization. Does realization ever lead to exhaustion?

Topper OCT. 17, 2011 AT 9:33 AM
Nature's fury is often indicative of inner turmoil—in fictional works, especially 19th century English literature. See my blog entry, Stormy weather: Brontë's Wuthering Heights.

Slice OCT. 17, 2011 AT 9:48 AM
Could Teva at least keep Isaac from tipping overboard while he naps?

SHOW MORE COMMENTS

A Polynesian in Amish Country

Entry No. 558 - POSTED: OCT. 18, 2011

I awoke to a dawn of golden light spreading from the canopy sky to the waters' horizon. The rest of the crew was awake and still paddling. Conversation was low and intermittent. I could tell energy was being rationed. From the row ahead, Vaea filled me in on what I had missed. The storm had pushed the craft off course, but luckily the stars had become visible and allowed Anapa the Navigator to ascertain our position relative to that of the constellations.

"We are headed to our island again," said Vaea. I nodded and did a big stretch. Somehow I had managed to sleep without falling overboard. (Would Teva had pulled me back if I had started leaning seaward?) I should have been exhausted. Actually, I was worn down, yet the excitement of the trip kept me going. True, a protein bar would have helped even as the sea was becoming my world.

Teva noticed my movements and said in a neutral voice, "Ia Orana. Maita'i oe?"

"That's hello and how are you," murmured the alert and always relaxed Arenui, the Big Wave, behind me. "Say 'Maita'i vau, mauruuru,' back. It means 'I am fine, thank you.'"

I tried my best, though I think I was off by a few consonants. Teva stopped rowing a moment, shook his head, and gave out a chummy laugh. I started to chuckle as well. He stopped laughing and I brought my frivolity to a skidding stop.

"Good try, Thinks Out Loud," he said. "You speak our language like a burping seal." I took that as almost a compliment. "However, I do admit during the storm, you showed more bravery than I was expecting from one so weak and worn down like an old coconut tree."

I didn't want to tell him my appearance was due more to being in shock than outright assuredness of spirit. "Thank you," I said and changed the subject. "Could you tell me how you ended up in Amish country?"

"Ah, the Amish, our American cousins in thought and deed, though not so much of the loins." Teva was looking skyward as he spoke and paddled. "Members of a group called World Connections came to our island and invited us to visit the Amish peoples. Vaea thought it would be a good idea to see how these others lived, so I was selected to spend six months with them." A member of the World Connections non-profit group provided a few months of English instruction. Teva explained about the shock of traveling by large boat and airplane to reach America. The size and scope of American cities nearly did him in. He was relieved when he reached Amish Country with its horse-drawn carriages and rural lifestyle.

"Like us, they believe in working with one's hands and heart and not depending on those machines of yours. They grow food, raise animals, and build shelter with a joy and energy as I feel in my people. Their dress, I admit, was different, covering the whole person. And they did not share our love for the beauty of the body, but I found the Amish to be good people, wise in their ways."

"Did you make any friends?" I asked.

"Yes and no. I was a stranger in their land. My size and my serious manner and my occasional war cry when chopping wood caused the Amish to always be watching me. At first. But there was a Jacob who treated me like a brother. He was short and, how do you say, wiry, with a beard but no hair above his lip. He asked me a lot of questions about my life on my island. He walked with a sure step. He would have been a good paddler and fisher."

I was about to ask a follow-up question when two crew on the port side raised their oars toward the horizon and announced, "Fénua!"

"The Land," interpreted Vaea for me. Straining my eyes, I could barely make out a low line where the sea met the sky.

"You guys must have built-in binoculars," I said. With renewed energy the men paddled forward. I lent my oar to the effort.

To be continued...

[*Message sent via DrumBeat, island-to-island communications.]

LABELS: AMISH CUSTOMS, BACK TO THE LAND, LOINS

VIEW COMMENTS (38)

Lux OCT. 18, 2011 AT 9:12 AM

I have some Amish cousins and spent two weeks with them one summer when I was twelve. I've never worked so hard. Realized farming wasn't for me. Ended up with five BurgerBurger franchises.

DoughNut OCT. 18, 2011 AT 9:39 AM
Isaac's blog should tie in with the Tahitian Chamber of Commerce. Run travel banner ads.

SHOW MORE COMMENTS

WHIMSY WITHOUT REGRET

tallboy is a BlogaMight

Entry No. 559 - POSTED: OCT. 18, 2011

Eddie: Brother tallboy started his new job (BlogaMight) a couple of days ago at AltaSystemics, and he says he won't have time to do an entry, so once again, I'm here to help out. I'm just glad I can offer my digital skills and knowledge to keep the blog going. And to add some of my own personal touches, although I admit I'm more used to communicating through tweets and Instagram.

I haven't been this involved in my brother's life ever. He's almost ten years older than me, so by the time I would have gotten to know him, he was in high school and then off to college. I do remember him taking me out for ice cream when I was six or seven at a place on Queen Anne Avenue that later got replaced by a juice bar. He seemed so old. I was a little scared of him. He'd come home and visit during college, but his friends would be over and I'd barely see him. Not exactly a strong brotherly bond. I even liked it when he teased me because it meant his paying attention to me. So, now I'm kind of getting to know him for the first time. (And vice versa, I hope.)

After his first day, tb mentioned he didn't have an office or cubicle at AltaSystemics. Instead, he was directed by Prime Mover, the company's head, to literally wander around and soak up what's happening. PM gave him an iPad and sent my brother on his way. A Connector (not sure exactly who these guys are) showed tb around and introduced him. "People would say hello and then get back to their projects," tb told me. "I could see how committed they were to their work. You know how IT people are called nerds—these AltaSystemics employees feel more like aliens."

I'll have more stuff tomorrow. Actually have to study for a quiz and finish a paper. I mean, I am still going to college!

Enabler OCT. 18, 2011 AT 11:01 AM
I heard about a CEO who gave up his office and roamed the building during the
day. He says he stayed in touch. (Bet the staff were a little more tense.)

MasterMind OCT. 18, 2011 AT 11:30 AM
When I worked at a major high-tech company on the other side of Lake Washington, there were no offices, only open seating. We used earbuds a lot.

○ ○ ○   **THINKS OUT LOUD**   ✕

BEYOND BANTER / WHIMSY WITHOUT REGRET

The castaway learns more about his rescuers

Entry No. 560 - POSTED: OCT. 19, 2011

As we paddled steadily toward the island, it slowly became more distinct
and pronounced on the horizon with bands of tropical sun-drenched
green and spots of deep browns topped with a sharp, rocky peak.

"Vaea, I never asked you the name of your land."

Speaking over his shoulder, the leader answered, "Do you wish to ask me
now?"

"Yes, yes, I do." I was discovering how these people of many ceremonies
did not stand on ceremony. They were direct when I tended to be
indirect and were capable of being subtle when I was being insensitive
and loutish, which seemed to be my default setting.

"We call our island Tiaré or Flower. You will soon see why." I nodded.
I wanted to keep rowing with the group, but I was drained of energy.
The easy rising and falling of the outrigger lulled me into a near-dream
state. I was about to begin dancing on a giant computer keyboard when
the head of a paddle nudged my ribs.

Teva was regarding me with a solemn expression. "You will eat well on
Tiaré. We will fatten you up." I wasn't sure about that goal. Was it for my

own good or to fulfill an ancient rite? They hadn't thrown me overboard, so was I being saved for a special feast? I quickly deleted such thoughts from my memory bank.

I still wondered about the experiences Teva had had during his six-month stay with the Amish. "Teva," I blurted out with all the friendliness I could muster, "what happened with you and the Amish?"

"More questions!" I didn't think he was going to answer. Looking out to sea, he continued. "Have you ever spent half a year among those who started out as strangers and then became your friends?" he asked. "That was the path I found. Gradually I was accepted by most all the people. I helped to build a barn, to repair wagons, to seed and weed the crops. Their chief even said that if I were willing to follow their god, I would be able to settle on fertile land and take a bride." Teva almost smiled. He had a hint of memory in his eyes. "There was one young woman, tall and graceful, long of hair and___." He stopped himself. "But I missed the great water, the mountains rising inland, the curving palm trees, and my people." So, after the six months of visitation, Teva said an emotional goodbye to his new friends and returned home.

His eyes grew lighter for a moment. "You should have seen their faces the night I performed one of our dances. The elders made me stop after I began to shake my lower body, but the next day a few of the young people asked me for a private lesson." Teva yawned and said he was tired of talking so much and wished to focus on paddling. I thanked him for the recounting of his time with the Amish and let him go about his work. Teva, I thought, the outside agitator.

To be continued...

[*Message sent via DrumBeat, island-to-island communications.]

LABELS: CALORY COUNTING, WAYS OF THE AMISH, VIRAL GUEST

VIEW COMMENTS (29)

The Good Doctor OCT. 19, 2011 AT 9:01 AM
A balanced diet, fresh air, lots of exercise. Both societies are doing all the right things.

Carrotty OCT. 19, 2011 AT 9:50 AM
How many Amish does it take to screw in a lightbulb?
None. They use candles. (Is that in bad taste?)

SHOW MORE COMMENTS

Beyond the cloud environment?

Entry No. 561 - POSTED: OCT. 19, 2011

Eddie: Okay, back. tb has thrown himself into his new job, so I'll relay what he's told me. The employees refer to AltaSystemics as The Hive. (Does that mean there are workers and drones? What about a Queen Bee? I guess the Prime Mover guy fits that role.)

Dress is "obligatory casual" which means most of them are in khaki or other light colors. tb says one group is dressed all in white robes. He's not sure what they do.

tb says he's impressed by the company's focused workplace culture and the employees' unified identity. What he's still processing is exactly what AltaSystemics does.

I don't know if this helps, but this is from the company website:

"AltaSystemics: developing sensate clairsentience systems for the ultimate in collective consciousness paradigms."

"Beyond the cloud environment with quantum/flux engagement."

"Psychometric applications for post-sapien modalities."

And: "Incorporating synthesis rather than eclectic derivation to form the basis of our openness to social, cultural and para-digitalistic phenomena." That one sounds more like it was pulled from academia.

Tomorrow, I'm going to bring up their site in my History of High-tech Seminar and see if anyone can figure out what's going on over at AltaSystemics.

Time to check Newser.

LABELS: CLOUD COMPUTING, HIGH-TECH JARGON, BEE BEHAVIOR

VIEW COMMENTS (35)

Anonymous OCT. 19, 2011 AT 11:55 AM
The job could be worse, like writing about the company's commitment to environmental concerns.

FactSeeker OCT. 19, 2011 AT 12:15 PM

Dolt. That could be his next assignment. I'll bet you don't compost.

SHOW MORE COMMENTS

BEYOND BANTER / WHIMSY WITHOUT REGRET

Landfall

Entry No. 562 - POSTED: OCT. 19, 2011

We neared the island, with its inviting lush lowlands and craggy mountain center. I'd seen photos of this kind of Polynesian paradise, but the real thing was pure enchantment. The canoe was making great time, and soon the beach began to dominate my view.

Vaea leaned toward Anapa, our navigator. "It is time." Anapa reached down and brought up a huge conch shell. Bringing it to his lips, he blew long and vigorously. The he repeated the note, a full, rich tone, a French horn of the sea. "We signal your arrival, Isaac," said Vaea.

Our sturdy outrigger rode a strong, long wave onto a wide beach filled with a score of curious locals. With raised paddles, the men of the canoe gave a victory cheer as they leapt from the boat and pulled it with practiced moves onto shore. Like an abandoned puppy, I sat alone in the canoe. Vaea motioned with his head for me to disembark, and I crawled more than leapt over the side.

Surrounded by what I assumed were family members and friends, an older, but still muscled and tall islander came forward and stood at the top of the beach. Teva called to him and indicated me. "We announced you to my father, our ruler," said Vaea. I was trying to take it all in: the spread of beach backed by palms and tropical forest, sturdy grass shacks above the water line, the warm sun and touch of relaxing salt-scented breeze. "Come," said Vaea as he moved up the beach. I followed on shaky legs.

We advanced to the solemn greeting party, my eyes focused on the leader, his headband sporting plumage of colorful birds, his walking stick planted in the sands. He looked at me with a studied expression before Vaea cordially embraced his father. Oblivious to everyone else, they began to confer in their language.

Vaea turned to me. "Keoni, Righteous One, my father, elder of our family, source of wisdom for all the islanders, greets you, Isaac with an open heart and welcomes you to the island of Tiaré and the village of Inas." Keoni had deep set eyes and pronounced grey eyebrows, a high forehead and a tuft of close-cropped grey hair. I felt as if I were standing in judgment but wasn't sure what I was being judged for.

"Tell your father I am really grateful for your having rescued me, and I am honored to be a visitor on his beautiful island and his village," I said as the team of paddlers formed a semicircle behind me. "What does Inas mean?"

Not answering me, Vaea and Keoni spoke for a minute or two. I tried not to stare at any one point around me, but I didn't want to look nervous. Behind Keoni stood three young dark haired women in airy sarongs, two with smiles, one her head atilt as if she were also judging me.

"Keoni, my father, offers you all of the hospitality, the lodging, the companionship within the realm of this island," said Vaea as Keoni nodded twice. "He also says we are to fatten you up." From behind me came a nudge. Teva.

As if they'd received a signal, the islanders livened up, approached and began to shake my hand and offer greetings, all except the non-smiling raven-haired woman who continued to stand beside Keoni, a buttery yellow hibiscus tucked comfortably in her hair. Was she some kind of advisor to the chief?

With gentle prodding, the islanders commanded my attention as they began guiding me toward what looked like an outdoor dining area. "Let the feast begin," I thought, the aloof woman now hidden from view by my kindly hosts. They don't seem so scared of outsiders, I quickly decided.

To be continued...

[*Message sent via DrumBeat, island-to-island communications.]

LABELS: POLYNESIAN CULTURE, POLYNESIAN CUSTOMS, BE OUR GUEST

VIEW COMMENTS (33)

Creature OCT. 19, 2011 AT 8:45 AM
Doesn't all this remind you of *Mutiny on the Bounty*, except there hasn't been a mutiny, yet?

2Spacer OCT. 19, 2011 AT 9:15 AM

No, Creature, not at all. Where's the mutiny? Where's the Bounty?

Heiress OCT. 19, 2011 AT 9:27 AM

Polynesians are famous for their warm hospitality, which is more than I can say for blogging culture.

SHOW MORE COMMENTS

Feasted in high Polynesian style

Entry No. 563 - POSTED: OCT. 19, 2011

What a feast! I tried to pace myself, not easy after having achieved semi-starvation. I couldn't resist what lay before me in a flower bedecked open circle touching the beach. Large wooden bowels rested on long wooden tables. My hosts pointed out the delicacies: breadfruit, taro, seafood. Fruits piled high: coconuts, mangoes, papayas, pineapples, limes, oranges, grapefruit. And hoisted from a central pit covered with what turned out to be banana leaves: a roast pig.

The women took over and sat me at an outdoor banquet table of smooth wood similar to the design of the outrigger. They placed before me three full plates of food, beverages hot and cold, fruited and alcoholic, and then stood back to await my reaction. I couldn't be impolite, so I sampled the cornucopia of Polynesian cuisine. The flavors—fresh, succulent, tender—my mouth couldn't believe the range of tastes and textures. Had I ever had real food before this meal?

"You haven't tried the poisson cru," said one of my hosts.

"Please, join me," I called to all. And the islanders did. I couldn't get enough of the marinated fish. But I noticed the worthy crew members of the canoe were not present. Chief Keoni sat across from me, to his right, the serious and silent woman I had noticed earlier. She studied me as if I were a laboratory specimen.

"Chief," I said with heartfelt thanks, "this is delicious food. You folks should publish a Polynesian cookbook. Where are the canoe members, by the way?"

A gentle girl with a warm smile translated my question. She introduced herself as Kohia and awaited the chief's answer, which he said between bites. "They will come," translated Kohia. "Right now they rest from the labors of their travel."

I nodded my understanding of their near continuous paddling to bring me back from their sacred island. The feast continued, heightened by much laughter and merriment. The chief added a comment, again with my kind translator completing the communication: "Do not eat like a boar. Save room for dessert."

Again I nodded, adding a nod to the woman examining me, which she chose to ignore. Her skin was flawless, her eyebrows dark and arched in a permanent state of haughtiness.

My companion on my right pointed out the fresh pineapple. "Yes, yes, a digestive aid," I said for no good reason.

From behind me came more celebratory exclamations and now I was presented with po'e. My translator, who added her name meant Passionflower, explained it was a sweet pudding of taro root accented with banana, vanilla, and papaya and then topped with a silky coconut-milk sauce, a dish fit for MasterChef. I didn't think she was more than a teenager, but talking quickly, she was eager to display her knowledge of English. Her face was animated and expressive. *"Hina'aro oe e inu?"* she said and self-translated, "Do you want a drink?"

"Please, no more," I said, patting my hands on my belly, which hadn't been there an hour ago. Everyone laughed. As the dusk turned to night, torches were lit, the drums came out, and the dancing began. Since I had had a lesson back on the other island, when my time came, I was excited to show my prowess. I took my place with a half dozen young lads and tried to follow their running in place, hands slapping chests, and some tricky sideways kicks. I tried my best. However, when they went left, I tended right. A full stomach didn't help.

From the shadows, new figures appeared, arms folded, watching. I tightened up until I realized it was the revitalized crew. As a group, they eased into the light and added their seemingly choreographed running, kicking and percussive chest slapping. Then, as if on cue, all of the men folded back, leaving me front and center as a dozen maidens, now grass-skirted with a bra-like top, glided onto the dance space, an open area of smooth sand. The drumming began again, more robust this time. Everyone laughed hard as I tried to mimic my hosts' moves.

Teva shouted out: "More *ori* than *'ori*," and everyone but me laughed.

I was about to politely beg off when the music stopped as if power had been cut to an amplifier.

My dance companions took several steps back and I followed their retreat. Onto center stage, walking as if she were a princess, came the serious one. With an authoritative glance at the drummers, she held a pose for just a moment, a Polynesian statue, a counterpart to a Grecian Aphrodite. Drums began, not as fast as before but with a new level of complexity between the instruments. She joined her motions to the syncopated beat. Her figure was taller in frame than her sisters and friends, not quite as curvy. When the drumbeat shifted into high gear, the men literally let out an "oomph" of desire. Maybe the Baptists are right about the lethal power of dance.

With a series of swift turns and twirls that sent her about the dance "floor," she tilted by me and I thought I caught her eyes probing mine. I didn't have time to react for the entire group of dancers jumped into motion. The drums throbbed, the chants turned to urgings, pounding, building, mingling with torchlights and waving of hands and the crushing smell of enchanted flowers, all merging into a single heated thunderclap followed by stillness, silence and the caress of the night ocean's soft breeze.

"Inas, it means *Wife of the Moon*," a voice whispered to me.

To be continued...

[*Message sent via DrumBeat, island-to-island communications.]

LABELS: POLYNESIAN FEAST, POLYNESIAN DANCE, POLYNESIAN ALLURE

VIEW COMMENTS (52)

EscapeGoat OCT.19, 2011 AT 11:27 AM
Dance can lead into a trancelike state of mind, if you let it. Or even if you don't.

JourneyMan OCT. 19, 2011 AT 11:40 AM
Isaac is getting in over his head. That might be good for him.

BlueBaby OCT. 19, 2011 AT 11:50 AM
It can be dangerous to gorge yourself after being on a limited diet.

SHOW MORE COMMENTS

Readers' turn

Entry No. 564 - POSTED: OCT. 20, 2011

Hi, Eddie here. There's a lot going on right now, both here in Seattle and in the South Pacific. Kind of like a Bond film where on cue the scene shifts to a different exotic location and an intrigue is developing and a woman catches Bond's eye or visa versa. Plus add a chase scene. You've got to have a chase scene.

Like you, I can't figure out how Isaac is blogging from a remote island (or a canoe). How has he had time to ruminate on his adventures? And even on the island of Tiaré, it sounds like there's no electricity or wifi. And yet...

Over here, tallboy is becoming really dedicated to his blogging job at AltaSystemics. He keeps raving about how they're going to be the next Google.

Anyway, sorry I don't have time for a full-length blog—midterms call.

Say, why don't we give over our blog to our readers today and catch you up tomorrow with the latest from Seattle and/or Tiaré?

FisherKing:
I have been reading this **Thinks Out Loud** blog for a couple of weeks now, and I think it's high time to call its bluff. This "Isaac" blogger supposedly takes a break in early August and goes on vacation and invites guest bloggers to fill in. Fair enough. Even plausible, to a degree. As if on cue, we start receiving reports by his "guest bloggers" that Isaac is visiting some institute in the Ukraine or biking Asia's Silk Road. Then he's in the South Pacific. Then he falls or is pushed overboard from a freighter during a typhoon and is swept up on a deserted island (from which he continues to blog!), and he gets rescued by some mythic Polynesians and brought to their flower-scented island, where he's worried he's going to be served as the main course at a tribal banquet. True? I think not!

PunctureProof:
Whoa, man, take a breath. Either this blog is true or it's not.

Heiress:

The true "idiots" here, are those who think this is a well-written blog. It lacks a post-modern feminist perspective. I should know.

VincentFrederick:

I think it's real, so far at least. Bloggers are burning out all the time. People get shipwrecked. People get hired for a job, but they don't really know what that entails until they begin working at the place. And no one can figure out what most high-tech companies are actually doing anyway.

LABELS: READERS' FORUM, TRUTH VS. FICTION, COMMENTS ARE US

VIEW COMMENTS (50)

BlueBaby OCT.20, 2011 AT 9:27 AM

Not complaining here, but who got to decide who the guest commenters would be?

Freezone OCT. 20, 2011 AT 9:30 AM

Does it matter, Blue? We can comment here.

Rookie OCT. 20, 2011 AT 10:00 AM

You guys can comment, but it would be nice to say something germaine to the subject.

Freezone OCT. 20, 2011 AT 10:10 AM

Like you just did, Rook?

SHOW MORE COMMENTS

○ ○ ○   **THINKS OUT LOUD**   X

BEYOND BANTER / WHIMSY WITHOUT REGRET

After the feasting

Entry No. 565 - POSTED: OCT. 20, 2011

I awoke from strange dreams: A brown, furry creature, all body, no head, was running in tight circles around me. And I was addressing it as if it were an untrained pet. "Bloggy," I was shouting, "sit!" But the wild creature continued to ignore my commands.

"Isaac, are you all right?" asked a deep voice in the early morning light. I was in a grass hut and lying on a comfortable bed of matting. "You were jerking about and shrieking as if insects were upon you."

"Yes, yes," I said, "just a dream."

"A dream is never just a dream," said the voice. I worked my eyes fully open to see Teva in shadow at the hut's other side. He seemed more relaxed than usual.

"So I guess Vaea thought I should room with you." I eyed a stone figure opposite my bedding. Large eyed and squat, it looked like an alien.

"That was his intention," Teva answered. "He has determined that we can learn from each other. But I must admit, I do not know what you have to offer me."

"We'll see," I said as I stretched and pulled myself up. I felt drained. "You folks certainly know how to party."

"It is part of our Way," Teva said as he stood and faced toward the open hut's fronting to the ocean.

"You islanders are great dancers. By the way, who was that woman who took the solo?"

"Vaitiare. Her name means Water Flower."

"Yes," I said also taking in the blue lagoon and beyond. "She is a very adept dancer."

"Indeed," Teva said as he turned without looking at me. "Let us join the others for our morning meal."

As we walked out of the hut, he muttered, "Ori not 'ori," and laughed to himself. Feeling the butt of a joke I didn't understand, I was working up the courage to ask him to explain the jest.

Already at last night's feast area, a score of villagers were enjoying a host of fruits and assorted dishes. I did not see the dancer Vaitiare.

Just as the night before, I was treated like a long lost family member. I had the feeling they didn't entertain non-islanders very often and felt like a media personality. My plate was filled and refilled. Conversation, in Polynesian, was light and bubbly. Several jokes, I think, were directed toward me with gentle laughter coming at what I assumed were the punch lines. Two children mimicked my awkward hip shaking dance style.

"They say you dance like a man who walks on hot coals," offered Teva. "You are the first male on our island to try and perfect the female way of dance."

"Okay. Fair enough." I accepted the banter and made a note to keep my hips on hold in future performances.

"Teva, if I may, why did you say I ori rather than awry?" That got another hearty laugh out of him.

He explained that *ori* means dance, but *'ori* which he said with a stronger emphasis on the first syllable means to wander aimlessly, which would describe my overall dance style and more.

I changed the subject. "Teva, how do I say, 'This is very good.'?"

"The meal? *'E mea maita'i roa teie.'*"

I tried to copy Teva's pronunciation when I said the phrase only to have the islanders stare at me until Teva repeated the words correctly. Then they all nodded and smiled.

"Teva, what did I say?"

"You asked the women to join you in a two-day love ritual."

I felt warm. "Wait, tell them I meant no offense."

Teva let out an even louder laugh. "No, Isaac. Your words sounded like an unruly wave splashing against rocks."

After breakfast, the islanders dispersed. Even Teva excused himself and went toward the boats. I sat on the wide beach and watched the waves roll in. I could get used to this.

I must have become half-hypnotized; I wasn't even aware that a man was standing next to me. "Isaac," he said. I gazed up and saw Vaea.

"You have a wonderful island, Vaea." He gave a slight nod. "I am indebted to you for saving me from slow starvation."

"You are welcome."

"You know I made a lot of notes while I was on your other island. If there were some way to send those notes as blogs back to my readers— course you don't have Internet access here, do you?"

Vaea crouched beside me. "Isaac, those messages have already been sent. And read by those who follow your words."

I laughed and said that was a good joke. But Vaea was serious. "Let me join you," he said, "and I will explain. I advise you to listen without letting your inner voice block out my words."

To be continued...

[*Message sent via DrumBeat, island-to-island communications.]

LABELS: POYNESIAN HUMOR, BLOGGING WITHOUT A COMPUTER, PARADOXES

VIEW COMMENTS (38)

DexTerra OCT. 20, 2011 AT 12:05 PM

Did I read what I thought I just read? I mean, I am reading these posts from someone shipwrecked, without a computer, etc.

Caruso OCT. 20, 2011 AT 1:10 PM

Maybe it's because they're on the other side of the International Date Line, but that would put them in the future compared to L.A.

iSite OCT. 20, 2011 AT 2:15 PM

Coconut oil. That's all I need to say. Visit CocoTrails to learn about all the benefits of this magnificent gift from the tropics.

2Space OCT. 20, 2011 AT 2:22 PM

Actually, Polynesia is on the same side of the Date Line at the U.S., but I don't think that's what Vaea is alluding to.

SHOW MORE COMMENTS

○ ○ ○   **THINKS OUT LOUD**   ✕

BEYOND BANTER / WHIMSY WITHOUT REGRET

Communicating to off-islanders

Entry No. 566 - POSTED: OCT. 20, 2011

Vaea and I sat on the beach (lighter than the dark sands of Fénua) and gazed at the glittering South Pacific. He began to tell me how they communicated with the outside world. Vaea explained that his island was at the end of a chain. If they needed to contact others, they used drums. "Our drummers live at the other side of Tiaré, closest to our neighbor island, Ponui or Big Night," said Vaea. "We use a method passed down from generation to generation. Based on the number of beats, the silence between passages, and even the particular sound of a drum touch, we can send many basic messages: help, warning, festival invitation, and so on."

I couldn't help but interject: "You know, Vaea, I love a good drum beat, but today's smart phones and other social media devices could run rings around your system."

Vaea acted as if he hadn't heard me and went on to relate that around a hundred years ago a new method was introduced by Westerners for more complex messages. "It was Dot-Dash," he said, "and our drummers were able to send word messages by doing combinations of long and short drum strikes.

Goodby cell phones, hello Dot-Dash. Did that mean I'd now be able to deliver my messages to the world? Vaea said he would walk me over to the drummer circle and show me how it was done. "Then I can send out blogs finally!" I said.

"Yes," said Vaea slowly, "but we ask that you respect our traditions. It is not our way to speak loudly about ourselves to others. We do not promote Tiaré to strangers as some of our sister islands do."

"Of course, Vaea," I answered, wondering why they were even allowing me to stay with them.

Vaea returned to the subject of sending messages. "You probably wonder, Isaac, how a message goes beyond our island chain." I nodded. "We use the Morse brothers, who also understand the Dot-Dash system."

Well, I didn't understand.

Running some sand through his fingers, he continued: "The drum message is repeated island to island until it reaches Poe, meaning Pearl, the island furthest from us in the chain. That is where Morse Brother the Elder lives."

Vaea explained the two brothers, now both in their late eighties, had fought in World War II. They had monitored Japanese troop positions in the Philippines and radioed the info back to Allied bases. After the war, the elder settled on Poe, the other, the younger, in Hawaii. They stayed in contact via what I realized was ham radio and Morse Code, which I knew lately had fallen out of favor as a communication means for ships and other vessels now that we were in the age of satellites, and even more recently, WiFi.

"So, your message will reach the elder on this chain. And he will in turn use Dot-Dash to transmit it to the younger in Hawaii," summarized Vaea. "Then, your modern methods can send the message elsewhere as you instruct the brothers."

That sounded great to me; I couldn't wait to try it.

"And that is also how your brother, tallboy, got his message to us asking to find you," added Vaea, "except it went from tallboy to the younger in Hawaii to the older on Poe and then by drumbeat to us."

"Ah, my brother." I didn't have the will to go into details about tallboy.

Vaea turned his head my way. "Do you miss him?"

"He lives within me," I said. "Now, Vaea, didn't you say my messages, my postings had already been sent and posted? That's impossible." I searched my companion's expression for an indication of humor or even mischievousness.

"Yes, including the reply you sent to your brother, tallboy, who asked you several weeks ago for what he called a 'letter of recommendation'."

Now I was sputtering. What letter had I sent to tallboy?

"Isaac, this is the moment for you to listen with an open heart and consider the great sea before us," said Vaea. "How you only see the surface and not the depths."

Actually, I was noticing Vaitiare over at a nearby hut. She went back and forth from staring up at me with her authoritative look to doing some sort of weaving.

Vaea, noticed me noticing her. "Ah, my proud sister."

An invisible hand slapped my face. "Your dad—the Chief—his daughter...therefore...and a very good dancer, I might add."

"All the men on the island were heart sick when she became betrothed to the equally proud Teva."

If my face hadn't been so tan, Vaea would have seen me redden. "To Teva. Well, congratulations are in order." My hutmate could have told me this earlier when I was asking all those questions about her.

"Yes," said Vaea as he studied me. "I advise you to be light of foot in her presence."

I didn't fully appreciate what he meant but nodded anyway.

"Isaac, have you ever been married?"

"Once," I sighed. "And divorced. We were young. My ex-wife says she thought she had married a man but got a boy." I felt my stomach tighten.

"I see. The currents of life can be like that," noted Vaea, who added that he had a wife and two boys. "Very well. Now, let me tell you about your messages that have already been sent."

To be continued...

[*Message sent via DrumBeat, island-to-island communications.]

LABELS: DRUMMING AS MESSAGING, MORSE CODE LIVES!, POWER OF CONFUSION

VIEW COMMENTS (33)

Crepdejour OCT. 20, 2011 AT 4:20 PM

.... . ._.. ._.. _ _ _   .. ... ._ ._ _._

HighFive OCT. 20, 2011 AT 5:15 PM

I thought I read an article about the Morse brothers, or at least two brothers who did radio communications in the Pacific during WWII.

SiteSeers OCT. 20, 2011 AT 5:49 PM

Hunkered down in jungle, day after day. . . How did they stay sane?

SHOW MORE COMMENTS

○ ○ ○   THINKS OUT LOUD   ✕

WHIMSY WITHOUT REGRET

What do they do at AltaSystemics?

Entry No. 567 - POSTED: OCT. 21, 2011

Eddie here. tallboy is practically working all the time at the startup. I don't know when the guy sleeps. He says he's getting deeper into Hivelife. So, I'm still on blog duty at Thinks Out Loud.

Anyway, as I said last time, both tb and I are still trying to pinpoint what goes on at AltaSystemics, although I seem more curious about the company's mission than tb is. I think he's just happy to have a job. I had my History of High-tech seminar classmates look at the company's website, which is heavy on soft focus photos and light on particulars. Even totally nerdman Eric shrugged his rounded shoulders. "No idea," he murmured. Professor Stevens didn't add much during our research. He doesn't believe in providing answers. "I'm more interested in the questions," he likes to say. That's because he's the one asking them.

So, things got a little wild in class. We were tossing out ideas like taglines at a branding session. "The company is deep into high-energy particle physics," said Chen, who is a chem major. Professor Stevens gave a thoughtful nod in the student's direction.

"They want to be the next Facebook," added Jeremy. He always has a Frisbee with him that he twirls on his finger until the prof asks him to "give it a rest."

"It's the next step in digitalizing text," said the usually quiet Alex. "All knowledge stored in some kind of super cloud."

"That's it! They found a way to store immense amounts of data within vapor molecules," theorized Gregor, who always has a sci-fi book near his person. Some classmates snickered.

By class's end we were still unclear about AltaSystemics. The mood had turned a bit sour around the fabled RoundTable.

"Maybe, they don't actually do anything," surmised Angela, one of only two girls in the class. "It's all a front of some sort."

Professor Stevens, who used to work in the industry, lifted his head and his eyebrows. "Class, I honestly don't have the answer to this one. Eddie, maybe your brother will be able to fill us in as he learns more." He pocketed his Droid RAZR. "Take care, all." With that we were done and people started filtering out of the seminar room while I lingered over my laptop and stared at the AltaSystemics About Us page. It had sparse content and those ethereal pictures, and I felt like I was trying to read a poem I couldn't understand.

Someone was behind me. Emily. Keep breathing, I said to myself. Emily, with her short, shaggy light brown hair and her half smiles and her green eyes—Emily made it hard to concentrate on AltaSystemics. I'd never talked to her outside of class and barely said a word to her in the seminar.

"Eddie, I have a theory. But it's going to sound really weird," she was speaking to my back. I looked away from the computer screen and couldn't get words to rise from my dry throat. So I just nodded pathetically. "Notice the words they are using to describe their systems: clairsentience, collective consciousness, para-digalistic phenomena."

I think I got out a 'mmmmmmm.'

She came to my side and leaned toward the computer. "I have this crazy theory. Say, do you think your brother could get us into the Hive, let us take a look around?"

"Emily, I don't know if we could get in," I said as my vocal chords began working again.

She nodded as though she agreed how tough it would be and then kept going. "Hey, how about if we get the whole class to take a tour?" she asked, her green eyes impossibly bright.

"Well, tallboy just started. We should probably give him a couple of weeks to settle in," I suggested.

"I think the sooner we do a tour the better. Are you in?"

I stood up. She straightened up. We were facing each other. I tried not to stammer. "Do you think you'd have time to get a latte with me?" she asked. "We could work on the plan together."

LABELS: CLOUD COMPUTING, STUDENT SEMINARS, HATCHING A PLAN

VIEW COMMENTS (35)

Genuwine OCT. 21, 2011 AT 8:45 AM
Maybe Isaac's Cloud Computing entry [#503] is turning out to be more prophecy than satire.

DexTerra OCT. 21, 2011 AT 9:15 AM
High-tech companies almost always use the broadest terms possible to explain their reason for being. It gives them wiggle room in case their latest offering falls flat.

Millenio OCT. 21, 2011 AT 9:45 AM
Wish I were a student again, taking seminars, going on field trips…These student loans are killing my options.

SHOW MORE COMMENTS

○ ○ ○   THINKS OUT LOUD   ✕

BEYOND BANTER / WHIMSY WITHOUT REGRET

It takes a wide mind

Entry No. 568 - POSTED: OCT. 21, 2011

On the edge of an enchanting beach, bathed in soft morning sunlight that filtered through the palms, Vaea and I sat and talked. He finally explained how I've been able to send blog postings that I haven't yet finished. It seems the elder and younger Morse brothers, in addition to being a cross-Pacific communication team, are also examiners of how the universe works.

According to Vaea, over the years they had developed ideas and ways of seeing that were new to Western thought. "Their discoveries have been accepted by our islanders who feel and experience many levels of being," said Vaea, his thick brow rising and falling as he spoke. "You think us primitive," he added, "but in some ways our minds are wider than yours." I didn't say anything to that.

Continuing his explanation, he related that the Morse brothers are Seers, what I realized as he continued his explanation would be called accomplished amateur physicists. Actually in the time I had spent with my rescuers, both on the sacred island, the sea passage and here at their home, I was beginning to perceive that the line between amateur and professional was blurred in Polynesian culture. They might have one person who excelled at navigation, another at fishing, but all islanders were considered to be equal contributors to the group's functioning and survival.

It did not seem unnatural to them that the Morse brothers had been using their thousands of miles of separation to test the ebb and flow of what Vaea called the unseen Pieces of the All. I came to understand that I think he meant they were using quantum physics in a way to navigate the currents of time. That would be a rattling big discovery!

Vaea did his best to convey what the brothers were doing. Even he was impressed by their rigor and intrepidness. "They use this very fast Part of the All to weave communications back through time. Using those pathways, they will be able to do the same for your messages, which I have indicated will be sent, will have been sent from the now to the then."

"And then published in the then?" I asked. Aloft in a current of transforming ideas, I needed to deeply inhale this incredible story. Certain that Vaea was telling the truth as he understood it, I slowly floated back down to the beach and the sea and the warm touch of a breeze. A few puffy clouds drifted toward the island.

"So, Vaea, these notes that I have, I can, in essence, have them sent from the past."

"That is one way of saying it, Isaac," said Vaea. "We islanders already see the yesterday in today and the today in tomorrow. In some ways, it has taken your people all this time to reach our shores."

"Let's do the time warp again," I said. Vaea ignored my idle comment as he wiped sand from his legs.

"And, soon we can go to the drummers and begin to send messages that will end up in the past?" My blog would be resurrected!

Vaea nodded to that. "Yes, but not so soon," he said as he looked me up and down. In addition to the actual message, he said we would need to tell the brothers the day I wanted to message to go out on. They would do the rest. That sounded too good to be true, but I was more than willing to try what I considered to be an iffy experiment.

As we rose from the beach, Vaea recommended I spend the rest of the week organizing my writings so I would be ready when we took the walk across the island. Plus, he added as he looked me over, I should keep eating and gaining weight. Thought I saw a flicker of dance in his eyes. "And one other shall accompany us. She has business in the same community of the drummers." He pointed toward the huts. "My sister, the proud Vaitiare."

To be continued...

[*Message sent via DrumBeat, island-to-island communications.]

LABELS: FASTER THAN LIGHT, SPACE TIME CONTINUUM, THE TIME MACHINE

VIEW COMMENTS

MasterMInd OCT. 21, 2011 AT 12:06 PM
I've got some messages I'd like to send. How do I get in contact with the Morse brothers?

Aladden OCT. 21, 2011 AT 1:22 PM
Is there a black hole scenario coming?

The Good Doctor OCT. 21, 2011 AT 2:54 PM
Time travel—even just of information—could have complicated implications.

SHOW MORE COMMENTS

Touring AltaSystemics

Entry No. 569 - POSTED: OCT. 23, 2011

Eddie here: With my brother's help (he hesitated at first until I reminded him it was my support that had led to his taking the job), my History of High-tech class was invited to tour AltaSystemics. A seemingly innocent chance for students to get a first-hand look at a cutting-edge company, we had another motive. My insightful and cute classmate, Emily, had thought up the tour idea so she and I could try and find out what REALLY went on at that mysterious company.

A slightly distant tallboy met us at the entrance to the building, its outer surface in that terracotta look that dominates Pioneer Square. Usually the slightly nervous type, he now radiated a pronounced calmness. Weird.

I introduced my class and Professor Stevens to AltaSystemics' BlogaMight.

"What are you blogging about?" asked Professor Stevens as tallboy ushered us into the vaulted-ceilinged reception area.

"Well, I just started," said my brother. "So, I'm working my way around the company and doing preliminary research," he said in a softer version of his usual talking pattern. "I think my first blog will reference the great employees and their commitment to the AltaSystemics Vision."

Professor Stevens nodded slowly. "I see," he said politely.

A thin door seemed to materialize right out of the wall and a tall, young, engaging man walked toward us. I noticed Emily studying him. "Hi," he said, "I'm Ted, an AltaSystemics Connector. It will be my pleasure to show you around the Hive today." He pointed upward to show the upper floors' honeycombed design that stretched skyward from the lobby. He was also too damned calm.

After we put on VIP buttons ("Visitor-in-Person," said Ted), he asked us to follow him into a bronze-plated elevator. As we were being herded in, Emily whispered to me: "When I flirt, do your independent research!" I opened up my palms outward and silently mouthed "What?" as the elevator closed and we went up a couple of floors.

As we followed Ted around, it was hard to tell when we were in hallways, large rooms or connecting rooms, hence their term Hive for their environment. As we passed (white robed!) employees walking en route to meetings or what not, Ted would say, "Hi, Shanti." or "H'lo Rahul." And they'd softly hello back. Everyone was calm, very calm.

With what seemed like a well-practiced commentary, Ted pointed out the HiveAlive room, for meetings and presentations, the Bibliotech, resource library (without any books), and the Honey Room or cafeteria. It all seemed fairly predictable for a high-tech/non traditional company. Emily practically hugged Ted's side throughout. The other students were making comments and going wow and looking left and right. I was watching Emily and Ted.

"Let's meet a Hiver," said Ted. "At AltaSystemics, we believe in Mind Power." I was wondering where tallboy had gone off to. Ted knocked twice at a non-door door, only a thin outline indicating a break in the pale blue wall. He paused and knocked again. The 'door' slid into the wall and opened. "Patricia, we've got visitors." On a white cushion on a white floor in a spacious cubicle of a room with white walls and a large gossamer thin-curtained floor-to-ceiling window, there, dressed in a hooded white robe, was a figure, head down. Slowly the head came up and revealed a dark-eyed woman with a serene expression and a hint of a smile.

"Welcome to the Hive," she said in a low voice, almost a whisper. I couldn't place her accent. I also couldn't tell if she was on some sort of break or actually working.

"Patricia is one of our Intuitives or Sensate Projectors," said Ted as if we all knew what that meant. Emily leaned even closer to him. "Excuse me, Ted," she began, "sometimes when one is deeply involved in a particular field, he or she starts to take for granted certain phrasings and meanings inherent in that sphere. It's called the Curse of Knowledge." Ted seemed mesmerized by Emily. With her playful eyes and raised eyebrows momentarily darting my way, Emily, I think, wanted me to do something. She continued, "Could you tell us a little more about what Patricia and the others do?" She tilted her head again.

Ted, calm as he was, puffed up a bit. "Sure."

Emily bounced an elbow out of Ted's line of sight to indicate to me that

I should what? Then I got it: initiate my independent research. As Ted talked about 'alternative dimensional interstices,' I slowly back away from the group. "Watch it," said Alex. "Sorry," I responded. At the door, I eased out and acted like I was looking at my phone messages.

I returned to the elevator, stared at the choices and pressed the button D+. I already had my excuse if I were caught: just looking for the bathroom.

Down I went. And down and down. Was I below ground? I exited and took a right. Indistinct lighting in the hallway emanated from the walls. A soft vibration, almost a hum, was a constant. I increased my pace; the hallway seemed to have no end or junction.

About to turn back, I literally bumped into a wall—the end—so subtle in shading that I couldn't tell space from solid. But my bumping caused that section to vibrate and slide open to reveal a room with much harsher lighting, currents of cold air, and deep pulsating sounds. I squinted and had put my hands up in front of my face to block the intense light when a body from behind shoved me into the room. "Just looking for the bathroom," I stuttered as I sheepishly turned around to face—tallboy.

My brother looked both surprised and concerned. "Eddie, what are you doing here? Why aren't you with the tour?"

I didn't know where to start.

VIEW COMMENTS (40)

Distaunt OCT. 23, 2011 AT 10:01 AM
Will tallboy help Eddie or turn him in?

Etruscan OCT. 23, 2011 AT 10:14 AM
Quite a company. . . . . .talented team. . .great concept.

FixTure OCT. 23, 2011 AT 10:44 AM
I worked for a high-tech startup in the late '90s. Also in Pioneer Square. Their product was called a uPOd, and it was going to revolutionize the Internet by providing a hand-held, non-computer access module. (Sound familiar?) Trouble was the technology hadn't caught up to their idea. We showed up to work one day and our computers were locked and an hour later we met in the Group Room and were told the money had dried up and thank you for your service. My take, years later? A dead-end branch of the Tablet Evolutionary Tree.

SHOW MORE COMMENTS

Beyond the tour

Entry No. 570 - POSTED: OCT. 23, 2011

We stood face to face in the brightly lit room. tallboy leaned in close, breathing hard, no more Mr. Calm. "Little brother, are you trying to get me fired?"

This fact-finding mission wasn't supposed to have gone in this particular direction. What was I searching for anyway?

tallboy continued to glare at me.

"Of course I'm not trying to get you fired," I said in an unsteady voice. "I need to tell you some stuff that may sound crazy." Because the throbbing base issuing from the room was so loud, we were almost shouting. "When you said you weren't sure what went on at AltaSystemics, my classmates and I did a brainstorming session to identify what the company does."

I told tallboy how Emily had developed a theory about the company, and she wanted to test her hypothesis, so we had this idea to take a fact-finding tour of AltaSystemics.

"That's coming here under false pretenses," said tallboy.

"Maybe," I said. "You've been here over a week. Have you figured out what the company does?"

tallboy pulled back and eyed a flashing panel in the equipment-filled room's center. "Sure. After interviewing employees for my blog, I'm finding a strong sense of dedication and purpose." But he still couldn't tell me in explicit terms what went on there. He looked past me as if he were gazing out of a window (in this windowless room). "I can tell you this: people are doing new things in new ways."

"I'll grant you that," I answered. He still wouldn't look at me. "And I'm all for change and exploration. Still, doesn't this place strike you as a little bit strange?"

I thought I saw a slight head tilt on tallboy's part, yet before he could respond a shadowy figure appeared at the door. He identified himself as Akira, apparently another Connector, one who was several inches taller and far broader in the shoulders than Ted, our tour guide. "Eddie, are you perhaps looking for a restroom?" he asked with a trace of a smile.

Not waiting for my answer, he motioned for us to follow him. tallboy walked head down, shoulders bent. He knew he was about to be terminated. As soon as we left the energy-filled room, the door zipped closed behind us.

We took the elevator and didn't stop at the tour's floor. Instead we went right to the top—the eighth level. Akira again motioned for us to exit and follow a curving walkway toward yet another hive honeycomb room. A quick glance beyond the walk's railing and all was pure space of the atrium to the first floor. The tour group? I had no idea where they were.

At another thinly outlined door, we stopped. In pale blue relief were the letters PM. The door slid open. "Inside," ordered Akira. We entered yet another room, the only one that wasn't white-walled. Instead, I took in the wall of red, the wall of green, the wall of brown. I knew where we were. Behind an uncluttered desk that seemed to hover, sat whom I assumed was the boss of AltaSystemics. To our right, sitting in the palm-shaped chair tb told me about from his interview was Emily managing to look both defiant and guilty at the same time.

The only person around here not robed in white or wearing pressed khaki was this bulldog of a man in a silver silk suit. Speaking on his smart phone, he motioned for tallboy and me to have a seat as two more burgundy palm chairs rose gracefully out of the floor. I took the one closest to Emily.

"You're probably wondering why I asked you here today," he said with a hearty laugh as he put down his phone. "Allow me to introduce myself. I'm AltaSystemics' Prime Mover. Candy?" He offered us a bowl of M&M-style treats, imprinted with either an 'A' or an 'S.' tallboy helped himself to a handful; Emily and I said no thanks.

LABELS: HIGH-TECH MYSTERY, ENIGMATIC STARTUP, THE BOSS IS IN

VIEW COMMENTS (49)

MasterMind OCT. 23, 2011 AT 2:00 PM
I warned them not to go snooping. They are dealing with proprietary information.

Ringside OCT. 23, 2011 AT 2:09 PM
Would I be willing to sneak into a high-tech company if I thought something sinister was going on?

○ ○ ○   **THINKS OUT LOUD**   ✕

BEYOND BANTER / WHIMSY WITHOUT REGRET

More than a guest?

Entry No. 571 - POSTED: OCT. 23, 2011

Anxious as I was to travel to the other side of the island and meet the communication drum team, I was still weak from my solo island experience. Taking Vaea's advice, I slept in for several mornings while the islanders went on with their daily life.

I ate and rested on warm sands and made some more notes and walked around the village and swam at a nearby lagoon and started to regain strength and energy. "This is just like a vacation," I thought. "I'm like any American on a Polynesian vacation." That left a bad taste in my mouth.

I think the excitement of my arrival had worn off for the villagers who returned to their routines of food gathering on land and sea, general upkeep of their houses and canoes, and their ongoing celebrations.

I didn't know if I were expected to help out or just stay a guest so I asked Vaea what I could do. "Get stronger," was his response. But the way Teva eyed me when he came ashore after fishing led me to think I needed to be more than a visitor.

"Vaea, can I at least help with cleaning?" I asked after another bountiful lunch.

He finally nodded. "Ask Teva what you can do."

I tracked down Teva on the beach where he was mending a fishing net. "Teva, is there something I could do, for example, neaten up the hut?"

He continued working and spoke to the netting. "The hut. Can you thatch a roof?"

"Not exactly."

"Strengthen the window frame before the next big wind?"

"No."

"Use a broom?"

"Sure."

Teva paused in his work and finally looked at me. "Good." He went back to fixing the net. Taking his answer for a yes, I backed away, returned to the hut, and looked for a broom. Now the hut felt like a tree house to me, except it was on the ground. With its palm wood siding, minimal furnishings, grassy roof and straw floor, we're talking basic. Didn't see a broom. What was I supposed to use to sweep out the sand Teva and I had brought in over the past couple of days?

The princess and a group of her friends were two huts down.

I walked over and tipped my head into the open window. Then I realized I should have at least knocked. The women were seated in a circle and doing some kind of necklace making out of shells.

"Hi, ladies."

They all stopped as if on cue. A stern Vaitiare said, "Feeling any stronger after your time on our sacred island?"

I tried to remain polite. "Yes, much stronger. Thank you. In fact, I was wondering if I could borrow a broom to clean the hut."

Vaitiare said something to one of her companions, who rose gracefully and left. Was I supposed to follow or wait? The women had gone back to their craft making.

"Those shells will make beautiful necklaces," I said.

"They are part of our tradition," said Vaitiare. "We believe in our traditions."

All I could think of to say was "Traditions are good." It sounded stupid.

Vaitiare did not respond. She and the others spoke softly in their language. A few of the women glanced up at me, at my head still sticking through the open window. I pulled back and let out an inward sigh. What was I doing here?

The villager returned with a broom that had a back-to-nature look. Of course, it was made from palm fronds.

"Take good care of our broom. A lot of attention went into its making," said Vaitiare's voice from the hut.

I thanked her and returned to my hut. It was a good broom. Firm. Responsive. Efficient. With quick strokes I worked my way from the far side to the door where I returned to sand to the outside. There. At last, I had made a contribution.

To be continued...

[*Message sent via DrumBeat, island-to-island communications.]

LABELS: ROLE OF THE GUEST, MAKE YOURSELF USEFUL, BROOM CONSTRUCTION

VIEW COMMENTS (33)

<u>Explica</u> OCT. 23, 2011 AT 5:10 PM
That's more than he ever did around the house.

<u>Krishnaman</u> OCT. 23, 2011 AT 6:05 PM
In Eastern traditions, sweeping can lead to higher consciousness.

<u>Ringside</u> OCT. 23, 2011 AT 6:25 PM
It may be a baby step, but Isaac is on a new path.

SHOW MORE COMMENTS

○ ○ ○   **THINKS OUT LOUD**   ✕

WHIMSY WITHOUT REGRET

A little chat with Prime Mover

Entry No. 572 - POSTED: OCT. 23, 2011

Prime Mover had us. It was as simple as that. Our plan to sneak around his company and find out what goes on had failed. Even worse, my brother was also in trouble and was probably about to be fired. So there we sat in the founder's eloquently sparce office—tallboy (very quiet), Emily (wish I could have given her a supportive hug), and me.

I wanted to Tweet in the worst way possible, but something told me that activity would not be well received by our host.

"Shall we get started?" Prime Mover asked politely. He had a broadcaster's smooth voice. And not waiting for an answer he continued speaking in a jarringly friendly manner. Balding and short and stocky, he looked more like an old-time, behind-the-scenes politico than the mastermind of a high-tech company. "I like people who show initiative. Boldness. Drive. Creativity." He gave each of us a pointed look. "What I don't like is subterfuge and trickery. Be honest with me, and I'll be honest with you." He leaned back in his tufted executive chair.

"Let's begin with you, tallboy." My brother could barely keep his head up. "You were hired to blog about AltaSystemics. That means we want you to explore the Hive, to pollinate the company buzz, to convey to our website readers what makes this place so special."

"Yes, sir," mouthed tallboy; no sounds came out.

"In fact your first blog just went up a couple of minutes ago," proclaimed Prime Mover.

"It did? That's great!" said tallboy. "What did I say? I mean, all I had was a draft so far."

"Yes," said Prime Mover, "and it was a really good draft. It's live."

With the press of a button on the arm of his chair, the green wall morphed into a video screen the size of New Jersey. Prime Mover brought up the page from the AltaSystemics site: "BlogaMight Direct" said the heading. "Happenings at AltaSystemics" read a subhead.

Then came the text, what I guessed was tallboy's blog. It started with his saying this was his first blog for the company and how excited he was to be working with all these great Hive members. Then he wrote how he'd been wandering the Hive and talking with everyone and that he was getting a sense of how committed they were to the mission. And he went on to describe several Hive members and how central their roles were to fulfilling the company's initiatives. And he ended by saying he'd be back soon with the latest updates.

That was it. I cleared my throat and studied my stained running shoes.

Bold Emily spoke out. "No offense, tallboy, but that blog doesn't say anything."

"Well, it's my first posting," he answered defensively. "There will be more details coming soon."

"tallboy, your blog is…" said Prime Mover as he rubbed his chin, "is just what I want. You are managing to write in a way, as Emily noted, that brings an inviting warmth to the page."

"Did I say that?" Emily asked. Prime Mover ignored her.

tallboy looked paler than a mannequin, though he managed a shy smile.

Prime Mover turned his attention to me. "Young man, some friendly advice: I appreciate you taking initiative, once. I don't recommend you do it twice."

All I could do was nod in agreement.

"Now, young lady, I suppose if you had been blogging, your content might have been a tad different. Don't you have a little theory about AltaSystemics?" Prime Mover had turned his attention to her.

She let out a sigh. "You have an interesting company. I don't really have much to add."

"Come now, don't be so modest," said Prime Mover. "Let's hear what you've got."

"Emily," I blurted out, "you don't have to do this. We can hire a lawyer. We can…"

"It's okay, Eddie," she said, giving me a warm look that made me dizzy. "I might as well play my part."

"The floor is yours, Emily," said Prime Mover with a royal wave of his hand.

A deflated tallboy and an anxious me could only look on as Emily faced this challenging moment. Leaning forward in a way that emphasized the curve of her back, she spoke in a serious voice, almost as if she were delivering a lecture, with just the slightest hint of hesitancy as she sometimes searched for the right word.

"Well, first of all we have cloud computing and cloud storage," she began. "That allows businesses and individuals to access software and memory via the Internet rather than from the traditional hard drive in someone's computer. The data and the software are kept on servers at locations remote from the user. It seems very abstract until you get used to it, which doesn't take very long."

Not bad, I thought.

Emily paused and gave me a half smile with raised eyebrow. "Now, as for AltaSystemics. When I saw the terms you were using to describe your mission and purpose, I was as confused as everyone else—those words and phrases such as *clairsentience, psychometric applications, collective unconscious paradigms*…It all sounded like gibberish. But then, with a little research on Wikipedia and a quick read of a recent issue of *NuConnexions: Beyond Earthly Realms*, I began to put it together. Add what I saw here today—everyone dressed in white, people seeming to be meditating rather than working—and it all fits together."

We waited as she pulled her left leg under her palm chair. His hands folded before him, Prime Mover was satisfied to let Emily offer her evidence.

"So, AltaSystemics is developing the means to operate software and store information in another dimension," she said, "one that is open to those with psychic abilities." I tried to keep breathing for myself and for her. "Your Hive people are working *and* they are meditating. That is, their meditation is their work. And in the process, they are opening up pathways to this other reality. And in that other reality, hmmm this is a bit hard to explain, in that other reality, time and space have different definitions from what we find in our dimension." Emily turned her right palm outward, her thumb massaging her fingers. "I suspect it's possible to store vast amounts of information in an infinitesimally small quantum of space slash time."

Even though I didn't fully understand what Emily was driving at, I was still impressed by her presentation. This could have been a Ted Talk.

"Well," said Emily, "we've seen this rapprochement between quantum-based physics and the intuitive universe in recent years. And the way physicists describe sub-atomic particles is closer to Eastern philosophies than traditional science."

Prime Mover raised his chin and studied Emily with penetrating eyes.

"When you say you are, and I quote, 'developing sensate clairsentience systems for the ultimate in collective consciousness paradigms,' you mean you are doing what I described—storing information in another dimension." Emily rested her case.

But only for a moment. "So why are you toying with us like this? Why are you using tallboy? Why do you use such slippery language on your website to describe this incredible breakthrough?"

"Those are excellent questions," said Prime Mover. "You know, I judge a person by the questions she asks, not the answers she gives, although your answers were pretty good." He continued, "Tell you what, let's adjourn to the CenterSphere and continue this little conversation, and, Eddie, no Tweets, not yet."

Even though I didn't work there, I felt like a dressed-down employee. We rose as a group, the palm chairs retracted back into the floor, and the thin non-door door slid open.

"Eddie," said Prime Mover, his eyes beckoning me, "I believe you know the way—the room you visited in our Underground Chamber. Lead on."

With a hesitant step I moved into the hallway, the troupe behind me. "Time for a, what did Emily call it? a quantum/flux engagement," I thought. Cue the atmospheric John Williams score.

To be continued...

LABELS: PSYCHIC POWERS, LOST IN THE CLOUD, THE FIFTH DIMENSION

VIEW COMMENTS (33)

Seequince OCT. 23, 2011 AT 7:10 PM
So, I don't understand everything Emily is saying either, but she sure got Prime Mover's attention.

Carrotty OCT. 23, 2011 AT 7:40 PM
Don't want to get in the middle of this; however, doesn't this remind you of some murky startup that makes grand promises and then skips town when the product they are supposed to be introducing turns out to be pure hype?

HindSite OCT. 23, 2011 AT 8:05 PM
Sure, Prime Mover could be a huckster. But what if he has made an incredible discovery?

SHOW MORE COMMENTS

○ ○ ○   **THINKS OUT LOUD**   ✕

BEYOND BANTER / WHIMSY WITHOUT REGRET

Anthropology 101

Entry No. 573 - POSTED: OCT. 24, 2011

I wish I had paid more attention in my Intro to Anthropology class in college because I am now going to offer my observations of the peoples on Tiaré, their customs, social interactions and belief systems. Ha! Right!

Well, actually I have noticed some items of note. (Is that redundant?)

Now that I am better rested, I have begun rising with the others, sharing their first meal of the day at the outdoor dining area. Ripe fruits. Banana bread. Fresh fish.

Their population probably numbers a couple of hundred. After breakfast, some head out to fish, others work on fixing netting or other tools. A group of women walk inland to gather fruits and vegetables. If any repairs need to be made on the huts, a crew apply their skills. The children follow along and mimic their elders. And each day, mid-afternoon, the kids, fifty or so, make their way to a hut slightly removed from the rest. An old man greets them, the oldest person I've seen on the island. They make a semi-circle around him, and he proceeds to speak in an animated voice. Stories, Vaea told me later. Hoanui is their teller of tales. He imparts to the children the stories about life on the island and what came before. Oral culture. I remember that term. I hung around behind the kids and listened, even though I couldn't understand the words. Sometimes the hand and body motions he made gave me an inkling of the subject, such as a great storm or a fierce beast. He's good, I thought, he's very good.

To further acquaint myself with the islanders, I started learning some basic Tahitian vocabulary. The language has a vibrant rhythm and is fun to speak:

'a 'oa'oa (smile)
himene (song)
nehenehe (beautiful)

An aside: I continue to bunk in Teva's grass hut. This is an excellent way to study the Polynesian male up close. He generally remains aloof but seems a little softer around the edges as when he asked me if I missed my homeland. That caught me by surprise.

"Good question, Teva. I feel like I should be missing my home greatly. My life there is very different from yours here," I said. I was so happy to be engaged in conversation with him I was practically running at the mouth. "I do not have a lot of close friends. I mostly communicate through my blog. I don't exercise enough. And my diet could stand improvement."

He asked me if I had a woman. "Well, we don't 'have women' where I come from. We mostly meet through online dating services and sometimes we marry. Right now, no, I don't 'have' a woman." He nodded and changed the subject to net fishing.

The role of nature is quite important on the island. Nature is all and everywhere. Humans are a part of it all and they interact with Nature in a, well, natural way. For example, one morning I was by myself at the lagoon, its pure blue waters contrasting perfectly with the rich mossy greens that layered the dark volcanic rock walls, all ceilinged by apse-like palm fronds. I was floating in the water, contemplating nothing, when I felt what was definitely a fin brush my back. Shark attack! I panicked and began flailing more than swimming. Anticipating the shark's powerful jaws chomping down on my legs, I cried out. Then it surfaced and I felt pure relief. I was eye to eye with Flipper! Curiosity replaced fear. The dolphin and I were definitely staring at each other. Intelligence and calmness in that eye. I tentatively put out my hand and touched the dolphin's head. Smooth and rubbery. The dolphin made one of those playful dolphin squeals, circled around me a couple of times, and slipped away.

Engulfed in calmness, I floated around for a few more minutes and swam back to shore.

Thought I saw someone watching in the shadows of the palms, but when I looked again he or she was gone.

So, surrounded by all this bounty, beginning to move at my host's calm but steady pace, I am gaining a greater appreciation for the way the Polynesians focus on the basics of life—and in a way that gives them great enjoyment.

To be continued...

[*Message sent via DrumBeat, island-to-island communications.]

LABELS: POLYNESIAN LIFESTYLE, ISLAND LIVING

VIEW COMMENTS (38)

Closer OCT. 24, 2011 AT 8:24 AM
Good try, Isaac. But a true anthropologist would be discussing social status, customs, religious beliefs, arts, morals, and laws.

Slice OCT. 24, 2011 AT 9:00 AM
Storytellers play an integral role in non-literate societies. They are like the tribe's memory.

Dexterra OCT. 24, 2011 AT 10:30 AM

Anthropologists walk a fine line between studying and affecting the societies they are observing. The Tiaré islanders bring Isaac, who is more an intruder than a scholar, to their home at some risk to their Ways.

Enabler OCT. 24, 2011 AT 10:44 PM

Often a shark's [first] bite is more exploratory than the start of a meal, a way to find out what it is dealing with.

SHOW MORE COMMENTS

In the belly of the beast

Entry No. 574 - POSTED: OCT. 24, 2011

Eddie here (still at AltaSystemics):

Leading the way, the obligatory James Bond pulsing film score in my head, I took our little group back down to the subterranean floor I had been exploring before I was interrupted first by tallboy and then by the Connector, Akira. When the elevator opened, there stood Akira to escort us to the pulsating CenterSphrere.

No one spoke as we moved through the white hallway, not tallboy, not Emily, not Prime Mover.

At the entrance to the room, I waved my hand before it, as if I worked there, and the smooth white door slid away. The room was still glaringly bright and filled with that sub-woofer bass throbbing.

"Thank you, Akira, we'll be fine," said Prime Mover. Akira nodded and faded back into the hallway, the door sliding shut upon his departure.

"This way, please," said Prime Mover as he indicated the centrally located device that looked like a projection machine out of a planetarium. "Lights, half power," he commanded. "Elemental bass, one quarter." The systems obeyed his directive.

The entrance door slid open again and a white-robed person entered. "Patricia," said Prime Mover, "thank you for joining us." It was the meditating woman we'd met on the tour.

Prime Mover spoke matter-of-factly, again praising Emily for her astute observations of what takes place at AltaSystemics. The only recognition she gave him was a slightly delayed eye blink. "As I said, this is our CenterSphere, containing our MosaicMedium, the axis point for psychometric collection, distillation, and, ultimately, trans-dimensional storage."

If we were really in a Bond film, this would have been my cue to swing into action and destroy the central nervous system of the whole place with a carefully placed explosive device I'd been hiding in my shoelace. Alarms would be screaming; armed guards would be firing at us; Emily would be pivoting and firing back with a laser weapon she pulled from her back pocket. But this wasn't a film. Instead I kept listening to Prime Mover as he continued to describe the operation of his super-psychic hive workers and their ability to move data into a realm beyond our normal reality.

"Would you like to ask Patricia any questions?" Prime Mover invited us. "She has the Power."

Emily jumped right in. "Patricia, is this true? Can you sense this other reality and interact with it?"

Patricia pushed back her hood. Her long jet black hair contrasted sharply with her white robe. Her voice was almost too calm. "Yes, Emily, I can. It's hard to describe in words. I go into a meditative state and use my breath and inner light to make the transcendence." She reached into a deep pocket, pulled out a handful of those candies, and delicately placed them in her mouth.

A phone's alert interrupted the conversation. We all looked to see if it were our phone. Prime Mover was the winner. He motioned for us to keep talking as he took his call.

"So you can deposit and later access information?" Emily asked. Prime Mover was watching her as if Emily were a prize race horse. I felt powerless.

"Yes, hello, Pablo," said the executive to his phone companion. "Yes, both of them…Yes, I know they are in different locations. You've got your marching orders. They'll be a wonderful addition to my, hmmm, Team. Ciao." He put the phone away and watched Patricia approvingly.

After she had swallowed her treat, Patricia answered Emily's question: "Yes, I can manipulate information in that way."

"This is great blog material," tallboy exclaimed as if he had just discovered the power to speak.

"Indeed, indeed," Prime Mover agreed as he clicked his fist lightly on the planetarium-like instrument. "Blog, tallboy, blog!"

"Can I cover everything you've been showing us and what Emily and Patricia have been saying?" He seemed to be coming back to life.

"Yes, yes. All of it. Get the word out!" This was the most excited I'd seen Prime Mover. He looked as if he were about to crow.

I had to contribute my bit: "No one is going to believe a word of any of this. It's all a big joke!"

Emily's eyes went saucerlike. tallboy came round to offer big brotherly protection.

"Possibly," said Prime Mover who showed no offense at my brazen words. "In fact, Eddie, you can do your own blog. Take me to task. Pull back the curtain on my wizardry."

"All right, I will," I said.

"How can I blog and report on what AltaSystemics does while you do a blog that denies everything?" questioned tallboy.

"Um, brother fought brother in the American Civil War," I offered.

"It's okay," Prime Mover said. "Blog, post, tell your friends on Facebook everything, whatever you want, the more outrageous the better. Create buzz, rev up the controversy, get people talking. In other words, Eddie, go Tweet and blog to your heart's content. In fact, you already have and you always will if I have my way."

LABELS: ESP, MASTERMIND OR MANIAC, IN THE LAIR

VIEW COMMENTS (40)

SeenIt OCT. 24, 2011 AT 11:54 AM
He should hire Emily. But she'd probably say no.

TS OCT. 24, 2011 AT 1:04 PM
Okay, let me get this straight. This Prime Mover has made the discovery of the century and he wants pro and con blog postings to go out?

Etruscan OCT. 24, 2011 AT 1:33 PM
If only this were a Bond film. But it's not. It's just a bunch of kids basically way out of their league. Don't they see how the dimensional storage idea/invention

will benefit humanity?

SHOW MORE COMMENTS

○ ○ ○   **THINKS OUT LOUD**   ✕

WHIMSY WITHOUT REGRET

Prime Mover in fine form

Entry No. 575 - POSTED: OCT. 25, 2011

Eddie: Deep under the Hive in AltaSystemics hidden control room, Prime Mover had essentially given us carte blanche (Is that the correct term?) to write whatever we wanted—good or bad—about his enigmatic company. tallboy was thrilled to still have his job and was primed and ready to support the AltaSystemics Way. Emily wore a poker face I couldn't read. I was wondering why PM would let me rip into his, well, whatever all this was. He maintained he didn't care what we communicated. Yet he didn't seem indifferent. In fact, it looked like what he wanted to have us do was create a kind of smokescreen about AltaSystemics with all kinds of competing commentary and reports so that you couldn't tell fact from fiction, fantasy from reality.

It was brilliant. Prime Mover was so Bond-villainesque.

"How's everyone feeling?" asked Prime Mover as he began to herd us out of the CenterSphere room. "Do you feel more relaxed now that you know the truth about AltaSystemic's mission?" tallboy was standing tall. Emily stayed quiet and evenly calm

"Trying to figure me out, Eddie?" asked the wily but perceptive PM, his hand motioning for us to continue down the glowing white hallway. For a compact, stocky figure, he had a light, flowing walk. "Consider this: How has Isaac been able to send his blog postings from a deserted island?"

I said I didn't know. It was a mystery.

"You must have fallen behind in your reading of Thinks Out Loud," he continued.

I didn't want Prime Mover to know he was getting to me. "Actually I was wondering what happened to the rest of our tour group," I said.

We approached the elevator. "They finished up some time ago," he said, "received a free facsimile meditation wheel, and, I assume, are probably home by now enjoying dinner while discussing my fascinating company." PM looked at his wristwatch, a massive gaudy golden piece that was more jewelry than timepiece.

We rode the elevator back up to the main floor. As we crossed a now quiet high-ceilinged lobby, I took up PM's previous question. "So, how has Isaac been able to send blogs he couldn't have written yet?"

Prime Mover was pointing us toward the double door exit, two husky Connectors chatting quietly and watching us from the lobby's 'Determination' desk. "Oh, that. Eddie, when was the last time you read Isaac's blog from Polynesia?"

"I've been busy." I admitted.

The exit doors glided open. Early evening traffic noise bounced into us. Quickening my pace, I couldn't wait to escape the Hive.

"When you get a chance take a look at his recent postings," PM called to us. "That should help answer my question about Isaac's blogging. See you tomorrow, tallboy." Like glass curtains, the doors slid shut and the three of us huddled in the middle of crowded Pioneer Square. We were physically free of the Hive but emotionally held captive by its mysterious inner workings.

To be continued...

LABELS: VILLAIN OR JUST MISUNDERSTOOD, CATCH AND RELEASE

VIEW COMMENTS (36)

FunGus OCT. 25, 2011 AT 11:19 AM
If this guy is for real, then I, for one, am officially nervous about what he's up to.

BlueBaby OCT. 25, 2011 AT 1:14 AM
Actually, I get it. Prime Mover is using a marketing technique of bringing atten-tion to his product (psychic storage) by intentionally creating controversy. Buzz is buzz.

SHOW MORE COMMENTS

Vaea talks about outsiders

Entry No. 576 - POSTED: OCT. 25, 2011

"Vaea," I said in the morning when he was coming out of his hut, "would this be a good time…" I caught myself being overly polite and went for direct: "Could you tell me what you reported to your people after your stay in Hawaii?"

Walking toward the beach, he answered, "Yes, this is the proper time, now that you have been among us for some days." Vaea went on to explain that after living among the Hawaiians and tourists, he had returned to Tiaré and told of his experiences, offered his general impressions, and made his recommendations.

Although he admitted some Polynesians had been caught in the attraction of modern ways both for practical and entertainment purposes, Vaea saw the price other islanders, including many Hawaiians, had paid in the withering away of traditions and the loss of the "View of the World" and how some of them were trying to reclaim their heritage.

With the press of modernity encroaching on the island, Vaea urged his people to continue to limit contact with non-islanders. "We still wish to follow the path of our ancestors." I stared intently at his home as he spoke.

"One of the younger men accused me of wanting Tiaré to become a museum. I did not deny that, but I said there was value in at least one of Polynesia's islands continuing to live by tradition." Vaea paused a moment and finally looked at me. Deeply.

He said that after a full day of discussion, the islanders took a vote and it was nearly unanimous in favor of eschewing technologies. "We made a few exceptions, such as for island emergencies. Thus, we have a site where an aircraft can land. And we have a rusted short-wave radio, seldom used. We also allow those who wish to visit off-island to do so. And our sewage system has been updated—we now have what you call outhouses."

He added that a few years before people "from Hollywood" had come by helicopter and asked if they could do a program with outsiders trying to survive on one of the rougher parts of the island. "We were to receive a bounty of money, but we said no."

I didn't have the courage to divulge to Vaea how much time I spent on modern devices, how I blogged and Tweeted and YouTubed and Facebooked. Instead I said, "Much of what Teva told me about his time with the Amish fits quite well with what you've just explained to me."

Seagulls were circling above us as if they wanted to express their opinion of outsiders.

"Yes," said Vaea, "Teva returned to us with a report of his appreciation for the Amish, our cousins in thought and deed."

"So why, when you rescued me, did you bring me here?"

He stopped at the water line. "You had lived on our sacred island. We wanted to see if that had somehow affected you."

"Do you think it has?"

"We do not know, yet."

To be continued...

[*Message sent via DrumBeat, island-to-island communications.]

LABELS: MODERN VERSUS TRADITIONAL SOCIETY, BALI H'AI

VIEW COMMENTS (39)

JourneyMan OCT. 25, 2011 AT 3:30 PM
They should be protective of their culture. Maybe give Isaac some kind of amnesia drug and drop him off on Tahiti.

Enabler OCT. 25, 2011 AT 3:53 PM
I went on Wikipedia and typed in Tiaré. The entry said it was a small Polynesian island at the end of a chain of islands off the coast of Tahiti. A mountain peak stands in the center of the island. There are two villages. Not much is known about the inhabitants who tend to be isolationist, unwelcoming and resistant to change. There is little trade with other islands and no major industries. Tourism is not promoted.

SHOW MORE COMMENTS

Out of the Hive

Entry No. 577 - POSTED: OCT. 25, 2011

Eddie: Released from the innards of AltaSystemics, like windup toys set free, tallboy, Emily, and I haltingly wandered past Pioneer Square's ornate bricked 19th-century buildings with arched stone entrances—many now housing high-tech companies. Places with secrets like AltaSystemics?

The streets wet from an earlier rain, we breathed in the nighttime air with its marine scent from nearby Puget Sound. tallboy was in a surprisingly upbeat mood, considering our earlier activities of practically being kidnapped and held against our will. Emily walked quietly beside me, wearing not a blank expression but more one of being lost in thought. For once, I didn't feel like Tweeting.

"Anyone hungry?" asked tallboy.

"No," said Emily and I in chorus. Just then we were caught up in the midst of a crowd who seemed to have come out of nowhere. Gazing in all directions, they flowed around us like a slow moving river, we the rocks in their current. "Next on our stop of Underground Seattle is a subterranean passage that once was the city's main thoroughfare," said a burly fellow, the tour guide I assumed. The tourists moved on, a couple of stragglers speaking in Russian making up the tail end of the group.

"I need to eat," demanded tallboy. He went in and out of being calm.

"Okay," said Emily and I, again in unison and without any enthusiasm. We entered Bistro Paloma. With fuscia colored walls and red paper lanterns hanging at different heights from the ceiling, this whimsical eatery was the opposite of the Zenlike purity of AltaSystemics. We sat at a corner table near the large front window. I took the wooden bench seat facing into the dining area, a raised stage at the back empty except for the covered piano.

"There's a tuba on the ceiling," said Emily, looking for a distraction from recent events.

"The art of whimsy, a physical example," I said.

"It's hard to pull it all together," said Emily after a studied silence. She felt her theory about using psychic power to store data could be true, but then again, it was all pretty far fetched.

"Emily, you are impressive. Your insights and ideas," I said. She seemed uncomfortable with the praise. I couldn't get over her mix of shyness and boldness. For a minute we were all quiet, except for tallboy's humming. I studied my plate and silverware. "Prime Mover may be a con man...or a genius."

"Or both," said Emily. "And his employees are kind of weird.

"Those Connectors are basically security guards," I said.

"And the Hivers, like that Patricia, have gone way beyond yoga and meditation.

"Now that I think about it," I noted, "how do we know any information is being stored? Does AltaSystemics actually have real clients?"

We realized we had more questions than answers.

"I like working there," said tallboy as he dipped a wedge of pita into some hummus.

"You've only done one blog so far," I said, "and it was mostly written by Prime Mover."

tallboy nodded. "It's a start. The company is doing good things. Good people doing good things. Good things from really good people. I gotta go pee." He backed out his chair, got up and crossed over to the bistro's other side.

I looked at Emily, her wonderful high cheek bones, her large intelligent eyes. She had a quiet beauty accented by an aura of intelligence. Go ahead, said my inner voice. "Emily, not to change the subject, but I've been meaning to ask you something."

She cocked her head. "What?"

I tried to keep breathing. "I know this is way off subject. I still feel as if I've been lost in a not-so-funhouse, but are you seeing anyone?"

She seemed affronted. "How can you ask that when we've just gotten away from almost being kidnapped?"

"Well," I started, but couldn't think of anything to add.

Pursing her lips she said, "I guess you could say I'm seeing someone. A business major. We don't actually do a lot. Movies. A party now and then." Her eyes, unblinking, searched mine. "Why, why do you ask?"

This was my moment. tallboy had come out of the bathroom and was walking slowly back to the table. He seemed a little off to me.

"Emily, with all this stuff we've been doing—actually and even before___"

Emily was watching my mouth, which wasn't working properly, and tallboy had reached us and immediately returned to the hummus that neither Emily nor I had touched.

Concern, warmth, and hope took turns on Emily's face. "You look a little pale, Eddie," she said. "I'm as shaken up as you. But we can't drop this AltaSystemics mystery."

I groaned inwardly and tried to reboot my mind to reopen the AltaSystemics folder. "Prime Mover suggested I read Isaac's latest blogs—how is he managing to post from a deserted island?"

"Let's go back to your place and review his postings," suggested Emily.

My heart went into overdrive. "Sure," I said. "Good idea."

LABELS: DEBRIEFING, SCENIC PIONEER SQUARE, ROMANTIC PIONEER SQUARE

VIEW COMMENTS (40)

Seattlebred OCT. 25, 2011 AT 1:39 PM
I love that restaurant! Didn't know it was still open.

RoseCity OCT. 25, 2011 AT 2:12 PM
I took the underground tour and got separated from the group and ended up going into the basement of an office building, in the dark, so I had to use my iPhone as a flashlight.

BlueBaby OCT. 25, 2011 AT 2:31 PM
People, Eddie and Emily have stumbled onto what may be a new way to control reality (and us) and all you can comment upon are restaurants and underground tours?

SHOW MORE COMMENTS

Getting sort of closer to Emily

Entry No. 578 - POSTED: OCT. 26, 2011

Before riding our bus to the U District, Emily and I made sure tallboy got on the right bus to get him up to his Capitol Hill apartment. Calmly, he said he'd be fine. He wanted to go home and do some blogging for AltaSystemics. He seemed so dazed; we asked the fifty-something driver if he'd make sure tallboy got off at 15th and Pine.

Emily and I caught an express to my neighborhood near the University. "It's not much," I told her. "I share the place with three other guys, so it will be messy." She said that was okay. During the ride, when we went over a bump my shoulder nudged hers. She didn't pull away.

My apartment building, a block from the bus stop, was unique to the area: stucco with a red tile roof. I was told the original owner/builder had imported the style from his previous home in Santa Barbara. "Nice," said Emily as we entered the building through an archway. Inside the apartment, amazingly, no one else was around. I grabbed my laptop, set it up amidst clutter on the dining room table and went straight to Isaac's blog. Emily sat next to me.

"Want anything to drink?" I asked. "Wine or beer?"

"Water would be great." She was warm and friendly and just a little restrained, like she was holding something back.

Water glasses in hand, we got caught up on Isaac's blog. Since we had been having our own adventure, we'd fallen behind in his Polynesian adventures. And word that the Morse brothers had developed the ability to send messages from the past while written in the present in what Isaac realized involved a theoretical approach to physics or something like that. "Prime Mover was hinting about that," I said.

"That's similar to what researchers claim to be doing in those Large Hadron Collider experiments," said Emily. She reminded me that an institute in Geneva had discovered a sub-atomic particle being able to travel faster than the speed of light. But could that mean that somehow someone in the present could have a message sent from the past? That kind of stuff always makes me dizzy.

"I also read the experiment needs to be verified," Emily said. "It isn't actually proven yet. Suppose the Morse brothers are working on a similar or related theory. That would explain how Isaac was able to blog from the deserted island—he wrote the blog after the fact and then had the brothers send it back into and from the past."

We were both excited. Leaning toward the computer, we had somehow joined hands. As if we simultaneously discovered we were holding dry ice, we dropped hands and pulled back.

"Emily, I…"

"I've got a boyfriend. Sort of."

"I know, I know."

"Eddie. You're great. You're smart and cute and I like…" Emily actually grimaced. "I don't know."

"Emily, I don't have any easy answers here. I like you. I like having you as a partner as we try and figure all this out." We were nose to nose, then mouth approaching mouth.

"Eddie, my man!" New voices invaded the dining room followed by two of my roommates. "Oh, you've got company," said Mike. He pulled off his hoodie and brushed at his long blond hair. Ashton, a gangly and serious guy, stood right behind him, trying to see what was going on.

"Mike, Ashton, this is Emily. We're both taking the History of High-tech class."

"Right," said Mike as he slid over to the fridge and found a beer. "A study date."

Emily was rising, "I'll see you in class, Eddie." As she moved toward the door, I followed after her like a puppy.

I caught up to her in our entryway. I wanted to kiss her, but she was looking toward the street.

"Emily…"

"Don't say anything Eddie. Not right now."

I paused to show I was changing the subject. "I'm going to contact the Morse brothers and see if they'll send some of my postings from the past like they did for Isaac. That would be so cool. tallboy figured out how to get in contact with them when he was searching for Isaac."

With a brief nod, Emily moved down the steps to the sidewalk.

"Walk you home?" I volunteered.

"No. It's not far. I need some time." And off she went into the night, taking my hopes and dreams with her. Does that happen in Bond movies?

LABELS: COLLEGE ROOMMATES, ROMANCE IN HIGH-TECH AGE, RUMORS OF TIME TRAVEL

VIEW COMMENTS (52)

JohnsBrain OCT. 26, 2011 AT 11:04 AM
Eddie and Emily are actually making a lot of progress.

FisherKing OCT. 26, 2011 AT 11:16 AM
If the Morse brothers are right, they deserve a Nobel Prize.

SHOW MORE COMMENTS

○ ○ ○   THINKS OUT LOUD   ✕

BEYOND BANTER / WHIMSY WITHOUT REGRET

Off to see the drummers

Entry No. 579 - POSTED: OCT. 27, 2011

It was a quiet morning; Vaea greeted me at the hut as I was awakening. "Today is the day we travel to meet the drummers," he said. I realized I didn't know what day of the week it was. I'd been on the island for a while now, that I knew, but was this day 8? 9? 10?

"I'm ready, Vaea," I said. He informed me our walk would take the rest of the morning and into the afternoon or so, depending on how much rest I needed. I assured him I would do fine. After a quick breakfast, we packed a lunch of island delights and readied to leave. I'd soon be able to send messages back to my world. And if Vaea had been speaking the truth about playing with time, you've already read my messages.

"My notebook. I need my notes," I remembered. "Back in a second." I jogged over to the hut and grabbed my notebook from my small collection of personal belongings. Upon my return, Vaea rose. Have I mentioned how graceful these people are? Beside him, studying me as usual, stood Vaitiare, who wore a pale yellow sarong I tried to avoid staring at. I nodded to her and readied to follow their lead.

From a nearby grass hut, Chief Keoni emerged. With him, Kohia, his translator. He spoke to us in his dialect and she offered the translation. "May your journey be a good one. May you find what you seek." He added in English, "Goodbye." Keoni waved. Kohia waved.

With Vaea a few paces in front, we took a path that curved away from the beach and into a grove of palms, flowering bushes, and ferns. Dappled morning light, a warm, soft breeze, and the knowledge of where we were headed put me in a sparkling mood.

Then Vaitiare, who was walking a few feet ahead of me, with a smooth, steady, swaying gait, threw a question without turning to look at me: "Isaac, you have lived alone on a sacred island, paddled with our men across the sea to our home, and have been living with us since the New Moon. What do you think of us?"

I almost froze but managed to keep walking. "That's a very interesting question," I said, stalling for time. What did I think of these islanders? I told her I came from a very different land where modern machines dominated our lives. We were also quite busy a lot of the time, at least we seem to be busy. "On this island," I said, "you and your friends and family live at a different pace. It's almost as if you are always dancing. And you seem more contented than the people from my land, even though you have a lot less." That didn't sound right.

"A lot less, you say," chimed in Vaitiare. "Do we seem primitive and poor to you."

"No, no. You just don't seem to need as much to make you happy and satisfied. You don't need gadgets and toys and professional spectator sports."

"Is that so bad?"

"No, not at all." I paused. "Having only been here a, what, a couple of weeks plus a couple of months by myself on the other island—

"Our taboo island."

"Yes, your taboo island. Having been a visitor in your world a short time, I have already developed an appreciation for your way of life."

She momentarily tilted her head toward me. "Perhaps you are here for a reason, but is it for the Good or the Bad?" she questioned as she pushed aside a tall bush's branch which slapped back into my face just as I passed. It stung.

To be continued...

[*Message sent via DrumBeat, island-to-island communications.]

LABELS: POLYNESIAN TRAVEL MODES, FORMER CASTAWAY, CULTURAL RELATIVITY

VIEW COMMENTS (44)

Just Saying OCT. 27, 2011 AT 8:12 AM
I hear you, Vaitiare. It's not just the Polynesians who are trying to find a way to simplify.

Gregorian OCT. 27, 2011 AT 8:29 AM
I love the word 'taboo.' I think the word originated in Polynesia.

Explica OCT. 27, 2011 AT 8:34 AM
Good job, branch.

SHOW MORE COMMENTS

○ ○ ○   **THINKS OUT LOUD**   ✕

BEYOND JESTING / WHIMSY WITHOUT REGRET

Lunch at the lagoon

Entry No. 580 - POSTED: OCT. 27, 2011

As we weaved our way into the interior of the island, while skirting its central peak, I didn't let Vaitiare's brusque treatment of me affect my mood. After all I was in paradise. Our soft path sometimes drifted upward to a gentle hilltop and then curved downward toward pools fed by cascading waterfalls. Wild pink, yellow, and violet flowers overran the sides of the trail. I was mesmerized.

I regarded a waterfall. I'd seen plenty of waterfalls before, really majestic ones like in Yosemite that seemed never ending. But this fall caught my attention. Surrounded by dense foliage and maybe thirty feet high. An arm's length wide. Pretty but not spectacular. Coolness of air surrounding it. I stared at the top third of the fall and saw a blur of water. Then a thought bounced into my head, and I decided to follow a section of the water as it fell. Instantly the look of the fall changed. Rather than blur, I saw a piece of the water moving like an elevator down the course of the slope until it splashed into the pool below. It was stunning! Two ways to look at a waterfall, I realized. The whole and the part. Two different realities.

"Let us stop here for lunch," said Vaea as he halted at a sun-warmed group of flat rocks near the edge of the deep green lagoon. He brought me back from my reverie. "*Haere mai,* sit."

"Looks good to me," I said. Vaitiare settled gently onto the rock closest to the water's edge and drew her legs under herself, Vaea on her left, me on the right. I was hungry and had to pace myself. "This is fabulous food." I searched my mind for the Tahitian word…"Delicious, *ma'a.*" Vaitiare gave me a nod.

"Of course it always tastes better outdoors. This vanilla accent is to die for." My two companions looked at me as though I had begun grunting like a wild pig.

Finally Vaitiare, staring into the water as it danced away from the fall, addressed me. "Isaac, I have heard everything you have said, but still, what do we know of you? You essentially appear out of nowhere, alone, barely alive. You tell us little about who you are, about what is important to you. What are we to make of you?"

Vaea let me answer as he continued to enjoy his lunch.

I nodded. "Good points, Vaitiare. I do feel like a mystery man. Here I am in the middle of a beautiful island, enjoying your company, so far from my home and other life. I'm even beginning to wonder if that other was even real."

Vaitiare gave me a glance. Did she detect if I was roaming among clichés? She combined power and allure in her look. "So, who are you?" she asked again.

I didn't want to disappoint her. "I've had a varied career in public relations and communications. I helped companies explain what they do to targeted audiences. If a thorny situation came up, I huddled with the CEO and other managers to resolve the issue with a series of explanatory communications…"

Vaitiare wasn't even looking at me.

I tried again. "I'm Colorado born and bred. Denver, the mile-high city, right at the entrance to the lofty Rocky Mountains."

This got a reaction from her. "So, you are of the mountains."

"Yes and no. I did a lot of hiking in the summer and skiing in the winter."

Her eyes wandered back to the lagoon. "Isaac, what moves you, what makes your soul flutter?"

"I don't know," I admitted. "I guess writing. I've always liked to write. At least since sixth grade when my teacher, Mrs. Milton, had us compose stories using the words in our weekly spelling lists. She always called on me and my best friend Carl to read ours. Been writing ever since."

"And what do you write?"

"So, besides the job stuff—that I do for pay—there's my other side: a score of short stories, three published, a novel in progress, and this blog that I started five years ago."

"So, Isaac," said Vaitiare, "you find happiness in writing, in telling stories."

"Yes, I guess I do."

She was back to watching me, her almond eyes drawing me into a trance state again. "Yet you gave up the blogging to travel and come here. Why?"

I had to listen hard to make out her meaning. Had I gone beyond blogging? Why had I felt the need to push my words out into etherspace? Here I sat on this rock, by this entrancing water, the entire island singing a seductive song to me. I stood up. I wanted to wade into the lagoon and submerge myself in the enveloping waters. I stepped forward.

"Isaac, watch out!" warned Vaitiare. I could barely hear her.

"Come back," jabbed Vaea. His words bounced off me.

I was in the pool, warm water up to my heart. Almost home. But like a burst bubble, the sense of rapture was broken. "This would make a great spot for a zip line," I blurted.

Vaea ignored my statement and rose. Something about the way he—all these people—manifested a larger energy surrounding them. "You can swim later. If we wish to reach the other side by the early afternoon, we should continue our journey."

We hit the trail.

Walking just ahead, Vaitiare said back to me, "Isaac, you are like a flower that has never fully opened. Perhaps that is why you have come to the island of flowers. Perhaps it is time to blossom. Or to be picked."

To be continued...

[*MESSAGE SENT VIA DRUMBEAT—ISLAND-TO-ISLAND COMMUNICATIONS]

LABELS: LIFE JOURNEY, POLYNESIAN ADVENTURE, TAKE A HIKE

VIEW COMMENTS (42)

Crepedejour OCT. 27, 2011 AT 9:10 AM
Isaac is on a journey into new realms (for him). Sleeping parts of him are awakening.

Specialist OCT. 27, 2011 AT 10:15 AM
Isaac, you should have studied the culture, history and religion/myths of the Polynesians before setting foot on their islands.

SHOW MORE COMMENTS

○ ○ ○   **THINKS OUT LOUD**   ✕

WHIMSY WITHOUT REGRET

Trying to focus

Entry No. 581 - POSTED: OCT. 27, 2011

Eddie: Before I could enlist tallboy's help in contacting the Morse brothers, I first had to go to school for a couple of days of classes, finish some overdue papers. And my part-time job, at a dorm's dining place. I felt as if I were stumbling around in a Seattle drizzle. AltaSystemics. Prime Mover. Emily. tallboy acting like a drone. Food server to hungry freshmen.

"Thanks, but I didn't order the burger," said a student customer as if she had already told me twice what she wanted. "The Bahn Mi, please." I made the switch. Focus, focus.

I wasn't much better in Social Media 101. Then came the History of High-tech seminar, the group that had taken the tour. I got there late, in keeping with my day of disorganization. Everyone was seated around our oval Round Table, including Emily, who was peering into her phone. I sat at the only open spot, next to her. She gave me a quick glance, a minimal smile.

Professor Stevens, still a nerd at heart who had trouble making eye contact, was asking students if they had any comments about the AltaSystemics tour. Chen said it had been interesting, but he still didn't know what they did there. I held in a laugh. Eric said he had a theory: The company was developing software for computers that were about to achieve self-consciousness. That idea impressed the class. "Eddie, what about you and Emily,' said our teacher, "Didn't you go on an extended tour?"

Emily looked up and gave me a "well-what-are-you-going-to-say" look.

"Right, the extra part of the tour," I said. "Because my brother, tallboy, works there, they showed us his blogging station and some other rooms, all white, by the way."

"So, what do they do at AltaSystemics?" asked the professor.

I was about to divulge it all when Emily cut in with, "Advanced storage using a super cloud configuration."

"But what about all that psychic stuff?" asked Angela.

"It's all just marketing hype," said Emily.

"Well," said Professor Stevens, "thank you for arranging the tour. It added a real-life component to the theoretical side of class. Eddie, tell your brother I look forward to his next posting. Now, let's continue with Apple's early years, when a lot of what it was offering was likewise hard to describe and a bit mysterious."

After class, Emily cornered me. "You were about to tell them what happened."

"No," I said, "just a summary."

"They wouldn't believe us if we told them the truth. This has to be our secret for now." She certainly was engaged again.

"Okay." I told her I needed to go meet with tallboy to send off my posts that would supposedly appear in the past. "Want to join us?"

She said no, she had another appointment and to let her know how the messaging went. Before I could reply, she was mounting her retro, big-fendered, yellow bike and pedaling away.

tallboy and I were supposed to rendezvous at a nearby Starbucks. I had my laptop, but I needed his knowledge because he had actually been in communication with the Morse brothers, who had helped him contact Isaac's rescuers. Not to mention they had conquered time or at least found a way to hitch a ride on its currents. Walking in a couple of minutes after my arrival, tallboy wandered around the crowded café and totally missed where I was parked at a back table. He was wearing more white these days: both pants and long-sleeved shirt. Standing before me but looking away, he finally noticed me when I tugged on his shirt. "tallboy!"

"Eddie!" He sort of glided into his seat.

For the third time I explained why I needed his help. He was following the ebb and flow of customers and occasionally nodding. "tallboy, can you guide me to the brothers?" I indicated my computer.

"Do you want to contact Isaac?"

Frustrated but acting calmly, I spoke softly and slowly. "Not exactly. I just need to reach the brothers."

I told him to hold on a second and half ran, half stumbled to the order counter for my triple, no foam. tallboy said he didn't need coffee anymore. "My energy is kind of constant these days." I redirected his attention to contacting the Morse brothers.

"You want to Skype with Morse the Younger in Hawaii?" tallboy didn't wait for my answer.

With some quick strokes of the keyboard, he brought up the Brother's account, just text, and explained that his younger brother, me, wanted to ask a favor.

I got on the keyboard and thanked the brother and his brother for helping to save our co-blogger, Isaac. And I had one more favor. Would they be willing to send a couple of my postings from past dates that are related to Isaac's postings?

There was a lag before Morse the Younger answered. tallboy sat next to me and was paying more attention to the ceiling's track lighting than the communication at hand. I didn't know how long I should wait for an answer before resending. As I was about to ask again, the Younger's reply came in. "Will do. Forward postings when convenient." I said I'd be sending them in a couple of days and thanked the brothers again for their kindness. Younger gave me his email address so I could send the posts. I was set. This was going to be fun.

Bent over in his chair, tallboy looked asleep. I wasn't convinced about his constant energy. After I nudged him, he opened his eyes and said he'd been meditating. By choice or by force, I wondered as I helped my brother to stand and head out into the drizzly night.

To be continued...

VIEW COMMENTS (62)

BlueBaby OCT. 27, 2011 AT 9:50 AM
Eddie is his brother's keeper. Then we have the Morse brothers helping each other. The Polynesians have brothers, although that hasn't been a theme here.

2Spacer OCT. 27, 2011 AT 10:05 AM
This all just got more complicated with Eddie joining in to manipulate the past. He makes it sound so innocent.

Etruscan OCT. 27, 2011 AT 10:22 AM
The Morse brothers sound like remarkable men. Would like to meet them.

SHOW MORE COMMENTS

○ ○ ○   **THINKS OUT LOUD**   ✕

BEYOND BANTER / WHIMSY WITHOUT REGRET

Let the drumming begin

Entry No. 582 - POSTED: OCT. 27, 2011

By midafternoon we had reached the village on the island's other side. Framed by palms, beach, ocean, and sky, thatched grass huts in a wide semicircle flanked a dining area and dancing circle. Very similar to Vaea's village. Just behind the huts, on a rise bare of trees stood a group of drums poised like sculptures. The communication system.

People grouped near the water or beside the largest of the huts. They noticed us and began to approach with a lot of pointing and clapping and animated language.

"You are a topic of conversation around here," said Vaea. As if being entertained, Vaitiare stood beside me and was content to see how I was received. An elder, perhaps the village chieftain, came before me and exchanged a head nod with Vaea. His villagers clustered around him and craned their necks to get a better look at me. "How DO I look to them?" I thought. I hadn't really paid much attention to my appearance since arriving at the island. I hadn't even seen my reflection in a mirror.

"*Maeva*, welcome to Manua, in your language Bird Messenger of Happiness," said the elder in passable English. He wore a bright blue cotton shirt and white clam digger style pants. He was short, but, again as I had seen in many of the older islanders, full-chested and sturdy. "We wish you a restful and peaceful stay with us."

"Thank you," I answered. These folks were really cordial. I didn't want to press the communication motive for coming here, but I couldn't help eyeing the drums. "Your village is charming."

Vaea added the introductions. "Isaac, this is Aitu or Priest. He serves two roles for the village—leader and spiritual head. "Aitu, this is Isaac, who has traveled here to visit and to make use of our drummer messengers."

With nods and smiles all round, we moved toward the outdoor dining courtyard where, once again, beautiful fresh fruit and vegetables beckoned.

"Please," said Aitu, "dine with us."

"My pleasure," I said, and we were soon sitting and eating and talking (not that I understood much) and enjoying the festive moment. The Manuans seemed to already know about me and went from shy to friendly in a matter of minutes. The kids were pulling on my arms as I tried to eat and were shooed away by their parents.

After the late lunch (my second of the day), Vaea beckoned me toward the beach. Vaitiare chatted with a trio of the village's young women who glanced over to me and then laughed. "Inas, our village, looks east," said Vaea.

"Wife of the Moon," I said.

Vaea studied me and then continued. "Manua looks west. We greet the sunrise. Our brothers offer the day's farewell." I could see some land that didn't look very far away. "Our neighboring island of Ponui or Big Night, the island I spoke of when you first came to Tiaré that receives our messages. They in turn send the message to their nearest western island and so on until the message is received by Morse the Elder of whom I told you."

"How far away is Ponui?" I asked. Vaea said not far, close enough to hear the drum messages from Manua. I guessed a mile or two. I couldn't believe the sound could carry that distance. He told me the drums were designed to send forth sound like gulls flying from island to island. "Hearing is believing," I said. Vaea paid no attention to my comment.

Accompanied by a gaggle of laughing and pointing children, Vaea and I followed a short trail up the rise to the hill's flat top. Six men stood by six percussion instruments, three of the drums looking like hollowed out logs and three upright, three-foot high drums, all beautifully carved and decorated. Five of the men were strong and big, the sixth was lean and hungry looking, a rarity around here. All wore white loose shirts and white 'Bermuda' shorts. Several sported tattoo designs running the length of their arms and legs. They stood motionless and solemn.

"You admire the drums," said Vaea. "We make the upright ones of coconut wood, shark skin, and coconut rope."

Vaea then greeted the drum team in their Polynesian dialect. They murmured back some kind of response. From behind me, Vaitiare appeared. "Vaea, I would be honored to translate what Isaac wants to say to the Messengers." He stepped back.

"Tell them I have come many miles and finally am able to fulfill my duty—to send messages back to my people, to tell my story," I said to the men. Vaitiare translated in a voice soft yet confident. The men nodded at first but then, as she continued speaking, began glaring at me. Only the lean one remained calm.

"Vaitiare!" shouted Vaea in a scolding voice.

"Vaitiare, what did you tell them?"

"Only that you intended to have them drum shameful stories of our society for all to hear."

I felt as if I were falling. "No," I groaned. "That's not right! Why would you tell them that!"

"Because I still don't trust you," she said shifting into full haughtiness. "Isn't that what you intend to do? To paint an unflattering portrait of us as simple-minded heathens cut off from the rest of the world?"

"Not in so many words," I said under my breath. Trying to regain my composure I told this vexing woman that I was mostly going to send reports of what has been happening to me and how her tribesmen saved me and treated me so well.

"Tribesmen!" Vaitiare actually took a step toward me.

Vaea had had enough. With a stern shout he silenced all of us. "Vaitiare, you forget Isaac is our guest." And addressing me, he said, "You must know our rituals are sacred. We ask that you respect our beliefs and spiritual practices."

"No problem," I said. "Have I actually seen anything sacred?"

Both Vaea and Vaitiare let out a deep sigh. Vaitiare spoke slowly. "Isaac, everything we do is sacred."

Now I was totally confused. "I haven't seen you praying and doing religious activities. You are more the dancing and partying type."

"Oh, Isaac, you do not understand us," said Vaea with a touch of sadness in his voice. "What we do—our eating, our singing and dancing, even our sleeping—is of a sacred nature and of a Oneness with the All. For us the body and its senses are the gateway to the Eternal."

"But if all you do is sacred, then anything I mention in my messages will be sacrilegious. I can't send anything!"

"Perhaps I can be of assistance," said Chief Aitu as he reached the top of the rise. He had donned a brightly plumed headdress. The drummers offered him a nod of respect. Uttering several sentences in his native language, he then self-translated for my benefit. "I have come to feel," he said, pinning me with his dark eyes, "that how one says something is as important as what one says."

To be continued...

[*Message sent via DrumBeat, island-to-island communications.]

LABELS: POLYNESIAN PERCUSSION TECHNIQUES, SOUTH SEAS CUSTOMS 2

VIEW COMMENTS (44)

AFriend OCT. 27, 2011 AT 11:06 AM
Isaac is at what I call a Moral Moment, where he has to decide what he thinks is Right.

Anonymous OCT. 27, 2011 AT 11:34 AM
I sympathize with the islanders. They are hosting this lost soul and this is how he pays them back, by posting all their secrets?

○ ○ ○   **THINKS OUT LOUD**   ✕

Let the drumming really begin

Entry No. 582 - POSTED: OCT. 27, 2011

Our entire group was staring at the chief and waiting. The drummers stood next to but did not touch their instruments. Surveying his audience, Aitu began, speaking first in Polynesian and then in translation for me. He said that for generation upon generation the word of the elders and the chief was law and could not be challenged. During and after the Great War in the Pacific, the influence of other cultures' ideas washed over the islands, even this island, which is the least touched by outsiders.

Imported by these outsiders, the new ways tugged at the ancient Polynesian traditions, which underwent a series of changes, such as the sharing of power with more of the villagers, including the right to express themselves and even differ with the opinion of the tribal leaders. "Here on Tiaré," he said, "we keep closer to the older ways, but even we allow a fuller flowering of thought than before."

That being said, Aitu stressed how respect for the earlier ways was still an important foundation for village life on Tiaré. "Let the messages of this Thinks Out Loud be sent," he said, in a tone that sounded more a suggestion than a command. "All I ask," he said turning to me, "is that you be aware of what you are saying and how it can affect those of us who call this island our home."

I wanted to applaud. Vaitiare, Vaea and the others remained silent. I could hear a nearby bird's lilt, the soft murmur of the waves. And I found Aitu gazing steadfastly in my direction. "Chief, Your Honor, I thank you," I said. "And know that I, as a blogger, will speak of the experiences I have had with your peoples. It will be my opinion and will probably reflect more poorly upon me than you of Tiaré." I wasn't quite sure what I was saying and I should have stopped, but I kept going. "The blogging tradition requires that I be true to myself, that I convey what I know, that I contribute to the General Conversation."

"Let it be," Vaitiare said, her haughtiness level having dropped by twenty percent, though she still seemed less than pleased with the outcome.

The chief gave a royal wave of the hand and returned to the large grass hut below us. As he walked down the hill, he added, "The brothers send their greetings and look forward to your messages, Thinks Out Loud." (He had somehow confused my blog's name with my name.)

Vaea said he was going to visit with some of his friends down near the water. That left Vaitiare to help me with organizing the drummers. "I shall aid you, Isaac, or do you prefer Thinks Out Loud. That does not mean I have to approve of what you are doing," she said.

We were off together at the side of the hill, the drummers at their station, talking among themselves. "You judge me too severely," I said, getting lost in her eyes again. "You know ever since I landed on this island, you've been…" I checked myself and took another turn. "Anyway, authors used to say at the beginning of their works that any of the mistakes made were the result of their own ignorance and not to be attributed to anyone else. I'll take the blame for whatever I write."

"Words can produce unforeseen results," she answered. "Come with me." She walked toward the drummers. "I am still trying to see if your thoughts and actions run as one or pull away from each other like hungry birds fighting over food."

Now, finally, we could begin. Vaitiare introduced me to the men, who still maintained a serious demeanor. "You will work most closely with Ari, whose name roughly means Friendly Song of the Deep Waters," she said, pointing me toward the scrawny drummer.

"Hello, Ari," I said slowly and in louder voice, hoping he could understand me. "I would like to send messages across the Great Water."

He shook his head and almost laughed. "Forgive me, Isaac," he said in a perfect aristocratic British accent. "I do not mean to laugh, for you must know I have traveled and studied in Europe and America."

"Oh," I said, quickly lowering my voice, "that's great. You must really love drumming."

He had a slightly narrower nose and thinner face than his drumming brethren. Were some of his ancestors European? "Yes, I love drumming. I was the Fellow in Percussive Studies at Kensington University, and I also had an opportunity to lead a tour of the Tahitian Drumming Society in America, Japan, and Western Europe last year."

I felt smaller than a feral rat. Vaitiare was more than content to let Ari take it from here. I showed him my notebooks and the sections I wished to send. Since I would supposedly be able to have my messages sent back through time, courtesy of the Morse brothers, I had dated each entry to create a sense of chronological progression.

"Is this doable?" I asked. "Does it seem like a lot of work?"

"Messaging is what we do. You have more content than the average message. Still, we can accommodate you," said Ari, just shy of boasting. He explained that like a symphony conductor he would direct how the drummers would play. In this case, they would drum in Morse Code, longer drum beats standing for the code's dashes, shorter beats for the code's dots. Apparently the team, though not fluent in English, knew which combination of dots and dashes made up the letters of the English alphabet. So, if Ari "conducted" them to do "hello," they would do the code for each letter. E, for example, was a simple, short drum beat representing "dot."

My job was to feed Ari the sections I wanted to send. He might also pause the drumming to ask me a clarifying question about the text. I said that was great. "Let's do it."

"Ah," said Ari. "First we must signal our drumming brothers to be ready to receive a message. They have my counterpart who will hear and transcribe the code and then take the message to his island's other side where another drumming team will send your messages to the next island."

Wouldn't it be easier to just get some cell phones, I was thinking.

"You find this an antiquated system," said Ari.

"Well," I coughed. "It is, unique."

"Yes, unique and a way of staying connected to our heritage as Aitu was explaining before. This very process becomes a part of the message. Plus the sounds of our drummers carry not only to the next island but they run through us as well. That drumbeat is our pulse."

And so we readied ourselves. On Ari's crisp command, the drummers came to life and sent a percussion blast toward the neighboring island. A minute later echoed a reply that sounded like controlled, splintered thunder.

"We may begin," said Ari.

I gave Ari a posting, he conducted, and much more rapidly than I thought possible, my words were turned into an almost danceable and vibrant drumming beat.

To be continued...

[*Message sent via DrumBeat, island-to-island communications.]

LABELS: GREAT PRECISION DRUMMING, SOPHISTICATED POLYNESIANS, FOOT IN MOUTH

VIEW COMMENTS (48)

JustSaying OCT. 27, 2011 AT 1:44 PM
Circle drumming is incredible. We have a pod here in Portland. Our Full Moon Lunacycle is not to be missed. Never thought about sending messages though.

Sleeper OCT. 27, 2011 AT 2:59 PM
That Vaitiare is one powerful woman.

SHOW MORE COMMENTS

○ ○ ○   THINKS OUT LOUD   ✕
WHIMSY WITHOUT REGRET

tallboy visits his old blog
Entry No. 583 - POSTED: OCT. 28, 2011

Hi, all. I know I have been away from Thinks Out Loud for a while as I continue to progress in my BlogaMight position at AS. And I know some readers may be wondering about my relationship to this company. Let me assure you: Everything is fine. I've got lots to write about and a very supportive CEO. While starting a new job can be both exciting and a bit tense, I feel remarkably relaxed about the whole thing. I feel relaxed just about everything.

The other day, when eating in the Honey Room, I was approached by one of the Connectors who asked to join me, sat down before I could answer, and proceeded to ask me questions about me, which was funny, because I've been the one asking everybody questions. Anyway, we proceeded to have a great conversation. Halfway through the meal, he got a text message, said he had to go, and popped up from his chair. Still it was fun to have someone take such an interest in me!

The tour (and sneakiness) my brother devised is now old history. Prime Mover has assured me that there are no hard feelings. In fact, he mentioned that there might be a place for Eddie and his friends at AS down the road. The guy is a visionary!

So, that's it for the moment. I am off to go meet with Patricia, the Sensate, who is going to give me a demonstration on how she links up with alternate dimensions.

LABELS: CORPORATE BLOGGING, START-UP CHALLENGES, JOY OF WORK

VIEW COMMENTS (40)

JustSaying OCT. 28, 2011 AT 10:34 PM
Being relaxed is one thing. Always being relaxed, that's another.

SpecMan OCT. 28, 2011 AT 10:50 PM
tallboy seems oblivious to what is going on around him. Is he really that naïve?

Etruscan OCT. 28, 2011 AT 11:14 PM
I think tallboy is fitting in wonderfully.

SHOW MORE COMMENTS

○ ○ ○   **THINKS OUT LOUD**   ✕

BEYOND BANTER / WHIMSY WITHOUT REGRET

A day in the village

Entry No. 584 - POSTED: OCT. 28, 2011

After three hours of near continuous drumming, Ali and his men simply stopped as if a light had been switched off. Wiping his brow, Ali said the group would continue to send my postings the next day.

"You have a lot to say," he said. I couldn't help being aware of his refined British accent here in the middle of Polynesia.

"Well, these messages do go back over several months. But I really appreciate what you're doing."

Ali motioned for me to be silent. From a distance I heard the return of drumbeat. "That tells us the messages have been received," he said. "And also their drummer leader Moeata or Sleeping Cloud, added, 'Have a pleasant evening.' He is an entertaining fellow."

I had been quite impressed by the drummers' talents and their stamina. The only break they had taken was halfway through the day's messaging when a whirlwind of shirtless kids had run up the hill to bring fruit and beverages. We paused and watched their energetic approach. One of the kids did a poor job braking, lost his balance, and was tottering on the hill's steeper side.

I was the closest adult; before I could think it out, I'd jumped toward him, grabbed his torso, somehow pivoted around and threw us both down in the dirt at the hill's edge. We regarded each other. I was waiting to see if he would laugh or cry. Instead he jumped up, said something in Polynesian, and ran to join his friends. I stood up, dusted myself off, and went back to the drummers. Nobody made a big deal out of my actions, so I didn't either.

Now, in the golden glow of the late-afternoon sun, the drummers walked back to the village below, their movements casual as if they'd spent the day strolling the beach and looking for seashells.

Vaitiare and I followed the group down. "That was good of you to keep Rahiti—Rising Sun—from falling off the hill."

I said it was nothing. I was the closest to him.

"I was trying to give you a compliment, Isaac."

I stopped walking. She *was* trying to be nice to me. Having built up so much antagonism against her, I had missed a friendly gesture on her part. "Vaitiare, you're right. I'm sorry."

We started walking again. "Why is there so much tension between us?" I asked.

"You do not know, do you?"

"Umm, you think I'm here to bring about the downfall of your society?"

Vaitiare chose her words carefullly. "You may be a danger to us. Many call this paradise, yet each year, the fish supply lessens, the garbage from passing cruise ships washes up on shore, even the potential of rising ocean could affect our lower lying lands. We attribute this to the Moderns, such as yourself. Yet little by little I am seeing other sides to you." Almost smiling, Vaitiare caught herself and returned to her regal, raised head posture with the distant look in the eyes. Almost. There was the subtlest shift in her manner. Just a minute pullback from her coolness toward me. Then she stopped walking, put a long finger to her chin and said she had an idea. An energy began to radiate from her, one I had first felt when she had danced before me my first night on the island.

"Come with me, writer of Thinks Out Loud." We walked over to one of the larger grass huts. The three shy girls she'd visited with earlier were inside, sitting on grass floor mats, and playing some kind of game with shells. Vaitiare spoke to them in Polynesian, and they all giggled and nodded. Standing up, the three young women approached me and kept murmuring and laughing. They guided me out of the hut and over to a small pool of clear, fresh water. And then they pushed me in. And then they followed.

Over the next hour I was gently bathed and dried, given a haircut and a shave. I have never, never experienced such attention. I joked in my language. They didn't understand, but they laughed anyway. The women were free of self-consciousness. When they were done, they pushed me back to a hut and had me stand before a gilded, oval mirror. I stared at this deeply tanned, lean stranger's face, narrower than the faces I'd been looking at for days. "Who is that?" I asked. "Thinks Out Loud!" shouted my personal makeover artists. They were starting to call me that rather than my given name.

"I am impressed," said Vaitiare from the hut's entrance. It was then I realized I wasn't wearing any clothes. Vaitiare gave a command and one of the women left the hut. I tried to look nonchalant. "Your bottom is white, the rest of you bronze," said Vaitiare. "Thinks Out Loud, modesty is not one of our ways," she added.

Before I could respond, the woman on her errand had returned with cotton pants and a flowery-patterned shirt. "We'll let you dress," said Vaitiare as she and the others left the hut.

A few minutes later, down at the beach, I found myself surrounded by the kids. They were pointing at my face and hair and speaking quickly. I was trying to watch the setting sun, but they wanted something.

"Why don't you tell them a story?" said Vaitiare who had joined us from the closest grass hut. "I'll translate."

I eyed the kids. They looked to be anywhere from six to ten, I guessed. Full of movement and chatter.

"A story. Let me see." I sat down on the warm sand, the last curve of sun on the horizon, a mild salt-fragrant breeze coming in from the ocean. "Okay. Here's a story. It takes place in a land of tall mountains, taller than the mountain on your island. A land where the mountains are covered in snow in the winter." I interrupted myself. "Do they know what snow is?"

"Not exactly," said Vaitiare. "I will tell them it is like frozen water but soft and fluffy and comes to lands that are very cold in the winter."

"That's pretty good," I said. (I really needed to start learning more Tahitian.) "Okay, so in the summer, the snow melts except at the very tops of these high mountains. One summer day a young man took a long walk up one of the high mountains on a trail that curved back and forth between the trees."

Vaitiare translated and then nodded for me to continue. "The young man decided to leave the path and follow a stream up the mountain," I continued.

A little boy raised his hand to gain my attention and spoke to Vaitiare. "He wants to know why the walker left the path."

"Okay. Well, he wanted to see where the stream went." I continued. "Soon, the rocks got bigger and he had to pull himself up to keep going. As he reached up to a large flat rock next to the stream, his head inched above his hand and he froze."

Another kid raised her hand. Vaitiare: "She wants to know if the cold froze him since you mentioned snow."

"No, it wasn't cold. You can also freeze out of fear." Vaitiare relayed that information.

"So he froze, from fright because right beside his head, taking a drink, was a huge cougar, a mountain lion."

Now the boy, the one I'd caught as he almost fell off the hill, asked Vaitiare a question.

"Rahiti, Rising Sun, wants to know what kind of animal that is."

I spoke directly to the alert boy, who leaned forward eager to hear more.

"Rahiti, do you have cats here?"

He said yes.

"The cat the young man met is called a cougar and is huge, larger than, say, 30 or 40 of your cats put together." The kids' eyes got bigger. Some were holding their breath. "It's hard to describe. So, the mountain lion stopped lapping up water and looked at the young man. The cougar's eyes were the most beautiful golden color the young man had ever seen. The cougar and he were gazing into each other's eyes. Just looking. Slowly the young man eased back down the rock. Now if that cougar had wanted to, it could have easily pounced and used its sharp claws and sharp teeth to rip the man into tiny pieces and then devour him."

Three of the children screamed. Two began to run toward the hut.

"Wait, that didn't happen. The young man climbed down the way he had come and didn't see the mountain lion again."

Rahiti again via Vaitiare: "I know what happened."

"What, Rahiti?"

"The man and the cat stood together rather than apart."

That sounded wise. I'd need to think about Rahiti's answer. Vaitiare gave him a nod of approval.

A call came for dinner and all the kids jumped up and ran to the dining area. Vaitiare stayed behind. "Not bad for your first story."

I walked with her toward the dining area. "I don't know. I think I scared them. And I needed Rahiti to finish it, although I'm not sure what he meant."

"Perhaps we have a different way of being with other animals than you do," she said.

To be continued...

[*Message sent via DrumBeat, island-to-island communications.]

LABELS: POWER OF STORY, POLYNESIAN BATHS, COUGER BEHAVIOR

VIEW COMMENTS (57)

PecMan OCT. 28, 2011 AT 8:26 AM
Isaac, seems as if you are beginning to adapt to Polynesian ways. Beginning, I say.

○ ○ ○   **THINKS OUT LOUD**   ✕

BEYOND BANTER / WHIMSY WITHOUT REGRET

A day in the village, Part 2

Entry No. 584 - POSTED: OCT. 28, 2011

After another bountiful dinner, some of the villagers made a fire and stood near it to talk and relax. Vaea was in light conversation with several of his friends over near the pool I'd bathed in. I found myself walking toward the beach with Vaitiare.

"I am still trying to decide if you are here to harm us," she said as we followed the top of the wave line. The ocean before me, the palm trees and flowers and distant mountain behind, this intriguing woman beside me, I felt as if I were inside a Gauguin painting.

Her arm and hand were brushing mine. Accident or on purpose? Leaving the village, we were now the only two on this long curve of beach that tilted us toward the east. From out of the ocean the nearly full moon was rising. Our companion. Vaitiare's sarong had drifted to fit low on her perfectly round hips. The moon and its reflection off the dancing ocean cast a soft light for me to see the gift of her body.

"Vaitiare..." She stood inches from me, unabashed, cool, open.

I wanted to touch her, kiss her. I started rambling about the differences between the structures of the English language, including references to Indo-European, and Polynesian.

It was worse than babbling, as if I were teaching an introduction to linguistics course. And it was especially hard to explain that Indo-European was a highly inflected language, where the ending of the word determined its syntactical function, whereas English had done away with those endings in favor of placement of the word within a sentence to determine meaning, usually subject/verb/object. "I'm only beginning to learn Tahitian," I said, my voice faltering. "I like how all your words end in a vowel sound: *māuruuru* for thank you, *nānā* for goodbye."

"Must we talk?" Vaitiare put her hand to my mouth. Perfume-scented fingers.

I managed to say, "I was under the impression you were going to marry Teva."

"Yes, that is the plan." She dropped her hand.

"Okay, if you are engaged, then I don't think this is such a good idea."

Vaitiare pulled back. "Why not?"

"Well, because you two are an item, a couple."

"Among my people, we can enjoy each other's company and can join as we like before we marry."

"Oh, boy," was all I could say. I averted her gaze and looked out to sea where reflected moonlight broke the rolling water into wavering sparkles of gold.

"You are afraid of Teva? You think he would challenge you to a battle to the death and snap you like a twig?"

"Do your people do that kind of thing?"

She ignored my question. "Come with me."

"But, but I'm…"

"Join me."

My mind said a pointed "No!" My heart said a soft, "Follow."

To be continued…

[*MESSAGE SENT BY DRUMBEAT, ISLAND-TO-ISLAND COMMUNICATIONS]

LABELS: MOONLIGHT, BEACH WALK, POWER OF ATTRACTION

Anonymous OCT. 28, 2011 AT 10:24 AM

I believe that fate draws people together.

Specialist OCT. 28, 2011 AT 10:30 AM

The Tahitian dialect is a part of a larger family of Polynesian languages that range from Hawaii to Borneo. Most of the vocabulary is based on the particulars of the islands, including plants, topography and weather conditions. It is interesting to note that the words are not by themselves the subject, verb object or qualifier. The role of the word depends on its placement in a sentence. For example, [the man kisses the woman].

Topaz OCT. 28, 2011 AT 10:39 AM

Specialist, Isaac and Vaitiare are sharing a special moment and you're giving us a lecture on the structure of language?

SHOW MORE COMMENTS

○ ○ ○   **THINKS OUT LOUD**   ✕

BEYOND BANTER / WHIMSY WITHOUT REGRET

The day after

Entry No. 586 - POSTED: OCT. 29, 2011

I awoke at dawn on a cool bed of beach grass, stood as if being raised by a crane, and walked unevenly down to the sea. The foamy water beckoned. With a stiff sprint I ran into an oncoming wave, dove through it, and resurfaced a few yards offshore. I paralleled the shoreline for a minute and then let another wave carry me in. The mild air temperature, even in early morning, felt refreshing. That's the way to bathe, I thought.

I returned to the grass bed, retrieved my shorts and shirt, and headed to the village.

It was breakfast time, and forty or so villagers were sharing a community moment. A couple of the kids saw me approaching and ran to greet me. Everyone else stopped eating and simply gave me a look. I returned a brief wave and approached one of the picnic-style tables. People went back to their meal, so I sat down next to one of the drummers. I didn't see Vaea or Her.

"We finish drumming today," I said to my burly table mate, who nodded even though I don't think he fully understood me. I'd gotten a late start at breakfast, and I felt as if I'd not eaten for a week. The other villagers, who had finished by now, watched me help myself to seconds and thirds of fruit, veggies, and dried fish. I could hear murmurings, comments in Polynesian, that I knew were about my dining unfinesse. Finally lean Ari, the head drummer, motioned for my percussion companion and me to join the troupe.

We returned to the hilltop, the drummers positioned their instruments, and, as if we were about to give a concert, Ari tapped on a boulder with a short stick to gain his men's attention. As before, they sent out a heads-up drum signal to the neighboring island. After a few minutes, came the somewhat faint throbbing reply. And so we went to work, me feeding the pages to Ari who directed the drummer's rhythms. Behind me, the kids sat and listened, some copying our efforts on old coconuts.

Today's messaging was shorter by half from yesterday's. After an hour and a half, we were done, including the recommendation, to be sent as an email, tallboy had asked me to do for a blogging job. I was also wondering if tallboy was still doing guest blogging for Thinks Out Loud.

Quite a trick, being able to send messages from the present into the past. I'd just sent new messages that I'd written over the past couple of weeks. Now they would appear on the blog in a timely (past) manner. I wasn't changing anything, just filling in some gaps. But what if I went one step further and rewrote some ill-conceived messages (emails, letters) from the past, corrected some mistakes, headed off some misunderstandings before they became misunderstandings? What if I wanted to use my knowledge to make some investments?

Shaking my head, I shoved the ideas out of my brain. A dangerous path.

Thanking Ari and his team, I added, "From now on, I'll have a couple of posts a week, all from the present. You guys are terrific!" As the men moved downhill, I asked Ari how I should compensate them for their work.

He didn't seem to understand. "It's what we do," he said. Stay with us long enough and you will understand. You will find what you do."

I lagged behind as the drummers and kids moved back into the village. "What to do? That is the question."

"What are you talking about, Thinks Out Loud?"

It was Vaea, from behind me. I don't know how he had gotten there. He was also using my blog's name for me.

"Hey, I was thinking out loud!" Vaea was watching me carefully. "Actually, Vaea, I was considering moving over to this side of the island. Easier to send blogs from here."

"I see. Of course, you could enjoy the walk from our village once or twice a week across island to send your messages. Very good exercise for mind and body." He stopped walking and feeling his pull, I paused.

"Yet I could also live over here and walk back to your village weekly or every other week to visit."

"So, ease of sending messages once or twice a week would be reason enough for moving away from all your new friends on my side of the island, the ones who traveled far across the sea to find and save you, the ones who fed you so that you would regain your strength and manhood."

Vaea was coming on strong.

My mouth felt like a waterless well. "It might be easier for me to think over here."

"To think but not to act, Thinks Out Loud?" There he went, seeing into my soul again. "This is an island: You cannot run from yourself without running into yourself. Come back with me and complete your path." He stopped and seemed to grow before me into a giant among men. I had never observed Vaea so determined in a course of action, in this case mine. With a sigh, I agreed to return with him. We took some provisions, said goodbye to everyone, and headed out, the kids following us for a half mile as a sort of sendoff party.

"Wait, Vaea, we left without your sister."

"She returned to our village earlier this morning. Like one of our gulls arcing back to its nest. You seem to have had some effect on the princess," said Vaea as we moved deeper into the island. "Remember when I warned you to be wary of her?" He didn't wait for my answer. "Perhaps I should have warned Vaitiare to be wary of you as well."

To be continued...

[*MESSAGE SENT BY DRUMBEAT, ISLAND-TO-ISLAND COMMUNICATIONS]

LABELS: TIDES OF LIFE, SANDS OF TIME

VIEW COMMENTS (60)

SummerThyme OCT. 29, 2011 AT 8:30 AM

Thinks Out Loud (Isaac) is playing with fire, or at least matches.

Topaz OCT. 29, 2011 AT 8:54 AM
This would make an incredible reality TV show, except they need to add people getting kicked off the island.

SHOW MORE COMMENTS

○ ○ ○   **THINKS OUT LOUD**   ✕

BEYOND BANTER / WHIMSY WITHOUT REGRET

Caution: Entering new territory

Entry No. 587 - POSTED: OCT. 29, 2011

Vaea and I made our way back to his village's side of the island. Although the isle was as enchanting as ever with its pastel wild flowers, curving coconut trees and hillside waterfalls, I couldn't stop replaying recent events in my mind and worrying about future ones.

"You don't have much to say, Thinks Out Loud." My companion gave me a studied look, which was becoming his default way of observing me.

I admitted I had been lost in thought. "Sorry, Vaea, it's just, I'm entering new personal territory here, and I don't know the rules." I kicked at the path.

He nodded as we topped a small hill layered with high grasses. "Yes, you are now swimming in deeper waters beyond the breakers. Stronger currents. Larger fish."

"That reminds me," I broke in, "by any chance, did you ever hear about the fate of a sinking ship, the Bogsworth, the one I fell overboard from during that storm?"

"I think I did. There was a damaged tanker that was towed to one of the larger islands. They reported only one casualty."

I snorted more than laughed. "That would be me."

"I will have our drummers send them a message that you survived after all. That was very unworthy of them to throw you overboard as a human sacrifice. Very old fashioned," Vaea was really thinking this through. "But apparently it worked," he concluded and I couldn't tell if he were joking or serious.

"I wasn't sacrificed," I answered defensively. "I fell off the tilting deck. Besides, one of the crew threw me a life raft that saved my life. I'd like to thank him."

"Maybe he reads your blog messages."

I rubbed some sweat off my forehead. "You know, I was also thinking of changing where I sleep. I've burdened Teva enough for a while. He needs a break from me."

Surprisingly, Vaea didn't challenge my statements. Did that mean he agreed?

It was still early afternoon when we arrived at the village. Sitting by the trail, two robust teenage boys met us as we approached. They seemed to know when we would have been arriving. "Ah, my sons," said Vaea. "Lani, Sky, and Fetu, God of Night." Shirtless, they came forward to give their father a hug.

"*Ia orana!*" They shouted in unison. I knew that meant 'hello.'

Vaea explained that they had been on a coming-of-age quest, five days at some caves several miles distant. "You should try it some time," he said.

"Doesn't my experience on the sacred island count for something?" I countered.

"Yes, yes it does, Thinks Out Loud. A good first step."

As I was rolling up my gear at Teva's, he entered without noticing me. That gave me a second to try and blend into a darkish corner. Right behind him came Vaitiare. And, as usual, she was wearing a patterned batik sarong that accented her figure. They were engaged in conversation—Polynesian—and the tone was a little strained. I didn't want them to think I was spying, which I was, so I cleared my throat and stepped out of the shadows. Teva wheeled around, and assumed a defensive crouching position, hands up and ready for striking. Vaitiare titled her head and simply watched.

"Teva, Teva, it's me. Isaac, you know, Thinks Out Loud!"

Stomping, arms still rigid, Teva advanced. Here it comes, I thought.

"So," Teva said, his right arm cocked for a decisive chop, "you have returned from sending your messages." He gave me a firm but not lethal pat on the back. "And other activities."

"Are you going to kill me?"

He looked over at Vaitiare and back at me. "Why would I do that?"

"Well, because, you know, you two are engaged, and I, that is, Vaitiare and I…"

"You still do not understand our ways," Teva said.

Vaitiare interrupted us. "Hoanui, Big Friend, our storyteller is looking for you, Thinks Out Loud."

To be continued…

[*MESSAGE SENT BY DRUMBEAT, ISLAND-TO-ISLAND COMMUNICATIONS]

LABELS: TAHITIAN CUSTOMS, TROPICAL ISLAND LIFE, ON OR OFF THE PATH

VIEW COMMENTS (62)

JustPlainHank OCT. 29, 2011 AT 11:19 AM
Isaac, you are acting like a wimp who doesn't deserve the princess's attention. Grow some backbone.

Seequince OCT. 29, 2011 AT 12:23 PM
Vaitiare, sister, I am with you in solidarity.

RepoMan OCT. 29, 2011 AT 12:35 PM
Vaitiare, here I am, babe.

VincentFrederick OCT. 29, 2011 AT 12:45 PM
Repo, something tells me Vaitiare would not pay any attention to you.

SHOW MORE COMMENTS

○ ○ ○   **THINKS OUT LOUD**   ✕

WHIMSY WITHOUT REGRET

Boy texts girl

Entry No. 588 - POSTED: OCT. 30, 2011

Eddie 6:36pm: Emily what are we supposed to do now? Whats our next step?

Emily 6:47pm: Eddie you're putting me in a tough situation I dont want to hurt him

Eddie 6:48pm: Think of all the people he's hurting and all the other people he might hurt

Emily 6:51pm: I dont know what u mean he's not cruel or anything we just have different interests

Eddie 6:52pm: Not cruel? Look how controlling he is

Emily 6:57pm: Eddie thats going too far I actually think he wants to do good in his own way

Eddie 6:57pm: Good? Emily you were practically kidnapped by him!

Emily 7:06pm: Well he tried locking me in his bedroom near the beginning of our relationship but he later apologized and never did anything like that again

Eddie 7:09pm: Relationship? What? You knew Prime Mover before the tour?

Emily 7:15pm: Prime Mover? I thought we were talking about my bf. omg!

Eddie 7:17pm: Oh I see wait Emily sorry. What should we do about AltaSystemics?

...

Eddie 7:24pm: Can we talk face to face after class?

...

Eddie 7:41pm: OK, see you in class Emily ttyl

[No reply. End of text messaging thread.]

LABELS: HIGH-TECH ADVENTURE, BUMPY ROMANCE, TEXTING ERRORS

VIEW COMMENTS (64)

Airborn OCT. 30, 2011 AT 11:10 AM
Leave it to a Millennial to insert texting into a blog.

Creature OCT. 30, 2011 AT 12:19 PM
Funny but not so funny.

SHOW MORE COMMENTS

The Princess Who Cast No Shadow

Entry No. 589 - POSTED: OCT. 30, 2011

In search of the storyteller, whom I'd seen once before, I crossed the grassy expanse between the dining circle and a row of grass huts. "Thinks Out Loud," called a young woman as she ran up from the beach. Was everyone going to call me that now? It was Kohia, Passionflower, the teenager who had served as my main translator. Like her sisters and friends, she wore a sarong, yellow, and in her long, black hair sported a flower, bright red. She reached me. "I can help you talk with our storyteller." She studied me. "Your beard is gone. I liked it. But your chin is nice, too."

"Thank you, Kohia," I said politely. "If you have something else to do, I'll use my fractured French and some hand signs."

"Don't be silly, Thinks Out Loud." She moved in front of me and led the way. "By the way, how old do you think me?"

That was always a dangerous question in any culture. "Seventeen, maybe eighteen."

"I'll be twenty next full moon."

I didn't believe her.

We found the storyteller on the dry, warm sands at the top of the beach, a collection of children sitting on each side of him. He was clearly the village elder, his short hair totally gray, his body shrunken from its brawny earlier days of youth.

Kohia re-introduced us. "Thinks Out Loud, this is Hoanui, Big Friend, our village teller of stories." We nodded to each other. (Did he remember me from before?) He smiled, open mouthed; I didn't see many teeth. And when he tried to speak, his voice came forth almost a whisper. Kohia explained that Hoanui, recovering from an illness, was still weak.

She continued, "That is why Hoanui has invited you here. He heard about the story you told to the children of Manua, and his heart would be warmed if you would consent to take his place today and tell another story for these children."

Everyone sure seems to know just about everything about everyone around here, I thought. "Kohia, tell wise Hoanui that while I would not presume to be able to take his place as a teller of stories, I would be happy to stand in his shadow for today and provide but a pale imitation of what he does so well."

Kohia gave me a quizzical look, shrugged her shoulders and offered the translation. Then as an aside she said to me, "A simple 'yes' would have served."

Hoanui didn't seem bothered by my praise and indicated to Kohia that my storytelling was welcome. He directed the children's attention toward me. I looked them over and said "Ia orana."

I began and Kohia translated. "Once upon a time—Kohia do they know that phrase?" She said they didn't, but she translated it anyway. I continued, "Once upon a time, on a faraway island, there was a great ruler, a king, no, a chief, an *ariki*, who was loved by his people." Kohia smiled when I got the Tahitian word right. He had a young daughter, Princess—," I paused and whispered to Kohia, "How do you say hibiscus?" She answered, *"purau."* I continued, "Princess Purau, whom he was very proud of. Since the chief did not have a male heir, the princess would assume rule of the island. He often spoke of how she would someday be a fine and grand queen."

Kohia said, "The young ones do not know 'heir.'"

"Okay," I answered. "How about something like, 'Since the chief did not have a son that meant his daughter would someday be queen.'?"

Kohia went back to translating.

"Princess Purau loved her father. He would take her to court—"

Kohia again halted my exposition.

I restated the line: "He would take her to the meeting of elders and have her sit by his side during his chiefly duties of running the kingdom. When she wasn't at the chief's side, the princess sat with her mother and the ladies in waiting."

Kohia gave me her look, a combination of mild frustration mixed with what I would call a motherly reprimand. She whispered: "These are children of this island who do not know your ways, your words."

"Okay," I whispered back. "So, as I was saying, the ladies who served the princess, showed her how to do a queenly wave, a queenly nod, a queenly curtsy."

Curtsy? I tried to illustrate. The children made faces of twisted mouths and eyebrows low. I was losing them.

"Purau was so busy learning how to be a queen, she never went outdoors." That got a gasp out of my listeners.

"One day her teacher—"

"Thinks Out Loud, in our village we have no teacher, all of us serve that purpose in various ways," said Kohia.

"Okay," I said too loudly. "One day she was outside for the first time and everyone started pointing at her because she didn't have a shadow! Everyone else did."

The children began looking under themselves to make sure they had a shadow. I actually looked behind and under myself, just to check, and realized the adult villagers had gathered round, including my rescue crew, Vaea, Chief Keoni, Teva, his arms folded across his broad chest, and, of course, Vaitiare. I wanted to call it a day.

One of the bolder children made a comment. "More," translated Kohia. "What happened to the princess without a shadow?"

I glanced at Vaitiare, whose face gave no indication of approval or disapproval. "Continue with your tale, Thinks Out Loud," she said evenly.

I didn't know where to take the story, but words came out on their own. The chief and queen were called. Everyone was in shock. The chief asked other elders how to fix the problem. One recommended a magic potion.

The kids wanted to know what a magic potion was. "A fun drink," I said, adding that the villagers in the story hoped it would give the princess a shadow. She drank it, made a face, and waited. No shadow appeared.

"'You look but do not see, Sire,' said the court jester, who was dressed in feathery robes like a colorful bird. 'You see but do not look.'"

Everyone was giving me the "what is a court jester?" look. "The jester is an advisor to the king, I mean the chief, who talks in jokes and riddles but truth is embedded in what he says. Got it?"

Some people nodded. Others sighed.

Then I had the island's best warrior suggest this was a plot from a nearby island to cause confusion and keep the islanders from properly guarding their beach so the invaders could come one shore.

Chief Keoni broke in: "We have not warred for generations."

"Right," I said. "And that's when the court jester, remember him, said 'Sire, you hear but you do not listen. You listen but you do not hear.' That confused the chief. But not the queen.

"She addressed her husband. 'What do you see when you look at our daughter?'

"The chief raised both arms as if it were obvious. 'Why I see the Princess, the future queen.'

"The queen said, 'You see a princess but you do not see your own daughter. You look but you do not see. You hear but you do not listen.'

"The chief was speechless." *What should I have the clueless chief do?*

"For a long moment he was still and silent as he gazed upon the princess. Then he tapped his forehead and opened his palm toward the sky, slowly, he walked toward her and crouched down. 'Purau, I am so sorry. I see you are my daughter first and a princess second. How could I have been so blind, so deaf?' And with that he gave her a big, warm hug.

"'Sire,' said the jester, look at the ground next to the princess.' All gazed at the grassy spot and slowly a shadow appeared. From that day on, the chief treated his daughter like a daughter. She still learned the ways of a princess and future queen, for now she knew she was loved by her parents not because they were chief and queen, but because they were her father and mother. And from that day on, she cast a beautiful shadow, which she saw often because she was now free to go outside into the bright and warm light of day."

Silence. Total silence, except for the sound of surf and a bird chant or two. The children continued to stare at me as did the adults. Then a few of the children began to laugh and soon the entire community was bubbling away. A lot of people were standing in front of me; I couldn't see Vaitiare or Teva.

Chief Keoni called for attention. He spoke deliberately and solemnly.

I looked around for Kohia to translate. Was I about to receive the Key to the Island, have a banquet held in my honor, enjoy another bath? Kohia worked her way over to me. There was a huge shout from the population.

"Was your tale a reflection on how our chief has treated Vaitiare?" Kohia whispered.

"Of course not," I shot back. "I kind of enjoyed telling the story. You know I'm starting to feel more and more comfortable here on Tiaré. I can send postings. I'm learning about your culture. I love the weather."

Finally, I asked Kohia what was going on. "The chief says the time has come to decide whether you are welcome to stay longer or be escorted off the island, never to return," she told me. "We hold a council tomorrow to determine your fate." Then she added, "I enjoyed your story, except I would have made the princess less timid. She and the court jester could be more aware of why she had no shadow. And it is important to always know your audience."

To be continued...

[*MESSAGE SENT BY DRUMBEAT, ISLAND-TO-ISLAND COMMUNICATIONS]

LABELS: ORAL TRADITIONS, LITERARY INTERPRETATIONS, FAIRY TALES, SURPRISE COUN-CIL MEETINGS

VIEW COMMENTS (58)

Gobbler OCT.30, 2011 AT 8:23 AM
Good kids' story. I've got more at my blog, CatchingUP.

iSite OCT.30, 2011 AT 8:45 AM
Have the islanders been planning this kind of 'trial' since Isaac came to the island?

Mipper OCT. 30, 2011 AT 8:58 AM
Would it have been better for Isaac if he had known he was being so closely observed?

SHOW MORE COMMENTS

Deciding the fate of Thinks Out Loud

Entry No. 590 - POSTED: OCT. 31, 2011

After the chief's announcement that the next day a village council would be held to decide if I'd be allowed to stay on the island, I wandered along a quiet stretch of beach.

For once, the soft sun-warmed sands, the pure, late afternoon light, the color-drenched tropical vegetation didn't hold my attention. Instead of being in the moment, I reviewed my life since being shipwrecked on their sacred island: my semi-successful attempts at survival; the arrival of my rescuers who brought me back to Tiaré, my getting to know these South Seas people who were trying to maintain their customs while the rest of the world went about Tweeting, downloading apps, and, yes, blogging. More recently, there was my journey to the island's other side with principled Vaea and alluring Vaitiare and the sending of some apparently controversial blog postings via drumbeat; my tense and now more complex relationship with the Polynesian princess who seemed both interested in and leery of me; my apparent talent for telling stories—where did it all lead? To some kind of trial to determine my fate.

As the afternoon drifted into early evening, I stayed apart from the others. I didn't even have an appetite for dinner. Much later I wandered back to my hut, snuck in, and fell into a fitful sleep filled with disjointed dreams and a lot of tossing and turning. Could I have become so attached to this island, these people, so quickly?

This morning a conch shell, calling all to the council, broke my unrestful sleep. I ventured out to find the village crowded with more people than I had seen at any one time. Was the whole island here? Everyone was standing on, and overflowing from, the performance area. Seated in the center on a tall wooden chair was Chief Keoni. Kohia found me and once again volunteered to be my translator. "Stand tall," she said.

Dressed in his finest pareo and bird-plumed headdress, the chief spoke loudly for all to hear. "Let us begin." He motioned for me to position myself to his right, his family, including Vaitiare and Vaea on his left. Two drummers began a fast-paced sort of introduction. No one danced to the intense beat; everyone was looking at me.

Chief Keoni motioned for the drumming to cease, and they stopped on the beat as if of one mind. He explained that I would be judged this day to determine if I would be allowed to stay among the villagers or be taken off-island to parts unknown. All who desired to participate could do so, to be followed by a vote of those who had passed the Coming of Age Rite of Passage. If I wished to, I could speak last.

It was kind of like a South Sea Quaker meeting—speak if you're moved, remain silent if you wish. There was no prosecuting attorney or the equivalent of a lawyer for the defense. Reminded me of the time I went before a dorm conduct board at college. I'd tried to stop a fight between two roommates, but the floor monitor thought I was the instigator!

Vaea went first, he who had counseled me the most. Looking from person to person and finally zeroing in on me, he said he had never met anyone quite like me. At times he thought me a pretender, at other times a kind of explorer. When he and his rescue crew had found me, I seemed like a lost child. But he noted that even though I was weak after being alone on their sacred island, I did try and paddle with the rest of the men and engage the crew as they took me back to Tiaré. During a sudden storm, Vaea said I had not panicked very much and had contributed what I could to help keep the canoe afloat.

He said my inner me seemed to be in battle with my outer me, like a black duck pecking at itself. He said I might be at the beginning of a path that could take me to a greater understanding of myself, but he was not convinced I had the desire or the fortitude to make that kind of journey. With a hand motion, Vaea indicated he had finished. Could have been worse, I thought. People murmured among themselves.

To be continued...

[*Message sent via DrumBeat, island-to-island communications.]

LABELS: POLYNESIAN CUSTOMS, JUDGMENT DAY, PEOPLE'S COURT

VIEW COMMENTS (66)

Aladden OCT. 31, 2011 AT 8:30 AM
Isaac is in a tough spot. Is ignorance of the 'law' excusable in this case?

Anonymous OCT. 31, 2011 AT 9:23 AM
He needs a good lawyer. Oops, too late!

JohnsBrain OCT. 31, 2011 AT 9:30 AM
What if he were to plead guilty and throw himself on the mercy of the court?

SHOW MORE COMMENTS

Let the vote be taken

Entry No. 591 · POSTED: OCT. 31, 2011

The islanders continued to speak to determine if I should stay or leave. Technically, I hadn't made a request to stay. Of course, I hadn't asked for transport to Tahiti either. Anapa, the navigator, the one with piercing black eyes, came next. "I shall be brief," he said. "I say this not with mean thoughts but only by seeing his actions. Thinks Out Loud, so far, lacks skill as a sea traveler. Even though stronger than when we found him, he is not made for active island life." He nodded to the Chief and returned to his place among the villagers.

"I shall speak." It was Teva, the tall, muscular one, who had not hidden his disdain for me since we first met on the sacred island. I still thought he did not care for me. Other factors were at play as well.

He stepped to the front of the congregation. "I have spent time with Thinks Out Loud, first on Fénua, Taboo, then I answered his endless questions during the canoe trip home, and most recently endured his erratic behavior here on this island, including his stay at my hut." He went on to say his main impression of me was that I didn't take anything seriously. "All Thinks Out Loud wants to do is play games, like a child. He even plays with us in the ways he studies us." He gave me a look of pity. "I do not hate him. Rather I now find him an example of what not to be. My greater fear, like that of my fellow islanders, is that he comes to our island and his presence is like a new breed of invading bird that pushes our native birds out of their nests and feeding areas. That is the danger he presents to us. And his stories cause the children's eyebrows to sit low on their foreheads."

As soon as Teva finished, Kohia, my translator, practically jumped into the open area before the Chief. "I must defend you," she said, and she added she would offer me the English translation at the end of her testimony. She spoke in her native tongue, and I tried to catch a word or two. Then she turned to me and said one last line. There was silence after she stopped. Some of the islanders smiled, others remained free of expression.

Returning to my side, she whispered her translation: "You are not evil. In the time I have served as your translator, I have known you to be kind, considerate, and helpful. It's true you do not know how to fix fishing nets, rethatch a hut's old roof, or find medicinal herbs in our jungles. It would seem you are of little use. Still, you have other talents. I think you write about us because we have something to teach you." She looked up at me as she re-delivered her last line: "And many of us have grown to like you. Oh, and you have potential as a storyteller."

The next speaker came forward—Princess Vaitiare, as regal as ever. "Our meeting tonight has a great bearing on our future as a people," she began. "We must decide wisely and carefully. Less than a moon ago, a mysterious outsider was brought into our midst by our brave paddlers who had found him marooned on our sacred island."

She went on to relate that from my first day on Tiaré, the islanders were uncertain about what to do with me. I came from a world of fleeting images, of things that give momentary but not lasting pleasure, of seekers who have no idea what they really seek. Vaitiare continued, "Some of us wondered if our visitor were to spend time with us, might he become more like us and less like the Others? That is a good question. With our care and attention, he is on his way to regaining his health and vitality. He has also had complete freedom to come and go as he pleased." She paused. Was it for dramatic purpose?

"He observes us," Vaitiare continued as she briefly eyed me. "He asks many questions of us and is hesitant to answer our questions about him. His main goal seems to be the sending of messages to those who live beyond our shores. Several of us have tried to let Thinks Out Loud know why we do not like to promote ourselves and our way of life to the Others, why we do not want to bring attention to our island, why we did not want the Others overrunning Tiaré with their non-island ways.

"I should mention the good Thinks Out Loud has done" she continued. "I witnessed his reaching out and catching a running child about to fall off the Great Hill of the drummers. Twice I have heard Thinks Out Loud tell tales to both our young and old. He also made a connection with one of our dolphin brothers." So, she had seen me that day at the lagoon.

Now, she looked at me and held her gaze. "I have had the chance to be alone with Thinks Out Loud during which time he did not once mention blogging, but he was probably thinking about it." She paused like a prosecuting attorney readying the last of her summation to the jury.

"However, even if some of us find some value in having Thinks Out Loud on Tiaré, we must decide if his presence here will lead to the eventual end of our ways. That is what all this discussion is really about. Not Thinks Out Loud's but our future." Vaitiare turned toward her father, the chief, and took her place by his side.

Chief Keoni asked if anyone else wished to speak. None came forth. He turned to me. "Thinks Out Loud, do you have anything you wish to say?"

Clearing my dry throat, I said I did. "Let me thank all of you for your care and attention," I began. "I am alive today because of you. I also want to say this trial, this judgment took me by surprise. I didn't know you were trying to decide if I should stay or go. I also didn't know I was perceived as a threat to you. I just thought I was recuperating and along the way getting to know you better and wanting to get back to writing and sending my blog writings. It's true, though, that I couldn't write about my experiences on your island without including you. If I have offended you, I apologize." I paused. "If you think me a kind of poison in your system, I can't fully disagree with that. In a way, you are right. For example, here I am standing before you and being judged as to my worthiness to remain in your presence, and what is going through my mind? Thoughts about how intriguing this posting is going to be!

"Perhaps I do represent change. Or at least the prospect of change. Maybe my being here is a kind of opportunity to consider other ways of being. And likewise, maybe what you offer me and others like me are new ways of thinking and feeling. I'll abide by your decision this day. That's all I have to say."

"Very well," said the chief. "The time has come. All who would have Thinks Out Loud remain, stand toward the interior of the island. All who believe Thinks Out Loud should be cast out, stand closer to the sea." With a deep silence, the islanders began to move, some inland, some toward shore. The brightness of the setting sun prevented me from seeing which way Vaitiare was heading. I stayed by the chief's now empty chair.

"The vote has been taken," said the chief's voice from a direction I couldn't pinpoint. "The islanders have spoken."

[MESSAGE SENT VIA DRUMBEAT, ISLAND-TO-ISLAND COMMUNICATIONS.]

LABELS: POWER OF THE VOTE, FAIR AND BALANCED, BLOG-STYLE SUSPENSE

VIEW COMMENTS (82)

Peligroso OCT. 31, 2011 AT 10:30 AM
Guilty. Guilty as charged. That's what I bet.

Emily's fury

Entry No. 592 - POSTED: NOV. 1, 2011

Eddie here. Emily wasn't in class today, and I really needed to speak with her. I thought about texting, but she's been distant lately. Talk about distant, tallboy is acting like he's from another planet. I wonder if they put something in the bottled water over at AltaSystemics.

After class, I retreated to the espresso café inside the gothic Suzzallo Library. Over a latte, I took out my laptop and went onto the blog. The Polynesian islanders were deciding the fate of Isaac (Thinks Out Loud), and it wasn't looking very promising.

I got down to where the chief was about to announce the big decision, and the blog came to a halt, except for reader comments. And nothing followed today. I'm concerned. What is going on on Tiaré? Is Isaac in danger?

"How could you!" I gazed up from my computer screen to see Emily practically leaning into me. She issued an order in a loud whisper: "Outside, now." I slapped my laptop shut without turning it off (will that hurt it?), grabbed my backpack, and followed her back to Red Square.

She found a private spot near some stone steps leading down to a dungeony locked library entrance. When she turned to face me, I smiled. She didn't. In fact, she managed to look beautiful and really angry at the same time. She told me her boyfriend had been reading the blog and the parts about her and me, including the recent posting of the texting between us. "He read about how I'm thinking about breaking up with him. You put our texting right into the blog? How could you?" I started to say something about texting not being really private, but she kept on talking about how she felt like she was in some kind of blog reality TV show.

"Do you want me to delete it?"

"It's too late."

I stared at Emily and tried to come up with something to ease her pain, but in all honesty, I was happy her boyfriend was finding out about me. Had I been so clever to have set the stage for his reading of the blog to bring about this very scene between them? No. However, for the first time, I did perceive how what I put in a blog could influence and affect the people who read it. Somehow I'd been ignorant of that.

I was treading water. "So, are you two still…an item?"

Emily gave me an intense look that seared my brain. She grabbed the back of my neck as you would a kitten's and pulled my lips onto hers. I lost track of time and space. I felt my laptop slipping from my grip. "No," she said into my mouth, "I don't think Justin and I are an item anymore." Then she pulled back, pointed down to my computer and said, "Don't drop it."

A couple of minutes later we were back at the café, and I was showing her Isaac's most recent posting. "Is Isaac, even in the midst of his trial, creating reader suspense by ending where he did? I was expecting his next posting today," I said.

Emily read and reread the entry. "Maybe Isaac didn't write a follow-up because the verdict went against him, he's been escorted off the island, and he didn't have time to do a new posting."

"Knowing Isaac, or what we know of Isaac, he'd find a way to blog," I said.

"All right," theorized Emily, "what if Isaac wrote a posting but it never made it through the drumming channels?"

"That's possible," I said. "Maybe the drummers refused to send his posting."

We both thought that unlikely.

Emily drew in a breath. "Or what if it has to do with one of the brothers. What if one of them had a heart attack or a stroke?"

I still had their email addresses from contacting them about sending some of my blogs out of the past, as they had done for Isaac, which I never got around to. I dashed off a quick message to both of them. "Let's see if they respond," I said.

2Spacer NOV. 1, 2011 AT 1:00 PM
Most likely, the break occurred after the event took place and after Isaac had the message sent. It's more a back end transmission problem, which would happen after the drummers did their job.

Creature NOV. 1, 2011 AT 1:10 PM
And we still don't know how the islanders voted!

The Kid NOV. 1, 2011 AT 1:20 PM
Changing the subject, Eddie is doomed. Emily has animal magnetism...I should know.

Tangerine NOV. 1, 2011 AT 2:03 PM
I fell for a guy like Eddie. He just needed a little push in the right direction. Trouble was, he didn't stay long and continued on his previous orbit. If only there'd been more friction between us.

SHOW MORE COMMENTS

○ ○ ○　　　　　　　　　THINKS OUT LOUD　　　　　　　　　X

WHIMSY WITHOUT REGRET

They came in the dark of night
Entry No. 593 - POSTED: NOV. 3, 2011

Eddie here. I invited Emily to our apartment's weekly spaghetti (and meatball!) party, and as soon as I did I regretted it. What on Earth prompted me to have her spend time with my mildly insane roommates? Either two things would happen: After seeing the company I keep, she'd have a lower opinion of me, or in comparison to these guys, my stock would be higher. I was hoping for the latter outcome but wouldn't be surprised if she went with the former. I also invited tallboy, mainly because I wanted to keep closer tabs on him as he continued to fall more and more under the influence of the AltaSystemics cult (as I saw it).

When Mike heard I was bringing "a special guest," he said he'd take charge of the pasta. Actually, he was a good cook. Ashton volunteered to a make his "signature Caesar Salad," which was surprising because he usually says he has to study rather than be a part of Spaghetti Night. Interestingly, Ashton was dressed all in black, a nice counterpoint to tallboy's new white look.

tallboy and Emily arrived at the same time. I could tell she was a little nervous because she looks around more and smiles more when she feels pressure. tallboy, on other hand, was supremely relaxed. Have they got him, I wondered?

Two other guys joined us this week, friends of Mike, both business majors. I think one of them already owned an apartment complex. They looked like models out of Maxim.

We crowded around our dining room table, introduced our guests, and dived into the pile of spaghetti. "That's my own garlic mushroom tomato sauce," Mike offered.

"Sauce compliments pasta," tallboy intoned as if he were delivering a really important message. But he didn't stop there. "M and M get the royalty treatment," he said. Emily and I exchanged a glance. Everyone else was eating and talking.

"The past isn't past," spurted tallboy. That got everyone's attention, the way you notice but pretend not to notice when someone's behavior, say in a movie ticket line, is out of context.

Mike drew our attention away from tallboy. "So, Emily," he asked, "what do you see in that guy?" With his fork, he pointed to me.

"Eddie kind of grows on you," she said with a smirk and a glance my way. She did look great in her gray and white striped sweater and these bright orange jeans.

"Yes, I guess he does," Mike said. "Great salad, Ashton." We all continued to eat. The business majors talked to us about real estate opportunities in the Puget Sound "designated market area."

"Not to be disturbed," tallboy said to no one in particular. Emily and I exchanged another, longer glance.

After several servings of pasta, more toasted garlic bread and salad, we were done. I volunteered to do dish duty. Emily said she'd join me. As we washed the dishes of assorted collections and silverware, we exchanged a quick kiss and a playful touch of noses. As if on cue, tallboy wandered into the kitchen. He opened the refrigerator and spoke into it. "Honored guests," he said.

I asked tallboy what he was talking about. He didn't seem to hear me. Closing the refrigerator door, he left the room.

"Weird," I said. "It's like he's under some kind of spell."

Emily nodded. "Did you ever hear back from the Morse brothers?"

"No," I said. "No answer to my emails. That's strange too." Emily stopped drying a plate, poked my shoulder and scooted out of the kitchen. A minute later she dragged tallboy back into the room.

"tallboy," she said, facing him and trying to get him to look at her. "tallboy, pay attention. Who are the honored guests at AltaSystemics?"

tallboy looked offended. "Trade secret," he said. What was Emily doing to the poor guy?

She kept after him. "tallboy, I'm ordering you. Who are the honored guests?" He grimaced as if he were under some sort of psychological torture.

"They came in the deep of night," he said. "Behind closed doors."

"Who?" Emily probed. "Who came to AltaSystemics?"

tallboy almost started crying. "Hard to blog about."

Emily kept up the interrogation, but with a gentler tone. "What's hard to blog about?"

"Them," he answered and added with a clenched mouth, "The brothers."

My head felt as if motor oil had been poured into it. I seemed to be speaking in slow motion. "tallboy, this is important," I said. "The brothers—do you know their names?"

tallboy seemed to be at war with himself. Twice he tried to say something but held back. Finally, in a whisper out came, "Morse. Special guests. Morse brothers. Do not disturb." He coughed and brought his hand to his mouth.

"Wow," I said.

"It's okay," Emily spoke soothingly to tallboy.

"That's why Isaac's postings stopped," I said.

"And why they didn't answer your emails," added Emily. Head down, tallboy seemed deflated, but he'd given us important information.

○ ○ ○   **THINKS OUT LOUD**   ✕

WHIMSY WITHOUT REGRET

Retreat is not an option

Entry No. 594 - POSTED: NOV. 5, 2011

Eddie here. I was stuck. Two days after the pasta dinner I had no plan, no ideas, no energy. I was worried about tallboy. I was worried about what Prime Mover was doing with the Morse brothers.

I was dimly aware of Emily's face, like a close up, staring right into my face, speaking so quickly I couldn't keep up with what she was saying.

Something about traveling to the South Seas to find Isaac and bringing him back here to help us. Sending me to Polynesia.

The suddenness of the idea prompted my defensiveness. "Why should I go get him? Why should I do anything? AltaSystemics is winning. First they've developed a way to store information in another dimension, which is an invitation for all kinds of sci-fi style trouble. And now they're probably going to learn the secret to message time traveling information, whatever.

"Eddie, we've gone too far to quit now," Emily said as she took too big a sip from my Machiatto. "You are in a position to help your brother, the Morse brothers, and all those hypnotized staff members," she said as she studied me. "But you look as deflated as your brother did the other night."

I said it was all too much. Besides, how would I get to Polynesia? I had enough money for a bus trip to Portland, maybe.

"Courier," Emily had been waiting to spring this one on me. "I've signed you up to be a courier for a package that needs to be personally delivered to Tahiti. From there, you'll motorboat over to Tiaré. My contribution." She kissed me on the cheek.

Negativism dominated my thinking. "What if I find him and he doesn't want to leave?"

"According to that last posting, he's about to get kicked off the island anyway," she countered.

"Why should I bring him back here? How can he help us?"

"Granted, you'll have to bring him up to date about what's going on at AltaSystemics. Still, he's the only person we can trust who has a relationship with the Morse brothers. If you think about it, Isaac is the center piece of all this; everything is connected to him."

I felt this slight, slight ray of hope. "So, I bring him back and we work together to save the brothers." Ah, I was swimming in a Bond film. "And somehow neutralize Prime Mover before he gains total control over the Morse brothers. I never thought I'd say a sentence like that."

"There's one more thing," Emily said. "See if you can bring back some of the villagers."

That also caught me off guard. "Why?"

"Because they are smart and strong and loyal, and I believe they will be immune to whatever spell Prime Mover is able to cast." Emily had thought of everything or at least a lot.

I finished my drink and we left the café. The first stage of the plan, so far, was just to get Isaac back to here. "We still don't have a way to save everyone," I said, "and disrupt AltaSystemics."

"You'll have something to think about on the flight. You depart SeaTac at 11:45. Here's the address for the package pickup in Fremont. Oh, you're also bonded, courtesy of the Couriers R Us website."

"Wait," I practically shouted. "How will we get back?"

"I'm still working on that part," she said. "Let's stay in touch as much as possible through email or texting," Emily added, as she took my arm.

Was she a little sad that I was leaving?

"But they don't have WiFi or cell phone access on the island," I said. There I was going negative again.

"I know," Emily said. She could hardly contain herself. "I got a compact satellite hotspot from Professor Stevens. I, um, borrowed it."

LABELS: SATELLITE HOTSPOT, JAMES BOND, IMPROBABLE RESCUE PLANS

VIEW COMMENTS (77)

Carroty NOV. 5, 2011 AT 9:12 AM
At this point we don't know if the Morse brothers have been 'debriefed,' or if they have voluntarily told Prime Mover how to send message back in time. Or if they are still alive.

Anonymous NOV. 5, 2011 AT 9:42 AM
I've been a courier. Mostly medical stuff from hospitals and health centers to labs. Good pay. Long hours. Time pressure. ASAP! STAT!

SHOW MORE COMMENTS

○ ○ ○　　　　　　　THINKS OUT LOUD　　　　　　　✕

Emily chimes in
Entry No. 595 - POSTED: NOV. 6, 2011

Emily here. I guess it's my turn to do a posting. Got a text from Eddie when he was switching planes at LAX. He's now on his way to Tahiti. He asked me to keep an eye on his brother and to try and find out anything else about the situation with the Morse brothers. Aren't I supposed to be in school?

I think all these high-pressure events are having an effect on me. For example, my two roommates, Jennifer and Scarlett, both asked me if I'm doing okay. They have NO idea! I told them I was tired from a lot of studying, and they sort of believed me. Up until recently, my study statement could have been true. Now I find myself in a world, which, if someone else were to say this is what's happening to them, I wouldn't believe a word they were saying. ESP data storage. A power-hungry CEO who somehow hypnotizes his staff. And now, time travel. Course I am getting to know Eddie better. (Plus, I'm minus a previous non-working relationship. Sorry, Justin.)

Different item. Here's an excerpt from a recent posting tallboy (or his boss via tallboy) did for his AltaSystemics blog:

"An article in the *Seattle Times* business section took this high-tech startup to task for making exaggerated claims about its purpose and working model. The reporter said, 'No benchmarks, under capitalized, no proof of concept, no links to cloud oriented architecture. The AltaSystemics concept is too good to be true.' The article was based on half-truths, out of context anecdotes and misquotes. We have since invited the writer to re-visit our company, and we're excited to report she has decided to become part of our Connect/Marketing team after she comes back from an introductory sabbatical in Eastern Europe.

"In reality, AltaSystemics is providing a revolutionary way to bring all of your data streams into one storage lake for the best ROI in data mining and big data aggregatology. We are making use of cutting-edge matrices and thinking not just out of the box but beyond the usual dimensions. That's true. And we're also including a human element as we go beyond traditional (and limited) cloud confinement storage."

tallboy certainly has the lingo down. But I know what I saw. Or I know what I saw isn't what tallboy is promoting.

I'm tracking Eddie's flight over the Pacific. Looks like his plane is about to start its descent to the islands.

Take care, Eddie.

LABELS: CLOUD COMPUTER STORAGE, ESP, HIGH-TECH MYSTERY

VIEW COMMENTS (75)

Ringside NOV. 6, 2011 AT 8:55 AM
Thus, the Innocent One rides the currents of the Winds in search of Truth with Hope as companion.

SpecMan NOV. 6, 2011 AT 9:08 AM
Uh, right, Ringside, anything you say

Etruscan NOV. 6, 2011 AT 10:13 AM
Emily, it's true you and your friends weren't out looking for this challenge. But now there is no turning back. Bring it on.

SHOW MORE COMMENTS

First stop, Papeete

Entry No. 596 - POSTED: NOV. 7, 2011

Eddie in Polynesia: Here at the Papeete Tea and Coffee, I've got access to WiFi, a coconut latte, a view of a busy street and a glimpse of ocean a block away. Am experiencing e-x-t-r-e-m-e jet lag. I want to sleep, but it's early afternoon. Think I need two more shots in this latte.

Was able to read Emily's recent posting. (Shout out to Emily!) I hope tallboy doesn't disappear entirely into the Hive. I hope she finds a way to keep tabs on the Morse brothers.

Tahiti, or at least Papeete, is different from what I expected. It's a city with Western-style apartments and businesses. The streets have French names like Rue du Général De Gaulle. And they have cars and electricity and big tourist hotels. There are thousands of people here— from everywhere. The ocean's blue is extraordinary, and the beach is beautiful, although it's black, from volcanic rock they tell me. And the Polynesians, who are still in the majority, are cool. But it's kind of a funny mix of traditional with modern times. And I think the modern may be winning. If I were coming for a vacation, I'd move on to a smaller, more secluded island. Like the one I'm going to—though I'm not on vacation.

Oh, first thing after landing at the modest airport (with roofing that echos a grass hut), I delivered my courier package to its intended address, DeepSee, a Polynesian start-up that's focusing on finding and salvaging undersea wrecks (treasure) by using satellite long-range cameras coupled with historic maps of these islands. Their office was more a storage room for diving equipment with a prehistoric Powerbook G4 in the corner. Got to talking with Tony, their CEO, dressed in a flowery red and white Hawaiian (Polynesian?) shirt, and as I was leaving, he asked me if I'd be interested in being part (all?) of their IT team. Tempting, except I'm still (sort of) in school.

Tomorrow morning, I board the boat that will take me to Tiaré. Have no idea what I'll find there. Isaac knows little or nothing about the AltaSystemics mess and why we need his help. Actually, he doesn't even know me, except indirectly. Once again I think: Maybe this isn't such a good idea.

VIEW COMMENTS (79)

SeaSalt NOV. 7 2011 AT 8:24 AM

Came back to the blog to see if it had gotten better. It has.

FreeZone NOV. 7, 2011 AT 8:42 AM

How dare the Tahitians modernize! As if they don't have the right to be more financially secure, to reside in more comfortable homes and have access to more products and services. Shame on them!

JoeCurr NOV. 7, 2011 AT 9:00 AM

I was going to be deep-sea diver, but I couldn't stand the pressure.

Emily NOV. 7, 2011 AT 9:16 AM

Good Luck Eddie! You do your part, I'll do mine.

SHOW MORE COMMENTS

○ ○ ○   **THINKS OUT LOUD**   ✕

WHIMSY WITHOUT REGRET

Casing the joint

Entry No. 597 - POSTED: NOV. 7, 2011

Emily here again. I think I have some private-eye ability. This morning, I tailed tallboy to work. (At some cost to my studies, probably.) As I watched from across the street, right on cue he entered the stone-faced Pioneer Square building. tallboy was dressed all in white—both pants and shirt—and he walked lightly. I went back to his Capitol Hill apartment he'd moved into recently and did some snooping. Finding the building superintendent, I explained I was tallboy's girlfriend (just a ruse, Eddie), and needed to get something from the apartment. Being a post-feminist feminist, I only felt a little guilty about using feminine wiles to get my way; a soft voice and a smile do continue to work wonders.

The forty-something guy with two-day stubble and rodent eyes said, "Girlfriend, huh? Why hasn't he given you a key yet?" I laughed as if he'd made a funny and clever joke. That seemed to win him over. He added, "First time's free. This way." (Did I ever mention I'd taken a year of Hapkido in middle school?)

He led me up to the second floor unit, knocked and waited for an answer that didn't come, unlocked the door, peered into the space and gave me a dopey smile. I thanked him and darted inside. "Let me know if you need anything else," he said. I thanked him again and shut the door.

tallboy's apartment was surprisingly neat. He was a guy after all. But he was a guy who was under the influence of some kind of AltaSystemics spell. The place's sparseness made it easy to 'case the joint.' I found some bills and junk mail at the kitchen table next to a bowl of those M&Ms lettered with 'A' and 'S.' On a magnetized white board attached to the side of the refrigerator, in large blue letters, were the words 'Hear today, blog tomorrow.'

All was quiet. I thought I heard the handle on the apartment's front door turning, and I was readying a reason to be there. No one came in. (The super hanging around in the hallway?) I turned my attention back to my mission. Which of the three bedrooms was tallboy's? Two were on the messier side so I went with the one that had the perfectly made bed. On the small bedside table, I saw what looked like a marriage announcement. Actually it was a printout of an email invitation, which read: "Tallboy, in recognition of your service and loyalty to the AltaSystemics Way, we are pleased to announce your acceptance into our Receivers program. You are hereby entitled to begin a residency at the AltaSystemics nesting singularity. Welcome!"

"Oh, brother," I said aloud, "and they didn't even get the non-capitalization of his name right." If tallboy got absorbed into the Hive, we might never get him out. And we would lose our essential link to AltaSystemics.

Stumped, I sat at the kitchen table. Somehow, he needed to be pulled out of that trance. Hadn't one of the blog's readers suggested an intervention? To do that, without Eddie here, I needed help from someone I could trust. I mentally scanned my acquaintances' faces. What about Angela from our History of High-tech seminar?

Time to leave. Opening the door of the apartment I found myself staring at a pudgy guy. Roommate. He tensed up. I forced myself to stay relaxed. "Do I know you?" he asked. "Doubt it," I responded and raised a pointed finger as if to make a point. "Just here from apartment management to ensure your double pane windows have been properly installed. They have been. Have a good day." Before he could respond, I was heading (not too fast) down the stairs.

LABELS: POST-FEMININE WILES, WATCHING THE DETECTIVE, COMMUNAL LIVING

VIEW COMMENTS (70)

FixerUpper NOV. 7, 2011 AT 11:09 AM

I'm a super and I resent the way this one is represented. Supers have feelings, too.

VincentFrederic NOV. 7, 2011 AT 11:29 AM

I'm sure you're a great super, but this super is not being 'represented.' This is just who he is as reported by Emily.

Etruscan NOV. 7, 2011 AT 12:10 PM

I thought for sure tallboy was going to come home early and find Emily there. Not!

SHOW MORE COMMENTS

Bound for Tiaré

Entry No. 598 - POSTED: NOV. 8, 2011

Eddie: [message sent via remote when I was unobserved]

After spending the night in a nondescript place Emily found for me, I left Tahiti at eight in the morning on the Ebb Tide, a high-speed hydrofoil. On the way to Tiaré, we made a half dozen stops at other islands where groups of tourists disembarked. They were from all over—New York, Japan, Russia (many Russians)—but the visitors all had three things in common: lots of tubes of sunscreen, loud flowery shirts, and smart phones. And most were all staying in the large cabin, playing on their phones, and enjoying a light meal. I was doing the same for the first hour or so.

To stretch my legs, I went out onto the passenger deck. One of the crew had stepped out from the bridge above onto a metal walkway. He was staring at me in a very judgmental way, I thought. Returning the stare of this bosun or whatever they're called, I felt as if he were sending me a message. After some seconds, he turned his attention to the horizon, and I did the same. I heard a cough. The crewmember. I felt the strong breeze as the ship cut through the sea. I breathed in salt air. Across the aquamarine waters was our first island, rising in mist like a surfacing sea creature. I was so tempted to take a photo, like the older couple next to me. I held back. The sailor looked down at me, gave a quick salute, and disappeared back into the bridge.

Almost on the hour we made our stops along the row of islands, and each time passengers went ashore. The sea had been surprisingly calm, which my stomach appreciated. By mid-afternoon, only a dozen of us remained aboard. When we reached a long, low island that a passing crewman called Ponui, that rang a bell. Yes, according to Isaac's earlier posting, Ponui was the island next to Tiaré that received the drum messaging.

The ship headed back out to sea with me as the lone remaining passenger. We had actually landed at the north end of Ponui and continued to follow its length before a relatively short crossing to Tiaré. But, again, from Isaac's posting, I knew we needed to reach the village at the southeastern side of the island, which took another half hour. Isaac, you are my guide.

Beach dominated the shoreline, and I noted a wall of cliff that met the sea. When we entered a broad lagoon, I felt the engines throttling down, and the ship slowed. The end of the line. The ride had been so enchanting, I'd forgotten, again, I wasn't on vacation but a mission.

"We don't call here very often," said a voice, an Australian accent, from behind me. I turned and saw the crewmember who'd looked at me earlier. "Captain Lawrence C. Kuborn, at your service," he said. He sported a full gray beard and bushy mustache. His face was lined and tanned. Still trim even though he must have been around 60. "Occasionally we drop off a package. We seldom deliver visitors to Tiaré."

"I'm meeting another American here," I said and kept it at that.

"The mate who was shipwrecked and rescued a while back?"

I tried not to act surprised that he knew. "Guess the word's gotten out," I said. He smelled of aromatic pipe tobacco.

"News travels fast among these islands." We were gliding toward a worn dock. "Pardon me while we make port." The captain nimbly climbed the nearby metal stairs and entered the bridge. In a minute or two we were parallel to the dock; the engine was cut as a deckhand jumped to the dock and caught a thick rope from another hand at the bow. On shore, a crowd was gathering. Beyond them lay a gradually sloping beach, then curved palms and bushes of vibrant flowers.

"Thanks for the ride," I called up to the bridge. The captain opened a hatch and motioned toward the island.

"You are no longer in our century. Be advised."

I didn't know what to answer, so I waved. Another deck hand helped steady me as I crossed a narrow metal plank onto the dock. "Step lively now," he said. He was serious.

One figure broke from the crowd of onlookers and advanced toward me. He looked familiar even though I'd never seen him. But I had read about him. Sturdily built. Grey at the temples. And the closest thing to a friend that Isaac had here.

"Hello, Vaea," I said.

"I do not believe we have met," he said, scanning me from head to foot.

"No, but I've read about you in the Thinks Out Loud blog."

"Ah, it begins," said Vaea. "And who are you?"

"Eddie, tallboy's brother."

Vaea really searched my face now. "Thinks Out Loud did not mention he had another brother."

I was confused for a second until I remembered Vaea thought them brothers, and Isaac had not corrected him.

"I am the youngest brother," I said, which was true. "I come in search of my brother." And I meant that in a large sense of the word.

"That would be difficult," Vaea said. "He is no longer among us. I suggest you get back on board your ship and sail home."

LABELS: UBIQUITOUS SMART PHONES, UBIQUITOUS TOURISTS, GANGPLANKS

VIEW COMMENTS (77)

HighFive NOV. 8, 2011 AT 8:39 AM
That captain knows something.

WatchYourBack NOV. 8, 2011 AT 8:52 AM
Eddie, probably best to be up front with them. Oh well.

SHOW MORE COMMENTS

Retrieving tallboy

Entry No. 599 - POSTED: NOV. 8, 2011

Emily: I am thrilled Eddie has been able to send a blog posting after he landed on Tiaré, although his reception had started off kind of rough. But right now I need to focus on saving tallboy.

Angela is olive skinned, tall and leggy with prominent cheekbones and dark, almond shaped eyes. Most of the students in the History of High-tech class are intimidated by her. I think our professor is as well. Yet I had this feeling she could be of help. I needed her cool brand of energy.

I caught a bus back to campus and got to class just as it was ending. Meeting Angela at the door, I asked, "Got a minute?"

She listened quietly as I gave an abbreviated version of events relating to AltaSystemics. "That explains why you guys disappeared during the tour," she said in a husky voice. "But why are you telling me all this?" Why am I telling her this, I asked myself. I could have shown her the blog postings. But that would have taken too long. She could read them later.

I continued talking at the pace of a non-profit phone solicitor and introduced tallboy's transformation from a blogger to a cult-like follower. Then I told her about the Morse brothers and their being kidnapped and their time-travel secret.

"This is unbelievable," she said, her eyes showing interest. "So where do I come in?" I was impressed by her willingness to not immediately consider me insane.

I explained what we needed to do to short circuit the plans of Prime Mover. I said we had to work fast. Like tomorrow night. Could she gain the attention of tallboy?

"Sounds like fun," she said as she checked her iPhone.

LABELS: CULT INTERVENTION, EXPANDING THE CIRCLE

VIEW COMMENTS (80)

Iris7 NOV. 8, 2011 AT 12:29 PM

Emily rules!

Mipper NOV. 8, 2011 AT 12:45 AM

Every person added to their inner circle both weakens and strengthens their hand.

Fate NOV. 8, 2011 AT 1:35 PM

I disagree. They grow stronger, unless it's an AltaSystemics plant. (And I see no evidence of that in Angela.)

SHOW MORE COMMENTS

○ ○ ○   **THINKS OUT LOUD**   ✕

WHIMSY WITHOUT REGRET

Brother in search of brother

Entry No. 600 - POSTED: NOV. 8, 2011

Eddie on Tiaré: Noting everyone's stiff body language, I think I got off on the wrong foot with the villagers. After Vaea greeted me at the dock, he and I had walked to the beach where all were watching and waiting. I immediately recognized the tall, alluring (sorry Emily, but she is) Vaitiare, the friendly translator Kohia, the strong Teva. I knew about them through Isaac's posts. They knew nothing of me. And that seemed to be a problem. Where the sands met the village grasses, two human-sized wooden carvings stared at me. They looked like antique robots or aliens with elongated heads. Taking a breath, I introduced myself. (Not to the statues but to the villagers.) Vaea added I was Isaac's other brother, and with that bit of mis-info the villagers relaxed a little.

Vaea then addressed the group. There were assorted gasps and shocked expressions all around. "I told them," he said to me, "you are in search of your brother."

"I, Eddie, would like to see Isaac," I said, speaking loudly and slowly to the group.

"Oh, please," said Vaitiare, who wore a soft pale yellow sarong. "Do not treat us like children. You are as bad as your brother."

I apologized and tried again. Vaea translated for those who did not speak English. "Can you tell me where Isaac is? On the island? Somewhere else?"

No one answered. I tried to explain that I needed to find him because an evil person back in America was being mean to his other "brother" tallboy as well as many other people. The mean person had also kidnapped the Morse brothers. At the mention of the Morse brothers everything changed. The villagers gathered around me, many speaking rapidly in their tongue. Vaitiare asked for quiet.

"If we lead you to Thinks Out Loud, you may endanger him," said Vaitiare

I said I didn't understand. (Should I have been calling him Thinks Out Loud?) Why was this mission so hard?

"At our assembly to determine the place of Thinks Out Loud, the vote was so close," Vaea said, "we could not come to a clear decision of whether to send Thinks Out Loud out to sea in a canoe filled with provisions or welcome him into our family. It was Vaitiare who came up with a solution."

Now she spoke: "I recommended Thinks Out Loud go on a vision quest. In seclusion, he may experience a Way that will show us all what his true path is. If you interrupt a person on quest who is in a trance, he or she may never be able to join our world again."

I rubbed my forehead. I felt a headache coming on. Asking if I could go somewhere quiet to think, I added that I needed to send a message back to a partner.

"You wish to use our drum messengers?" Vaea asked. He acted as though I wanted to steal the drummers' souls.

"Without the Morse brothers, those messages will never be able to travel from the drummers to my friend," I said.

"Then how will you send your messages?" asked Teva as he moved from the front of the group right up to me. I was looking up at him.

"With this," I said, showing my laptop and solar-powered iHAL27 remote satellite Internet access terminal. Now that we were getting to know each other I wouldn't have to be so secretive.

"I'm sorry, brother of Thinks Out Loud," said a stern Teva, "but we can't let you do that."

Heading back out to sea, the Ebb Tide revved up its engines and let out a deep blast of its horn. I thought I saw Captain Kuborn offering a salute from the top deck.

VIEW COMMENTS (80)

HindSite NOV. 8, 2011 AT 4:13 PM

Eddie, in his innocence, puts not only his foot but his entire leg in his mouth.

DoughNut NOV. 8, 2011 AT 5:33 PM

If I were Eddie, I'd be covertly videoing all this for a reality show.

SpecMan NOV. 8. 2011 AT 5:54 PM

In a way, the islanders are being protective of Thinks Out Loud.

SHOW MORE COMMENTS

○ ○ ○   **THINKS OUT LOUD**   ✕

WHIMSY WITHOUT REGRET

Hypnotism, moles and Facebook

Entry No. 601 - POSTED: NOV. 9, 2011

Angela and I were in Pioneer Square standing across the street from AltaSystemics and waiting for tallboy to leave work. "He arrives and goes home like clockwork," I told Angela. "Are you ready?"

She loosened a button at the top of her sleeveless red shirt. "A trance for a trance. Ready." Once again I felt a little guility about using our physical nature to control men, but a lot was at stake here.

Right on time, tallboy exited the building, turned right, and drifted toward his bus stop. "Go," I said. Angela crossed the street and quickly took her position just behind him. I followed from a few feet back. At the red light Angela moved into action and 'accidentally' bumped into tallboy. At first he barely seemed to notice her, but she persisted. I watched her body language, the way she leaned toward him, the way she titled her head and playfully wiped at her long hair. The light changed and they walked together. Rather than going to the bus stop, they continued toward a pier just above the ferry terminal on Puget Sound.

tallboy took out a bag from his pocket and offered Angela what looked like hard candies. They continued to talk and walk further up Alaska Way. Gradually Angela's stride began to parallel tallboy's, a light floating step. Good, I thought, make him comfortable. Then they sat at a park bench facing toward the Sound. I casually walked by, behind them, and slowed to hear their conversation. They were talking in whispers. Okay, Angela, is gettting on his wavelength.

I walked a few feet past the bench, turned and made another pass, this time in front of them. Angela had a glazed look in her eyes. And an empty smile. What was going on? Rather than pulling tallboy back into our reality, he had somehow pulled Angela into his dream state! Some intervention!

Angela saw me—I was standing right in front of her—and purred, "Candy?"

Frustrated, upset, disappointed, I stomped right up to Angela, grabbed the candy package out of her hand, and threw it to the ground. Taking a very deep breath, I tried to calm down. You would think she would have reacted in some way to my aggressive action, but Angela looked at me as if I had just done her a favor. I was about to begin berating her when I glanced at the candy wrapping again and it all became crystal clear. "Angela," I practically shouted, "did you eat some of those candies?" She tilted her head and began humming what sounded like a Mozart piece. "tallboy, have you been eating these candies?" He momentarily turned my way and then gazed up at the partly cloudy sky which was tilting toward evening.

I tapped my hand on their shoulders and motioned for them to look at my face. "tallboy, Angela, watch my fingers," I said as I began to conduct the tune Angela was humming. tallboy tried to rise from the bench, and I gently pushed him back. They slowly started to focus on my movements. I spoke to them in a calm, quiet voice and told them to relax, relax. After a minute or so they both closed their eyes.

"Very good," I said. "Now listen carefully. Angela, you are going to let go of your current condition. It is a false feeling of contentment. Let that contentment seep out of you through your pores. Good. You are returning to your usual aloof way of being. And you, tallboy, you are also breaking free of the chains that bind you, the chains of obedience to AltaSystemics. You are becoming free again."

I hoped I was getting through to them. Continuing, I said in a firmer voice: "Do not, repeat, do not eat any more of the AltaSystemics candies. They taste terrible to you, like paste." Then I said I'd count to five and with each number I uttered they would begin to come out of their hypnotic state.

"One, you are beginning to become more alert. Two, you will awaken refreshed and clear headed. You will not remember what I have told you, but it will live within you. Three, continuing to awaken. Four, begin to move your fingers and toes. Five, you are now awake. Open your eyes."

I heard a seagull at the end of a pier. The ferry bound for Bainbridge Island gave a blast of its deep horn. tallboy and Angela opened their eyes and acted as though nothing had happened. "Hi, guys," I said. "Let's go get a bite at Pike Place."

"Great, said tallboy, I'm starving." He turned to his bench mate. "Do I know you?"

"Angela, a classmate of Emily's." They stood up and began to walk up the street. Bending over, I grabbed the candy package and noticed a few of the M&M-like pieces were inside. I needed a chemist.

LABELS: SECRETLY DRUGGED, HYPNOTIC POWERS, CANDYLAND

VIEW COMMENTS (80)

Fleecer NOV. 9, 2011 AT 8:09 AM

THE CANDIES. OF COURSE! WHY DIDN'T I SEE THAT?

Hummer NOV. 9, 2011 AT 9:00 AM

Have tried several times. I can't be hypnotized.

Aladden NOV. 9, 2011 AT 9:20 AM

Actually, you don't realize it, Hummer, but you probably go into a light hypnotic state several times a day. We call it daydreaming.—So, should I have my own blog?

Heiress NOV. 9, 2011 AT 9:40

Emily, at least on this point I am in solidarity with you. As a post post post feminist, I totally approve of using whatever means are necessary to gain control over men, especially those who dominate the blogging world.

SHOW MORE COMMENTS

WHIMSY WITHOUT REGRET

Eddie pleads his case

Entry No. 602 - POSTED: NOV. 9, 2011

Yesterday, on the beach, my travels caught up with me. I sure lack ambassadorial skills, I was thinking and growing limp at the same time. The islanders didn't want me to visit with Isaac/Thinks Out Loud, who was on a quest; plus, they didn't want me to send messages with my high-tech equipment. They'd actually suggested I leave (as the boat that brought me motored out of the harbor). I felt waves carrying me away. That was when I found myself passed out on the beach, Kohia and Teva beside me trying to offer aid. Teva actually carried me over to a hut, Kohia had me drink water, and I fell asleep again.

Apparently I slept into and through the night. With morning's light airy breeze and sun warming the hut, I finally awoke. Kohia was by my side, Teva in the background. I told them I felt better and was actually hungry. They said that was a good sign. While I was enjoying an outdoor breakfast, people began to gather around me, including Chief Keoni. Unfinished business.

Part of me felt like giving up. Then young Kohia, spoke. "Friends and family, it is true we do not know this Eddie who has suddenly come to our island," she said, translating her words back into English. "At least, it seems suddenly for us. The situation, I just realized, is not the same for him." She asked me how I knew so much about Tiaré and its people.

I said it was because I had read the blog postings of Thinks Out Loud—until they had suddenly stopped. I said I felt as if I knew the islanders and what they valued and wouldn't have come if it hadn't been an emergency "that could affect the entire world, including these islands." I continued to address the group. This was the most I'd ever said before an audience, any audience. I told them more about what had been going on where I was from. "All of this may sound strange or maybe it won't," I said. I explained about tallboy's job as a blogger for a mysterious company. The way the owner of the company uses people and even puts them into a trance.

"We value the trance experience," said the chief with several nods from others.

"This is a different kind of trance I think," I explained. "It's a forced trance." I went on to describe the capturing of the Morse brothers to use their knowledge of time to rule the world or at least make a lot of money in an unfair way.

"Why would someone want to rule the world?" Vaea asked. "What a foolish idea."

I said I agreed, but added that certain individuals do attempt to do so from time to time. Especially in the movies. *Dr. No. Goldfinger. Skyfall.* Again, no response beyond dismissive stares.

"So why are you here?" Teva asked.

"None of us volunteered for this mission," I explained. Why did this feel as if I were on trial? "It was kind of thrust upon us. We're just regular people. I'm a college student," I said. "There are only a few of us we can trust. Unfortunately, tallboy, my brother, is under the spell of this evil man. If we try and tell others of the threat, they will not believe us. We need Isaac, I mean, Thinks Out Loud. He knows the power of the Morse brothers. He is the leader of our blogging group." I paused and added one more reason: "In the time he has been here with you, he has learned much about how to live and what is right and how to be strong." The group sat up straighter. Even Vaitiare seemed touched.

"Will you lead me to Thinks Out Loud?" I finally asked. There was a long moment of silence. I saw the chief eye Vaea and Vaitiare. Then he looked at me.

"You ask much of us, brother of Thinks Out Loud," said the chief. "But you ask more of Thinks Out Loud. He should be allowed to choose what he wishes to do. We will lead you to him."

I thanked the chief and the islanders. Vaea said we would leave first thing in the morning. That would give me time to rest, to eat, and to figure out how to deal with Thinks Out Loud if he were indeed in a deep trance.

"One last request," I said. "Chief, may I use my machine to contact the others in my group?" And I added in a quieter voice, "And to send out a couple of blog postings?"

The chief didn't quite get my meaning. But Vaitiare did. She walked right up to me, and I thought she was going to strike me or yank my equipment away.

All she said was, "If you must. At least wait until the village sleeps."

"Come," said Kohia as she took me by the hand, "let me show you our home."

LABELS: DEBATE CLUB, HOME TOUR, POLYNESIAN ATTRACTIONS

VIEW COMMENTS (80)

GeorgiePorgie NOV. 9, 2011 AT 11:49 AM
I value the trance experience!

CrashSite NOV. 9, 2011 AT11:58 AM
Eddie had to rise to the occasion, and I think he did.

SHOW MORE COMMENTS

○ ○ ○   **THINKS OUT LOUD**   ✕

WHIMSY WITHOUT REGRET

Report from Post Alley

Entry No. 603 - POSTED: NOV. 10, 2011

Emily: Sometimes a remote chance of success is all we have, in all areas of life. It would certainly have been easier to call it a day and go catch up on schoolwork. Would that make us quitters?

Haven't made much progress since my last posting yesterday, except for one thing that happened. tallboy and Angela had come out of their trances, and we were eating burgers and fries at the Pike Place Bar and Grill. The open-air market, a half block closer to the Sound, was basically closed for the night.

"Our waiter is our age," Angela observed. "Wonder if he's in college."

"This is fun," said tallboy, who was more alert than I'd seen him in a long time. Angela was also more relaxed now that she didn't have to entrap him. Did I mention she's statuesque? That's a word pre-blog writers used to describe a tall, curvy woman. And her bold Italian-design glasses only accented her strong presence.

Trying to think about what to do next, I was the most tense. "Let's figure out a game plan," I said. "Does anyone know any chemists?"

Angela peered over her glasses. "What about Chen?" she asked, referring to our History of High-tech classmate. "I think he's a chemistry major." The candy package still in my purse, I made a mental note to have a conversation with him as soon as I could.

tallboy put down his burger. "I'm not sure which side I'm on now," he said slowly. "I like blogging for AltaSystemics. I think I look good in white. And even though Prime Mover has ways of controlling us, maybe we just don't see the big picture. What if the company is ahead of the curve? What if our two elderly visitors came on their own accord to see what we're doing?"

I didn't try to argue tallboy's points weak as they were. I was just happy to see him beginning to think again, even if his powers of reasoning were still in need of recharging. Then Angela broke in. "tallboy, you're on the inside and sometimes that colors your view of things."

He asked what she meant by that.

Now I broke in. "I think none of us has all the answers. There is one man, though, who does. Prime Mover."

"There he goes," tallboy said offhandedly as he downed a handful of fries.

"There goes who?" I asked.

"Prime Mover. He just walked by the restaurant."

I slapped down whatever money I had, grabbed the arms of both tallboy and Angela and pulled the two of them out the door. tallboy managed to flip his burger off his plate and catch it in mid-air. I thought I heard mild applause.

"Which way, tallboy?"

"To the right, toward the water."

Weaving around a crowd of Japanese tourists, we accelerated past Rachel, the Market's mascot, a full size brass pig/piggy bank, zagged past the front of the popular Pike Place Fish Company, where fish are literally thrown around, and slid around the corner into the narrow Post Alley.

We slammed on the brakes. I always found this place spooky, the way the old brick buildings lean in toward you.

"Is that him?" Angela asked, pointing toward a short but sturdy bulldog of a figure dressed in a silver silk suit. Walking as if with a purpose, he was about 30 feet ahead on the uneven brick road.

He didn't pay attention to the wall of gum, known as the, well, The Gum Wall.

"Not too close," I whispered, even though I knew he couldn't hear me. Or could he? Prime Mover stopped at a doorway and after a momentary halt to check something, opened the door, and stepped inside. Seconds later we were there.

"Unexpected Productions," tallboy read on a worn sign. Beneath the wooden sign was a placard: Classes begin this week.

"They do improv shows here," Angela added. "And I guess offer classes."

"Angela," I said, "Prime Mover knows us. He doesn't know you. Go check it out."

Pursing her lips, she studied the sign's class schedule. "I was in my high school senior play. We did *Harvey*. I was the nurse," Angela said. We stepped back as she entered the bricked theater.

"Break a leg," I said.

LABELS: PIKE PLACE MARKET, HARD CANDIES, POWER OF REASON

VIEW COMMENTS (75)

The Good Doctor NOV. 10, 2011 AT 8:30 AM
Coincidence that Prime Mover should just happen to walk by? I think not!

Anonymous NOV. 10, 2011 AT 8:45 AM
I was there at the Market. The Fish Guys do toss the fish around. Not to the customers, though. Well I suppose you could intercept one of their passes.

SHOW MORE COMMENTS

○ ○ ○　　　　　　**THINKS OUT LOUD**　　　　　　　　×

WHIMSY WITHOUT REGRET

To the Quest Cave

Entry No. 604 - POSTED: NOV. 10, 2011

Eddie: Kohia gave me a very nice tour of her village. After a filling dinner of island specialties and some general conversation about my life in America (and a little more wriggling when it came to talking about my "brother" Thinks Out Loud), I waited until things had quieted down to set up my equipment and check in to the blog. I chose a spot under a palm tree just off the beach. The moon provided soft light. Reading and writing with the soothing background sound of rhythmic surf, I could see how addictive this island could be.

Early this morning, after Vaea woke me from a deep sleep, we ate a quick breakfast and headed out. With me were Vaea, Teva, Vaitiare, and the chief. Oh, Kohia came along as well. Our pace was constant and quicker than leisurely but not so fast I couldn't take in the island's beauty: the gradual rising and falling of the trail past collections of flowering bushes, small ponds and groves of palm trees. Great overviews of green hillsides rolling up and away from the beaches toward a steep inland mountain.

I found myself walking next to Vaitiare who was surprisingly quiet. Teva and Vaea were talking animatedly. "Island politics and local goings-on," said Kohia. The chief occasionally made a comment in English for my benefit. Not exactly small talk. More, I think, his way of being inclusive. Periodically Kohia, just ahead of me on the trail, would point to a flower or bush or piece of land and tell me their names in Polynesian. I occasionally could see cuts of ocean view beyond the trees.

I wanted to find out something that had been gnawing at me. "Vaitiare," I finally said, "I can't help but be curious about the vote to decide Thinks Out Loud's fate. It was a public vote, right?"

She took several seconds before answering. "Yes. The results are known to all islanders."

The others moved ahead as she paused and looked at something in the distance. The glimpse of mountain beyond the trees?

 "When I first landed on the island, you said it was a close vote."

She regarded me with a direct gaze as though I were also being evaluated. "Yes. Very close. A tie. We didn't feel right about making any decision."

"And it was your idea to send Thinks Out Loud on a vision quest."

She stopped on the trail as the others continued. "It seemed the only way to find our and his Answer."

"So you must have voted for him to stay?"

A long, long pause. I could hear birdcalls all around us. "My vote was for Thinks Out Loud to leave."

I actually gasped. I mean according to the postings, they had a relationship. Then I realized: Not everything is in the postings!

"Well," I stumbled on, "Teva certainly voted Thinks Out Loud off." They'd had a tense relationship since first meeting on the sacred island where Thinks Out Loud had been marooned.

"No, he voted for him to stay."

Now it was my turn to be silent. We started walking again, faster, to catch up to the others, who had paused at the top of a rounded hill to wait for us.

We reached them. "Halfway there," said Vaea.

Another idea took hold of me. "Vaitiare, would you be interested in my giving you a summary of everything that's been happening to those of us in Seattle since Thinks Out Loud has been here?"

"Not really," she answered. "Your troubles are of little concern to me."

She had surprised me again. "Don't you care about the fate of the Morse brothers?"

"I don't send messages off-island," she said as she glanced at some nearby orchid-like flowers.

"But I read the earlier postings where you said your people were concerned about the actions of non-islanders—the cruise ships, the new technologies."

"We have our ways of dealing with them," she said curtly.

I tried again and reminded her about the mastermind Prime Mover and his goal of controlling time and the way he controls people. In spite of her protests, I continued to describe how we—tallboy, Emily and I—had infiltrated the strange AltaSystemics company, our discovery of Prime Mover's evil plans, and the steps we were taking to stop him.

"Yes," said Vaitiare. "And your need to take your brother back with you to help fight this enemy."

"Right!" I said. "That's why I'm here." And as I said this I realized what Vaitiare wasn't saying: She didn't want me to take Thinks Out Loud away from Tiaré. She feared he would never return. But she had also voted him off. Had something recently changed her mind?

I lost track of time, but I would guess we'd been walking, with occasional rest stops, for a couple of hours. With a turn in the path, we moved directly toward the ocean. I could hear breakers.

"The cave is up ahead," said Vaea. We had reached the cliff-like edge of the shore, the wild section of the island I had seen from the boat as we followed the coastline to port. "Let us pause and make certain we approach Thinks Out Loud in a way that does not send him so deeply into his trance he is lost to us."

"It's the kava root," Kohia whispered to me. "A stronger version of it taken during this time of testing. It can be dangerous."

Vaea recommended Vaitiare try and awaken Thinks Out Loud with a special ritual used in these circumstances. Even though she knew the ritual, she said she'd never been asked to break a trance. They asked me one last time if we should attempt this. My chest tightened. I nodded.

We stood a short distance away. "Everyone ready?" asked Vaea. "One other item," he said. "If Thinks Out Loud awakens in a fiery state and begins running toward the edge of the cliff, we must tackle him and bring him down before he thrusts himself onto the rocks down below. Use caution, for his strength may seem to be that of five men. Let us go."

LABELS: VISION QUEST, RUDE AWAKENINGS

VIEW COMMENTS (78)

Toddler NOV. 10, 2011 AT 10:01 AM
They should handle Thinks Out Loud with kid gloves.

HindSight NOV. 10, 2011 AT 10:22 AM
Wake him up. Let's see if he's a sprinter.

JourneyMan NOV. 10, 2011 AT 10:37 AM
HindSight, why don't you go find another blog?

SHOW MORE COMMENTS

Opening the Psychological Trunk

Entry No. 605 - POSTED: NOV. 11, 2011

Emily: Angela joined the improv class Prime Mover was taking. tallboy has come out of that candy-induced trance and has agreed to be our mole at AltaSystemics. And Chen from our class, who is indeed a chemistry major, is testing the candies to find the trance-inducing ingredient. After class I had walked with Chen, a relaxed guy who also manages to look like he's always thinking. He became the next of our student group to learn about what we're facing. "Are you in?" I'd asked. Other students passed right by us, totally unaware of the import of our conversation.

"Even if you are making this all up, I'll analyze your candy specimen," he'd said with a tone that was surprisingly casual given our situation. "Where did you say Eddie was?"

"An island in Polynesia. Here's the candy. Do NOT try one. Did you see where Angela went? I need to talk with her."

Chen pointed me toward a campus espresso bar. I caught up to her as her mocha cookie crumble frappuccino was called out.

"I can't believe I haven't taken an improv class before," she gushed. "Carl, the instructor, is great! He had us spread out on this stage and open up a pretend chest and pull out anything we found in there and say aloud what it was. The game is called 'Letting go of baggage.' We were all reaching in to our chests and pulling out items. I found my American Doll collection, a worn soccer ball from fifth grade and, um, what was my mother's favorite recipe book." A single tear welled in her eye. I didn't know what to say, so I stayed quiet. She took a sip and slowly continued. "Turns out improv can be more than just funny."

After a moment of shared silence, I felt I had permission to continue. "What about Prime Mover?"

"He was pulling out all kinds of stuff. Couldn't hear exactly. Caught a little: comic books, a trapeze. He actually shouted the words. Carl said great job and had us close the trunks and get into an Identity Circle, where we learned three main rules of improvisation: Don't negate, make your partners look good, don't TRY and be funny. Then Carl asked us to go around the circle and say why we were taking the class. There were a dozen of us. Prime Mover was opposite me. He was glancing at me, but I didn't make much of it. He couldn't remember me from the tour could he?"

I said I didn't think so.

"When it was my turn I said I was taking improv to stimulate my mind and give me a break from school. Hey, that's kind of true! When Prime Mover's time came, he said he'd had some showbiz experiences when he was a kid, though circumstances had led him into the sciences as a career. He wanted to get back in touch with his artistic self.

"Carl told Prime Mover, who introduced himself as Art, that he was in the right place," Angela added. "The teacher made everyone feel relaxed and capable. We're putting ourselves out there after all," she said. "He makes it okay and safe to go for it."

I reminded Angela of why she had attended the class.

"I know, I know," she said. "And I want to go back next week. That way I can keep observing Prime Mover."

Her drink finished, she said she had a midterm in an hour and headed out. I sat at her table and sent a text to tallboy. Time to see what he'd been up to. Simultaneously, a call came in. My mom. Due back today from an eco-vacation in Guatemala. I debated whether to take the call and have to listen to her rave about the trip nonstop for twenty minutes. Except this time, if I'd wanted to, I could have topped her. She had no idea what her little girl had been up to.

LABELS: WHOSE LINE IS IT ANYWAY, POWER OF IMPROV

VIEW COMMENTS (85)

Mipper NOV. 11, 2011 AT 8:22 AM

Did improv in my late twenties when I lived in Santa Barbara. Kind of fell into it: I was sent to write a feature story on the local performing group, Scriptless. When audience members were invited on stage to participate, for the sake of the article, I volunteered. With the others who joined in, we became the Sound System, an orchestra of funny instruments conducted by one of the group's leaders. I played and supplied the sound for an angry lawn sprinkler. The audience laughed and applauded. I showed up next week and the next. Eventually I became the only dues-paying member of the group. A year later it all fell apart due to a mix of clashing egos, too much planning (for an improv group) and people moving to LA.

○ ○ ○   **THINKS OUT LOUD**   ✕

WHIMSY WITHOUT REGRET

The Awakening

Entry No. 606 - POSTED: NOV. 11, 2011

Eddie on Tiaré: We stood at the edge of the cave set in a cliff above a rocky shoreline. The cave had a wide opening and sloped backwards into a dank darkness. I could barely make out a figure crouched or sitting against the rear wall. While the rest of us remained at the entrance, Vaitiare advanced slowly, singing a haunting song that sounded surprisingly modernistic. I realized it had a hypnotic effect, or maybe an anti-hypnotic effect to pull Thinks Out Loud out of his trance. Vaea motioned for us to fan out and follow Vaitiare at a slight distance. The outside light barely entered this deeper half of the cave, but my eyes started adjusting to the near darkness. When Vaitiare was ten feet from Thinks Out Loud, she stopped walking and sped up her chant/song. Even in the darkness, I could see the outline of Thinks Out Loud, who sat crosslegged like an Indian guru. Now his lowered head began to rise from his chest, and his breathing became expansive. Vaitiare ceased singing and made a blowing sound, like a beckoning wind. Thinks Out Loud tilted his head; I couldn't tell if he saw us or if he even had his eyes open.

Vaitiare took several steps forward and raised her arms as if she were about to take flight. Thinks Out Loud slowly rose to his feet and also let his arms come up in a wide expansion. Vaitiare moved her right leg to the side and planted herself. Thinks Out Loud mirrored her movement. "So far, so good," I thought. Just like Simon Says.

She emitted a higher pitched "ooooh" that reverberated in the cave. Thinks Out Loud cocked his head again and uttered a loud "Huuuugh!" I felt Vaea, Teva, the chief, and Kohia go tense. Vaitiare also pulled

207

back and moved into a crouch. Thinks Out Loud gave an even louder "Huuuyuuuh!" and planted his other leg with a firm stamp. Out came his tongue and more shouts. Vaea said something quickly in Polynesian. "Careful," he said to me."

As if released from the starting post at Churchill Downs, Thinks Out Loud surged forward, a fierce expression reforming his face. Closest to him, Vaitiare tried her best to slow him down by grabbing at his torso, but he moved effortlessly past her like a practiced running back and continued toward the mouth of the cave. My other four companions met Thinks Out Loud's charge, Vaea aiming at the legs, the chief and Teva at body center and Kohia trying for an arm. It looked like one of those Godzilla movies, with Thinks Out Loud as the giant monster easily flicking his adversaries away.

No one remained between him and the edge of the cave. Except me. He was picking up speed, and I was directly in his path. An image of Thinks Out Loud smashing into me and sending us both over the cliff chilled me. I'd heard people in this kind of situation report a slowing down of time, of noticing of all the details of the scene. I could see the expansion of Thinks Out Loud's chest as he drew in a breath, the churning movement of his four limbs, even the non-blinking eyes as he approached. Behind him, the others were stirring though too far away to help. Vaitiare cried out, "Thinks Out Loud!"

Who would blog about our end, I thought with gallows humor. But that was it! Physical counterforce was not working. I had one last option. Literally face to face with him, I yelled, "Thinks Out Loud, your blog just passed a million page visits!" It was as though an invisible shield had been erected. He reared back as if his jockey had suddenly yanked on the reins. One of his curving arms caught me, and we both hit the hard dusty cave floor. Thinks Out Loud was mumbling about the million hits, and I felt groggy myself. The others clustered about us, Vaitiare gently touching his hair. I thought I heard Teva grunt. The only other sound was the crash of waves below us. As if waking up from a deep sleep, Thinks Out Loud raised his head and tried to look at me.

"Do I know you?" he asked, as he pulled himself up. Brushing off a layer of dust, I rose as well.

"Thinks Out Loud, it's me. Your brother, Eddie." I tried to give him a private wink.

He shook his head and seemed to be processing information new to him.

"I don't have a brother named Eddie."

Vaea and Teva came forward. "He's confused," I said. "Coming out of the trance, you know. He's still in a different state of mind." I winked again.

"Perhaps," said a guarded Vaea. "Or he really does not know you."

For a brief second I wondered if it would have been easier (and more mythic), if Thinks Out Loud and I had gone over the cliff.

LABELS: THE TRANCE STATE, GREAT RUNNING BACK MOVES, WHITE LIES

VIEW COMMENTS (87)

EveningMist NOV. 11, 2011 AT 10:29 AM
Americans know nothing about the trance-mind. The closest they come is by staring into their 'smart' phones!

WayOut NOV. 11, 2011 AT 10:49 AM
Actually, Evening, some Americans do know about the trance-mind.

Hummer NOV. 11, 2011 AT 11:48 AM
I could have brought Thinks Out Loud down with an upper leg tackle. Worked for me at the Orange Bowl.

SHOW MORE COMMENTS

○ ○ ○   THINKS OUT LOUD   ✕
WHIMSY WITHOUT REGRET

A big chunk of fiction
Entry No. 607 - POSTED: NOV. 12, 2011

Emily in Seattle: While waiting to hear from Chen about the chemical composition of those candies, and while waiting to see if Angela learns anything useful about Prime Mover in the improv class, and while waiting for tallboy to burrow deeper into the foundation of AltaSystemics, and after listening to my mother's non-stop recounting of her eco-tourism trip to Guatemala, I guess you could say I'm in a waiting period.

Taking a break from reviewing for my anthro mid-term, I reread the past 40 entries in Thinks Out Loud. Interesting to do that all at one time. With everything taking place, both here and on Tiaré, I had a realization: These events seem hard to believe, something several readers have remarked upon.

EdSell calls the postings "delightful, but a story."

DebbieDoesDuluth says "It's all fiction!" (Jeannie, is that you?)

And MasterMind is just plain skeptical about everything.

I can see their point. What Isaac, tallboy, the others, and I are experiencing would seem an assortment of fictions, of story upon story, to a reader (outsider), but to me, the predicament of tallboy, Isaac's identity crisis, and the power urges of Prime Mover are all as real as the upcoming presidential primaries. Anyway, isn't truth supposed to be stranger than fiction? (Not to say there aren't supporters. Etruscan, for example, admits to being a doubter at first but has come around and now is a strong believer "in these events, however extraordinary they seem to be."

"Hey, Emily, how's it going?" asked a voice from behind my chair. I pivoted and saw Chen, a smile spread from cheek to cheek. The guy is nice looking, just shy of a model's too perfect Adonis face.

"I've compiled the results of the candy analysis. Got a minute?"

"A minute?" I whispered motioning for him to sit beside me. "I've got ten minutes if you've got answers."

"Right," said Chen as he joined me, "although sometimes apparent answers can lead to more questions."

LABELS: FICTION VERSUS REALITY, BETTER LIVING THROUGH CHEMISTRY

VIEW COMMENTS (80)

Redo NOV. 12, 2011 AT 8:28 AM
What is reality, eh, Emily? For that matter, am I real?

Anonymous NOV. 12, 2011 AT 8:40 AM
I was real, once, but I gave it up for pretend. Gave me a lot more freedom of movement and plot possibilities.

AdamsRibEye NOV. 12, 2011 AT 8:50 AM
Everyone tries to be a joker in this comments section. No joke.

SHOW MORE COMMENTS

My brother's keeper?

Entry No. 608 - POSTED: NOV. 12, 2011

Eddie on Tiaré: I was at one of those pivotal moments most of us do our best to avoid. Coming out of his trance, Thinks Out Loud (Isaac) did not recognize me as his brother, which made perfect sense because we weren't related, and we'd never met in person. The five islanders gathered around us at the mouth of the cave were looking at me and awaiting an explanation. I could have maintained the fiction that Thinks Out Loud was confused, which is why he thought me a stranger. Or I could tell them the truth and suffer the consequences of being a falsifier and confirming their belief about the hypocrisy of off-islanders. I was locked in a moral dilemma!

"Do you have anything to tell us?" Vaea was giving me the chance to come clean. All eyes were on me, including the semi-glazed ones of Thinks Out Loud.

"I know that lying about one's nature is unacceptable and not appreciated in your culture," I began. "But where I come from, we bend the truth many times a day. It actually becomes a habit."

"Perhaps it is time to break that habit," said Vaitiare, giving her penetrating stare.

I rubbed my forehead and looked out to the deep blue ocean beyond the breakers lashing the rocks below us. "Perhaps it is," I said. "Could we go back inland and find a place to sit? I'll try and explain it all to you." That relocation would at least buy me some time.

Quietly, solemnly, the islanders filed out of the cave. Vaitiare helped guide a still shaky Thinks Out Loud, who was walking with a tilt toward the cliff's edge. I followed last. A hundred yards down the path and away from the cliff, we stopped and sat cross-legged on a bed of compressed waist-high grass that was softer than I expected.

Out came the truth. I told them that Thinks Out Loud and I had misled them. We were not brothers. Thinks Out Loud and tallboy were not brothers. tallboy and I were actually brothers. tallboy had been hired (well more of an internship) to write blog postings while Thinks Out

Loud took some time off for travels and others pursuits. I had only gotten involved after tallboy had gone wacko when he started working at AltaSystemics. Today was the first time I had met Thinks Out Loud. tallboy has never met him, although we felt as if we knew him. And we see him as the leader of our, well, his blog. (I didn't go into how you can develop electronic relationships with people without physically meeting them.)

Vaea was shaking his head. Teva's face was immobile. Vaitiare had a wistful look, and Kohia's mouth was downturned. Only the chief seemed relaxed.

"Why did you feel the need to create this false story about brotherhood?" asked Vaea.

"I wish I could say," I answered in a soft voice. "It started sort of as an accident when you assumed they were brothers back when tallboy contacted you to do a search and rescue for the marooned Thinks Out Loud. For whatever reason, Thinks Out Loud did not correct your assumption. And once it was in play, I didn't correct anyone either when I landed on Tiaré. Do you know how a lie can take on a life of its own?"

As a group, they said no. I thought I saw the chief briefly smile.

"Uh, okay. Well in our culture lies can be very hard to eradicate, especially in dating, modern political campaigns, and IPOs. Anyway, I thought I'd have a better chance of getting Thinks Out Loud off Tiaré if you thought I was his brother. You see, we really need Thinks Out Loud to come help us fight Prime Mover. Even though he doesn't know us personally, Thinks Out Loud is our Prime Blogger. That's the true part."

Chief Keoni faced us. I hadn't really paid much attention to him. Although he wore the casual orangish board shorts and a flowery shirt, like Vaea and Tiva, Keoni's short but thick gray hair, his gray intricately designed tattoos on arms and legs, the solid line of eyebrow, the weathered face—he still radiated 'leader.'

Standing before us and with Kohia doing an immediate translation, the chief said, "I have observed Thinks Out Loud on our island. I have observed you as well." He nodded in my direction. "I have heard your confession. And this is what I know: You may not be brothers in blood, but you are becoming brothers through deed. Go to him."

A chemistry lesson

Entry No. 609 - POSTED: NOV. 13, 2011

Emily in Seattle: Sitting next to me at the long library table, Chen began to rattle off the ingredients of the candy Prime Mover was using to control his Hive. "They're basically M&Ms," he said. I didn't catch all the components. He did mention sugar, cocoa butter, various artificial colors. "Normal stuff; however, that's not the interesting part."

He paused for effect. "Hexamethylene diammonium adipate. You can imagine my surprise when that turned up." Chen finished with a shy half-smile.

"Yes, I certainly can," I answered. "Chen, I have no idea what you are talking about."

"That's a chemical used in the production of nylon. Don't you see?" He was incredibly earnest. And earnest was what we needed right now.

I told him I was still confused.

"Look." He pulled a paper napkin from his pocket and began to sketch the molecular make-up of the chemical.

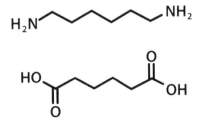

"See the adipic acid is partially oxidized via the pathways of lipid metabolism. That's the key to this guy's mind control." Chen again rested his case.

"Chen, can you just tell me in plain English what you discovered?"

He opened his mouth to speak and out came the voice of Angela: "Guess what we learned in improv last night!"

Chen and I both turned to see Angela standing behind us.

I couldn't help but blurt out: "How to behave like a wayward nylon molecule?"

She wrinkled her nose and said, "I have no idea what you're talking about."

"Could you guys take it somewhere else," said a nearby student in a gruff whisper. "I've got a math midterm in 20 minutes."

*   *   *

Chen, Angela and I found a table in the back room of Allegro. The coffee spot is wonderfully old—old brick and old wood siding. Only the event posters covering the back wall are new.

Continuing where he had left off, Chen explained that the chemical found in nylon, hexamethal something or other, binds with the artificial colors in the candies. "That produces a hypno-psychotic response that makes the recipient extremely open to suggestion," said Chen, pointing toward his head for emphasis. "Someone had to add that chemical to the candy recipe."

"I get it," I said.

"Guys, I want to tell you about my improv class," Angela broke in. "We did an improv called Three Word, where we had to say only three words of dialogue each time. Our teacher gave us a topic: Applying for a job. I was the employer, Prime Mover the applicant. I felt very weird, but the improv gave me permission to take on this role."

Angela had our attention. "One of the conditions of improv is to 'be here now.' So that's what I was—there—now. We're also supposed to really listen to each other. So, Prime Mover says, 'I need work.' And I say, 'Got any experience?' He goes, 'Lots and lots.' I wanted to laugh but forced myself to stay in character. We went on for a couple of minutes, and we both knew we needed to bring our bit to an end. He said, 'Am I hired?' And I answered with, 'We'll call you.' The rest of the class applauded."

"Wouldn't that be four words?" Chen asked.

Angela responded, "What do you mean?"

Chen said the 'we'll' in Angela's line was a contraction for 'we will' and that would equal four words.

Angela gave Chen a nasty stare that would probably have even stopped a charging Polynesian warrior in his tracks.

"After class, Prime Mover came over to me as I was putting on my black fleece vest. He said he'd really enjoyed doing improv with me, and he asked me if I was a student. I said I was. He asked my major and I told him computer science. He said he was impressed I, a woman, was in that male-dominated major. Did I mention that Prime Mover can be quite charming? He's short but he glows with presence and confidence. He was all smiles. Well, he almost casually mentioned that his high-tech company was looking for interns and if I were interested all I had to do was call their number, ask for the Initiator, tell her I'd spoken to him and I'd have the internship." Letting her hands do a physical 'ta da,' Angela looked pleased with herself.

"Actually, Angela, that is good news," I said. That makes you a second mole at AltaSystemics." As long as you remember the post-hypnotic suggestion I gave you: Don't eat the candies, I thought.

Angela stood up and addressed us as if she were a lawyer delivering her final argument. "I knew this improv class would pay off. Now, I'll be doing improv in a slightly different location. Gotta go. Big test in my A.I. class tomorrow." She'd left the room before Chen and I could say goodbye, good luck.

LABELS: CHEMISTRY 101, IMPROVISATION 101

VIEW COMMENTS (84)

FactSeeker NOV. 13, 2011 AT 8:30 AM
This candy hypothesis is purely conjecture. A controlled experiment is necessary to establish the role that particular chemical might play. Chen should know better.

Heiress NOV. 13, 2011 AT 8:45 AM
Oh, please, FactSeeker. Give Chen and the others a break. They don't have time for the niceties of the scientific method. Besides, he did isolate the only chemical

not normally found in the candy. Go back to the outdated video game of your choice. (Do I get any points for defending you guys?)

Etruscan NOV. 13, 2011 AT 10:30 AM

In addition to its pure entertainment value, improvisation is also useful as a confidence building tool in a host of settings, including business, education and self-improvement seminars.

JoeCurr NOV. 13, 2011 AT 10:45 AM

I was going to be an improv comedian but I kept forgetting my lines.

SHOW MORE COMMENTS

○ ○ ○   **THINKS OUT LOUD**   ✕

WHIMSY WITHOUT REGRET

The path into darkness

Entry No. 610 - POSTED: NOV. 13, 2011

Eddie on Tiaré: We headed back to the village, Vaea setting a quick pace even as twilight began to soften the sky. Walking next to Thinks Out Loud, who was humming Talking Heads tunes, I thought he might benefit from a summary of the postings we'd sent out from Seattle during his time on the island.

"Sure," he said, halting his rendition of *Burning Down the House.* "Did I miss much?" He was this combination of naïve and deep.

I asked him if he remembered giving that recommendation for tallboy to work at AltaSystemics.

"It was after the fact but the Morse brothers lent a hand. Did he get the job? Isn't this early evening air fresh and warm?" TOL was paying more attention to the island's charms than our conversation.

Pressing on, I said tallboy was now the BlogaMight at what was turning out to be a mysterious high-tech company.

"What else is new?" TOL asked. "High-tech companies are always guarded about their trade secrets." He sniffed the air.

"Right," I said. "With AltaSystemics it's a lot more than trade secrets."

Letting out a slow deep breath and seeming to will himself into paying attention, TOL asked me what the company did.

"That's the tricky part." We weaved into an even denser part of the island. Others in the group were ahead of us and not visible when the path took a turn or climbed a hill. Kohia was the closest to us, and if we were in view, she would periodically look back to make sure we were not falling too far behind.

"Thinks Out Loud—Isaac—did you know your posting about your trial was interrupted during its transmission?"

"Not at first." He paused and I didn't know if he was going to continue. Then he started up again: "The day after the big meeting when they voted on my fate, we got a message from the drummers on the other side of the island that something had gotten blocked. They said the Morse brothers had gone away." He didn't seem very concerned about the disruption.

"That's because the Morse brothers got kidnapped."

TOL stopped walking. He brought a nearby branch closer to smell. "By who? Or is it 'By whom?' I should know that."

"Prime Mover, the head of AltaSystemics, tallboy's boss." I tried to give my statements a sense of gravity by speaking in a deeper than normal voice.

TOL titled his head as he listened to me. He put his hands on his waist and kicked up some dust with his sandal. "Just supposing for a moment that your Prime Mover would want the Morse brothers, how could they help him? Does that company deal in Time and Space vortexes?" Was he serious or trying to make a joke?

"Actually it does. Prime Mover wants the brothers because of their time-travel theory. We believe he has already developed the ability to store information in another dimension, and___"

TOL held up a hand to stop me. "You've been reading too much science fiction, brother." He was almost patronizing with that addition of 'brother.' Maybe he should have stayed in the cave longer.

"No, I saw it for myself," I explained. My foot tapping, I was losing my patience. "To tap into this other dimension he has to control the mind of the Hive members."

"Hive members?"

I hadn't fully realized how much TOL didn't know. "Prime Mover's staff. They all dress in white and are really good at meditating. Anyway he controls them, including tallboy, but lately we (Emily and I) have made some progress to neutralize that."

In a flat tone he asked who Emily was. A good friend I told him. I added details about our History of High-tech class and Emily's help in sneaking into AltaSystemics, and how we got caught, but then we learned a lot, and with tallboy's mind being taken over by Prime Mover how I had been blogging on the site.

"You've been blogging on my site?" Thinks Out Loud sounded more surprised than angry. We were walking again, slowly.

"I had to, to keep the blog moving forward. See, we could read your blogs, and we had lots of stuff going on in Seattle. We have to stop him."

"tallboy?"

"No, Prime Mover. In fact, that's why I'm here. Emily is back in Seattle, and I'm here for you."

Thinks Out Loud put his hand on my shoulder again. I was waiting for him to say how much he appreciated what I had done. Instead he shifted away from me and began jogging down the trail. "I've got to get back to the village!" he shouted as he disappeared into the gathering darkness.

LABELS: LOST, CONFUSION PLUS, NIGHTS IN TAHITI

VIEW COMMENTS (84)

Platter NOV. 13, 2011 AT 8:39 PM
Thinks Out Loud is still coming out of his trance. Give him some time.

Etruscan NOV. 13, 2011 AT 8:50 PM
Want to know what I think? I'll tell you anyway: Thinks Out Loud is toast. No good to anyone. Prime Mover holds all the cards. Everyone else should fold.

SHOW MORE COMMENTS

Bonding with other villagers

Entry No. 611 - POSTED: NOV. 14, 2011

Emily in Seattle: My mom, Katherine, is really beautiful. I think it has defined her whole life. She's gotten everything she ever wanted. Almost. Thanks to that Miss America-wide smile, sparkling, large eyes and hourglass figure...she was Miss America. Almost. As Miss Texas, she garnered second runner-up and winner of the swimsuit competition. A celebrity of sorts. My mother was one of the former contestants featured a couple of years ago in a *People Magazine* "Whatever happened to the almost Miss Americas" cover story. Autograph seekers still come up to her at airports and in restaurants.

Back from her trip, she texted me to come over for dinner. Her house sits right on Lake Washington north of Seattle in Lake Forest Park. It's a three-bedroom ranch, dark shingled with lots of fir trees on the non-water side, and a nice wide back deck almost level with the lake. The view is to die for: a vast expanse of water with tree-covered foothills on the opposite shore, the Eastside, several miles away, and snugly rising beyond the hills the dramatic line of the Cascades. It doesn't have a beachy feel cause there's no beach here. But the lake water when it ripples with wind can be hypnotic.

Mom had dinner ready when I arrived by bike. For most of her adult life, fashion had been important to her, but in the last year she had gone casual, such as nondescript jeans and a non-designer name blouse. Even without makeup, though, she still looked gorgeous. Great bone structure, they said.

We hugged and she led me to the dining room with an oak table larger than it needed to be. My mom is very physical and likes to touch the people she's talking with. She was actually holding my hand as we sat and sipped a Merlot, her favorite wine.

"You're home," I said.

"Let's just say I'm back at the house."

Mom had a point. This was a house not a home. As a family, we'd moved here two and a half years ago, right before I started college, so I didn't really ever get a chance to call this home. My off-campus apartment was more a home. Then dad had moved out after six months. "The shock of my life," my mom had said at the time. He'd gone to Europe with his golfing partner, Stewart, and had only come back to finish the divorce. Mom got the house.

"Dinner's ready," she said as I gazed out at the lake at dusk, the dining room window more a wall of plate glass. Mom returned with salad, mini tortillas and rice and beans, "a Guatemalan recipe." She proceeded to tell me again of her trip: an eco-vacation of southern Guatemala. Her fourth or fifth tour to a less developed country in the past year.

"It's a poor country," she said. "And the peoples of Guatemala, many of them descendants of the Mayans, have endured countless dictators. But the climate—always spring—and the beauty of the land and the warmth of the people we met. I want to go back!"

She explained that her American group, a mix of young and older adults, spent most of their time in the smaller villages meeting and interacting with school children and parents. "We shared parts about ourselves, helped out in their gardens, took weaving lessons at the central market and delivered an assortment of tools, packages of seeds, and other things we hoped they could use." And everyone made music together and took a boat trip with the kids of a village, called Panachchel, across Lake Atítlan in the Western Highlands to a national park that had a really long zipline, which my mother said was scary but fun. And they walked in the shadow of volcanoes and watched the villager's ceremonies. "We really bonded with the townspeople," she said.

Mom opened the silver cover of her iPad and showed me a slide show of her adventures. The Maya kids she posed with looked cute and a little sad, even though they were smiling.

"And it wasn't all a one-way street," she said. "The villagers young and old were welcoming and friendly. There was something more; we began to catch the rhythm of how they live. They look deeply into each others' eyes. And our eyes as well."

As usual she hadn't asked me about me, which this time was probably good. What would I have said? Oh, just trying to save the world.

"You look tired, Emily. You are going to spend the night," she said in a half-question, half-statement tone. For a split second, she had a vacant look that quickly reverted to a raised eyebrow and smile. I carried our plates into the kitchen, remodeled with granite top counters. I did have a room in the house, one I rarely slept in.

"Sure," I said. "Got an extra toothbrush?"

○ ○ ○   **THINKS OUT LOUD**   ✕

WHIMSY WITHOUT REGRET

Where is home?

Entry No. 612 - POSTED: NOV. 14, 2011

Eddie on Tiaré: I was the last one to make it to the village last night. Luckily a moon just past full allowed me to track the path. By the time I arrived, the villagers were gathered around a campfire and talking and singing. Barely able to keep my eyes open, I fell into my hut and slept the night through.

And would have kept sleeping if Kohia hadn't peeked into the unscreened window and called, "Eddie, the morning is leaving you behind."

I grunted and stretched and Kohia pulled away from the window to allow me to dress. But she met me at the door. "Eddie, how old do you think I am?" Her toe circled in the sand.

I actually took a good look at her. Energetic. Smart. Young. "Younger than the twenty you told Thinks Out Loud."

She momentarily copied Vaitiare's haughtiness. "Okay, I'm almost eighteen."

"Kohia, you are a great translator and you are playing an important role in this situation."

That helped.

As we walked to the dining area, Vaea saw us first. "Ah, Kohia, you have brought the unbrother over to us. Well done."

I didn't see why he had to remind everyone about my having admitted I wasn't the brother of Thinks Out Loud. Then I realized he had just made a joke.

"Eddie, come this way," Vaea said. We followed him to a nearby grass hut. Villagers we passed who were in conversation grew silent and stared at us. I tried to maintain a confident look. On the side of the hut facing the beach, Thinks Out Loud was standing with a semicircle of children at his feet and the other villagers massed behind the shirtless kids in a larger semicircle.

Things Out Loud seemed to be at the beginning of some kind of presentation. "I should be his translator," said Kohia as she shifted into her village role. Another wahine who had been translating stepped aside. Thinks Out Loud spoke mostly in English and Kohia gave the Polynesian version.

Here's the gist of what Thinks Out Loud had to say:

I have followed your custom and gone on the vision quest. At first I saw nothing but bits and pieces of what I normally see in my head. During my last day in the cave by the sea, I sat very still and…and… I transformed into a dolphin, a young male filled with energy and a desire to be what I was supposed to be. I was not dreaming. I was that creature. The other young dolphins in my group seemed to have no trouble finding out who they were. Fin was fast and a good catcher of fish. Jumper could leap out of the water in the most beautiful way and was our dancer. Whistler made enchanting musical sounds, and she led us in song. Current knew the best places to swim and was our guide. They all looked at me and whistled in unison: Who are you? What is your purpose? What is your name? I whistled back an excuse that I had been practicing my turning techniques and had not yet decided who I was.

One day, feeling sad, I separated from the group and swam toward a nearby island. I entered a quiet lagoon. Without noticing I bumped into another creature, the two-legged land dwellers who sometimes try and swim in the sea. This one was too far out and was beginning to sink under the water. With my snout I helped him reach the surface. He was holding onto me, my fin, and breathing deeply. I swam on the surface toward the shore with him holding onto me.

We reached the shore, and I curved my body so that he could slide off me and onto the beach. Lying like a tired sea lion on the sand, he raised his head. We were eye to eye. He said something in a gentle voice. I shook my head, gave my tail a little pat on the water's surface and turned to swim out of the lagoon. As I neared the opening to the greater sea, I surfaced and looked his way one last time. He was standing now and had his upper fin up in the air moving in a wide arc. I took that as a good sign.

Swimming as fast as I could, I rejoined my group and told them what happened. They seemed interested. Finally, Thinker, an elder, said, "Now we know why you are here."

"We do?" I asked. I was so excited I could barely keep a steady pace as we all rose to the surface for a breath.

"Yes," said Thinker. "You are our Toucher, our link to others."

The other dolphins whistled and bounced their tales against the water's surface. They swam around me and nuzzled my sides.

"Toucher," I whistled. "I have a name and a purpose."

*   *   *

When Thinks Out Loud had finished speaking, all was quiet. The waves visiting the shore grew calmer. Even the ever-present bird chants had stopped. Chief Keoni came forward in the traditional dress of scarlet full-length cloak and a brightly plumed headdress. In one hand he held his staff, in the other a wide fan.

He spoke slowly and Kohia translated. "Thinks Out Loud, your light shines upon us. Your vision is now within us." He held out his staff. "Thinks Out Loud, welcome home."

Thinks Out Loud raised and lowered his head. He had a distant look in his eye. I scanned the faces of the villagers; even Teva and Vaitiare seemed pleased. One big fat question squatted before me: If Thinks Out

Loud was now home, how would I be able to convince him to join our defense against Prime Mover? It was ironic, he was more centered and focused than ever but now less likely to help us!

LABELS: POLYNESIAN CUSTOMS, SWIMMING WITH DOLPHINS, BEACHED

VIEW COMMENTS (82)

JourneyMan NOV. 14, 2011 AT 10:00 AM
The dolphin story is not that far off base. The creatures do exhibit the ability to specialize within their pods. And tales of dophins aiding struggling (human) swimmers are not uncommon.

Slice NOV. 14, 2011 AT 10:35 AM
Thinks Out Loud as a dolphin. Interesting choice. Do dolphins share stories?

SHOW MORE COMMENTS

○ ○ ○   **THINKS OUT LOUD**   ✕

WHIMSY WITHOUT REGRET

Angela meets the brothers

Entry No. 613 - POSTED: NOV. 15, 2011

Emily in Seattle: As I was getting on my bike, my mom stood at the front door of her lakeside house. "Sure you don't need a car?" she asked. It's part of our routine. "No, Mom, I'm fine." "Just thought I'd ask." We said a goodbye and I biked up the one steep hill between her house and campus. On the trail back, I was humming along and trying not to think about anything when a phone call intruded. It was Angela. She was talking so fast I couldn't understand most of what she was saying: Prime Mover something. Internship something. Inner sanctum something.

"Angela, slow down, please."

"Okay, sorry," she said. "So I've been interning at AltaSystemics."

"Right."

"And Prime Mover has taken a personal interest in me."

With those words, my antennae went on full alert. "Angela."

"No, wait. I know what you're thinking. He's interesting and bright and powerful and all that, but I can handle him. And I hardly even notice he's almost a foot shorter than me anymore. He does keep offering me candy though, which I have no desire for, so I pocket the pieces. Anyway, he took me on a personal tour of the company. We went floor to floor. He even introduced me to tallboy, who was working in this white windowless room. tallboy was cool, and we acted as if we didn't know each other."

"That's good," I said.

"Now listen to what the tour included—a visit with the Morse brothers. Can you believe it? Prime Mover said AltaSystemics was hosting some special guests, and he wanted to introduce me. I acted like I didn't know what he was talking about and said OK. He led me to this special area, the VIPZone, he said. And you know how he does that whisk of the hand in front of the doorless doors and they zip open? Well, that's what he did, and he led me into this pretty large white windowless space which sort of looked like a hotel room with beds, a wide-screen TV, desk, a wide blackboard filled with mathematical symbols, and, I think, a door leading to the bathroom. A suite."

"What about the brothers?"

"Oh, yeah, they were there. Very old. Quite friendly. Kind of sleepy. Dressed in white robes. One with a white beard, the other clean shaven. And eating candy."

"Oh, no!"

"So, he introduced me and I said hello. Prime Mover said they were researchers visiting the company. They had gentle smiles. I nodded my head and said, 'Great to meet you.' They were relaxed, very relaxed.

"One of the brothers, the bearded one, noticed me noticing the blackboard. 'Do you have an interest in higher mathematics,' he asked slowly.

"Emily, I've taken some trig and calculus, but these equations looked different.

"Before I could answer, Prime Mover looked at his watch and said, 'Time to go.' I said a quick goodbye and wished them luck on their project. 'Oh, we don't need luck,' said the clean-shaven brother. 'But we may need more chalk.'

"'I'll see that you get it,' said Prime Mover. He spoke in a friendly manner combined with an underlying urgency.

"As I followed Prime Mover to the elevator, he thanked me for coming and added I should return tomorrow to begin the actual internship. Then he was in the elevator and gone and there I was alone on the VIP floor. I casually walked back toward the suite and casually swiped my hand in front of the door and nothing happened. I tried again. Nothing. 'Try a circular pattern,' said a voice. I whirled around and saw tallboy!"

"You guys!" I shouted. A passing cyclist on the trail turned my way as if I were calling to him. I motioned for him to continue on his way.

Angela continued, speaking quickly: "I asked tallboy if he knew who was in there, and he said he did. He used the hand pattern and the door slipped open. 'Be quick,' he said. 'I'll stand guard outside.' I jumped in and the door closed. The brothers were staring at the blackboard. I tried to get their attention by touching their shoulders. They slowly turned and did not seem surprised to see me. 'I'm back,' I said.

"'Have we met?' asked the bearded one.

"'Yes, about a minute ago. Oh, never mind. I'm here to help,' I told them. 'You're not researchers visiting the company. You've been kidnapped!' They looked at me as if I were delivering a weather report.

"I asked them if they remembered about living in the Pacific and how they can transmit messages. They both rocked their heads to mean, I think, 'yes, more or less'. I pressed on: 'You've made some discoveries about time.'

"They both gave the slightest of nods.

"tallboy opened the door and leaned in, 'I hear footsteps. Let's go!' I told the brothers we'd be back soon. Both of them waved goodbye. The door was sluicing shut as two Connectors came around the curving hallway. tallboy and I acted as if we were talking blogging strategy. One of the Connectors turned our way and stared hard at us as he passed."

My phone buzzed. Another call. I asked Angela to hold that thought and checked the other caller. tallboy. Also talking faster than he had in months. "Angela took a big chance at AltaSystemics. If I hadn't been there, they'd have caught her trying to get into the Morse brothers' room."

"I know, I know," I said. "I'm talking with her right now. Don't hang up." I switched back to Angela and recommended we all get together tonight to compare notes. She agreed and I suggested the same to tallboy.

Totally energized, I bicycled back to the U-District faster than usual. Boy, it was a good thing those guards hadn't come by the brothers' room any earlier, I thought. Yes, timing is everything. Or nothing.

LABELS: HIGH-TECH LEVERAGING, STARTUP RUSES, VIP ACCOMMODATIONS

VIEW COMMENTS (83)

Anonymous NOV. 15, 2011 AT 9:00 AM

Hard to tell what the mental condition of the Morse brothers is. Seems to me if they get too doped up, they won't be able to finish the formulas, not that I'm trying to give Prime Mover any advice.

G&G in Jaipur NOV. 15, 2011 AT 9:40 PM

fantastic post and thanks for sharing this timely info. very helpful.

SHOW MORE COMMENTS

○ ○ ○   **THINKS OUT LOUD**   ✕

WHIMSY WITHOUT REGRET

Let the feast begin

Entry No. 614 - POSTED: NOV. 15, 2011

Eddie on Tiaré: Following the invitation for Thinks Out Loud to live on Tiaré, the chief announced a feast to celebrate the "awakening of the newest member of our community." Without a word, the villagers busied themselves with preparations, while I tried to talk with Thinks Out Loud who was surrounded by well wishers. Plus, the island's kids were pulling at him and asking for another story, and then everyone was taking a seat on the benches at the long outdoor tables.

At the feast, Thinks Out Loud and I ended up at opposite ends of the dining area. Bronzed, his dark hair in ringlets, he was chatting and eating and nodding and totally unaware of me. Kohia sat next to me and helped to translate some of the nearby talk. Surrounded by torch light, touched by a soft evening breeze, I lost my sense of purpose and couldn't help but enjoy the fruits, vegetables, and roast pig.

After a dessert of fresh coconut, mango, and pineapple, the islanders as a group began to move toward the dance circle. At some point everyone had changed into traditional dance clothing of grass skirts. When Thinks Out Loud moved past me toward the dance area, he was surrounded by young people, all laughing. Even he had gone the grass skirt route, while

I stood out in shorts and a Hawaiian-style brightly-colored shirt.

They certainly know how to make a bonfire, I thought. The dancing flames could have probably been seen twenty miles out at sea. Even with all this celebration, I still wanted to talk with Thinks Out Loud, now stomping and chanting with the men who alternated with the non-stop hip movements of the women, all to the beat of the throbbing drums.

At one point I tried to ask Kohia for help, though she only made hand motions for me to enter a dance circle. As if coming out of a trance, I wanted to shout to everyone to stop all this dancing and pay attention to why I was here. I was practically raising a fist in anger and frustration when another's hand caught mine. It was Vaea. "Let them dance. Tomorrow you can talk. Go, join them."

Before I could reply, three slim wahinis enveloped me and drew me into the body of dancers. There was a whole lot of hip shaking going on. I tried to mimic them, but my movements were closer to the vibrating of a washing machine on the drain cycle. Teva curved over my way. Although I'm around six feet tall (still shorter than tallboy), I had to look up to the muscled Polynesian, who danced with a lightness I wouldn't have expected.

"You move like a stranded dolphin," he told me and then he was gone.

Next came cool Vaitiare, and like all the other men, I fell under the spell of her movements. "Find Kohia," she advised me and then melted back into the shadows. I was actually still looking for Thinks Out Loud who might have been in the center of a nearby group.

I was about to pull out of the dancing throng when my backside bumped into Kohia. I couldn't help but turn and look her over. Her head was high, her eyes alert. "You are opposite the beat," she said as she closed in on me. Let your thighs take turns and the rest will follow."

The torches flickering around us, the drummers commanding the center, the rapid thrustings of the bodies. They were right. I gave in to the moment...

LABELS: SERIOUS FEASTING, THE RIGHT MOVES, THE WRONG MOVES

VIEW COMMENTS (84)

DexTerra NOV. 15, 2011 AT 11:10 AM
Eddie, you are on the cusp of losing Isaac/Thinks Out Loud. Don't falter.

JustSaying NOV. 15, 2011 AT 11:30 AM

What is it about Polynesian culture that we (Americans/moderns) find so appealing?

Freezone NOV. 15, 2011 AT 11:40 AM

JustSaying, you're kidding, right?

SHOW MORE COMMENTS

○ ○ ○   **THINKS OUT LOUD**   ✕

WHIMSY WITHOUT REGRET

Plan of action?

Entry No. 615 - POSTED: NOV. 16, 2011

Emily in Seattle: Back room of Allegro. 1900 hours. Attending: tallboy, Angela, Chen, myself. Our mission: Come up with a mission.

"So, we know the Morse brothers are being held at AltaSystemics where they've been drugged with those candies, which means we're running out of time before Prime Mover has his way with them," I said.

"Has his way with them?" echoed Angela. "I've gotten to know Prime Mover at improv class and he may be trying to take over the world, but he's not the Marquis de Sade."

"Okay," I said. Everyone seemed to be a in a bad mood. Including me. "Let me try again. tallboy and Angela, are there any delay tactics you can do to make it harder for Prime Mover to learn the Morse brothers time travel theories?"

Silence as we sipped our coffee.

"I know," said tallboy, "we could re-kidnap the brothers and hide them somewhere away from AltaSystemics. Like in the basement of my apartment building." He was a lot less robotlike, thanks to our intervention, though not fully back to his pre-AltaSystemics days. Or maybe he was.

"Since we're essentially brainstorming," I said, "I won't comment, yet." tallboy simultaneously looked hopeful and disappointed.

We took more sips of our coffees.

"Got it," said Chen. "We seduce Prime Mover. I mean we have Angela

229

seduce Prime Mover, and she gets him to take a romantic getaway to the South Seas to buy us more time."

Angela glared at Chen. She didn't have to say a word.

"My mocha is too sweet," said tallboy. "I told them light on the mocha. I like my mocha to advise but not control my beverage."

"That's it!" I shouted. My friends stared at me. "Sweets. Candies. Don't you see? Chen, can you formulate a copy of those AltaSystemics candies minus the drug ingredient?"

"No," he said matter of factly. That wasn't the answer I wanted to hear, but he went on. "I don't have to do anything in the lab. All you have to do is order them. They'll personalize their candies with whatever letters or message you want on them." He brought the pages up on his phone.

We took turns looking at the website. Personalized M&M's. Just what we needed. "That's fantastic," I said. "Chen, order us up a batch, half with the A, half with the S for AltaSystemics. Have them shipped overnight express." Before he could say anything, I added, "I'll reimburse you."

Then I explained phase two of the plan, once we had the non-drug candies. "tallboy and Angela, it will be up to you to get into the brothers' room and replace the bad candies with the good candies."

"I see," Angela said. "And that way, we'll wean them of the drug-inducing candy." For once I didn't have to overly explain a plan. Angela, at least, got it.

"Right," I said. "Once they start coming around, we'll fill them in on what's going on. I know you tried to talk to them, Angela, but they were too drugged."

"And then what?" Chen asked. Actually, he was capable of getting it as well.

We all drank more coffee. And then what?

tallboy stood up. "Then we enlist their aid as double agents, sort of like what Angela and I are doing now. The more moles the better."

"Yes," I said, awarding tallboy credit for a creative idea. Angela gave him a playful cuff on the shoulder. tallboy reacted with a self-conscious smile.

VIEW COMMENTS (82)

PumpedUp NOV. 16, 2011 AT 8:10 AM
Angela is starting to strike me as interesting.

Obserfor NOV. 16, 2011 AT 8:37 AM
I eat M&Ms for breakfast. Not every day. More on special occasions. Like after I've gotten a haircut the day before. A way to celebrate life's little moments.

SeenIt NOV. 16, 2011 AT 9:01 AM
Planning is hard.

SHOW MORE COMMENTS

○ ○ ○   **THINKS OUT LOUD**   ✕

WHIMSY WITHOUT REGRET

Heated sand, odd bedding

Entry No. 616 - POSTED: NOV. 16, 2011

Eddie on Tiaré: Teasing waves, heated sand, an odd bedding. I opened an eye to find I was face down on the beach, intertwined in soggy kelp strands. What a night.

"Comfortable?" asked a voice from above me.

I tried to answer but a mouth full of sand muffled my words. Turning over and pulling at the wet kelp, I looked up at Thinks Out Loud. From this ground level angle, he towered over me like a giant. Cleaning out my mouth with my fingers, I sat up.

"Thinks Out Loud, I've been wanting to talk with you." I continued to grapple with the sticky snake-like kelp wrapped around my middle.

"I know," he answered. "Kohia told me where to find you." Deeply tanned and dressed in his Tahitian best of grass skirt and a surprisingly new, clean white T-shirt, TOL continued, "Did you have a good time last night? Your dancing improved over the course of the evening. Did I see you trying to blog after the party?"

I ignored the questions and stood up. "Thinks Out Loud, what if I show you the blogs we posted while you've been here?" I explained about the solar powered satellite terminal and began heading unsteadily toward the equipment.

"After what you told me the other night as we were walking to the village—all that highly imaginative material about the high-tech company that's using psychics to store data and the kidnapping of the Morse brothers," Thinks Out Loud paused. "Very entertaining!" Although I didn't like the tack he was taking, he was starting to talk more coherently.

"I'm not making this up. It's really happening." We came to the side of the hut where I'd set up my equipment. One by one, I showed TOL the postings he'd missed. He read them without comment, except for an occasional sigh or a pause to rub his chin.

We reached the most current postings—including ones from me since I'd been on the island and other posts from Seattle, several of which I'd only now read.

"That Emily person sounds very responsible, very dependable," said my companion.

"Yes," I said, "she is." I logged off and shut the laptop. "Thinks Out Loud, do you see that this is really happening? How else can you explain the disappearance of the Morse brothers, for example?" I was running out of arguments. Why was he so skeptical?

"The disappearance of the Morse brothers is strange," Thinks Out Loud admitted. "And their time travel theories could be used for evil ends. Just imagine the possibilities. You could send back a message to buy or sell a certain stock or bet on a Kentucky Derby winner." Thinks Out Loud had a distant look in his eyes. "Who could resist that temptation? Let's hope the Morse brothers are made of firmer stuff."

TOL regarded the ocean for a long time. "Eddie you do seem to have some challenges," he said, talking more to the sea than me. "But why do you need me? I am now of Tiaré. This is where I need to be." Thinks Out Loud began to walk with a kind of quiet confidence toward the outdoor dining area. I was left, staring at the empty emerald waters stretching to the darker blue horizon. I don't know how much time had passed when a thought played across my mind. I had one last argument, one last appeal to make before I left Tiaré, if necessary by myself, to join my compatriots in Seattle.

LABELS: THE GREATER GOOD, TEMPTATION, ART OF CONVINCING

VIEW COMMENTS (82)

Spirit NOV. 16, 2011 AT 11:04 AM

Spirit NOV. 16, 2011 AT 11:04 AM

Why is TOL/Isaac really afraid to go back to Seattle? Does he have some unfinished business there? Is he running away from something?

Topaz NOV. 16, 2011 AT 11:35 AM

It's what they used to call 'Going native.' Don't think you can say that anymore. Not sure what it's called now.

Specialist NOV. 16, 2011 AT 11:55 AM

I believe the anthropology phrase is something like "total immersion within a local population resulting in adoption of mores and belief systems."

SHOW MORE COMMENTS

○ ○ ○   **THINKS OUT LOUD**   ✕

WHIMSY WITHOUT REGRET

A last plea

Entry No. 617 - POSTED: NOV. 16, 2011

Eddie on Tiaré: Alone, I trudged back into the center of the village. Thinks Out Loud sat in the oval outdoor dining area, a cluster of kids in front of him. As I approached I could hear he was telling a story with Kohia translating. Basically a retelling of the Icarus myth, of the young man who flew too close to the sun that melted the wax in his artificial wings and down went Icarus into the sea. TOL set the story in Polynesia. And he gave it a happier ending. A dolphin saved the boy before he drowned.

After the children jumped up and scooted off to run around on the wide beach, I started toward TOL and then hesitated. Kohia was saying something to Thinks Out Loud, but I couldn't hear her words clearly. He appeared to be thanking her when they noticed me.

"Thinks Out Loud, could I speak with you one more time before I leave?"

TOL adjusted his t-shirt and nodded. Kohia opened her mouth but said nothing. As if on cue, Vaea and Chief Keoni came into my line of vision and joined the group.

Wishing I had been on the debate club in high school, I began. "Well, the time has come for me to return to Seattle, the city where I live, to face a crafty foe." Without asking, Kohia translated.

I continued. "Thinks Out Loud, I understand you have a new life here, a rich life centered around the people of this island. And I'm very happy for you. I think you have a lot to contribute to Tiaré. Still, I read in one of your blogs before you came here—the one on the day of the supposed rapture predicted by that guy named Camping. Remember that posting? Just to hedge your bets in case the rapture was real, in a post-modern sort of way, I think, you were apologizing for all the wrongs you had done others and then you wrote that life sometimes requires sacrifice, a giving up of one's personal goals for the good of others."

Other villagers, including Teva and Vaitiare, were attracted to our conversation and encircled us.

I took a breath, looked up at the faultless blue sky and back down to the island. "I know you don't know me or the others who've been blogging for you. And I know what I've told you and what you read in our blogs sounds far-fetched. But if my tales were just that—fictional stories—why would I have bothered to come here in search of you? Why would I be asking that you return with me to right some wrongs?"

I stressed that TOL had been the reason we even knew about the plotting of Prime Mover. "If you hadn't been looking for a blogger and decided on tallboy to intern for you, which gave him the experience he needed to be considered for the AltaSystemics blogging job, well, we wouldn't have ever known what was going on at AltaSystemics." I was rambling. That would be points off at the debate club as well as a challenge to translate. "You are our focal point, our connector…"

Time for the last pitch. "Thinks Out Loud, we need you. We need your wisdom, your energy, your coolness under fire. All of those qualities are even more evident now that you've been on your vision quest." I added one other appeal: "The Morse brothers helped you to send your blog postings for the world to read. Now the brothers need your help. We need your help."

TOL's head sunk back as though he'd lost the will to hold it up. Like an undercurrent, the villagers were whispering among themselves. "How did this Prime Mover even know about the brothers?" He threw the question out to the sea, followed by an, "Oh. My fault."

I didn't have anything else to say. I could hear the breakers thumping near the shore, the chirpy voices of the children playing on the sand.

Thinks Out Loud turned to face me.

"Eddie, you make a strong case for my return. That could be The Way. Yet The Way could also be fulfilled by my remaining here. I would like to consult with those around me. I will give you my answer in the morning." With a flourish of his grass skirt, he brought our talk to an end, turned toward the chief, and together they walked as companions to the water's edge.

LABELS: ART OF ARGUMENT, CONFLICTING CHOICES, THE UNRAPTURE

VIEW COMMENTS (81)

HindSight NOV. 16, 2011 AT 2:52 PM
Eddie, know when to fold. TOL is lost to you.

SpecMan NOV. 16, 2011 AT 3:34 PM
Eddie, you can't take no for an answer. Use those hard candies if you have to. Oh, you don't have them on you.

SHOW MORE COMMENTS

○ ○ ○   **THINKS OUT LOUD**   ✕

WHIMSY WITHOUT REGRET

Back to the table

Entry No. 618 - POSTED: NOV. 17, 2011

Emily in Seattle: It had been a Seattle-multi-level-gray-day until late afternoon when the sun made a meek appearance and then promptly hid away again. I was walking back from work, where I'd once again not had my mind on the subject. A block from my apartment, I got a text from Angela: White M&Ms on back order!

That was certainly a setback. Time to call another meeting.

A half hour later, Angela, Chen, and I were at our nicely worn coffee house table. tallboy joined us via Skype. He was telling us that Prime Mover had edited his latest AltaSystemics blog. "I wrote about the power of deep breathing and its positive effect on the workplace, and when I saw the blog it was all about how to boost creativity through improvisation exercises."

"Well it's true," said Angela.

"Can we get to the subject at hand?" I asked. "Anyone got a Plan B?"

Silence.

"What if we slipped the brothers some spirulina supplements. They're supposed to pull heavy metals out of the body," said Chen.

"I still think we could sneak them out of AltaSystemics and hide them in my apartment's basement," tallboy said.

"Somehow I have a feeling Prime Mover wouldn't allow that to happen," I said. Angela nodded in agreement. "Look, maybe we're in over our heads."

Chen began to protest, but my words marched over his. "We made a good go of it," I said looking over at Angela.

She caught my eye. "Yes, we did," she said solemnly. "I don't know about you guys—I'm falling behind in school. I'm tired all the time. And I've been thinking: Maybe Prime Mover isn't as bad as we think he is. Maybe he'll evolve into a force for good if he gets his way, I mean, if he's able to tap the knowledge of the Morse brothers."

Almost choking, Chen was aghast. "Listen to yourselves! Give up? Never! You guys can walk out, but I'll find a way to defeat Prime Mover!"

I brought my hands together. "Okay. Here's an idea. Let's lie low for a while. tallboy and Angela, keep observing the Morse brothers."

"Actually, I did notice Prime Mover put some pens and pads and even a Morse Code key sender in their suite," said tallboy. "If I just had an invisibility cloak."

"What about Eddie and Thinks Out Loud?" asked a calmer but still disappointed Chen as he crushed his coffee cup into a mound.

"I don't think we can count on them," I said.

"I'm thinking, maybe it's time for me to get to know Prime Mover a little better," Angela said with a frozen smile.

"Meeting adjourned," I said. "I'm going to bed."

LABELS: AYE OR NAY, REALISM VERSUS FANTASY, MEETING FATIGUE

VIEW COMMENTS (84)

Gym NOV. 17, 2011 AT 9:00 AM
Despair. It can be contagious. Reading the post, I feel it myself.

Dolfan NOV. 17, 2011 AT 9:25 AM

As a trained actor, I can emote despair when the script calls for it.

Etruscan NOV. 17, 2011 AT 9:35 AM

You kids gave it a good college try. Time to go back to your studies.

SHOW MORE COMMENTS

Passing the baton

Entry No. 619 - POSTED: NOV. 17, 2011

Eddie on Tiaré: It was still early in the morning, although most villagers would have been up with the dawn. Without pausing to knock, I entered the airy grass hut of Thinks Out Loud. Adjusting his grass skirt, he looked up and nodded as if he were expecting me.

"Thinks Out Loud, Isaac," I began quickly, "things aren't going very well for us back in Seattle. Prime Mover is winning. Our team needs—"

Thinks Out Loud commandingly held up his hand to signal silence. "Eddie, there is no need to offer more argument to affect my decision. This is what I am going to do."

Without blinking, he drew in a breath, raised his chin and was going to continue when Vaitiare entered the hut, also without knocking. In a hushed voice she said, "Thinks Out Loud, Hoanui—Big Friend—our teller of stories must speak with you. Right away. The Passing." She made way for him to exit.

He left, followed by Vaitiare. Left alone in the hut, I sighed and went to catch up with them as they headed directly to Hoanui's hut. A crowd of quiet villagers stood outside. The group parted to allow Thinks Out Loud and Vaitiare to enter and closed when I tried to do the same. Peeking over and around everyone, I tried to ease my way closer to the entrance.

I saw Kohia, who was just outside the hut. Calling her name, I attempted to get her attention, but she was peering inside, a tear glistening on her cheek.

"Kohia," I twisted and excused myself as I worked my way toward her. Everyone was very solemn.

"Kohia," I said again as I finally reached her. "What's happening?"

She could barely speak. "Hoanui, our storyteller…"

Trying to look in the hut, I couldn't see much. Even though it had wide open windows, the hut was dark inside and a smoky fire made it even hazier. I could make out the chief, Vaea, Teva, and Vaitiare standing near the bed where the storyteller lay. An old woman was crouched and chanting beside him.

Feeling left out, I asked again, "What's happening?" People wept openly.

"It's time for the Passing," Kohia said.

I assumed she meant his passing away. Now the old man slowly raised an arm and with great effort called one of the group forward. It was Thinks Out Loud. He lowered himself until his head was near Hoanui's. Vaitiare moved with TOL and was respectfully close but not atop them, I guess so she could translate. I couldn't hear what was being said, although I did see Thinks Out Loud tenderly touch the chest of the storyteller. I don't remember it happening, Yet Kohia's hand was in mine. Gripping my hand tightly. There was a momentary flash and the fire went out. It should have been darkish in the hut; however, glowing light seemed to flow in from the open-air windows. The men and women in the hut began singing in louder voices, a song of sorrow and sadness mixed with joy and peace. The villagers outside the hut joined in.

Slowly, the group from the hut came out and called for the attention of the onlookers. Wearing his formal robes and headdress, the chief spoke. (Kohia whispered the translation for me.) "Hoanui, our great teller of stories, has joined with those who came before us. We honor his life and his contributions to our people. In keeping with our traditions, Hoanui has made his recommendation. It is his wish that Thinks Out Loud receive the Passing."

Silence. Did that mean approval or rejection? What was being passed?

Everyone looked at Thinks Out Loud, positioned between the chief and Vaitiare. He stood tall, proud, calm. In clothing, posture, and demeanor, he was Polynesian. I was thoroughly confused.

Thinks Out Loud now spoke. "Chief and friends, I have been called to a new task, a new challenge. Hoanui has placed upon me a great role to play from this day forward." He momentarily glanced at me. "Although I cannot replace Hoanui, I can strive to follow in his ways. I humbly accept the offering and pledge with my heart to keep your traditions alive and to grow them as well. To be your teller of stories." Then he added with just a hint of a smile, "Hoanui also asked me to learn how to speak your language better." He turned to Vaitiare and said something I couldn't hear. She answered him in a low voice. Then he said to the people. "You will hear me asking this a lot: *Eaha tei'oa ote'ie?*" Teva grimaced at TOL's pronunciation and quickly pulled back into his serious expression.

Kohia filled me in: "What is the name of this?" A soft laughter had countered the silence. Two things happened at once. The villagers began to prepare for the water funeral of Hoanui, and they also clustered around Thinks Out Loud to affirm his new role. Head down, I turned and retreated from the village, my steps leaving a trail in the sands. I felt a tear on my cheek and couldn't tell if it was caused by what I'd just seen or by my failure to help my friends back home. Maybe it was both.

LABELS: POLYNESIAN RITUALS, PASSING THE TORCH

VIEW COMMENTS (86)

Mipper NOV. 17, 2011 AT 8:13 AM
Among the Dinizulu of Africa, the storyteller role is a specialized position, an essential one within the context of the tribe. The storyteller may not be the best hunter or leader, but he (yes, he, at least in earlier days) has the ability to entertain through the power of words. And body postures, if he's good.

Anonymous NOV. 17, 2011 AT 8:29 AM
Did I miss something, Mipper? Are you on the right blog? Storytellers exist in all societies and in all times. Nothing new here. Move on.

SHOW MORE COMMENTS

○ ○ ○   **THINKS OUT LOUD**   ✕

WHIMSY WITHOUT REGRET

A kind of sacrifice

Entry No. 620 - POSTED: NOV. 17, 2011

Eddie on Tiaré: I sat on the deserted beach, let my eyes rest on the turquoise-tinted ocean, and tried not to think about all the classes I'd missed. I'd definitely have to ask for some extensions or just withdraw entirely. As for Prime Mover's plans, I felt like I was in *Star Wars: Come over to the Dark Side.*

"Quitter," said a gentle yet firm voice.

Without turning, I knew Kohia was standing behind me. She came around and planted herself between the water and me. How, I wondered, do their sarongs manage to both hide and emphasize their form?

"Even if Thinks Out Loud chooses to remain here," she said, "you still have your duty." A lecture? What had happened to the giddy teenager who'd first given me a tour of the village?

I tried to again explain the challenges I was facing and the lack of progress I and the others were making.

"Stop! You are like a wild boar lost in the undergrowth. Pull back and see beyond the tree roots."

"I am," I answered. "I'm staring out at the ocean."

"Only with your outward eyes," she countered, "not with your inner vision."

"My inner vision is out to lunch."

Kohia gave me a puzzled look. "Sometimes your wordings come out like the wrong steps of a dance."

"I simply meant that I'm out of ideas. I'm confused. Maybe I was wrong to come here." That earned me a cold glare. For some reason I kept babbling. "I mean haven't you ever had a thought reversal, a sudden and complete change of what you believed was right?"

Softening, she held out her arms. "Rise. Let us go back to the village. The journey nears." With a sigh, I took her hands. Kohia stepped back and pulled me forward. We ended up in a hug.

Back at the village, conveniently, the main players were all gathered together down by the water. It was almost as if they were awaiting my return. Hmmm. I am at another part of the beach. I'm feeling sorry for myself. Kohia shows up and talks me into coming back with her...

We reached the chief, Vaea, Teva, Vaitiare. They'd been talking but grew silent upon our arrival. It was late afternoon, and the sun was casting a golden light across the sands. What did they know that I didn't?

"Final preparations are being made for our storyteller's next journey," said Chief Keoni (with translation courtesy of Kohia). "The question is: Who will go with him?"

I wasn't really paying much attention to what the chief was saying, but a couple of villagers seemed agitated as if they disagreed with him.

The chief continued: "Of those who make this journey, we ask a great deal, and we will feel their absence. Strong Teva, wise Vaitiare, intuitive Kohia. They will do well in that Other World."

Chief Keoni's words seem to coalesce around me; I couldn't believe what I was hearing. These damn old customs!

I was beyond aghast. "How can you?" I shouted at the group. "To send such fine young people who are so full of promise to accompany the storyteller on his final journey. It's an abomination!"

"Eddie," said Kohia, "we go willingly."

I almost fainted. "You are primitives," I sputtered. "This is beyond belief!"

"Someone calm him down," said Vaitiare. "We do what is asked of us, nothing more."

The chief peered at me with his deep set eyes but said nothing. On my right a surprisingly unconcerned Teva short circuited a laugh. I was impressed he could look death in the eye with such bravery. He spoke quickly in his native tongue, and all except me were grinning but trying not to grin. They laugh, I thought. They laugh at me for not appreciating their Ways!

"You are confused, Eddie," said Vaea. "That seems to happen to you a lot here." Before I could come up with an answer, Vaea pointed toward the huts. "Here he comes. This will clear up the matter." All I could see was Thinks Out Loud walking our way.

"Edward," he said to me as he reached us, "I see you are talking with those who will make the journey."

"Thinks Out Loud, you've got to help me help them. There must be another way."

"We've talked about it," answered TOL. "If I am to go on this journey, then I will need these good friends as well."

TOL as well! Even having just been named the storyteller? I was triple aghast!

"Eddie, are you all right?" asked Kohia as she touched my shoulder.

"I just don't want to see you all die."

"Die? Why should we die?" she asked.

The chief motioned for all to be quiet. "Eddie," he said through Kohia, "no one is dying. I was talking about the storyteller—Thinks Out Loud—and his decision to journey with you to America to combat the evil man you told us about." Chief Keoni went on: "Some of the villagers disagree with me and think they should stay here, but after conferring with other elders it is my judgment that your cause would be best served by having Teva, Vaitiare, and Kohia join you, even though we will miss them during their absence.

"Wait," I said. "So, Thinks Out Loud, you are coming back with me?"

"Yes, Edward."

"Plus, the islanders?" I specifically eyed Vaitiare, whose expression was calmly neutral.

"Yes," said TOL.

"I need to sit down," I said. "I had the wrong Bond script running in my head."

Oblivious to my ramblings, Chief Keoni addressed Teva. "Send a message by DrumBeat to ask for a boat pickup tomorrow morning." Teva nodded, and the chief spoke to all of us. "Today we mourn the loss of Hoanui, and tomorrow we send him on his last journey." He looked at me. "Alone, but with our love and gratefulness."

LABELS: SACRIFICE, A-TEAM, COGNITIVE DISSONANCE IN ACTION

VIEW COMMENTS (80)

CheckIn NOV. 17, 2011 AT 3:00 PM
A simple misunderstanding, Eddie, especially when you carry cultural stereotypes around in your head.

Energee NOV. 17, 2011 AT 3:22 PM
Eddie, I thought the same thing! Based on the evidence you had, you made a logical assumption.

Etruscan NOV. 17, 2011 AT 3:32 PM
The more the merrier.

SHOW MORE COMMENTS

Stop start, stop start

Entry No. 621 - POSTED: NOV. 18, 2011

Emily in Seattle: Eddie is coming back, and he's bringing some help, but will it tip the odds in our favor?

Over mochas, Angela and I were commiserating. "Yes," Angela said, "the Mariners have a better chance making it to the World Series than we do of succeeding. It's more likely the city will get a new basketball stadium and the return of the Sonics than we'll be able to stop that nefarious but bold Prime Mover."

"I didn't know you were into sports," I said.

"I play on the womens' soccer team, when I'm not trying to save the world. Speaking of Prime Mover, I've got a date with him tomorrow night. We're going to the Georgetown art walk. He says it's edgy."

I wished her luck.

"I'm both repelled and attracted to him," Angela said carefully. "Isn't that the way love is?"

Wanting to remind her he was the enemy, I let her carry on about his dual nature and difficult childhood, something about being the son of acrobats who died in a high wire accident.

While we were talking, tallboy phoned to say he'd checked on the Morse brothers and, as he related, "had some fun." I asked him to explain, and he said while trying to interview the nearly comatose brothers for his next blog entry, he noticed they'd added more mathematical computations on a big white board. "I'm pretty sure it had something to do with their time travel theory. What else could it be about?"

He had a point. That would mean Prime Mover was getting closer to acquiring the knowledge of how to send information from the past.

"So, here's what I did," tallboy said. "While the brothers were napping, I changed some of the plus signs to minuses and vice versa and a couple of the, what do you call them, the x with a floating 2 or 3 right next to it?"

"Exponents," I said.

"I mixed them up, too. I wasn't making much progress in the interview anyway."

"Right," I said quickly. "That's what you would have done if you had had the chance, but wasn't your subterfuge interrupted by the entrance of a white-robed attendant?"

LABELS: HIGH-TECH STRATEGIES, HIGH-ENERGY PARTICLE PHYSICS

VIEW COMMENTS (84)

HindSite NOV. 18, 2011 AT 8:10 AM
Good try, tallboy, but I'm still voting for PM to succeed.

Closer NOV. 18, 2011 AT 8:15 AM
HindSite, you better hope PM doesn't succeed.

SHOW MORE COMMENTS

○ ○ ○   **THINKS OUT LOUD**   ✕

WHIMSY WITHOUT REGRET

The next journey
Entry No. 622 - POSTED: NOV. 18, 2011

Eddie on Tiaré: Throughout the day, villagers walked over from the other side of Tiaré as well as arrived from nearby islands by canoe and motor boat for the evening funeral. People were weeping and smiling at the same time. Everyone was greeting everyone, and eventually all were present on the beach. Kohia stood by my side. She told me people were remembering Hoanui: his storytelling abilities and his gifts of friendship and his love for the children. In the crowd, I lost track of Thinks Out Loud, though I hoped he was close by.

Loaded with gifts and foods and brightly colored cloth, a solo canoe rested on the shore. Four silent, unmoving women in black stood beside the craft, two fore, two aft.

With the appearance of the night's first star, Chief Keoni called for silence. He was dressed in his finest tunic and headdress. Thinks Out Loud had quietly come to my side. Next to him were Vaitiare, who was dabbing her eyes, a stoic Teva and a calm Vaea. Kohia softly translated

"It is time to bid farewell to our beloved teller of stories, time for Hoanui to journey to his next life," the chief said. "We rejoice in his days with us and all that he shared. Tonight we send him forth to let him ride upon moana in the form of a blazing star."

With a nod from Chief Keoni, Vaitiare began to sing what had to be a lament in a clear and haunting voice. Male voices joined in, followed by the women. Bearing a torch, the chief approached the canoe. As the women in black began to slide the canoe the short distance to the water's edge, the chief allowed the torch to fall into the center of the boat. Joined by four men, also in black, the women moved the canoe away from the beach and into and over the breaking waves. From behind me, I heard drumbeats that echoed the rising and falling of the song.

Once past the waves, the canoe began to float out to sea on its own, the flames from its center spreading the length of the boat. One by one the islanders moved away from the beach until only a few of us—Vaitiare, Teva, Vaea, plus a handful of crying children—remained to watch the shrinking craft fade into the night like a dying ember.

"All," Teva said to the silent group, "tonight Hoanui makes his journey, and tomorrow, we make ours."

What followed was a feast, which was a remarkably happy affair, all things considered. Kohia told me this was a celebration of Hoanui's life, a time for joyful remembering. TOL seemed restrained. Sitting beside me, he ate some but not much and had few words for those of us around him. He was here but elsewhere at the same time. At one point Vaea leaned over to me. "Do not worry about your brother," he said without a trace of teasing or irony. "For once Thinks Out Loud needs to be silent to allow him to receive Hoanui's message." Nodding, I took in the starry sky, the scent of burning torches, the warmth of the night air, and the feel of a community balancing grief with joy.

LABELS: ANCIENT CEREMONIES, CYCLE OF LIFE

VIEW COMMENTS (88)

Topper NOV. 18, 2011 AT 9:20 PM
A long tradition in pre-literate cultures as well as a motif in sagas and epics—the fallen hero sent out to sea, aflame.

Millenio NOV. 18, 2011 AT 9:40 PM
Except he's an old man, an elder who had a full, rich life.

SHOW MORE COMMENTS

A date with Prime Mover

Entry No. 623 - POSTED: NOV. 19, 2011

Emily in Seattle: "Prime Mover has a fun side," Angela said to me as we walked away from our high-tech seminar class. (I'd let Professor Stevens know Eddie was still engaged, so to speak, in his special project. "Just as long has he's making progress," the professor had replied.)

Angela was going on and on about her date with Prime Mover. They'd dined at a new Vietnamese restaurant in Belltown. "At first I didn't know where he was taking me," Angela said. "We went down some stairs and along a gloomy corridor. I was remembering that I am bigger and probably stronger than this guy, when we came to the restaurant, brightly lit but sort of cramped. Prime Mover called it an *in place*."

I told her she didn't have to go into detail about what they ate, but that didn't stop her. Vietnamese pancakes, duck egg noodle soup, green papaya salad with grilled chicken. I asked her to skip the food part: My stomach was rumbling.

"Prime Mover was dressed in his silver suit," Angela continued as we took a bench seat off Red Square. "The waitstaff paid a lot of attention to him. Like he was a celebrity. I have to admit I was dressed rather strikingly, I thought, in my black strapless Conquesto knockoff. Anyway, Prime Mover talked a lot about himself. His parents were in the circus. Trapeze artists. Always on the road, except when they wintered in Florida. Tragically, they died in a terrible high-wire accident when a pigeon flew into the big top tent and landed on his dad's balancing pole and they lost it—Am I boring you?"

Angela charged ahead: "The circus dropped him in Burcharest under the care of an aunt. She made him live in a basement and pushed him to go into accounting with an engineering minor, but he said he'd never lost the desire to perform."

I may have said an uh-huh.

"Turns out he was previously married and has two boys nearing college age, but he never sees them. That's sad."

"Angela," I interrupted trying to get her back on track, "by any chance did you talk about AltaSystemics?"

"Only in passing. After dinner we skipped the art walk and went to the Comedy Underground. Prime Mover says he goes to the comedy club to pick up pointers. I asked him if he was serious about improv, the classes and all. He said if he weren't the head of a dynamic high-tech company and were twenty years younger, that, yes, he would probably go to LA and join the Groundlings. They're an improv group."

"Angela, you're talking about a megalomaniac who wants to control time and space."

"Oh, that," Angela touched my shoulder. "He says he's interested in what he can do as a post-interfacer to bring about positive change and allow humanity to reach its full potential."

The guy is so crafty, I thought. "Angela," I asked, "did he try and get you to take some candy?"

"Oh, actually he did. Some of his M&M-like candies. But I was too full from dinner." She patted her flat tummy.

She then rather quickly summarized the rest of the evening. "He walked me to my door and was angling to come up, but I said I had early classes the next day, and I gave him a peck on the cheek. He actually bowed and returned to his BMW as I went inside. That was it."

"Good work, I think." I said.

"Tomorrow I go to my internship at AltaSystemics. I'll try and visit the brothers," Angela said as she stood up. "Time to go to my electronics class."

She was gone before I could say anything else. I'll check in with tallboy tonight to see if he's made any progress, besides his so-called blogging. And there's also the upcoming return of the Polynesian contingent.

VIEW COMMENTS (80)

Aladden NOV. 19, 2011 AT 8:11 AM
The symbolism of spending an entire date underground is obvious. Repressed desire. Smoldering passions waiting for release. Below the belt organs.

Time to depart

Entry No. 624 - POSTED: NOV. 19, 2011

Eddie on Tiaré: Mid-morning: When I saw Vaitiare, Teva, and Kohia come out of their huts, I couldn't help staring. They were dressed like tourists—khaki pants, colorful cottony shirts, sunglasses. Each one had a black-wheeled suitcase, the kind that fits into airline overhead storage bins. Then came Thinks Out Loud—and he still appeared native, wearing only an ocean blue lava lava wrap skirt. And I realized how focused I'd become on the convincing of Thinks Out Loud to leave Tiaré. I'd gotten so involved that my exit-Polynesia mission had become the end all and be all rather than a step toward neutralizing our adversary. Time to recalibrate. It was time to return—with reinforcements—to Seattle and face Prime Mover.

"You look exhausted," Kohia said as she walked briskly by me on the way to the boat. Maybe so. Wasn't there always a down time two-thirds of the way in to a Bond film when the Evil Guy seems to hold the better hand and the good guys are regrouping and there isn't a real plan in place to defeat him? Time to cut to the next scene.

Vaea accompanied us as we headed toward the pier where Ebb Tide, the high-speed hydrofoil, was about to dock. Behind us, the entire village's population followed and within that number, the children.

"Like a curious group of puppies, those children," Thinks Out Loud said.

As we approached the pier, the children thronged forward. "Thinks Out Loud! Thinks Out Loud!" they called. They knew his name in English.

TOL stopped and faced them. He gave them a wide grin and a sweeping goodbye wave.

"They want more story," said Kohia.

The throaty blast of the boat's horn signaled it was time for us to depart. Thinks Out Loud looked up at the bridge and motioned a combination of wave and wait signal. I saw the bearded captain, the one who brought me here, give a two-fingered salute, but he appeared to be gazing at me.

"Kohia, could you translate?"

She nodded.

"Okay," said TOL, "this tale is called The Puppy Whisperer."

The children sat before him, the villagers standing in an arc behind.

This was the story:

"On a nearby island, on a plantation with big sugar cane fields surrounded by palm trees, three Border Collie puppies were born one sunny spring day. One was a mostly white girl puppy, one was a mostly black boy puppy, and the third puppy, a boy, had black and white spots. A young boy and his sister lived on the plantation. When the puppies were born, their father, who ran the plantation, told his children they would be responsible for raising the puppies.

"'The puppies can enjoy their puppyhood,' said the father, 'but then they will have to learn the ways of the plantation and take on responsibilities.' The boy and girl had fun with their puppies, who wanted to play all the time. The children and the puppies ran all over the plantation, past the pineapple groves, the mango groves, a big fish pond and the hills dotted with sheep."

"What are sheep?" asked a little girl.

"A recent animal import to broaden the Polynesian economy," intoned TOL.

Kohia didn't even try to translate.

"Fluffy animals that give us their wool so we can make clothing," amended Thinks Out Loud. "And so, after two moons, when the puppies had more than tripled in size, the father told his children it was time for the dogs to learn how to be helpers. The boy and girl began training the three young Border Collies. The white dog and the black dog took very quickly to the training and learned how to sit and wait and run after the sheep."

"Why did they run after the sheep?" asked a little boy.

"Trained dogs can move the sheep around," TOL answered. "They can run and bark and tell the sheep where to go."

Even the adults were listening. "The spotted dog, however, didn't seem to want to sit or wait or herd sheep. He still wanted to run around the plantation and play all day. The boy and girl tried hard to get the spotted dog to join his brother and sister, but nothing worked. The father noticed what was happening and said, 'If that spotted dog doesn't learn properly, we'll have to give him away.'

"'NO!' exclaimed the boy and girl. 'We want to keep him. We'll find a way to train him.' So they took the spotted dog out with the other two dogs into the field where the sheep were. The black dog and the white dog ran right up to the sheep and began to do their duties, but the spotted dog just rolled around on the grass and looked for a stick to play with.

"'Oh, no!' said the boy and girl. This was the last chance for the spotted dog."

"Oh, no!" shouted several young listeners in the audience. TOL gave a wink and continued with his story.

"Across the field on the dirt road leading to the island's main village, a bearded old man was slowly walking. Looking over at the working dogs and the playing dog, he stopped and leaned up against a worn wooden fence pole. 'How's it going?' he called to the children.

"'Not good,' they said. 'All one of the dogs wants to do is play and not work like the other dogs. If he doesn't begin working, our father says we'll have to give him away.'

"The old man thought for a moment and said, 'Mind if I have a word with your dog?' The boy and girl looked at each other and said, 'Okay.'

"The old man went through the gate and came over to them. He tilted his head and looked down at the happy, playful dog. 'What's his name?' he asked.

"'Lani,' the girl said, 'The Sky.'

"'Hmmm,' he said. He gave a whistle and said, 'C'mere, Lani.' The happy dog looked up and over at the old man and kept on playing in the grass. The old man called him over again with a more commanding voice and a movement of his hand, and the dog suddenly rose and as if pulled by an invisible force, walked right over to the man.

"'We've never been able to get him to listen to us,' said the girl as she copied the old man's hand movement.

"The old man bent down close to the dog and began to whisper into his ear. The dog listened patiently and wagged his tail. After a few minutes, the man straightened up and said to the dog, 'Well, go give it a try.'

"As if being released from a spell, the dog sprang up and ran barking towards the startled sheep.

"'How did you do that?' asked the boy.

"'Oh, I have a way with animals,' the old man said with a twinkle in his eye. 'Just a matter of explaining to them what they need to do. I told him that fun and games were all right up to a point, but he also needed to take on some responsibilities if he was going to be a plantation dog.'

"The boy and girl thanked the man and asked him his name. 'Just call me... ah...the Puppy Whisperer,' he said as he went back onto the dirt road and headed toward the village. '*Manuia*! To your health!'"

Thinks Out Loud had finished. At first everyone was silent, but then the kids began to laugh and shout. The villagers did the same. I thought I overheard Kohia suggesting TOL give the children in the story a more active role. The captain gave another tug on boat's deep horn, and, with lots of hugs and waving and some tears, the villagers escorted the travelers to the loading ramp.

Chief Keoni offered a blessing and directed his arms toward us. Vaea tried to get in some parting words, but it was hard to hear him above the jumble of conversations. Something about keeping connected to the Earth and each other.

Finally we stood on the boat's main deck and the captain gave the command to "cast off." The Ebb Tide began easing back as the engine went from idling to reverse. My friends (Can I call them that now?) were all gazing ashore at their friends and family. TOL was also silently regarding the islanders, especially the children. I looked from island to boat to island, and I tried to take it all in because I had no idea if I'd ever see this world again.

LABELS: JAMES BOND FORMULA, CHILDREN'S STORY CRITIQUE, ANCHORS AWAY

VincentFrederick NOV. 19, 2011 AT 10:28 AM

In all cultures, the power of story leads us into and beyond ourselves.

DogStar NOV. 19, 2011 AT 10:44 AM

Hey, people, the popular conception of an Alpha Wolf (i.e. most aggressive of the pack) is being rethought. Wolves survive in packs, true, but they are dependent on each other, which means they are cooperative much more of the time rather than fighting for top, uh, dog position.

FreeZone NOV. 19, 2011 AT 10:49 AM

Thanks for that invaluable information, DogStar, but what does that have to do with anything in this posting?

SHOW MORE COMMENTS

○ ○ ○   **THINKS OUT LOUD**   ✕

WHIMSY WITHOUT REGRET

Passage to Papeete

Entry No. 625 - POSTED: NOV. 19, 2011

Eddie, heading toward Tahiti: We all watched as Tiaré slowly receded into the expanse of the sea. Without a word, Thinks Out Loud turned and went aft and the open air while the rest of us retreated into the main enclosed deck area and sat on white plastic chairs around a plastic table. A snack bar with a bored attendant stood out at the galley's other side.

"There is no one else around," Teva noted.

"Anyone want something to eat?" I asked. None of our group bothered to answer. Why were we so glum?

"Welcome," said a man descending a steep metal stairway from the bridge above us. It was the gray-bearded Australian, Captain Kuborn. Dressed in a white, pressed uniform, he approached us and remained standing at our table. "You're on a non-stop express today," he said. "A direct flight to Tahiti." The captain looked at the aft bank of windows and saw Thinks Out Loud staring out to sea. "Ah, it appears Thinks Out Loud wishes to meditate. The ocean has always been conducive to deep thoughts."

Captain Kuborn asked if we needed anything and we thanked him and said no. "You are a very serious group of passengers," he said. "Well, enjoy the ride. We'll arrive in Papeete in about four hours. If you do get hungry, our snack bar features local cuisine." He turned to go back to the bridge and stopped a few steps from our table. "Oh, by the way, when Thinks Out Loud rejoins you, could you let him know that I heard from Hank, the second mate, now the first mate of the Bogsworth?" The captain went on to tell us that while the ship had been in dry dock for repairs, Hank had been enjoying the blog. "Hank says the story is quite entertaining," said a grinning Captain Kuborn. "He also says the Bogworth, now seaworthy, set sail for Seattle the previous week. How about that!" The captain left us to enjoy the voyage.

I felt as if I should say something to break the silence. "Thanks for taking us" was the best I could come up with. Teva was staring into space. Vaitiare sat with her hands clasped. And Kohia looked like she'd been crying.

"Is something wrong?" I asked. To be heard over the deep thudding of the engines, we all had to talk more loudly than normal, which gave our conversation a slightly forced manner.

Teva sighed and began, "We have a hard time leaving Tiaré. Whenever we go away from the island, we feel incomplete."

"The island sustains us and we sustain it," Vaitiare added.

"Then I am even more impressed you are willing to join Thinks Out Loud and me on this mission," I said.

Teva pointed toward TOL. "That one," he said. "Less than two months ago we found this limp shadow of a man on our sacred island. We brought him, a foreigner, to Tiaré, a move I resisted. And now look at him. Our storyteller. He dresses and acts more Polynesian than me!" Teva rose and went out the starboard doors and stood on the deck, the late afternoon sun highlighting his muscled right side.

"Kohia, Vaitiare, did I say something wrong?"

They looked at each other. Vaitiare also stood up and wandered over to the snack bar. Kohia spoke. "Not your fault. Teva's is a troubled soul. You don't know this, but a few years ago his mother left her husband, Moana or the Ocean, for another man." I practically gasped. "It was rare in our culture. In the old days he would have hunted her down and, well, anyway, she left with an American anthropologist who had come to the island to observe our customs. Moana was never quite the same. He could have taken another wife—in the old days he would have already had several—but he chose not to. He died not long after she left. He faded away. Teva took all this very badly and has not healed. He still carries anger toward his mother and anyone not of Polynesian descent."

I wanted to ask if this was the case then why Teva had voted for TOL to stay on the island, but I kept silent.

"Teva is on his own journey," Kohia said. "He must make his own way. He may surprise us."

Over the next several hours, everyone retreated to different parts of the boat. The captain saw me near the bow, taking the full brunt of the ocean breeze, and approached. "You and your fellow travelers are under some stress. During the time you are in Papeete, try and relax."

I thanked him for his advice. Directly before us, the fabled isle of Tahiti was growing on the horizon, the sea, the sky all aglow in the last of the day's light.

"One other little suggestion," said the captain. "You might mention to Thinks Out Loud that he change out of his native clothing before boarding your flight to Seattle."

LABELS: PAPEETE TOURIST SPOTS, UNSPOKEN FEELINGS, OCEAN DEPTHS

VIEW COMMENTS (83)

Rookie NOV. 19, 2011 AT 8:43 AM
Hmmmm. Am reconsidering my take of Teva. More complex than I had imagined.

Anonymous NOV. 19, 2011 AT 9:18 AM
Is there a Polynesian version of a therapist Teva could go to?

Krishnaman NOV. 19, 2011 AT 9:33 AM
His island probably has a traditional healer who makes use of herbs and rebalancing the body.

SHOW MORE COMMENTS

○ ○ ○   THINKS OUT LOUD   ✕

WHIMSY WITHOUT REGRET

Invasion plans

Entry No. 626 - POSTED: NOV. 20, 2011

Eddie in Papeete: When we docked yesterday, Teva led Thinks Out Loud to a men's store to outfit him for travel to the U.S. Off with the grass skirt; on with the pants and shirt. Kohia and Vaitiare were taking in the historic sites because, it turns out, they rarely visit Tahiti.

Papeete buzzed with human activity: cars, trucks, scooters, boats. Multi-story buildings blocked the view of the water. I know this island would seem slow-paced compared to a major American traffic-jam city, but after spending time on quaint Tiaré, I was a bit overwhelmed.

I was going to check in with Emily when we first came ashore, but I was hungry and a little tired from the trip. I wandered down Rue Gauguin and a few of the other downtown streets and ran into Tony, the guy who runs that high-tech salvage company I made the delivery to when I first arrived. He even recognized me.

"Hello, young courier," he said as I was about to cross the street. "You're back on the island." Taller and broader than me, he patted my shoulder. He had tousled blonde hair, a great tan, and a genuine smile of someone who really likes being where he is.

I said yes, I was here but for less than a day, on my way to Seattle.

"Lot going on there," he said, his eyes bright with amusement about something. "Lots of creative energy. Must be due to the caffeine. Well, if you make it this way again, drop by the shop. Didn't you say you were taking technology courses?"

I said I was but I wasn't sure what I wanted to do yet.

"No rush, no rush. Have a good flight." And off went Tony while I refound Papeete Tea and Coffee (and WiFi).

A latte, a chocolate muffin and baked banana vanilla custard before me at my table, I checked to see if my phone had recharged enough to work again. Then I had to go to the bathroom. And out of curiosity, I leafed through the island's newspaper, *Les Nouvelles de Tahiti,* but my French was limited to *"bon appétit."*

A little voice in me ordered: "Call her!" Emily answered after three rings.

"Eddy, what's your status?" She was all business.

I pulled back from my phone, and I know I had a quizzical look on my face because a customer two tables away was scrutinizing me.

"Oh, hi, Emily, and how are you, too?"

She spoke in a neutral tone. "Sorry, hi. We're holding our own over here. Trying to slow down Prime Mover's attempts to extract information from the brothers. We've realized he has to drug them to control them, but if they're too drugged, they won't properly write out their time/space theories on the white board in their room."

"Well, we're on our way," I said. I wanted to make some kind of contact with her. "How are you?"

"Busy." A pause of silence between us. She was waiting for me to continue.

"I'm bringing help," I said.

"I know. Good." I wanted to ask if she missed me, but I held back and said a quick goodbye.

LABELS: PAPEETE, WORDS NOT SAID

VIEW COMMENTS (88)

VincentFrederick NOV. 20, 2011 AT 10:33 AM
Now is the time for the group to stick together. Support one another. Keep your eye on the goal.

EveningMist NOV. 20, 2011 AT 10:50 AM
Feel the energizing power of the Great South Pacific. Let its waters and winds surround you with an aura of golden light. And check out my new electronic book, *Glow Your Own*.

SHOW MORE COMMENTS

○ ○ ○   THINKS OUT LOUD   ✕

WHIMSY WITHOUT REGRET

In-flight conversation
Entry No. 627 - POSTED: NOV. 21, 2011

Eddie: The first leg of our flight, Tahiti to LA on Air Tahiti Airlines, would take nine hours—time enough for a movie or two, a great Tahitian meal that included what Kohia called Chicken Fafa and a fish stew, some naps, some reading, and some talk. The plane was two-thirds full, mostly tourists and some business people, which meant we got a lot of attention and service from the traditionally-dressed flight attendants. The cabin smelled like flowers. "Gardenias," said Kohia.

There were five of us, and our seat choices were two by the windows or four in the middle. Thinks Out Loud chose a spot in the back by himself. I sat next to Kohia; I felt more comfortable with her than if I had been next to Vaitiare or Teva. Kohia always emanates an island's flowery fragrance, not exactly a perfume, more a part of her physical makeup— not applied makeup. Sort of Gardenia-like.

She had the window seat. "Kohia," I said, "I can't believe we're here."

"Here is where we're supposed to be," she said.

"Well a lot has happened to get us here. A lot can happen, even in a day." The flight attendant popped by and asked if we wanted to try their caramel-vanilla coffee. I said yes, Kohia said no. Kohia and she traded some words in Polynesian. "Island talk," she said.

I tried again. "Kohia, we're heading into the unknown, and we'll be joining up with some others."

"Yes, others." She was looking out the window at a combination of endless fluffy clouds and wide ocean below.

"You know, all of you have become very special to me," I said and immediately regretted my limp statement.

"That's nice," said Kohia.

I tried again only to have Teva punch my arm. "Eddie, want to switch seats for a while?" I'd never seen Teva so animated. He was sounding almost happy. "We are soaring. I had forgotten how much I enjoy leaving the Earth below."

We traded seats. Now I was next to a sleeping Vaitiare who put her head on my shoulder. I tried to quietly sip my coffee. I didn't think Vaitiare could hear me, so I said softly, "You know, Vaitiare, I am finding it hard to talk to Thinks Out Loud. He seems distant, like he's living in another land."

"Yes," answered Vaitiare in her own whisper. I almost spilled my coffee. She continued, "Yes, when he came to our island, I kept urging him to find his true inner self." She rubbed her head along my shoulder. "And now he has. And yet, and yet..." Vaitiare opened one eye that was only a couple of inches from me. "And yet, I find I miss some of the old Thinks Out Loud." Her eye closed and she folded back into a deeper sleep.

Sitting next to Vaitiare for the rest of the hour, I was thinking about Thinks Out Loud. It was great he had had that experience in the cave. But he wasn't in the cave anymore. Would he remain tethered to our world enough to face Prime Mover?

A little while later, coming back from the bathroom, I discovered that Teva had taken Vaitiare's place. She had relocated next to Kohia. They were whispering. I hesitated to sit next to Teva; there was an empty row just before him. When I slowed to begin my descent into that row, Teva motioned with his head for me to join him. Actually, that would afford me a chance to ask him my question.

We were silent at first. I tried to read. He peered outside the window. Searching? "Teva, could I ask you a personal question?"

"What do you wish to know, Eddie?"

"Okay, I've been wondering about this. Remember the vote about what to do with Thinks Out Loud?"

Teva expanded his chest and spread beyond the confines of his seat into my territory. "Ah, the vote."

"Yes, I don't want to pry..."

"Then do not ask."

Sometimes I thought Teva must be kidding, playing with me. Still, he wasn't known for his sense of humor.

"Teva, why did you vote for Thinks Out Loud to stay on the island after you seemed to dislike him so."

"Who said I disliked Thinks Out Loud?" He pulled back his head and slowly turned toward me.

I was gulping air. "Well, no one, actually. It's just when I read the blog postings Thinks Out Loud wrote when he mentions you there's always this tension between you two, and you know you can sound pretty gruff."

Teva spoke evenly, letting each word settle before going to the next one. "I do not want to see our island ways destroyed. Some would destroy us on purpose, others by accident. I cannot let that happen. I first saw Thinks Out Loud as an accidental destroyer. As I followed his actions and deeds, my mind turned and my heart softened. He has become one of us."

I wanted to ask, "You support TOL, even if he falls in love with Vaitiare, the woman you were to marry?" I held back.

"Ladies and gentleman," said a women's calm, professional voice with a touch of island softness from a loudspeaker, "please prepare for our landing in Los Angeles."

LABELS: HIGH-TECH SUSPENSE, TAHITIAN ROMANCE

VIEW COMMENTS (86)

Anonymous NOV. 21, 2011 AT 11:48 PM
Eddie, when it comes to women, you don't have a clue.

FriendO'Kierkegaard NOV. 21, 2011 AT 11:59 PM
As my favorite philosopher wrote: "Our life always expresses the result of our dominant thoughts."

SHOW MORE COMMENTS

○ ○ ○   **THINKS OUT LOUD**   ✕

WHIMSY WITHOUT REGRET

Welcome to Seattle

Entry No. 628 - POSTED: NOV. 22, 2011

Emily: When I borrowed my mother's Range Rover to go to SeaTac, she asked why I needed the car. "Picking up some Pacific Islanders, transfer students," I told her. It wasn't exactly a lie, if you think of life as a continuous learning process.

Traffic meant I was late reaching the baggage claim pickup area; I made a quick scan of the waiting passengers: Japanese tourists, reuniting families. Ah: A group too lightly dressed in colorful Hawaiian (Tahitian?)-style shirts—one American and four Polynesians. I stopped behind an orange Prius taxi in the lane next to the curbside lane.

I had spotted them, but they were still looking for me. "Hey," I called. "Over here." A dozen waiting and now hopeful arrivees turned my way. Then I saw Eddie recognize my head leaning out the window. He led the way over. Shoulders slumping except for one big fellow, they all looked as if they'd been traveling for almost 15 hours, which they had.

As I helped to load luggage, we made quick introductions. Teva stood above us all. I knew he was big, but I hadn't realized how graceful he would be as he picked up and deposited luggage in the back. Vaitiare, the princess, reminded me of Angela in her height and build, with an added grace that seemed natural. Kohia was giving me a deep penetrating look. The other Islander turned out to be Isaac now Thinks Out Loud! Even though I'd never actually met him, I could tell he was transformed—bronze skinned, curly-haired, a line of tattoos on his arms. And it wasn't just his looks—he carried himself as though he'd studied the Feldenkrais Method. He was a pleasant enough guy, but his eye was scanning the whole environment. And then there was Eddie. A thinner version, tanned, hungrier. Avoiding my gaze except for a quick, meager head nod, he seemed to be focused on watching the other cars leaving baggage claim parking. (Was he embarrassed to see me?)

Teva, Thinks Out Loud and Vaitiare climbed into the rear seat. Eddie and Kohia crowded into and had to share the front passenger seat, my leg touching Eddie's. A dour traffic officer standing in front of the car gave us a quick hand motion to move on.

 "Next stop," I began, "my mother's house. Just remember to say you are here to study. You are transfer students. Got that?"

"Do we look like students?" Vaitiare asked in a low voice.

A glance in the rear view mirror and I saw her almost smiling. "Some of you can be undergraduates, some of you working on your Ph.D."

"What's my major?" asked Kohia.

"Choose one," I said. "What are your interests?"

She answered after a few moments of thought. "The role of island women in Polynesian society."

As we passed Boeing Field, I nodded. "There's a good Women's Studies Department here."

Teva spoke. "I am interested in building things, things that will last through storms and the shaking of the earth.

"Construction Management," Eddie threw out as if he were on a game show—Name That Major.

"For me," Vaitiare began, "the law."

"Great," I said, "and tell everyone you also came to sample the coffee."

○ ○ ○   THINKS OUT LOUD   ✕

WHIMSY WITHOUT REGRET

Settling in

Entry No. 629 - POSTED: NOV. 22, 2011

Eddie: Emily's mom did look like a former Miss America with her wide smile and strong cheek bones. She didn't miss a beat when Emily shepherded all of us into the lakeside house and introduced the South Pacificers with their need to stay here until housing on campus became available.

"I'm Katherine. You must be starving, how about Thai?" Emily's mom was totally inviting and super friendly. "I've always wanted to visit the South Pacific."

"You would be most welcome on our island," Teva said with a courtesy nod of his head.

"Mom likes to go to places that haven't been Americanized," Emily added as she gave her mother a hug.

The house was deluxe—spacious, wood floors, wood-paneled walls, wood everywhere, plus great views of the lake. Emily kept things moving and showed Teva his bedroom, "which you can share with...Isaac or is it now Thinks Out Loud?"

Teva explained that 'Thinks Out Loud' had become Isaac's island name, part of his being welcomed into their society.

"Thank you for the honor, Teva. Here in Seattle, I'll answer to either name. They are both part of me."

"And I see we are roommates once again," Teva said in a lower voice. TOL walked slowly into the large bedroom and sat at a straightbacked chair beside a mahogany desk. "I'm not used to being in this kind of house," he said.

Emily's mom wasn't sure if that was a critique or a compliment, but she gave him a nice smile anyway.

Vaitiare and Kohia entered a second room. "It's got a view of Lake Washington," Emily added. The two visitors were quietly taking it all in.

As for me, I planned to ride a bus back to my apartment near campus. "Do you mind sleeping on our den couch?" Emily asked when others weren't around. "It's actually quite comfortable. We need to talk."

While everyone was getting situated, I sat down on another deep-seated couch in the expansive living room. Perhaps I had dozed off for a few minutes. I awoke to the front door opening with Emily's mom calling out, "Pad Thai anyone?" Katherine had gone all out with container (compostable) after container of food.

"So many new flavors," Teva said, after his second helping of everything. "A change from roast pig." We were all hungry.

"So you've come here to study," Katherine said to the South Seas islanders, who mumbled back yeses and kept eating. "And what are your majors?" Thanks to Emily's prepping, they were able to answer. I was starting to believe they really were students.

Then Katherine caught us off guard with one of her questions. "Kohia, whom did you interview with over at Women's Studies? I took a few classes there a couple of years ago."

Kohia chewed her food a bit longer than usual before beginning to answer that she couldn't remember. It had been several months ago.

"Was one of the interviewers a man?"

We all stole looks at one another, and I saw Emily give Kohia just the barest hint of a nod.

"Yes," said Kohia as she spooned more Pad Thai on her plate.

"Was it Chad, one of the adjuncts? A phone interview?"

In an attempt at redirection, I asked Emily's mom about the house. "It's so airy," I said.

"Thank you, Eddie. When we moved in, we did a remodel of the interior, brought down some walls, opened up the spaces." She repeated, "We." Then, with only one silent beat, she turned to Vaitiare. "Your island is called?"

"Tiaré, which means Flower," Vaitiare answered politely.

"Do you have family there?"

"Yes, my older brother and my father, Chief Keoni."

Katherine raised her eyebrows. "Chief? Does that make you a princess?"

Vaitiare brought her paper napkin up to her mouth. "Yes, I have royal blood in me."

By the time we were done with the banquet, Emily realized the group was too tired to plan and strategize. "You all need a good night's rest," she told us. "I'll text the others to meet us at the coffeehouse tomorrow."

I was still standing in the living room when everyone except Emily adjourned to their bedrooms. Emily led me into the den and indicated I should sit on the couch where she joined me. The lights were low. Now that I had seen her glamorous mother, I perceived Emily through a different lens. I mean she was dressed casually in jeans and a dark blue pullover and her hair was growing out from the pixie cut. And she also had her mom's high cheekbones. And some Miss America genes.

"Eddie...do you remember why we are here?"

"Sure, sure I do—to face Prime Mover and rescue the brothers from Prime Mover." Was this some kind of quiz?

"Good," she said as she casually wrapped her legs underneath her. "It's important to stay focused."

All I could do was nod. The rest of the house was silent except for the ticking of a distant clock. Through the large plate glass window that fronted the lake, I could see the constellation of outdoor lights on the other side of the water.

Even though I had read her blogs, Emily gave me a rundown on their activities here in Seattle while I was gone. "We haven't made all that much progress," she admitted. "With all of you here, I hope that's about to change."

"Did you miss me while I was gone?" I ventured to ask.

"Of course I did," she said while looking down. Had something come between us? As a test I leaned forward to embrace her only to have Emily turn to allow me to kiss her cheek. I wanted to ask if she had gone back to her ex-boyfriend.

Finally she blurted out, "You and Kohia seem to be getting along quite well."

I must have looked astonished because Emily did a kind of doubletake and caught her lower lip in her teeth. "Kohia? She's just a kid. Emily, she's become a good friend and a great translator."

Emily apologized and said so much was happening right now with Prime Mover and the Morse brothers and everything else, that it was hard to think about personal relationships.

"Like ours?" I asked. "Do we have a relationship?"

"A proto-relationship," she said, a hint of brightness returning to her eyes.

I told her I could barely keep my eyes open, and she let out slow breath. With us at opposite ends of the sofa, Emily helped me arrange the sheets. It's funny, here I was back in Seattle, yet I could still hear the rhythmic sounds of the surf on Tiaré.

"Get some sleep," she said gently and gave me a return peck on the cheek. I settled into the soft sheets, my eyes closed, images of Polynesian beach mixing with Pacific Northwest fir forests.

LABELS: LIVING ROOM DÉCOR, INDIRECT LIGHTING, RELATIONSHIPS

VIEW COMMENTS (84)

Tangerine NOV. 22, 2011 AT 11:34 PM
The calm before the storm. Not to mention a real rain storm. Not to mention stormy relationships.

SeattleStu NOV. 22, 2011 AT 11:49 PM
Interesting to see how these Polynesians will react to the Northwest.

SHOW MORE COMMENTS

Contemplation before dawn

Entry No. 630 - POSTED: NOV. 23, 2011

Thinks Out Loud: In the early morning hours, out on the back deck, I sit in a low-legged Andirondack chair and gaze across the calm, dark waters of Lake Washington. Above is a cloud cover backlit by the glow of the hidden crescent moon. All is silent except for the faint clicking of a mastline of a sailboat docked beside a neighbor's house.

Calm dark waters. I've adapted to spending most of my time outside, though it's like being in a refrigerator here in the Pacific Northwest. Living outdoors made me much more aware of the day's rhythms. I also find indoors confining. Gauguin would understand.

My name(s). Last night after dinner, Eddie said I should consider changing my name to Talks Silently. Perhaps he's right. For that's what I've been doing of late. My thoughts: It hasn't felt right to say them aloud. So many ideas are converging inside me—a mix of memories encompassing physical adventures and internal struggles, my undistinguished life before being marooned and my unexpected life on Tiaré. Teva. Vaitiare. The cave. The children.

Here in Seattle, I sense what is going on around me, even as I feel removed from the ebb and flow of current events. As if I am watching a movie, I am aware of the threat Prime Mover poses and the challenges my cohorts and I face in stopping him. Then there is Teva. It is good he is with us, even though I still do not fully understand him and his personal quest. Something is out there waiting for him.

tallboy—he who tried to take over my blog, back when I actually cared about such a triviality. Still it was my blog, a personal expression of thought and feeling. We've never physically met, even though he is responsible for contacting the islanders to search for me. He, too, is on a journey, although I think he would benefit from a Google maps for the Soul.

Emily and Eddie, who now blog in my place. You are having adventures of your own. I don't know if this will help or hinder you:

I hereby relinquish any claim to the blog Thinks Out Loud.

It is yours to do with as you wish. If you like, you can invite me to be a guest blogger from time to time. Either way, Thinks Out Loud is now yours.

I should probably go to sleep for the coming day promises to be full of import. Still, I wonder how the children are faring on Tiaré. Come what may, I'll have stories to share should I make it back to them.

One more thing. If I am honest with myself, I have somehow managed to live my life up to this point without really living, without facing a challenge, whether internal or, in this case, external.

It's about time.

LABELS: RUMINATIONS, WATERY DEPTHS , THE WEE HOURS

VIEW COMMENTS (85)

Explica NOV. 23, 2011 AT 6:29 AM

Can't think of anything sarcastic to say to my ex-husband.

SeenIt NOV. 23, 2011 AT 6:59 AM

Thinks Out Loud, Isaac, don't give up blogging! A sabbatical is one thing; leaving for good is another.

Miser NOV. 23, 2011 AT 7:29 AM

Is it my fault? Were my harangues too much? Hey, I was just playing a role. Isaac, c'mon. Keep blogging.

SHOW MORE COMMENTS

○ ○ ○　　　　　　**THINKS OUT LOUD**　　　　　　✕

WHIMSY WITHOUT REGRET

Mother knows best?

Entry No. 631 - POSTED: NOV. 23, 2011

Emily: I awoke to a mix of breakfast aromas: eggs, toast, coffee. My mother knew how to play the host. We were emerging from all corners of the house, and it was quite a show. Teva wore a fashionable pin-striped black pajamas (Dad's). Vaitiare and Kohia were robed in white. Thinks Out Loud had reverted to the Polynesian look of a sarong up to his waist. And poor Eddie had slept in his now wrinkled pants and shirt.

"Breakfast," sang out my mom. "What do you plan to do today? Don't some of you have classes to register for?"

"Of course they do," I answered quickly. "And I still want to show them around campus." (Plus time to gather together with the rest of our companions at the coffee house for our big meeting.)

Teva volunteered to bring dishes into the kitchen. He was asking my mother about the kinds of fish in Lake Washington and the varieties of birdlife in the area. Kohia and Vaitiare took their tea cups out to the back deck. It was a typical November gray day, though the rain was holding off. Thinks Out Loud seemed content to make notes in a small writing pad he kept with him.

Eddie approached and told me he was taking a bus back to his apartment and would meet us later.

"Three o'clock," I said, anticipating his question. He barely made eye contact with me as we talked. I didn't know how to lessen the tension between us, which I hoped wouldn't affect our mission.

As I was helping my mother straighten up in a far corner of the house, she fluffed up a pillow and tossed an unexpected question at me. "They're not students are they?"

Sucking in my breath, I thought about continuing the lie.

She continued: "They're like Polynesian CIA, the way they move in such a guarded way. The way they are watching everything."

"They're just new to the country, which is so different from their island."

"That may be true, but there's more going on here."

I dropped down on the partially made bed. "You wouldn't believe me if I told you."

"Try me." She was giving me that look, not exactly cold but penetrating.

And so I began. Took me ten minutes to describe it all. My mother, for once, listened without interrupting.

"That's why they're here," I finished. "It's stranger than fiction."

My mother sat down next to me. "Hard to believe," she said as she took my hand. "Honey, I know I haven't always been around when you needed me. And the divorce has been hard. What can I do to help?"

I started tearing up. "Can we borrow the car?"

"Of course," she said. "But I'm serious. If you're in trouble…"

I told her I wasn't in trouble. It was more a matter of taking on a responsibility I hadn't ever imagined I'd be dealing with.

"Are your friends up to the task?"

"I don't know."

"Well, this may sound like a cliché, but give it your all. And let me know what else I can do."

We hugged.

Two hours later I tried to round everyone up.

Eddie was gone. My mother said Teva had told her he would be walking along the shoreline. She didn't know if he'd gone north or south. Vaitiare and Kohia weren't in the house either. "They are looking for high ground to do a ceremony to give thanks for a safe arrival," my mother informed me. How did she know what was going on while I was supposed to be keeping track of everyone?

"What about Isaac?"

"You mean Thinks Out Loud? I'm letting him use my computer to type up some children's stories."

I was pacing the living room. "Mom, this is ridiculous. We've got important work to do!"

She advised me to relax. "Everyone will back in a few minutes. Emily, maybe they all need this time to ready themselves for the tasks to come."

I hadn't thought of that. When had my mother become so wise? Sure enough, as if on cue, within ten minutes Teva returned from his walk, Vaitiare and Kohia somehow materialized at the back deck, and Thinks Out Loud came out of the study. "Time to go?" he asked.

The trip to the U District was relatively quick. My passengers were looking in all directions as we drove from wooded Lake Forest Park to the more urban north Seattle. "Cars dominate," Teva said.

"If we had time, I'd show you the Arboretum, Seward Park and Discovery Park," I said. I did take them on a quick detour of Magnuson along Lake Washington. "It's a combo park—part grasslands, part waterfront, part playfields and facilities. Used to be a naval base. Oh, there's a great dog park that even has its own beach." We curved around the parking lot and drove back to Sand Point Way.

"A village would do well, here," said Teva. I didn't tell him that Native Americans had settled here before the coming of the White Man.

We headed toward campus. As I looked for a parking space on a side street of The Ave, I said, "So, this a planning session where you'll meet the other key Seattle people of our team."

"We look forward to it," Kohia said. She was soft spoken with an underlying energy and vitality.

"They're all Polynesian goddesses," I thought, as we walked in a loose group to the coffeehouse.

At the back table in the back room of Allegro, a cleaned up Eddie immediately saw us and waved. Next to him, a texting Angela looked up and gave us a serious appraisal. We made quick intros and retreated to order drinks. By this time, tallboy, looking sleepy, had arrived. A couple of minutes later Chen came in. More introductions were made. Everyone was a little stiff. We all sipped our drinks.

"Eddie, are you okay?" Chen asked.

"Yes, fine. Thanks for asking," Eddie answered.

Thinks Out Loud spread out his arms, his palms open. "It's good to have all of us together, actually, for the first time," he said with a laugh. That was the first time I'd seen him display a sense of humor.

"Now we can stick it to that Prime Mover," Chen said. He took a big gulp of his grande latte.

"He's not that bad," muttered Angela, "for a monomaniac, I mean."

"Angela, I'm starting to doubt your commitment to this mission," jabbed Eddie.

All of the islanders were silent. Teva and Vaitiare were looking at each other. Kohia glanced at Eddie. I could practically hear their thoughts: "Why are we here?"

Jumping in, I asked tallboy if he could update us on what was going on at AltaSystemics.

He took a long sip from his mocha. "I do have some stuff," he began. "Last week, Prime Mover was bragging to me that he was primed, pun intended, to discover a really big secret about the universe. But his mood soured as the week progressed. He has become increasingly frustrated with the brothers Morse I think. He must have figured by now they would have yielded their secrets. It's partly my fault because I've been changing the formulas they are writing on the whiteboard in their room. Course sometimes I just pretend to change the math, to keep things interesting. But yesterday, security got tightened up. No more pretending these are guest consultants. Now, two Connectors are posted at the brothers' door. I need some more coffee."

I urged tallboy to continue his report.

"Okay, so I did notice that the white-robed Hivers are now visiting the brothers. They are the only ones allowed inside."

"I'll bet Prime Mover wants to use those Intuitives to try and mentally extract the formula info from the brothers," I said.

"Not necessarily," said Angela. "Maybe the brothers are interested in ESP."

"Doubtful," I said, a knot forming in my stomach.

tallboy went on. "There's something else." He looked up and down the table. "Remember Jeannie who keeps getting kicked off our blog? Last night, PM found me just as I was about to walk out the door, and there she was, right next to him. 'Meet Jeannie,' he said. Her big smile felt like an icicle being jabbed into my stomach. PM said she was the new Social Media Maven and I would be reporting to her. We shook hands. She acted as if she didn't know who I was, and I did the same about her. Actually, she coolly said, 'Have we met before?' And I replied, 'I don't think so.' I felt as if I were in a play. Then she said she looked forward to working with me, and I don't know what she meant by that. She could fire me, you know."

"Oh great," Eddie said.

"Are there problems?" Teva asked.

"Someone who doesn't like us and knows about us is now in a position of power at AltaSystemics," summarized Chen.

"Maybe she won't hold a grudge," said tallboy.

"She is one big grudge!" countered Eddie.

Everyone was talking except Thinks Out Loud who sat silently with his hand under his chin.

I gazed up and down the table; some of our team had traveled from the other side of the planet to join in our struggle. The rest of us were locals brought together under these unusual circumstances made more challenging by Prime Mover's recent actions. "Friends," I said as I pushed my empty coffee cup away, "we need to reboot."

LABELS: A HICCUP, CIRCUMSTANCES BEYOND OUR CONTROL

VIEW COMMENTS (87)

Freezone NOV. 23, 2011 AT 4:39 PM
Pretty obvious that PM is winning. All he needs is a little more time to gain the formula.

AFriend NOV. 23, 2011 AT 5:50 PM
"Never give up, never surrender!"

SHOW MORE COMMENTS

○ ○ ○   THINKS OUT LOUD   ✕

WHIMSY WITHOUT REGRET

Pep talk

Entry No. 632 - POSTED: NOV. 23, 2011

Chen: This is the first time I've written on Thinks Out Loud. I usually post on Pinterest, but I wanted to get this down while it was still fresh in my mind. The members of our group were like a lab experiment gone wrong. Acid leaking onto the floor. The Bunsen burner melting a test tube. HazMat being called in to stop the spread of noxious fumes.

True, Prime Mover is wily and savvy and having Jeannie on his side does not help our cause. And so far we didn't have a winning strategy. Or any strategy. And he was taking stronger steps to get that formula out of the Morse brothers.

Still, and I emphasize this, all was not lost.

We were walking without direction on The Ave. I looked at our silent group and noticed that Thinks Out Loud had a trace of a smile playing about his lips. Did he know something we didn't? "Guys," I said, "we *can* reboot."

Teva was regarding me with the calmest of eyes. Such calmness—maybe that was the way. I spoke directly to Teva in a manner that invited everyone in. "Teva, you have faced great challenges in your life—on your home island, at sea, even in your personal life, if I may."

He was silent, the silence of someone willing to listen.

"We need your strength, your power to get us back on track."

Teva pressed his hands together. "Indeed, I have strength."

"Yes," I said quickly, "physical and mental strength. And you, Eddie, look at all you've accomplished in just a short while. You ventured to the other side of the planet and brought back Thinks Out Loud."

Eddie took my words as a compliment by silently acknowledging me with a half smile and a small outward movement of his hand as though trying to push away the praise.

Now that I had their attention, I complimented everyone in the group— Emily for her insights and planning ability, Thinks Out Loud for his expanded range of awareness and being, Angela for her bravery in interacting with Prime Mover, tallboy for his attempts to stall Prime Mover's plan, Vaitiare for her willpower and Kohia for her creativity and daring.

"If you think about it, we're quite the team. We all have something to contribute," I gushed.

"What about you," Emily said. "Why are you here?"

I could feel my tongue tapping the inside of my upper front teeth. "Right. Well, I'm from Brooklyn. Quitting is not in our vocabulary."

LABELS: RALLYING THE TROOPS, HIGH-TECH SUSPENSE, THE POWER OF THE COMPLIMENT

VIEW COMMENTS (84)

RoseCity NOV. 23, 2011 AT 5:19 PM
'Bout time Chen spoke out. Where would the group be without him? More lost, more confused, more dazed. And a lot less knowledgeable about chocolates.

Anonymous NOV. 23, 2011 AT 5:39 PM
Chen, if and when you get a spare moment, give me a call.

SHOW MORE COMMENTS

The Art of War

Entry No. 633 - POSTED: NOV. 24, 2011

Emily: Chen's words did re-energize us and not a moment too soon. We'd lost a day due to our own ill behavior when we succumbed to doubt and pessimism. Perhaps, though, the delay also offered us certain advantages. Chen had helped rally us. tallboy and Angela were able to gather more intell. Eddie and Thinks Out Loud said they were running over strategies. And now that my mother knew about our little project, she had offered her three-car garage as a staging area.

tallboy says Prime Mover is becoming more and more irrational and agitated, that he's walking around and yelling at everyone in the company. "He roared that I was weeks behind in my blogging, which is not true. I'm only one week behind," said a defensive tallboy. Then he admitted, "Actually, I don't know what to write anymore. And Jeannie, my new supervisor, keeps giving me conflicting feedback. First, she likes what I do. Then she totally changes her mind. I think she's toying with me."

"She's also spending a lot of time with Prime Mover," hissed Angela, who'd been at AltaSystemics yesterday as part of her internship. "She's so obviously trying to please him. What a bimbo."

I tried to remind Angela that Prime Mover was the enemy.

In the nearly empty garage, we created a rudimentary model of AltaSystemics formed out of cardboard from old moving boxes. "Please, everyone, say what you think," I said. "There are no wrong answers here. Every idea is a possibility."

"A direct frontal assault would be best," said Chen. Eddie volunteered he could create a diversion, but he didn't have one in mind. Thinks Out Loud said to adapt Sun Tzu's *Art of War*. "We must be able to respond to changing conditions." Angela voted for high explosives targeted primarily at "uppity females." Chen tried again: "Maybe entrance via a back door." Teva added we should remain calm and firm of mind. Eddie again: "Bond and his team would parachute in."

Then, all was silent. I could hear the hum of my mom's freezer unit at the back of the garage. Electricity. Energy. Power. Or not.

"That's it," I said. "That's our answer." The group stared at me. "Our answers. All of them. We can use it all!"

We set to work, struggled with ideas that ran off course, took a few detours, and made a couple of imaginative leaps. An hour and a half later, we owned a plan, more or less. Strong on goals. Moderate on details. Dependent on a certain degree of luck.

"Are we good to go?" I asked, closing up my black carrying case.

"As good as we'll ever be," answered Eddie. Others nodded. "Cue the John Barry climactic theme music," he added.

LABELS:

VIEW COMMENTS (88)

HindSite NOV. 24, 2011 AT 8:20 AM
"If you know both yourself and your enemy, you can win numerous (literally, "a hundred") battles without jeopardy." Sun Tzu, The Art of War

AdamsRibeye NOV. 24, 2011 AT 8:38 AM
These people are letting emotions get in the way. Right now they need to be made of steel, free of feeling, all focus and attention.

BlueBaby NOV. 24, 2011 AT 8:58 AM
Easy for you to say, Mr. Armchair General.

SHOW MORE COMMENTS

○ ○ ○   THINKS OUT LOUD   ✕

WHIMSY WITHOUT REGRET

tallboy posts

Entry No. 634 - POSTED: NOV. 24, 2011

We had a plan. I wanted to say something. Clearing my throat, I began, "I don't like to talk about this, but it might tie in with what we are doing. Eddie won't remember, he was just a baby, and I was about ten when I started getting short of breath and I felt a weight inside my chest. At first my parents and my doctor thought I had a cold, but I only got worse. They did an x-ray and the technician thought the machine was not working right because the image—my chest—was one big dark spot. Finally, my parents took me to the emergency room. Boom. Turns out I was in bad shape: Cancer. Called Ewings Sarcoma—develops very fast, very deadly. Anyway, I got put on this really powerful treatment plan and it took a year—chemo, surgery, radiation. At any point in the treatment I could have bought it. And it turned out, even as we seemed to be getting the upper hand of the cancer, that there were all kinds of other ways to lose: infections when the chemo lowered my blood cells, secondary illnesses, a negative reaction to drugs, you name it."

My voice got a little unsteady. "I managed to hold on, and here I am today. It could have gone the other way. Luck played a part. Hope. Being part of a team—parents, friends, doctors, nurses, specialists like the guy who did my MRIs. Some prayer. Some anger. Some confidence in yourself. I guess I learned life lessons that can be applied here. Like anything can happen anytime. You can lose, even if you've been winning all along. And it's hard to put this one into words, but don't get too solidified in your views or opinions, cause new info or experiences can really change things up. I guess we just need to be ready for anything."

No one said a word. Until Teva: "tallboy, you faced a supreme challenge and you are stronger for it. As for you then, for us today alertness is the key. May we all strive to keep our center of balance."

Emily reminded the islanders to bring their change of clothes. They answered they were ready. "The sea lion does not venture into deeper seas unprepared," said Teva.

Running down her mental checklist, Emily asked Thinks Out Loud if the rest was in place.

"It will be soon," he replied with a calm, clear voice, his gaze steady.

"My stomach hurts," admitted Chen. "Is this how it feels to go into battle?"

"I can attest to that," said Teva, briefly tapping his abdomen

"We happy few," murmured Thinks Out Loud.

"Dinner," called out my mother. We'd been so focused in the garage we didn't realize it was time to eat.

"Smells good," said Chen. He paused. "Isn't today Thanksgiving?"

We'd completely forgotten. My mother had not.

Tangerine NOV. 24, 2011 AT 10:20 AM

tallboy faced his mortality. And he did it as a youngster. My heart goes out to him.

Hummer NOV. 24, 2011 AT 10:39 AM

They are not exactly trained commandos, but they'll have to do.

SHOW MORE COMMENTS

○ ○ ○   **THINKS OUT LOUD**   ✕

WHIMSY WITHOUT REGRET

Gaining entrance

Entry No. 635 - POSTED: NOV. 25, 2011

Eddie: Black Friday. We began Operation Overboard. tallboy went to work as usual and entered without a hitch. Likewise, Angela reported for her intern duties. Ten minutes later, as Emily and I watched from across the street where we sat at a Paraguayan pastry shop's outside table, the Polynesians walked up to the AltaSystemics glassy front door. Dressed in their island ceremonial finest—colorful sarongs and plumed head bands—they gained entrance into the spare lobby and began their act.

Could the Polynesians pull this off? Unable to hear the trio, we could see them commandingly gesticulating. I thought I saw Teva do a stomp or two. They were answered with counter gesticulations coming from a growing number of AltaSystemics staff.

With the hand and body motions on both sides reaching a boiling point, Emily and I, both dressed in loose flowing white robes, rose gracefully from our seats, flowed across the street and eased into the building's lobby. By this time, several more Connectors had joined and added to the mounting imbroglio (Always wanted to use that word.). It was easy for us to apply our thumb print (actually tallboy's taped to our thumbs) and be admitted into the building proper. (Amazing what you can learn from a YouTube instructional video.)

Familiar with AltaSystemics from our earlier tour, we followed the curve of the first floor hallway to the elevator. tallboy had told us the section of the hive leading to the room holding the Morse brothers. We wanted to move quickly, though we had to maintain the calm pacing of an Intuitive. As we expected the door was guarded by two

Connectors. Pulling up our cloaks' hoods, we made our approach.

"Hold it," said a Connector. "Two Intuitives are already in the room." We nodded.

In a calm and soothing voice, Emily said, "Yes, of course, and to complete the energy flow, we need more power."

"This is the first time so many Intuitives have been called for," said the other Connector. He could have been a younger version of a Navy Seal.

"Right, and we haven't gotten the results Prime Mover is demanding," I said in the gentlest of voice. "Of course, if you'd like to have him come down and…"

"That won't be necessary," said the first Connector, and he waved his hand before the door, which opened with an air hiss and a pop.

We glided inside, the door whooshed closed behind us, and we tried to muffle our exclamations of surprise. Before us, seated at a card table were the Morse brothers and the two Intuitives—playing what looked to be a hand of poker.

"I'll see you and raise you," said one of the brothers.

"I should have seen that coming," said one of the Intuitives with mock surprise.

"That's what you said last time," teased the other brother.

Emily and I took several steps deeper into the room before both Intuitives looked away from their cards and regarded us. It was hard to see their faces with their hoods up. I guess the same could be said of Emily and me. The brothers didn't look as drugged as I expected. In fact, given their age, they were sitting up straight and following the gaze of the Intuitives toward us.

"Greetings," I said. "The time has come for the changing of the Intuitives. Prime Mover thanks you for your efforts."

The Intuitive on our right, a male, answered in the nicest of tones: "I received no message from the Prime Mover. Perhaps you are early."

"Right," I said in an equally nice voice. "But the Prime Mover has decided to shorten the sessions so that we can apply the strongest possible energies in this matter, so if you'll kindly return to your honeycomb."

"You folks sure babble a lot," said the brother at the far side of the table.

He was bald except for a ring of long white hair at the base of his head, from temple and behind to temple.

Emily and I ushered the other Intuitives toward the door, she guiding the female, me the male, who hesitated. He wanted to finish the hand. "Games relax them," he told me in a stage whisper.

"Later," I whispered back. "Time for the brothers to take a nap."

With the whoosh of the door's smooth opening and closing, the two Intuitives were gone.

"Nap?" scoffed the second brother, who sported a full gray beard. "How about some Texas Hold'em."

"Not now," I said. "I need to tell you something that's really going to raise the stakes."

LABELS: HIGH-TECH SUSPENSE, POKER TOURNAMENTS, INSIDE STRAIGHT

VIEW COMMENTS (86)

Topper NOV. 25, 2011 AT 8:40 AM
They're in! Per Teva, stay alert! Keep breathing!

FixTure NOV. 25, 2011 AT 8:48 AM
Yes, they're in. Question: How will they get out?

JoeCurr NOV. 25, 2011 AT 9:00 AM
I wanted to be an Intuitive, but I knew it wasn't going to work out.

Feeder NOV. 25, 2011 AT 9:08 AM
Wouldn't a high-tech company have scads of security cameras?

SHOW MORE COMMENTS

○ ○ ○   **THINKS OUT LOUD**   ✕

WHIMSY WITHOUT REGRET

Fatigues make the man, and woman

Entry No. 636 - POSTED: NOV. 25, 2011

tallboy: All I had wanted was gainful employment in the high-tech field, and a Samsung LED 8000 Series 65-inch TV, and a carbon endurance road bike. Now I found myself a double agent caught up in challenging a wild plot to take over space and time. I could see Prime Mover had been using me from the start as a sort of blog prop to present a false face for his bizarre startup. Or was I actually using AltaSystemics to advance in my career? Or were we using each other?

Since it's not unusual and even expected of me to wander the halls of AltaSystemics in search of blogging material, no one paid any attention as I approached the utility closet on the Basics floor. With a smooth, actually nervous, hand motion, I induced the door panel to slide open and entered the room with its rows of packed shelves along the walls and tight open space in the middle. It was like taking inventory—cleaning supplies, labeled boxes, even some old computer hardware. At the back shelf, I found what I needed: army green fatigues now worn by the Connectors. I took two sets, sized grande, and returned to the hallway where I casually continued on my way…until I got to a sharper curve in the route and came face to face with Jeannie.

"Been looking all over for you, 'boy," said my supervisor or Queen Honey Bee as she wants to be called. She eyed what I was carrying. Before I could say anything, she grabbed the clothes. "No, no, no," Jeannie admonished, "you and all of us in Communications look better in cream khaki." She stepped back and struck a modeling pose to illustrate her point, her silky khaki one-piece set off with a gold colored belt around her waist. "Trying to pass yourself off as a Connector?" She jabbed me in the ribs. "I want to see your latest posting draft in 15 minutes. And go get some better clothes." Offering her eternal smirk, she turned and lightly jogged away.

Sighing, I went back to the utility room and borrowed two more sets of fatigues. Now I was moving at a faster pace and took the back stairway up to Level Three where Angela was waiting for me at the minimalistic Hang Out room, with its glowing indirect lighting and Swedish-style sofas and chairs.

"You're late," she said. She had an appraising look in her eyes I'd never seen before.

"I got held up." I gave her one of the outfits. She retreated past the low-slung round tables and retro beach-style chairs to a corner of the room and motioned for me to do the same—at another corner.

"Don't look," she said.

I turned toward the wall and traded my street clothes for the Connector uniform. And I looked. How could I not? She was down to bra and panties. Tall and curvy.

In a tit for tat moment, no pun intended, Angela caught my eye. Actually, it was more than a catching. We locked eyes. Hasn't happened to me much, but it's when a woman, say in a room, even from the far side, looks at me, into me and we go into some kind of trance. And some kind of deep communication takes place.

Eyes locked. "I snuck a peek at you, too," she said softly. "Not bad, but our timing is off."

If I could have spoken, I would have agreed. All I could do was clear my throat and button my olive green shirt.

Now we were Connectors, at least in appearance. Side by side, we strode to the back stairs and went down to Level Two. The hallway was empty, except for the two Connectors at the entrance to the brothers' room. Remembering to breathe, thank you, Teva, I stopped before them, Angela beside me, both of us stern-faced.

"You are relieved," I said in my firmest voice as I tried to copy the blank expression of the guards.

"I don't think so," said the Connector closest to me.

"No, really," said Angela as she leaned forward. "You boys need a break, a chance to stretch those big muscles."

"Well," said the second Connector, rubbing his neck, "I am getting stiff."

"Go, relax, have a snack," said Angela with hint of a lilt in her voice. "We just started our shift."

The first Connector remained hesitant. "But we didn't receive official notification for this."

Angela was in great form. "Do you need permission for everything, or can you think for yourselves a little bit. Didn't the Academy teach you about taking initiative in the field?"

The Connectors both scratched their heads. "Sure, sure," said one. "C'mon, Kip."

As they disappeared around the curve of the hallway, Angela and I waited a few more seconds before opening the door. As if on cue, the Connectors came back; with a quick hand motion, I shut the door. I just caught a glimpse of Eddie and Emily straining to look toward me.

"Quick break," I said.

The Connectors were serious. "You," he pointed at me. "What's the password?"

It seemed as if it took forever for me to say something. I looked at two cold sets of eyes. "Well, actually, the password changed when we started our shift," I said as Angela slipped behind the two. "It's now *Venison*."

They pressed toward me. "Okay," said one. "What was the old password?"

I held out a hand in a friendly gesture and slid it before the door's entrance sensor. The panel opened, Angela lunged at the backs of the Connectors, and I reached out to pull them forward and into the room. The four of us ended up on the hard, white floor. I managed to yell a 'help' out to Emily and Eddie, who jumped into the pile. Everyone was grabbing everyone, but we had strength in numbers.

"About time you got here," said Eddie as he and Angela held down one of guards, Emily and I the other. They continued to struggle and curse us.

"Gentlemen," said Eddie to the brothers, "do you see any rope or thick chord?" Staring at us as if we were invading aliens, they didn't move from near the whiteboard. "Really," Eddie continued, "these are the bad guys. We need to tie them up."

The brothers said something to each other about the war days and began searching the room. Nothing. They came over to us, the two Connectors still trying to break free. One brother knelt down beside each Connector. A well-placed judo chop at the base of each connector's head and they were unconscious.

"That'll have to do," I said. "Grab your things. Let's get out of here." Then I added, "Wait a sec. Let's erase your work on the white board."

LABELS: HIGH FASHION, SURPRISE ENTRANCES, MARTIAL ARTS

VIEW COMMENTS (90)

DexTerra NOV. 25, 2011 AT 9:19;8 AM
Timing is everything. Or maybe in this case, everything is timing.

HandyMan NOV. 25, 2011 AT 9:47 AM
Would love to help! Slapping a strip of duct tape over the bad guys' oral cavities would do the trick.

SHOW MORE COMMENTS

Islanders crash the party

Entry No. 637 - POSTED: NOV. 25, 2011

Kohia: Readers, I wish to post. We do not often present a false face to others. However, to help our friends, we did so. Like sly eels we slid around the big glassy greeting room and forcefully said we were ready for our tour. Teva stood with legs boldly apart. Vaitiare never looked colder or haughtier. The attendant tried to be nice to us with a polite smile, but the scent of fear was upon her. When she could not find a record of our engagement after looking two or three times, she called for others who appeared in groups of twos and threes.

Teva actually seemed to have fun as he puffed himself up with more and more supposed frustration. He said this poor attention was "an affront to the Peoples of Polynesia." Vaitiare and I also offered looks of cold stone. "We have traveled thousands of miles to see this company," Teva continued. "Our leaders will be most distressed." Workers dressed in white tried to calm us down. Others in pale green uniforms looked as if they wanted to bite us.

"What's going on here?" We heard a gruff voice before we saw the speaker, a short but well-dressed man pushing his way through the crowd of employees. He walked like a chief with his head up and his chest out. Everyone parted for him.

He came face to face with us, except we were all looking down at him. "I am Prime Mover, and you are?"

We introduced ourselves and again said we were here for the tour. The Greeter spoke softly to her leader and said there was no tour listed on the day's activity list.

"All the way from Polynesia?" Prime Mover studied us. "Well, we do not want to disappoint you. Welcome to AltaSystemics." Transforming his posture from defensive to more welcoming, he then told his staff he would personally lead the tour. "Now I understand," Prime Mover said in a softer voice. "Follow me, please, and let me show you AltaSystemics," he said to us as he turned and walked quickly to a glowing closed door. He placed his hand over a flat screen, and the door slid open. "Right this way. It really is a pleasure to have you here," he said becoming more conversational. I believe 'charming' is the word that would now describe his new presence. He was asking us about our travel experience and how was the weather back home and mentioning how he loved *Mutiny on the Bounty*.

"Sir, would you like us to join you?" asked one of the serious men dressed in green.

"No need, no need," said Prime Mover and we followed him into a curving hallway. "Nice headdress," he said to Teva.

We were in…but Vaitiare whispered, "That was too easy."

LABELS: COMPANY TOURS, HIGH-TECH SECRECY, INTERNATIONAL RELATIONS

VIEW COMMENTS (91)

RepoMan NOV. 25, 2011 AT 10:05 AM
Oh, come on, I wouldn't trust Prime Mover even if he had been ingesting his own hard candies.

Belle NOV. 25, 2011 AT 10:33 AM
He is social and he does like to promote his company. Perhaps we judge him too harshly.

SHOW MORE COMMENTS

○ ○ ○   **THINKS OUT LOUD**   ✕

WHIMSY WITHOUT REGRET

Delivery boy

Entry No. 638 - POSTED: NOV. 25, 2011

Chen: Dressed like a pizza delivery guy, which is to say I was in faded jeans and a plaid shirt, I waited outside AltaSystemics a couple of minutes after the Polynesians started their bogus tour. Huge brown (compostable) pizza box in hand, I made my entrance.

"May I help you?" asked the Greeter with a false smile and still recovering from the Polinesian episode. She was dressed like a lab technician, which I identified with.

"Delivery for the Morse brothers," I said cheerily.

The Greeter looked away and back at me. "I'm afraid there's been some kind of mistake," she said as she re-checked her computer screen, her hands visibly shaking. "They are receiving all of their meals in-house."

I paused a moment for comic timing. "Maybe that's why they ordered this large AGOG with mushrooms, roasted garlic, goat cheese, Kalamata olives, fontina, mozzarella and parsley on olive oil with tomatoes after bake," I said reciting from memory of when I actually did delivery for Pagliacci—the 'G' is silent.

This wasn't the Greeter's day. She was like a computer program on its way to crashing. Her angular face unlined, she even sort of looked like an avatar image.

"Just buzz me through, tell me their room number, and I'll bring them the best pizza in town."

She tapped some letters on the keyboard and then touched a communication button. "Morse brothers," she said, "did you order a pizza?" I thought I heard the sound of muffled fast-moving steps and some whispered jumbled words from the speaker next to the Greeter's computer.

"Yes, yes, thank you," a voice finally said.

Somehow Greeter had regained her composure. "Fine," she said. "Oh, and let me check with the delivery person to see if he brought the right pizza. Which one did you order?"

After a short silence, a garbled answer came back. It could have been any mixed-up sound, like "Glphml."

"I'll need to have a Connector escort you."

"My pleasure," I said when this buff dreamboat in olive combat greens joined us.

"I'm Chen," I said, "and you're?" Without a word, my own personal guard led me to the entrance of the Morse brothers' room. Checking left and right, seeing no other Connectors, he went into high alert.

"Stay where you are," he ordered as he approached the closed entrance panel with the stealthy grace of a wild panther.

I followed silently.

He swished the door open to reveal an almost absurd scene: tallboy and Angela energetically erasing the number-filled whiteboard, Emily and

Eddie standing over two seemingly sleeping Connectors, and the Morse brothers playing cards.

"What's going on here?" my escort demanded as he went into some kind of kung-fu defense. Charming.

Everyone looked at him but no one said anything. tallboy caught my eye and titled his head toward our adversary. Did he want me to go into kung-fu mode as well? I shook my head. tallboy thrust his head forward more directly. I shrugged my shoulders. He torqued his head.

Aha! I charged the Connector, crunched into his muscled body, and pushed him into the room where he was grabbed and restrained by the group. One of the Morse brothers put down his cards, came over and gave the poor guy a sharp chop.

"Pizza anyone?" I asked. The empty box prop lay on the floor.

"Later," said Eddie. "It really is time to take the next step."

"What about the Connectors?" Emily asked as she pointed to the knocked-out guards.

I scanned the room. There they were stretched out in front of the whiteboard. "We'll feed them these," I said as I walked over and grabbed a handful of the AltaSystemics special edition candies. "Then the Connectors won't care where they are or about us."

tallboy and Angela helped me prop up the guards one by one and force feed them the candies that would keep them sedated. Emily looked upset about something.

"Okay, now we go," Eddie said again. Looking at the Morse brothers as we snuck into the hallway he added, "By the way, why aren't you two under the influence of those candies?"

"Apparently we were," said the bearded brother. "One-day tallboy warned us to stop eating them. He said they were bad for our teeth."

"Bravo, tallboy," said Angela as she gave his shoulder a playful punch. His face reddened and for a moment he looked like a cute five-year-old.

"Where to?" I asked.

"This way," Eddie said as he pointed down the curving corridor. He grouped us so that it looked as if tallboy and Angela in their Connector uniforms were leading the rest of us "to a meeting with Prime Mover."

I know this is serious business. Could I help it if I were having fun?

LABELS: PIZZA DELIVERY, BODY LANGUAGE, ESCAPE ARTISTS

VIEW COMMENTS (91)

MasterMind NOV. 25, 2011 AT 11:20 AM
If you apply a Critical Theory critique of negative dialectics to the rise and influence of AltaSystemics, it becomes quite evident that Progress in the form of the company's services is an example of corporate control of mind, body and spirit.

Carroty NOV. 25, 2012 AT 11:37 AM
They better work fast.

SHOW MORE COMMENTS

○ ○ ○   **THINKS OUT LOUD**   ✕

WHIMSY WITHOUT REGRET

Shadowland

Entry No. 639 - POSTED: NOV. 25, 2011

Thinks Out Loud: Lost and found in deep, dark places, such as this dank subterranean vault, not unlike the cave I knew on Tiaré.

Again I await a sign. Again I will rise as if from slumber and advance with a power I never knew I had within me. Or so I hope.

A faint light will direct me, us. In the meantime, I am free to wander among my memories. The blogging era (error?). Travels. Reaching the islands (luck? fate?). Struggle and rebirth. A teller of tales.

Vaitiare. I know she wonders where the 'me' she first knew has gone. I am still here sharing myself with my newer (older?) me. I am still a work in progress.

In some ways you could you say this situation is all my fault. Perhaps not fault but certainly the result of my actions, both premeditated and accidental, leading to an unexpected chain of events that brings us to this pivotal now. Therefore, I must not falter, not this time. Not with what is at stake. Things matter.

For the moment, though, I sit amidst darkness. And wait.

LABELS: STRATEGIES, ART OF WAITING

○ ○ ○ **THINKS OUT LOUD** ✕

WHIMSY WITHOUT REGRET

Back in the belly

Entry No. 640 - POSTED: NOV. 25, 2011

Eddie: With dramatic, tempo-quickening, volume-swelling Bondsian invasion-of-the-villain's-lair music playing in my head, at least I thought it was in my head until Emily nudged me and did a 'shhh,' we made our way along deserted hallways—coming across only two Sensates who barely noticed us through their meditative haze.

It seemed too quiet, but we continued to advance, the Morse brothers moving within the protective huddle of our bodies. When we reached the lower inner sanctum and stood before the entrance that would lead into the Hive's main energy room, we paused.

"See anyone?" I asked. Was the whole company on break?

tallboy leaned back and said, "No one behind us."

Emily carefully followed the hallway beyond our stopping point. "All clear," she whispered.

"Then in we go," Angela said crisply, sounding more and more like a secret agent with each passing minute.

tallboy performed his fluid hand wave, the door panel slid open and the hum of the power room massaged us as we slipped inside. We shielded our eyes against the glare of lights coming at us from all directions. Then I remembered Prime Mover's command the time he brought us down here.

"Lights, half power," I ordered. The lights dimmed.

287

"Look at these dials," Chen said as he pointed to a panel of blinking lights and meters. "I'm not certain, but it looks as if there's a lot of energy being generated around here."

"Right," said tallboy. "My next blog was going to be about how AltaSystemics is repurposing composting to create electrical power for the building. They are also capturing rain water for toilet use."

"There's a lot more than electrical power pulsating through this room," I said as I studied other readout panels. The Morse brothers seemed mesmerized. Angela guarded the door.

Emily called me over to the geometrically complex CenterSphere, ground zero of AltaSystemics. "Should we blow it right now?" she asked but with a degree of hesitation.

"I didn't bring any explosives, did you?" Bond would have all the firepower he needed for his mission hidden in his belt, tie clasp, or shoelaces.

She knew I hadn't. "But we could disable it," she continued.

Angela made a muffled sound and we turned to see a stern Connector holding her from behind, his hand covering her mouth. In the next instant, the Polynesians were being forced into the chamber by a squad of the guards. Almost anticlimactically, a silver-suited Prime Mover made his way past both parties and addressed us: "As they say in B-movies, 'We meet again.'"

I could feel Emily, tallboy and Chen tensing for battle. "Wait," I said to my friends as I hovered over the CenterSphere.

"Don't come any closer, Prime Mover," I said, my hand placed above a glowing red button, "or this room is history."

He laughed. He laughed in that stupid, insipid way that villains have always laughed. "Go ahead, press the damn button and see what happens. . ."

I slammed down on the button…a delay and then the sound of the room's vent fans whirring to a stop.

His Connectors herded all of us into a vacant spot near a lesser group of readout screens and blinking lights. I could see Teva was restraining himself and actually managing to make his body look smaller and weaker than it was. Angela had also gone passive. The poor Morse brothers looked uncomfortable and slightly put upon as they stood between Emily and tallboy.

Prime Mover was in fine form as he strutted about the room. "Did you think I was unaware of your feeble machinations? My surveillance cameras have been following your every move. I admit that tallboy's erasing and rewriting of the Morse brothers' formulas has slowed down my efforts to gain their time travel information, but I have had to be patient to draw you out—to reach this divine moment."

As if on cue, in walked Jeannie, dressed head to foot in a tight red high-fashion outfit. "Sorry, I'm late, darling," she said addressing Prime Mover. "I had to freshen up for our guests." She actually sneered at Angela who sneered right back. tallboy tried to move toward Angela but was held back by the two Connectors at his side.

"Quite all right, my dear," Prime Mover answered. "I was just explaining how amateurish the attempts of our friends here have been to try to, how shall I say it, to restrain us."

"You don't know everything," hissed Chen and immediately Emily shouted, "No, Chen!"

"Oh, but I do, I do," Prime Mover said. "I'm a loyal reader of your blog, Thinks Out Loud, have been since before I hired tallboy. How do you think I found out about the Morse brothers, by the way, and how do you like my screen name: Etruscan?" He stopped, pivoted and faced Chen. "Anything you want to add, young man?"

Chen pushed out his chin. "You'll never get away with this. Even if we fail, others will take our place."

"I doubt that, Scooby Doo." Prime Mover almost did a tap dance step he was in such a good mood. "A good many of your blog readers think this is fiction, a good read, but not possibly true."

The portal opened and two Sensates entered, one holding a large ceramic bowl, the other with a case of bottled water.

"Ah, I would not be the proper host if I didn't offer a little refreshment," Prime Mover said as he motioned for the Sensates to deposit the items before him.

"We're not thirsty," Emily growled. Prime Mover ignored her impoliteness.

"Actually, I do want to give you a choice," he said to all of us. "Heretofore you have been a proverbial thorn in my side, not that you haven't made the game more interesting. So, here's my offer, for I do respect your taking initiative in a cause you believe in." He bent down, placed his hand in the bowl and retrieved a handful of his signature candies. "Join with me as we take the next step in our evolution, a linkage to the multidimensional universe and the time vortex. Join with me and go beyond the mere human and transcend our physical limitations. Or..." Prime Mover paused and turned his hand. The candies, like sands in an hourglass, flowed back into the container. "Or, well, you know the effect of these fine treats, yes?"

"No way," Chen said.

Prime Mover acknowledged the comment with a raised eyebrow. "Why am I not surprised?" he asked. "Do you all feel this way?"

We murmured yeses. The Polynesians didn't exactly answer. They simply acted as though none of this concerned them.

With a simple hand motion, almost as if he were bored, Prime Mover pointed toward Angela and the two Connectors who now restrained her. She put up a good defense and was not easily dragged toward the bucket where a calm Sensate pulled on a pair of thin latex gloves.

"Bon appetit," said Prime Mover as he stepped away from the axis of activity. I caught Emily's eye. A dozen feet to my left, she gave the subtlest of nods and jerked free from her single guard. Adding a war yelp, Teva sprang into action and immediately the two Connectors nearest him were on the floor.

I expected Prime Mover to act concerned. Instead, he continued to seem bored. With a touch of his finger on a control panel, the main portal again opened and in charged another group of Connectors. Four tackled Teva. The rest helped the Connectors already in the room to re-establish control.

"Angela, you are no longer an intern at AtlaSystemics. You have broken our bond of trust, although I did enjoy the improv classes." Prime Mover had turned impatient, as though all the games were now over. "Give her the candies," he ordered and headed toward the exit panel. "Candy for all of them. Sweet dreams. C'mon, babe." He practically dragged Jeannie from the room. "Oh, and let's bring the Morse brothers, as well." A Connector each grabbed a brother and began to escort them from our midst. "No, wait," added Prime Mover, interrupting himself. "They also stay, for the sweets, but of a lesser degree."

As if he were having trouble leaving all this fun, Prime Mover leaned back into the room. "On second thought, or is it the third?, start with the big Polynesian."

The Connectors released Angela and went for Teva, who, surprisingly, didn't resist.

"Hey," said one of the Connectors as they led Teva to the bowl, "a martyr."

We were again under the control of Prime Mover. The brief turmoil, however, had allowed me to send a timely text message, at least I hoped it was in time. No answer came back. Maybe coverage didn't reach down that far. That would indicate bad planning on our part.

LABELS: ARCH VILLAINS, 007, HOLDING PATTERN

VIEW COMMENTS (94)

Spirit NOV. 25, 2011 AT 12:25 PM
Prime Mover holds all the cards. Or at least a winning hand.

HindSight NOV. 25, 2011 AT 12:39 PM
I knew PM would prevail. Sometimes good doesn't win.

JustIn NOV. 25, 2011 AT 12:54 PM
He does seem confident.

SHOW MORE COMMENTS

○ ○ ○   **THINKS OUT LOUD**   ✕
WHIMSY WITHOUT REGRET

Cavalry Time?

Entry No. 641 - POSTED: NOV. 25, 2011

Thinks Out Loud: *Ping.* One word: Now.

Focus. In the near darkness, I motioned for Hank, now first mate of the repaired Bogsworth. "*Forword.* Let's do it," I said. Hank clicked his flashlight on and off to signal his crewmates. Twenty brawny men, mostly in black, all here thanks to Hank and his desire to make things right after my ambiguous departure from their storm-tossed ship. He'd contacted me when the freighter had docked in Seattle.

Two of the huskier mates charged the old wooden door and in unison, like battering rams, they shredded the door and fell into a clammy and dimly lit hallway.

"We're in," Hank said. "Which way?"

tallboy had provided me with a crumpled drawing of AltaSystemics' layout. "Right. Should be a stairway not far from here," I said.

Pay attention to the here and now, I reminded myself as our group infiltrated the building. No one had been down here for decades since this level had become part of underground Seattle. Pushing through cobwebs, sliding on muck and breathing stale air, we reached the stairway or what was left of it—rotten wood planks, chipped brick walls, and the stairs angled, like a ship in storm.

"Men, let's do this one at a time," Hank suggested. He went first. I heard wood creaking and then cracking as he climbed. Then a pause. "I'm at the top. There's another door. It's jammed. Finch, Eduardo—I need your services again, mates."

With remarkable agility the two vaulted up the rickety stairs and applied themselves to the door. I heard two grunts and the sound of bodies thudding into thick wood. That must hurt, I thought.

"I'll help," I heard Hank say followed by an even louder thudding, followed by a combination of personal and inanimate objects groaning, a moment of pure silence and and a crash and a smash of a dense wood mass falling over and striking floorboards. Dust like falling snow wafted down to the rest of us.

"Now we're really in," called Hank. "Come on up!"

With each climber, the stairs groaned louder and louder. A wiry fellow made it halfway up and that was it—the stairs or what was left of them collapsed. Those of us still below jumped back as pieces of wood and the climber tumbled down.

"Everyone okay?" Hank yelled.

"Yes," I coughed. "By any chance do you have any rope?"

"We do!" said a shadow of Hank looking down at us. "We're taking this mission seriously. I mean there really is a mastermind guy here we've got to deal with, right?"

Hank fed us the rope, which we used to make the ascent.

"Actually, I've never met the fellow," I said, "although through the postings I caught up on, I feel I would recognize him at an improv show."

I reached Hank, who was steadying the rope. "What are you talking about?" he asked.

"Not important," I said, looking at the map again. "Down this hallway; we're getting close."

"Attack positions," Hank said in a stage whisper. "A lot of us guys are vets," he said to me. "Or former inmates."

In single file, we snaked down the hall, two scouts before us, signaling with a blinking light to keep coming.

"Hey, Thinks Out Loud," came a voice with a New Jersey accent from behind me. "Sorry about how we might have treated you back during the storm. No hard feelings, right?" How could I explain to him that my falling, or being pushed, into the sea is what led to all that came after—my solitary challenges on that island, my rescue and new life on Tiaré, and even this current assault against the mysterious Prime Mover.

The scouts rejoined us and pointed down the passageway. Two guards stood outside what we assumed was our target. "Get 'em," said Hank and four of our men stalked their quarry. Two went high two went low, and the guards went over. The rest of us moved up to the door panel. Hank gave another signal, and our two battering rams heaved into the door panel, which literally crumpled under the onslaught. Hank and I were the first to enter. For a moment the scene before us looked frozen—surrounding the rest of our team, more guards, two of them trying to force something down Teva's throat. With a vibrant shout, our men poured into the room, the guards shifting into defensive postures.

LABELS: ATTACK POSTURE, POWER OF SURPRISE, POWER OF APOLOGY

VIEW COMMENTS (95)

Ringside NOV. 25, 2011 AT 1:49 PM
They're in, well almost in, but they're in enough.

Can't we all just solve our problems peacefully with respect toward each other?

SHOW MORE COMMENTS

○ ○ ○   **THINKS OUT LOUD**   ✕

WHIMSY WITHOUT REGRET

Fisticuffs

Entry No. 642 - POSTED: NOV. 25, 2011

Eddie: Teva was swallowing the drug-candies by the mouthful with no apparent ill effect. His stern-faced captors actually looked down his throat to see if he were sneaking the candies out of his mouth like a magician. In response he smiled broadly and said, "More, please."

That enraged the Connectors. One was about to strike Teva across the face when the CenterSphere's door shattered like safety glass. Thinks Out Loud and his band of merchant mariners plowed in, as we had hoped they would. After a moment of shock, the Connectors locked into classic battle position.

Our men charged. With a piercing war cry, Teva erupted and floored the two guards next to him as if they were flimsy mannequins. All of us from the room joined in the attack. tallboy tackled a guard. Emily jumped on the fallen guard's back. Vaitiare and Kohia double teamed another guard who seemed stunned that women were willing to belt him. Thinks Out Loud, wiry and strong from his island days, was dancing before a befuddled guard. Chen was striking out in all directions as he tried to access a control panel. Angela, not to my surprise, was using martial arts moves on a guard. And I was wrestling with a grunting adversary who was cursing me as we tumbled about. In every corner of the room, up against light panels and other pieces of equipment, our team was making headway—until heavy footsteps vibrated the floor, and a wave of more Connectors entered the fray. We were out of reinforcements. Even the Morse brothers had disappeared.

I felt a surge within me, a jolt of energy I'd never experienced before. This was not gaming, not Mortal Combat—it was Real Combat. I actually had my adversary on the floor, his breathing deep yet fast, and was raising my hand to strike a hard blow when I felt fingers gripping my wrist. It was Emily. "No," was all she said. She joined me in a straddle over the fellow. He was about my age, maybe a little older, with cold, expressionless eyes and a hard smile, the kind of smile I'd once seen when facing a competitive pitcher in a city softball tournament, a look that said, "I've got you."

The seamen tried to stand their ground but were outnumbered. As the Connectors gained the upper hand, our men were pushed toward the walls. Teva was now dealing with four attackers, but how long could he keep fighting?

From out the corner of my eye, I detected movement near the busted door. Like two ancient cowboys, the Morse brothers were herding a group of unfocused Sensates into the room. They were even whoopin' and 'yee-hawing' as they directed the dreamy gaggle in the direction of the Connectors. The last thing I saw before my foe upended Emily and me was the Morse brothers guiding the Sensates into the backs of the Connectors. Over I went. The guard was atop me now, and there was no one to stop his fist from meeting my chin. I saw stars. Groggy and with half opened eyes, I could do nothing as he batted away a screaming Emily. He actually seemed to be enjoying this. Everyone in the room was moving in slow motion. Then he was gone. Teva. He helped me up. "Thanks," I said as two more Connectors rushed us. Using his arms like war sticks, he batted both of them away.

"Go find this Prime Mover," he said to me as he turned to face another guard. I'd completely forgotten about our target. With the Sensates bumping into and confusing the Connectors, our guys had a chance to rebound and regain the initiative.

I called over to tallboy, "Isn't it time for you to pay Prime Mover a visit after the way he used you?"

Pushing against a Connector, tallboy deftly sprang back. The Connector, inertia with him, jerked forward and struck a metal panel—hard.

"Right," tallboy answered. He, in turn, called for Angela, who had just dispatched a foe with a powerful leg thrust.

"Where to?" she asked, as she adjusted her shirt.

"We have a date with Prime Mover."

"Definitly not a date, but I hope his current flame is with him," Angela said as they backed out of the room and into the corridor.

"Let's take 'em mates!" yelled Hank, rallying the troops.

Pivoting over a prostrate Sensate, I rolled into the side of the nearest Connector, deflating his abdomen (a whoosh of air escaped from his mouth) and letting him trip over the Sensate.

At a long, wide control panel in a raised section back and center of the room, Chen, his face lit from the bottom by glowing dials like a flashlight on Halloween, urged me to join him. "Pay dirt, I think," he said, just before a Connector grabbed him from behind and yanked him away.

"Teva," I yelled above the din, "help Chen—he hit pay dirt...he's caught a fish of large proportions."

LABELS: BLOW BY BLOW, FIGHT SCENES, WHEN PUSH COMES TO SHOVE

VIEW COMMENTS (96)

Peligroso NOV. 25, 2011 AT 3:15 PM
A high-stakes brawl!

Anonymous NOV. 25, 2011 AT 3:28 PM
Am new to this blog. What is going on? Is this some kind of movie script?

SHOW MORE COMMENTS

○ ○ ○   THINKS OUT LOUD   ✕

WHIMSY WITHOUT REGRET

Ground zero

Entry No. 643 - POSTED: NOV. 25, 2011

Eddie: As the fighting continued, I crawled more than walked to where I'd last seen Chen before he got yanked from the control panel. Vaulting past me went Teva to offer his help. By the time I'd reached them, Teva was crouching and lunging and shouting and keeping four Connectors on the defensive. His one-man-army ferocity allowed me to pull the fallen Chen back to the panel.

"What did you discover?" I asked.

Chen's lip was bleeding. He wiped at it with his arm. "I think this is the amplification unit that concentrates the powers of the Sensates and allows for greater storage in that other dimension or wherever the information goes."

"Right," I said. "Whatever."

"I think I can neutralize it. I don't know what will happen to the Sensates, though, when the connection is broken." Chen's hands hovered over two glowing dials.

"We don't have time to analyze this."

Chen had just touched the dials when one of the Connectors fighting Teva squeezed by him and leaped at us. Chen flew one way, I the other. Dazed and looking up, I saw the Connector had actually landed face down on the panel. Raising my head from the floor, I heard hissings and poppings and saw sparks shooting up from the panel. I forced myself to rise and practically fell over the fallen Connector. He was literally on top of the malfunctioning unit.

"Roll him off." It was Emily from a corner of the room. She'd taken some blows and was holding her stomach.

With a groan, I pushed the guy to the floor just as the panel in front of me caught fire. Within seconds smoke was billowing up, flames licking at the length of the couch-long panel. The overhead lights started flickering. I backed up as sprinklers came on, but they had no effect on the electrical fire. "We need an exit strategy," I thought or even said aloud as a piercing alarm sounded.

*   *   *

tallboy: Angela and I reached Prime Mover's office and were surprised when a pass of my hand over the door panel's electric eye allowed us entry.

"Too easy," Angela whispered as we crept inside. Some soft non-descript world percussion music was playing. I went right, Angela left. Within seconds we realized the room was empty. I even looked under PM's desk.

"Not here," Angela confirmed. "Where to?" We turned to leave but I paused.

"This *is* too easy," I said, standing at the entrance. "Wait."

I re-entered the room, looped behind Prime Mover's desk, and scanned the row of buttons on a black plastic strip. I started pressing them. The music got louder, softer, the room's lights brighter, darker. And then the floor on the desk's other side parted and up rose the burgundy egg-shaped chairs. And in one of those chairs sat a hunched PM with Jeannie on his lap.

Angela gasped and laughed simultaneously.

Prime Mover used his hands on each side of Jeannie to help her up. He stood as well and pulled at his silver suit as if were about to make an entrance to a gala affair. "Well, well," he said. "We meet again, again."

With a quick glance and hint of a nod, I warned Angela to watch out for a gun. I in turn was poised to upturn and flip the desk at PM if I saw the vaguest hint of a weapon.

"tallboy, I'm impressed. Angela, you also," said Prime Mover, taking a step forward. "As I said, I like initiative. I like the bold move. I like you two." I thought I heard Jeannie say something derogatory. "Tell you what, how would both of you like to be part of the AltaSystemics Leadership Circle?" He held out his hands palms up, as if offering us the world.

"Sounds interesting," Angela said as she eased back into the room. She was now closest to Jeannie, who looked at her with tightening eyes. "Tell us more."

Prime Mover became all cheery and friendly and took one more step toward the desk. "Sure," he said, as he became a blur, kicking the desk into me, pinning me against the wall. He pivoted, grabbed Jeannie, and shoved her into Angela. Before we could react, PM sped out the door, which snapped shut behind him. A moment later a painfully loud alarm went off.

That's trouble, I thought as I pushed the desk away and ran to the door. It took a long second to open. Out of the corner of my eye, I saw Angela and Jeannie wrestling on the floor, but I didn't have time to offer Angela aid. Looking in both directions of the curving hallway, I had to decide which way PM had gone.

LABELS: HIDE AND SEEK, TRUST IS JUST A WORD

VIEW COMMENTS (97)

RepoMan NOV. 25, 2011 AT 3:48 PM
Warned you—didn't I warn everyone about Prime Mover when he first appeared in the blog...

FixTure NOV. 25, 2011 AT 3:52 PM
Hello! People, there's a fire breaking out!

SHOW MORE COMMENTS

Where there's smoke

Entry No. 644 - POSTED: NOV. 25, 2011

Eddie: Smoke, fire, alarms. It was hard to think. And breathe. A coughing Emily crawled over to me.

"We've got to get out of here!" she gasped. As if on cue, another panel burst into flame.

Not waiting for my command, Hank boomed, "Abandon ship!" and began marshaling his stumbling men toward the exit. Disengaging from the battle, the Connectors were also scrambling toward the door. The poor Sensates seemed more dazed than ever and were drifting in slow circles. The rest of our group were also pressing to leave.

"Teva," I shouted among the general tumult and confusion, "grab a Connector!" Despite the smoke, he charged the door and collared the nearest one like it was a lost puppy. A dangerous puppy. I got Thinks Out Loud and Chen to help me collect the Sensates. Sheep. Lost sheep.

"Keep one of those sheep with us," I said. Chen gave me a quizzical look. TOL just nodded.

"The Sensates. Make sure we have one," I shouted.

Emily grabbed onto the brothers. They held their hands over their mouths and chivalrously insisted Emily leave first.

As we squeezed out of the chamber, Hank was waiting, directing everyone down the corridor. I was twenty feet beyond the door when an explosion threw us to the floor. A surge of flame shot out of the room and chased us along the curving hallway.

Running, feeling rising heat behind us, we stopped as a group and stared down at a broken stairway and a dark floor below. Too much happening to compare to the obligatory-end-of-Bond-film-destruction-of-villain's-headquarters, which I guess I just did.

"No choice: Jump or burn," Thinks Out Loud said.

*   *   *

tallboy: Left or right—which way had Prime Mover gone? I voted for right, an easier, time-saving turn for the escaping PM to make. The pulsating alarm made it hard to think. I was leaving Angela and Jeannie fighting in PM's office but had no choice. As I followed the curve of the hallway, I thudded into someone. No. Two someones, Vaitiare and Kohia. "Keep going," I told them. "Go help Angela." I pointed from where I'd come, saw them nod, and was off again.

He wouldn't take the elevator, not with that alarm going. Had to get to the stairs, which I reached only to be thrown to the floor when the whole building shook. I momentarily thought it an earthquake, but that alarm told me otherwise. I fell more than ran down the metal stairs and reached the main floor—and main exit. A quick sprint brought me to the front desk where the confused Greeter was asking what was going on.

"Did Prime Mover come this way?" I demanded as I barely slowed down.

Looking nervously in all directions and holding her smart phone with both hands, she answered, "He just ran by me and left the building." Then, perhaps out of loyalty she reversed herself. "Actually, I think he went to our Recognition Room to make sure our awards are undamaged."

"Sure," I said as I headed toward the exit. "You better get out right away. And use your PA to tell everyone to leave right now!"

Flying through the door, I jerked to a stop at the entrance to the stone building and scanned the streets. Nothing but late afternoon traffic. Then I saw a glint of silver bouncing between other pedestrians on the sidewalk a half block away. I followed. From behind came a low rumble and more shaking. In the distance I heard sirens—fire engines trying to cleave through the rush hour mess to get here.

While running I texted Eddie but couldn't look down at my phone and keep my eye on the silver streak at the same time. He moved surprisingly fast: Out of Pioneer Square, sliding over to 1st (and crossing the street against the light, a Seattle no-no) and in the general direction of Pike Place Market. Slowly gaining on the silver figure, I realized my friends would have to take care of themselves.

LABELS: GOT GAME, FOLLOW THE LEADER, BURNING QUESTIONS

VIEW COMMENTS (96)

TeaTimer NOV. 25, 2011 AT 4:20 PM

I'm actually sympathetic to Prime Mover. He is trying to bring a dream into reality. And look how unappreciative these rebellious immature youngsters are!

Hummer NOV. 25, 2011 AT 4:30 PM

TeaTimer, you little troll. You're probably one of Prime Mover's mentally challenged Connectors.

Seattlebred NOV. 25, 2011 AT 4:44 PM

The thing about Pioneer Square, the buildings are old, a lot of brick and stone. It was the hardest hit area in the 2001 Nisqually Quake (6.8).

SHOW MORE COMMENTS

Actions and reactions

Entry No. 645 - POSTED: NOV. 25, 2011

Vaitiare: Readers, I shall speak. Kohia and I followed the curving hallway until we reached an office from which groans and shouts were coming. Inside we saw overturned furniture. In the room's center, Angela sat atop a seething Jeannie, that opportunistic woman, her hands pinned against the floor.

"Angela," I said as Kohia and I approached the fighters, "we must leave the building."

"Yes, run away, run away," shouted the pinned woman.

"*All* of us must go," Kohia said. "And now."

Angela nodded and began to rise. Not unexpectedly, Jeannie took this opportunity to try and escape. Kohia and I were ready for her move and were there to grab her. "We will escort you out," I said. Our restrained adversary gave us a withering look.

We felt the building shake again.

"Run!" I shouted and added, "Woman of the Prime Mover, it would be in your best interests to make peace with us."

"I don't think so, not after the way I've been treated by all of you," she answered as we charged down the hallway and found the stairway leading down.

"Prime Mover used you just like he did everyone else," Angela said to Jeannie as we ran down the stairs. "Wait," Angela added as we reached the main floor. We could smell smoke. She pointed upward at the honeycomb design. "There may be Sensates in the Recharging Cells." She turned back toward the stairs.

"The what?" I asked trailing behind her.

"Where they sleep and rest. Fancy name for a dormitory."

She was correct. We could not leave innocent people to perish. Kohia and I followed Angela back up the stairs, even as rumblings deep in the building continued to remind us of the destruction heading our way.

"Fuckin' A, I'll come too," our adversary said from behind us.

*   *   *

Thinks Out Loud: Heat and flame chasing us from above, friend and foe intermixed, we carried each other through the basement. The jump from the upper floor had led to sprained legs or other bruises. I couldn't see Eddie but heard him yell: "Teva, hold on to that Connector." More explosions came from above. Walls around us cracked, the floor shifted. When we reached the opening to underground Seattle, it was blocked by fallen posts. People shined their cell phones as flashlights on the close quarters.

"Either we work together or none of us gets out," I said.

We quickly split into groups of four and six and pushed and tugged at the beams. "C'mon, mates," yelled Hank, "heave to!"

Another explosion rocked the building. With a simultaneous groan, a half-dozen of us loosened a post enough to create a narrow space to squeeze through. Once on the other side, Hank and his men helped pull the rest of us to safety. The stale, dirty air of the underground passageway had never smelled better.

"This way," I said as the exhausted group moved away from whatever was left of AltaSystemics. We retraced the steps Hank, his men, and I had used. As we rounded a corner in the near dark, we ran into another body of people. The Underground Seattle Tour. "Didn't you hear the explosions? Do not go any further," I warned them." The flustered tour guide tried to ask us what was going on, but he and his group were swept up in our retreat.

"Here's the stairway!" Hank pointed to the steps back to street level. One by one we ascended the wooden stairs leading to open air. And a chaotic scene. Coughing, groaning, we—our group, Hank's crew, Sensates, Connectors, and the tourists—stood on the sidewalk and looked in the direction of AltaSystemics, two blocks away. We could see smoke lofting skyward. And we heard multiple sirens.

Eddie hopped up to me. "I got a text from tallboy, but it doesn't make sense. It says, 'hating 2 margret.'"

Perhaps it was some kind of code.

"I think he means 'Heading to Market," said Emily. She sent a text back to tallboy: "where r u?"

"We'll escort these fellows back to our ship," said Hank, indicating the roughed up Connectors. "The Merchant Marine is always looking for a few good lost men."

I surveyed our group—ash on our faces, clothing torn, dried blood—and an invisible fist slammed into my stomach. "Where are Vaitiare and Kohia?" Eddie's head jerked up.

"Saw them go the opposite direction when we were leaving that energy room," Chen said. "Looking for Angela, I think."

"I got another text from tallboy," Eddy said. "This one says 'PPM.'"

"Pike Place Market," said Emily.

As we were trying to decipher text, I noticed that Eddie turned and tried to slide back down the stairs. Still holding a Connector, Teva grabbed him with his other hand. "No," he said. "You would not survive."

LABELS: COMPANY IMPLOSIONS, THREE ALARM FIRE, BEYOND RESCUE

VIEW COMMENTS (98)

Vibrato NOV. 25, 2011 AT 4:27 PM
The old building is a fire trap.

Tangerine NOV. 25, 2011 AT 4:38 PM
Smoke inhalation—that's the danger Kohia and the others face.

SHOW MORE COMMENTS

It's late

Entry No. 546 - POSTED: NOV. 25, 2011

Thinks Out Loud: Hank and his crew (and the Connectors—future crew?) left for the ship docked just south of the downtown. I thanked them for all their help and also asked one last favor.

"I think we can arrange that, mate," Hank answered me as he guided his men toward the waterfront. They looked grimy but proud.

The rest of our group weaved up toward Pike Place Market. I said I would catch up to them. Emily, at the back of the group, made sure Eddie was ahead of her. I backtracked to AltaSystemics. From a block away, the structure didn't look so bad from the outside, except for smoke issuing from broken windows and the smashed front entrance. Fire trucks were everywhere. So were the police who had cordoned off the front area.

Sounding intentionally naïve I said to a fire marshal, "I need to get inside. My friends might still be in there."

"No entrance," he said gruffly. "It's an inferno. My crew can't even get in." Streams of water invaded the building from six angles. TV crews had taken up positions as close as they could get.

Someone touched my shoulder. Emily. She took my hand. We scanned the crowd that had gathered but only saw strangers. Another explosion shook the entire block.

"They might have gotten out," Emily said. I looked around to see if any firefighting breathing gear was nearby.

Emily knew what I was thinking. "Even if you got in, they could be anywhere," she said.

Still watching, we had drifted toward a darker street corner away from the main face of the building. It was hard to think clearly with all the hissing from the hoses, the clanking of arriving fire engines and the deep rumblings from the burning building. I felt impotent. Were the losses of my friends worth the destruction of AltaSystemics?

A hand tapped my shoulder, even though Emily was still on my right and holding my hand. Turning, I saw a group of sooty messes.

"Vaitiare?"

She nodded. Her clothes were in worse shape than mine. Same for Kohia and Angela. Jeannie was with them. And four Sensates, who looked ridiculously calm.

Emily gave the women warm hugs. Wanting to hug Vaitiare, I stood by and asked, "How?"

"Let's move away from this," Emily said.

As we trudged in the direction of the Market, Vaitiare told her tale. Angela had led them to the Sensate's room, where they found these four standing in a kind of trance. "There wasn't any fire on this floor, just smoke drifting in the hallway," Vaitiare said. "We tried to explain to the Sensates that we had to go. They seemed to be dimly aware of us."

Angela broke in. "I even slapped one. Didn't make any difference. We opened the door, briefly, but the smoke was getting too thick, so we put sheets at the bottom of the door."

Angela said they were on the second floor, toward the back of the building. "The windows were the kind that open at an angle and not all the way."

"That's when the Woman of Prime Mover had an idea," Vaitiare said.

"Hey," Jeannie broke in, "I am definitely not the 'Woman of Prime Mover,' and yes, I looked at the bunk bed frames and told the girls to shove one over to the window. Then we leaned it back and gave a collective push. Smash! And again. And again. We created an exit where a window had been."

"But you were on the second floor," Emily said.

"We had no choice," Vaitiare answered. "I showed the group how to go out onto the ledge and hang there so that your feet were lower to the ground."

Siren blaring, another fire engine charged past us.

Vaitiare said she went first and did a roll when she hit the pavement. Kohia came next. The challenge was the Sensates. Angela and Jeannie had to maneuver them one by one into position and hold them until Vaitiare said, 'Drop!' so she and Kohia could try and cushion their fall. Actually, being so relaxed helped their landings. Finally, Jeannie came down. That left Angela.

"Hold on a second. I need to get something," she said to the group below her.

She disappeared back in the room, Vaitiare said. "We didn't know what was going on."

Reappearing at the window, Angela said, "Here," and tossed out several bags that Kohia caught. "Coming down," Angela said, and she gracefully wriggled out the window and fell to the ground. The group immediately backed away from the building as another internal explosion shook the area.

"What did the bags contain?" Emily asked.

Angela answered: "Those special AltaSystemics candies."

LABELS: FIRE STRATEGY, BURNING QUESTIONS

VIEW COMMENTS (120)

Topaz OCT. 25, 2011 AT 6:12 PM
Thinks Out Loud has grown, no doubt about it. They all have.

Sleeper OCT. 25, 2011 AT 6:34 PM
Wow! I would have panicked in the Sensate's dorm with all that smoke.

Freezone OCT. 25, 2011 AT 9:28 PM
Just so we are clear on this, shouldn't the Sensates have known in advance that AltaSystemics was gonna blow?

Crepedejour OCT. 25, 2011 AT 9:40 PM
The Sensates are highly intuitive but that doesn't make them psychic.

SHOW MORE COMMENTS

The show must go on

Entry No. 647 - POSTED: NOV. 25, 2011

tallboy: Just as I was catching up to Prime Mover on 1st. Ave., he glanced back, saw me, and shifted into overdrive. Pushing roughly past tourists and locals, he slipped into the crowded open air section of Pike Place Market, ran through the Fish Market, intercepted a salmon being tossed by a fishmonger to his partner, and sent it my way. I ducked, the fish slamming into a middle-aged couple behind me. "Sorry," I said and turned back to see PM zipping further into the Market and knocking produce and souvenirs from the stalls into my path.

Finding my stride, I felt like a hurdler. Prime Mover exited the Market, leaped down some stairs and darted over to Post Alley with its uneven brick pathway. By the time I got to the alley, PM was at a doorway of an old brick building. In he went. I reached the door a few seconds later and, not knowing what to expect, slipped in. I entered a small lobby and could hear laughter from nearby. I'd been here before, once. Improv.

I passed into the musty theater and stood near the back. The house was packed. Onstage a group of actors were doing a scene with a guy rubbing his chin and looking perplexed. Next to him, a young woman was saying in a loud whisper, "I don't know him. Maybe he was one of Herb's friends from high school."

And standing between two other actors was Prime Mover, smiling and nodding. "Great party," he said. "Great hors d'oeuvres! What's for dinner?"

"This is a funeral," said the woman coldly as she sniffed and tried to hold back tears.

The audience thought that was funny. I made my way forward and reached some steps on the side of the stage. I could see PM watching me out of the corner of his eye.

"Well, for a funeral, this is a great spread," Prime Mover said and got another laugh.

I'd never done improv, never been on stage except for a musical in eighth grade, *Kokonut Kapers*. I played Captain Kidd.

No one was paying attention to me as I hesitated at the bottom of the four steps. Taking a deep breath, I mounted the stairs and stood on the stage. Bright lights from overhead made it hard to see the audience. All of the actors turned toward me and waited.

"Sorry to interrupt," I began, "but this man is wanted by the IRS. He doesn't believe in paying taxes." That got a mild laugh. "Mr. Pryme, if you'll come with me please."

PM edged toward the other side of the stage. "You must have me confused with someone else. I'm attending a funeral of a dear friend."

I advanced. "Yes, please pay your respects, and we'll be off."

"I'm one of the pallbearers," PM said. The audience liked that line.

I drew closer to PM who was almost off stage. "Come peacefully, I don't want to have to use force, especially at a funeral." That got a few chuckles. Maybe I had a little bit of talent.

"If you insist," said Prime Mover as he plowed into me. I was thrown back. The audience gasped. PM tried to exit the stage, but I reached out and clasped his ankle. I jerked him back, and the audience started clapping.

"Guys, help me out," Prime Mover appealed to his fellow improv teammates. "I only embezzled a few grand to open a daycare for homeless children."

Members of the audience applauded. A few said, "Awe."

The other actors had been frozen. Now they moved into action, and three of them grabbed Prime Mover's arms and tried to pull him from me. "Hey, you guys don't understand," I shouted. "This is a bad man. Bad."

"We protect our own," muttered an actor who wore one of those T-shirts made to look like a tuxedo. He wasn't acting anymore. But the audience was laughing and applauding.

"There they are!" came a shout from the back of the theater. Still holding PM, I tried to make out who it was, but the stage lights blocked out everything beyond the first couple of rows.

I heard the thud of running feet. Five bodies bolted onto the stage. Eddie, Teva, Chen, plus I think a frowning Connector and a sleepy looking Sensate. They joined my side and grabbed onto various parts of Prime Mover. From offstage, more improvisers, rallying to the cause, flew out and held onto their compatriots. It was a tug of war with PM as the object. He was screaming. And the audience just loved it. They were standing on their feet and applauding and going crazy.

"Teva," I shouted. "Do something." Releasing his hold on PM, he jumped into a crouched, leg-spread war stance and gave a tremendous cry. Everyone stopped. We all released Prime Mover who collapsed onto the stage floor. As a group, the audience had pulled back.

Teva picked up the unconscious figure as if he were a life-sized doll. "We'll be going now," I said. "You've been a great audience."

LABELS: IMPROVING IMPROV, ENCORE

VIEW COMMENTS (124)

HughMan OCT. 25, 2011 AT 8:07 PM
In improv, I advised my mates to make your partner look good and you'll look good.

Aladden OCT. 25, 2011 AT 8:38 PM
What's called tug of war actually comes from ancient tribal legal traditions where the outcome of the person on trial was judged by the winning pull of those who believed in his innocence vs. those believing him guilty. Sometimes it was a hung jury resulting in a split defendant.

SHOW MORE COMMENTS

○ ○ ○   **THINKS OUT LOUD**   ✕

WHIMSY WITHOUT REGRET

Nightfall

Entry No. 648 - POSTED: NOV. 25, 2011

Emily: Early evening. Behind us, the city's glassy high rise offices and condos. Before us, broad Puget Sound with car ferries coming and going to Bainbridge Island and Bremerton. Further, the sharp silhouette of the Olympics. We were standing in a small park just beyond the Market. A moment of calmness. We looked like miners who had survived a cave in. Our group (with the Sensates) had caught up to the other group (with a groggy Prime Mover who could barely stand).

"What do we do now?" Eddie asked. He could have passed as a homeless person.

"We should probably turn ourselves in," said Chen. "Or at least drop Prime Mover off at the police station."

People in the group—were we rebels of a sort?—roundly rejected that option. tallboy perceptively pointed out: "He'd probably end up having us arrested."

Then what do we do?" repeated Eddie. Teva and he were supporting the limp Prime Mover. Between tallboy and Thinks Out Loud, our Connector captive was silent, defeated. Kohia and Angela were trying to contain the dazed Sensates.

Vaitaire spoke. Despite her torn clothing, she still managed to look regal. "Just as we judged Thinks Out Loud on Tiaré, so should we now judge this Prime Mover."

"Better to let him be the dinner of the sharks," Teva said, motioning toward the darkening waters.

"I agree," Thinks Out Loud said. "With Vaitiare. Prime Mover should sit in judgment."

"I'd like to take part in this judging deal," Jeannie said, giving PM a piercing look.

She went directly up to Prime Mover to slap him, only to be blocked by Teva. "I just wanted to give him a love tap, like this," she said as she reached past Teva to caress Prime Mover's lips.

Teva advised her to back away. "You snap like an enraged sea turtle," he said. "Much as I agree with you, the group will decide the guilt or innocence of this Prime Mover."

Now I had an idea. "My mother's house. That will serve as our court."

"The brothers Morse," interrupted tallboy.

"What about them?" Eddie asked as he began to have the same realization.

Heads turning, we saw no Morse brothers and experienced a group panic. "Does anyone remember seeing them?" I asked. "I don't remember their leaving AltaSystemics."

"We ran up here pretty fast to help snag Prime Mover," said Eddie.

"This is not good," Chen said. He acted as though it were his fault.

"Okay, okay," I began. "We'll comb the area between here and Pioneer Square." I knew it was a dumb idea, but I didn't have anything better to offer."

"May I?" asked Jeannie, as she reached into a pocket of Prime Mover's jacket. Pulling out a small device, she showed it around. "A homing device. Planted on the brothers. Primy thought you might sneak the brothers out of AltaSystemics and he wanted to be able to track them and you." She pushed a button on the little black box and it started beeping. Looking at a readout, she announced, "Approaching the Seattle Center."

Thinks Out Loud, Eddie and Angela said they'd go retrieve them. Eddie grabbed the homing device. "Get the cars and meet us up there," he called back to us as they scooted away.

LABELS: DECISION FACTORS, SOCIETAL NORMS, REVENGE

VIEW COMMENTS (100)

StucKey NOV. 25, 2011 AT 8:50 PM
These kids never get a chance to catch their breath.

CheckIn NOV. 25, 2011 AT 8:58 PM
If they take Prime Mover to the house, they will then become guilty of kidnapping, of CEOnapping.

Topper NOV. 25, 2011 AT 9:08 PM
Some kidnappings are acceptable or at least necessary—if the kidnappee is guilty of heinous crimes against humanity.

SHOW MORE COMMENTS

○ ○ ○   **THINKS OUT LOUD**   ✕

WHIMSY WITHOUT REGRET

Observation Deck

Entry No. 649 - POSTED: NOV. 25, 2011

Thinks Out Loud: As Eddie, Angela and I closed in on the Seattle Center, Eddie monitored the homing device. "They're near the Science Center...they're heading toward the International Fountain...Looks like they're going up the Space Needle."

"What if they start talking about their time travel theories?" asked Angela. I was thinking about the same scenario.

When we reached the base of the Space Needle, since it was a grey November day turned night, the line to ascend was short. Before we bought tickets we self-consciously tried to dust ourselves off and just gave up.

According to the elevator guide, who gave us a quizzical look, it's a 43 second ride to the top. For us, it was long 43 seconds. When we reached the observation deck, I pushed my way past a group of students, sorry! and scanned for the brothers. To my right a modest crowd had formed on the outside ring. Below the cloud level, Seattle's skyscrapers formed a galaxy of lights. The Sound lay dark except for the toylike ferries, and on the horizon, the pinpoints of island homes. And there were the brothers doing their lecture thing. The listeners seemed divided into two groups: an apprehensive collection of Midwesterners who thought the brothers dangerous and/or homeless and the more accepting listeners (probably local progressives) who found these two elders in their singed robes prophets of some sort.

Angela suggested we "just grab them." Eddie and I exchanged eye contact and both said that probably wasn't the best solution.

I had an idea. "Back me up," I said, "but in a nice way." Saying "Excuse me," I worked my way to the brothers. One of them was discoursing: "Now as for the space/time continuum, here comes the good part," but I didn't let him get beyond that. "Ladies and gentlemen," I broke in, "I'm sorry to have to bring the brothers' lecture to a close, but they are late for an appointment with Bill Gates."

Before the brothers could react, Angela and Eddie were escorting them back to the elevator. The Midwesterners looked relieved and the progressives applauded politely as we left.

LABELS: RIDE THE SPACE NEEDLE, ELDERNAPPING

VIEW COMMENTS (120)

SeattleStu NOV. 25, 2011 AT 9:45 PM
Close one!

JourneyMan NOV. 25, 2011 AT 9:53 PM
Even more than Prime Mover, the brothers are the wild card here.

I wanted to be a time traveler, but I couldn't see any future in it.

SHOW MORE COMMENTS

○ ○ ○   THINKS OUT LOUD   ✕

WHIMSY WITHOUT REGRET

Together again

Entry No. 650 - POSTED: NOV. 25, 2011

tallboy: When I dropped the first passenger load off, including Thinks Out Loud, Teva and the Morse brothers, Emily's mom took one look at me, ordered me to stay, disappeared for a minute and reappeared with some clean clothes that I think had been her ex-husband's. A little short in the sleeve but better than the torn and smoked up pants and shirt I'd been wearing since the fire.

Emily brought back a couple of the zoned-out Sensates, Kohia, Eddie and Angela. And she placed the captured Connector in the back cargo hold. They all looked exhausted. In my trusty Toyota wagon, I retrieved the last of the group, Chen, Vaitiare, another Sensate, Jeannie, a strange smile playing about her lips, and in my cargo area, one recumbent Prime Mover.

No one spoke on the last trip. "Have you at the house in no time," I said, as I left the Seattle Center, where even in the late evening young people and some families were still hanging around. "Quite a day," I said to no one in particular. The only response I got was a snore from the back seat. The Sensate.

When we entered the forested area near Emily's mom's house, I thought I heard someone mumbling. "What's that?" I asked. The Sensate, her hood hiding her face, was saying something in a sad voice. I could make out a word here and there. Sounded like "Broken...Alone..."

We came to a four-way stop. The car to the right arrived at about the same time. So did a pickup truck on my left. No one moved.

"Why doesn't someone go?" Vaitiare asked.

"It is the Seattle Way," I answered. "We can be polite to a fault."

All of us began to inch forward simultaneously and all again stopped.

"See what I mean," I said and hand motioned for the other car on my right to go. The other driver was doing the same. The truck driver threw up both of his hands.

"This is ridiculous," I said as I hit the accelerator and hoped they weren't doing the same.

In my rearview mirror I could see the other two cars still waiting for the other to make a move.

I pulled into the driveway. "Let's get you guys cleaned up," I said. "Tomorrow we decide what to do with Prime Mover."

Emily met us at the door. "I think most everyone's asleep."

"Including Prime Mover," Jeannie said with a wink, as we pulled him out of the back of the truck.

"We're going to need to take shifts to guard him and his Connector," Emily said as our weary group rolled like a slow wave into the softly lit living room.

"He'll sleep like a baby," Jeannie actually chirped.

"How do you know?" Emily asked.

"Because when I went up to that asshole at the park near the Market, I fed him some of his own medicine—his candies."

"Oh," Emily said. "A little revenge for the scorned lover? I heard how he tried to run you over when he ran out of his office to escape the fire."

Jeannie was advancing toward Emily who held her ground. I shook my head and jumped between them. "Can we all just get some sleep?" I asked as they both halted within an inch of me.

"Okay," said Emily. "But no more candies for Prime Mover. We need him awake and alert for his judgment tomorrow."

"Of course," Jeannie answered as she sat down on the long couch. "Awake and alert, and in that order."

LABELS: RESCUE OPERATIONS, RE-ENTRY, REVENGE 2.0

VIEW COMMENTS (129)

FunGus NOV. 25, 2011 AT 10:10 PM

Sorry, Emily, but Jeannie is right this time. Keep that Prime Mover under seda-
tion.

HindSite NOV. 25, 2011 AT 10:25 PM
"Appear weak when you are strong, and strong when you are weak."

SHOW MORE COMMENTS

○ ○ ○   **THINKS OUT LOUD**   ✕
──
WHIMSY WITHOUT REGRET

Breakfast first, trial second

Entry No. 651 - POSTED: NOV. 26, 2011

Emily: People slept all over the house. Everyone woke up in a groggy
state except Teva who was still alert even after having stayed guard over
the surly Connector and the sleeping Prime Mover.

"Justin and I had a conversation last night," said Teva, indicating the
Connector, "and we came to an understanding that it would be in his
best interests to remain with us during the judgment of Prime Mover."

Now we kept the two in the living room within a circle of four of us. A
more alert but silent Prime Mover watched us watching him, his silver
suit now wrinkled. Justin, younger than I had expected, had thick dark
blond hair that made him look more innocent than he could ever be. He
sighed a lot and kept looking at the door, perhaps expecting his brethren
to charge in and save him? At the dining table, seated together, Thinks
Out Loud, Princess Vaitiare, and Teva spoke quietly to each other. I sat
next to a pensive Chen who sat next to them.

"Can you hear what they're discussing?" I asked Chen.

"Something about the Day of Judgment."

"Could I have everyone's attention, please," Thinks Out Loud said as he
stood up from the table. The rest of the group were in nearby stuffed
chairs or had taken a position in high-backed chairs at the breakfast nook
this side of the kitchen. "When I was living with the Tiarens, there came
a time, a day of judgment when the islanders decided whether I could
stay amongst them," Thinks Out Loud spoke solemnly. "Some of you
may have read about the experience in one of my postings." Most of our
heads nodded. The three Sensates, who looked only slightly less drugged
than before, vaguely watched the rest of us nod. "Vaitiare, Teva, and I

propose that Prime Mover be given his Day of Judgment, that all who wish to speak do so, including the accused, and that a vote be taken to determine his fate." Thinks Out Loud spread his gaze around the room.

"Teva," tallboy interrupted, "I thought you wanted to throw him in the Sound." I couldn't tell if tallboy was kidding or being serious.

"That may be the outcome, but only after the Day of Judgment has resulted in a verdict," Teva answered.

Chen spoke up: "Just to make sure I understand this process. We are taking it upon ourselves to basically have a trial. Is that legal? Is it Constitutional?"

Everyone started talking at the same time until Thinks Out Loud raised his hand to signal quiet. "Who outside this room would believe us?" he asked. "We can be fair. We do not bring the mob mentality to this matter."

Eddie chimed in: "James Bond is always dispatching his adversaries without taking them to a court of law."

"He had a license to kill," said Emily. "We don't."

LABELS: A JURY OF PEERS, ALL IN FAVOR, JUST DESSERTS

VIEW COMMENTS (122)

DexTerra NOV. 26, 2011 AT 8:03 AM
The legality of this version of justice calls to mind the potential of not exactly a mob mentality but more the power of the masses over the few. Be careful, ye who judge.

EveningMist NOV. 26, 2011 AT 8:22 AM
The team absolutely has the right to judge the man who would have used them for his own selfish ends. (Am I biased? You betcha!)

SHOW MORE COMMENTS

Day of judgment

Entry No. 652 - POSTED: NOV. 26, 2011

Emily: While we were turning the living room into a courtroom of sorts my mother stood in the background at the wide entrance to the kitchen. I thought she'd have something to say, but she just watched. Buttoning his plaid shirt, Eddie came out of the guestroom. He avoided my gaze and went over to join Teva who was setting up chairs in a broad arc. Thinks Out Loud and Vaitiare were talking at what I guessed would be the open area where those of us who wanted to speak would stand. It was right in front of the windows, beyond which the unexpected, still-bright morning did not reflect my mood.

I found Angela in the wood-paneled den that had temporarily been converted into another guest room. She was slumped on the black couch that had been her bed. "You okay?" I asked.

"I suppose so," she said, her eyes directed downward. "I was an idiot wasn't I? Didn't I give him the benefit of the doubt?

I cleared my throat. "No, Angela, no. That guy may be short, yet he's got a certain power over people."

She shook her head. "Well, at least this time we're the ones in control."

I didn't say it, but I thought, "I hope so."

Teva and Eddie were finishing up the living room arranging. They put one stuffed chair near the windows, facing the others. That's where Thinks Out Loud would sit if he wished. He was going to be our guide through this, along with Teva and Vaitiare.

Eddie and Teva stood back to admire their composition.

"Done," said Eddie with the first smile on him I'd seen in ages. I walked over and complimented him on the seating design. He wouldn't look at me. Then he would. Then he wouldn't.

"Your mom's been great," he said finally as though he'd decided on a safe subject.

317

"I know."

"Well, time for the judgment." Eddie moved away from me to a seat on the other side of the room.

It took a few minutes to gather everyone together and get them focused on the day's content. The Sensates were now acting less dreamy, though no one would mistake them for accountants.

tallboy stayed right by the side of the Connector who kept his shoulders hunched and eyes stern. The Morse brothers, looking far more alert than I had expected them to be, were talking to Kohia as though they were at a cocktail party. They could be charming.

"Where's Prime Mover?" I asked when I didn't see him in the perimeter we'd established.

"Said he had to go to the bathroom. Teva's guarding the door," tallboy reported. That sent me on alert.

"Eddie," was all I had to say. He zoomed out of the room. I followed.

Eddie banged on the guestroom's bathroom door. "Locked," he said and then shouted, "Prime Mover, it's time."

There was no answer. Without waiting for my permission, Teva pushed against the door, which gave way like a broken twig. The bathroom was empty, its window opened and de-screened. Teva shot past me, followed by Eddie.

"Prime Mover's gone," I shouted as I followed them out the front door. Others joined us.

"Spread out," Eddie said as he and Teva circled the house in opposite directions.

I caught up with them at the outside deck where Vaitiare was scanning the water. Raising her arm, she pointed at a kayak about a hundred yards out. Teva nodded and dived into the water. I had no idea one could swim so fast. In the meantime, I jumped into our dingy. Eddie joined me, all of our attention focused on the situation at hand. "Row!" I shouted as we took what seemed like an hour to point the bow in the kayak's direction.

Even though PM had quickened his pace, Teva gained steadily on him. When Teva was about to grab the kayak, PM tried to bean him with his paddle, which Teva grabbed and jerked away as if it were a toy. We were closing in as well. By the time we reached the two, Teva was actually towing the kayak back to land. I threw him a line, which he attached, and we became the towers. Teva, still in the water, held the kayak amidships. Prime Mover, his back to shore, gave some snorts, sighs, and even a pained laugh or two.

"You don't want to miss your own Day of Judgment," Eddie called to him as we neared the shore. We put in just beside the house. Prime Mover was helped out of the kayak, not gently, by tallboy who said, "Welcome back, you little piece of—"

"tallboy," I called out, "let him be. You can speak your mind in a few minutes." tallboy held Prime Mover's collar, which caused Prime Mover to have to walk on tiptoe, and we all moved back into the house. Someone got Teva a towel. And my mother found both of them clothes. Eddie was quiet.

At the back of the spacious room, with a view of the front drive through a narrow window, Angela served as a lookout, just in case…

"It is time," intoned Thinks Out Loud as Teva marshaled Prime Mover to stand next to him. For someone about to be judged for a series of crimes, PM now seemed imperially calm. All signs of having been force-fed those candies by Jeannie had worn off.

"Is there anyone who wishes to speak on the nature of Prime Mover's actions, his running of AltaSystemics and related activities?" Thinks Out Loud asked as he scanned the seated group.

"I have something to say!" It was Angela, who started speaking before she reached the front of the room. "We met at an improv class. He said his aunt, who raised him after his parents died in a tragic circus accident, had discouraged him from doing acting when he was in high school, so now he was finally going to give it a try. Anyway, we did some skits together, and he invited me to become an intern at AltaSystemics but intern in name only. From day one Prime Mover stalked me like a panther, a short panther. I finally agreed to go on a date, and I have to admit he did have a little charm, but honestly, could any of you see me with him? We're like two different species. Anyway, it was all an act. He didn't really care about me, especially after *she* came along." Angela practically growled at Jeannie. With a defiant step, she walked back to her chair.

"Is that all you've got?" asserted Prime Mover. "I give you opportunities, and you repay me by spying on AltaSystemics."

"Enough, Prime Mover," said Thinks Out Loud. "Who is next?"

"Me!" blasted Jeannie. "The *other* woman." She stood, arms akimbo, as though ready for a fight. "First I get kicked off the Thinks Out Loud blog," she had actually puffed herself up. "Then, well, I kept reading it, and when I saw that the action was shifting to AltaSystemics, I went over there and tried to make as much mischief as I could. I also caught Prime Mover's attention, and he put me in charge of the company's communications, including the blog." She cast a cold eye over at tallboy. "Boy was that blog awful. Anyway, I thought things were going pretty well, until…" Now she paused and let out a breath. "Until all those fires started in the building when everyone was running around and fighting. Until we were in Prime Mover's office and he was cornered by tallboy with that girl." She pointed to Angela. "But everything changed when Prime Mover made a run for it—to escape tallboy and the fire—made a run for it by pushing me out of the way so he could get away, the shit." She paused for emphasis. "But during the time I was in his good graces, I got to see him in action. I can truthfully say he is the most selfish, self-centered person I have ever met. Do you know he keeps an Excel spreadsheet showing which CEOs and heads of state he plans to feed hard candies! He'd already gotten to several Governors and a Justice of the Supreme Court.

Jeannie lunged at Prime Mover, but Teva came between them. She reluctantly returned to her seat.

Then came Chen who used a lot of hand motions as he spoke: "I was the one who analyzed the chemical makeup of the hard candies Prime Mover fed to his Hivers, as he calls his staff. The candies contained a drug that allowed him to control them, to create a drug-induced work force. I'm surprised no one overdosed." Chen began to go into the chemical makeup of the candies only to have Thinks Out Loud interrupt and thank him for his contribution.

"My turn," said an unfamiliar voice. "Do I get the chance to have my say?" The Connector Justin rose slowly from his chair and moved unaccompanied to the speaking place. Out of his beige uniform, and in street clothes, nice street clothes, he seemed less dangerous. Rough around the edges but lacking the power of his group now that he was cut off from them. "You people think you know everything. Well, you don't. For instance, I was a nothing. I mean I couldn't even pass classes at the community college. I spent time on the street. I know what it is to be hungry. Prime Mover found me standing in line for a free meal program and offered me a job, a real job. So maybe I didn't know what his company did. That didn't matter. I could still escort people around, keep an eye on things, and protect the company to the best of my ability. Prime Mover gave me a chance, which is more than any of you will ever do." He almost spat on the floor as he swung his way back to his seat.

The room was silent. "Maybe we should take a break," I said softly.

Thinks Out Loud looked at Teva and Vaitiare. "No," he said as he breathed out. "This is the moment. We must continue."

LABELS: JUSTICE FOR ALL, THE WHOLE TRUTH, USE YOUR WORDS

VIEW COMMENTS (134)

SpecMan NOV. 26, 2011 AT 9:39 AM
Granted, it's not exactly a court of law modeled on the traditions of modern democracies, but in a sense, rather than representative democracy, this method involves the full participation of the community, a purer form of democracy.

Anonymous NOV. 26, 2011 AT 9:54 AM
No trial needed. Waste of time. Guilty, as charged.

SHOW MORE COMMENTS

○ ○ ○ THINKS OUT LOUD ✕

WHIMSY WITHOUT REGRET
More testimony
Entry No. 653 - POSTED: NOV. 26, 2011

Emily: I could feel the tension, like a heavy cloud, in the room. "I'll go," said tallboy who rose and stood in the open area before us, the defendant to his right. Shifting his weight, he glanced at Prime Mover before he began. "When he hired me to be the AltaSystemics blogger, I couldn't believe how lucky I was to have the job of my dreams."

"You see? I am a force for the Good." Prime Mover interrupted, and rising, tried to advocate for himself only to be quickly blocked my Teva.

Thinks Out Loud held up his hand. "Prime Mover, we will take turns. This is not your time."

"Well it certainly isn't your time either!" Prime Mover shouted. "If the Morse brothers and I had been able to come to an understanding, I wouldn't even be here."

Again, Thinks Out Loud's hand went up. "Prime Mover, no more speaking out of order. Please continue, tallboy."

"Turns out Prime Mover didn't care about the blog I was writing. I was just a front to convey misinformation. I was like his puppet, a drugged puppet. And it wasn't just me. Everyone in his company was under his control as in taking away our freedom!" I'd never seen tallboy so worked up. "Plus to this day, I still don't know what the company did and what I was supposed to write about." tallboy aimed a dirty look at Prime Mover and returned to his seat.

"I refuse to take part in this ridiculous charade! I demand to call my lawyer!" bellowed Prime Mover.

Thinks Out Loud evenly addressed him. "You can keep interrupting other speakers and force us to tape your mouth shut or you can remain quiet until it is your time to speak. You decide."

"I'll come forward," said one of the Sensates. No longer in white, she wore soft pastels courtesy of my mother. "It is time to move into deeper realms of reality. I am Patricia. I was a Sensate at AltaSystemics," she began. I remembered her. She was the mysterious Sensate we had spoken with during our tour.

Patricia stood before us, her hands open as if inviting us into her world. Her formerly long dark hair was now close cropped, her face still dominated by large blue eyes. Looking like innocence with a capital I, she spoke in a voice deeper and fuller than I would have expected. It's hard for me to tell someone's age after they're thirty, so I would guess she was in her mid-thirties, or a little older or slightly younger.

"My role was to act as a conduit to another dimension, to transfer information from our world to the Other." She paused to allow us to try and absorb what she was saying. "It has always been a part of me—my ability to sense what others cannot. Meditation, yoga, and certain teas have strengthened that ability. It is another sense, one beyond taste, smell, sight, sound. You all have it to some degree. You just don't realize it."

I looked around. Everyone was transfixed by her words, Teva actually leaning in her direction.

"Prime Mover found me at a retreat, a weekend of silence, held at a rustic conference center not far from Mt. St. Helens," the Sensate continued. "He asked me if I wanted to be part of a great movement, an ascent of this way of knowing that would bring about a better world. I looked in his eyes, and..." She paused and bit her lip. "And, I'm not sure what happened next. I went into a kind of trance. The next thing I knew, I was in a white room, a cool white room, and I wore a white robe and I had some hard shelled candies in my hand." The Sensate seemed to be reliving the episode. "Connect—connect—connect—connect—"

"She's back in a trance," whispered Angela.

"Looks like she's done with her comments," Prime Mover offered. "Doesn't know what she's saying. I saved her, I saved that girl!"

"Silence!" commanded Thinks Out Loud in an authoritative tone I hadn't known he could manage. "I shall ask the Sensate a few questions." In a friendly but probing voice he asked, "Sensate, how did you store information in this other dimension?"

She moaned.

"Sensate, show us how you reached the other world."

She spoke even more slowly now and somehow there was a slight reverberation to her words. "I take it in. I become a storage matrix. And through me passes the information." She weaved a trail with her arms. "It opens and I send the information toward the light." Her hands went above her head, almost like a dance. "The information goes into the light."

"I see," said Thinks Out Loud. "And how do you retrieve the information?"

The Sensate froze. "It is there," she said in a weaker voice. "There it stays until..."

"Yes," said Thinks Out Loud gently, "until?"

The Sensate began to turn around slowly at first and then more quickly. She was like a wounded bird plummeting toward the earth.

"Enough!" It was Teva who ran up to the Sensate and let her fall into his arms. He carried her to the guest bedroom. I didn't know what to think. We were all exchanging looks and making questioning motions with our hands.

"I may as well speak," I said. "Tap me on the shoulder if I fall into a trance." My attempt at nervous humor went over like a proverbial lead balloon. "Sorry," I apologized. I faced the group, including Teva who had returned.

"This whole situation came out of nowhere. I was taking a seminar on high-tech history and there was this other student." I pointed to Eddie. "He was in the class and he was trying to figure out this confusing situation involving his brother at a high-tech company—Alta Systemics. It sounded intriguing to me, so, and I admit this, we came up with a plan to get inside the company to discover what it did. A fake tour." I went into detail about the tour and how Eddie and I had used it as a chance to see other parts of the building, about how we got caught and taken to the office of Prime Mover. "That's where he asked us what we thought he was doing and I gave him my theory, based in part on what we'd learned in the secret room we discovered. It was about the storing of information in another dimension, like the Sensate just said. Did I believe all this? I wasn't sure. But I could see that strange things were going on at this company, and people were not acting normally, like they were robots."

I continued to relate the events that got even more complicated when we learned the Morse brothers had been kidnapped so that Prime Mover could gain control not only of people but of time and space as well.

"It was a business arrangement!" Prime Mover said gruffly.

I kept talking. "To prevent Prime Mover from succeeding, we had to take action. I don't deny that." I took in a deep breath. "And I'd do the same thing again. But there's something that keeps tugging at me: Aren't we doing the same thing that Prime Mover has done: Taking away another's freedom? And then I realize the reason we are here is because he is the one who took those freedoms away." I walked back to my chair and practically fell into it. I felt drained. The room was filled with jagged conversation.

Thinks Out Loud clapped his hands to get us back on track. "Are there any other speakers?"

"Guess I'll talk now," Eddie said as he came forward from the other side of the room. "I'll try not to be too repetitive." We exchanged a momentary eye-linking, a precious second where he seemed to transmit an emotional charge that gave me a shiver. "I was just this student, taking classes, doing student things. When my brother, tallboy, got this blogging job at AltaSystemics, I was happy for him. But he began to change, once he started working there. He became a drone. That's when, as Emily said, we infiltrated the company. What a weird place filled with weird people. And in command was Prime Mover, very smooth, but very mysterious. I've thought this whole information storage in another dimension thing to be fiction, a way for Prime Mover to control people and probably take in investment money. Actually I doubt he even had any clients. It's all so bizarre. I think he created this shell of a high-tech company and was biding his time until he could get investors to give him their money. And eventually he'd run off—to an island paradise."

"Enough of this!" shouted Prime Mover, his clenched fist heading in Eddie's direction. "I am not going to just stand here and let this little peon—" Teva grabbed PM's shoulder and jerked him back.

Eddie continued. "As bad as it was how Prime Mover was controlling those Sensates and my brother and in the process of stealing investors' money, things got even more serious when he kidnapped the Morse brothers to learn how they send messages back in time and wreak who knows what kind of havoc with the world as we know it. We had to act. And we did, as Emily said. Prime Mover had to be stopped. Kind of reminds you of a James Bond adversary, yes?"

His head held high, Eddie returned to his seat. The room was silent.

"I'm speaking now," growled Prime Mover as Teva allowed him to step forward and address us. I've never seen a person so agitated yet controlled, so angry yet trying to look calm. "What is going on here? Are you going to find me guilty of being an ambitious and far-sighted entrepreneur? I'm not the one who should be on trial. You should be!" I think he meant all of us. "Entering a private company under false pretenses, spying, attempting to cause irreparable harm to the equipment and other parts of the company, trying to remove guests of the establishment against their will, and then actually invading the building resulting in its destruction and the breaking of expensive state-of-the art laboratory equipment. You misfits destroyed a viable business. That's a big sin in Seattle." He paused for effect. When he started to speak again, Prime Mover's tone took a softer turn. "Look, pioneers are always misunderstood by the society they live in. When you are ahead of your time, people fear you. And that is what has happened here. I was trying to better society, to bring us closer to that light that Sensate referred to. Incidentally, I provided shelter, clothing and food for my employees. Not even Apple or Google do that."

I looked at the group. Some were adjusting themselves in their chairs as though they felt uncomfortable.

"As for the Morse brothers," continued Prime Mover, "they are great discoverers. But they are also elderly. What a shame if their work should die with them. That is why we developed an agreement with them so that they could record their achievement for the good of humanity.

"Finally, I wasn't pushing anyone when I decided to exit the building. I am highly allergic to smoke and simply had to rush outside to breathe fresh air…Don't all of you value clean, fresh air where you can take a deep breath, hold it in, and slowly release it?"

He was talking in a low, calm voice about breathing and slowly nodding his head as he made eye contact with all of us, massaging the group with his dark eyes.

"Deep breaths, and a feeling of peace. That is what you feel," he said. "All is well. Breathe in and hold it. Now breathe out. Relax." Members of the group began to lower their heads. Even Thinks Out Loud, Vaitiare and Teva seemed affected.

"He's trying to put us under," I thought, "to hypnotize us." Feeling the pull as well, I desperately tried to think of a way to counter his deviltry.

"You were hypnotized at that high school party," I remembered. "And to come out of the trance…Think back."

"Your eyes are feeling heavy. You want to sleep," cooed Prime Mover.

And my eyes were feeling heavy. I was falling…There would come that moment…that point of no return when I would drift into sleep…and I wouldn't even be aware of that last moment…

I couldn't let that happen. "Snap out of it!" I shouted in my mind. In my head, I heard that crisp snap of my mental fingers.

That was it.

Eyes open, I saw the group, now trancelike and Prime Mover standing tall, as tall as he could. "Now, "I'm going to give you a suggestion, a very pleasant one."

Snap! and Snap! and again Snap! My snapping fingers broke into Prime Mover's hypnotic rhythm. Standing up, I shouted, "At the sound of the snap, you will awake!"

I felt strong hands grabbing at my torso. Not even bothering to look back, I jabbed hard with my elbow, added a flipper kick to the groin, and pivoted to face him. Prime Mover, shocked and in pain, fell back and began cursing me with short takes of breath. People were starting to pull out of the trance. Teva, who came back the fastest, took up an aggressive posture over Prime Mover.

We needed a few minutes to rebalance ourselves and bring order to the room. I checked on my mother who had collapsed along a wall. Rubbing her forehead, she said she was all right and added she couldn't believe what she was hearing. Prime Mover was now sitting on a hard chair, front and center. Thinks Out Loud called for a continuation of the Day of Judgment without referring to what had just happened. "Anyone else?" he simply asked.

One of the Morse brothers, the bearded one, rose slowly and came forward. "My brother and I are sorry about all of this," he said. "We were just trying to enjoy our golden years and provide a little communication help to the Polynesian communities. We probably shouldn't have gotten into the time adjustment realm, but it seemed so innocent when backtiming some of their communications. Forgive us. As for Prime Mover, his idea of a business arrangement is to capture us in the dark of night, bring us against our will to his lair, force feed us those damned candies, and try any means necessary to steal our information." He sat down next to his brother who put an arm over his shoulder.

"I must speak," Teva said. "tallboy, would you watch him?" Teva emanated a glowing kind of energy that made me pull back slightly in my chair, even though I was ten feet from him. "We of Tiaré were brought into this series of events because we were asked to help." He nodded toward Thinks Out Loud and Eddie. "Some of us did not wish to get involved. Our island is so far from this land and its way of life, so far from this man." He indicated Prime Mover. "But the taking of the Morse brothers, and the pleas of Thinks Out Loud and Eddie led us to join in his overthrow. Now that I have seen Prime Mover in action, I have come to understand him. His heart and his head are far, far apart. His heart is buried so deep within him that he cannot touch it. He acts without thought for others. He is his own world, a world without love or joy. I am almost sad for him, except that he causes others so much pain. And that pain would have been so much worse if he had gained control of the powers of the Morse brothers." Teva relieved tallboy and stood over Prime Mover, who was still recovering from my self-defense moves. Now he did look smaller, defeated at last.

Thinks Out Loud clapped and then said with a hint of a smile, "Perhaps I should have snapped my fingers." I noticed that Vaitiare distinctly raised her eyebrows. "Are there any other speakers before we proceed to Judgment?" All was quiet.

With one more look around the room, Thinks Out Loud said, "Very well, let those who find Prime Mover guilty of acts against humanity stand to my left." He paused and then finished with "Those who find Prime Mover not guilty stand to my right."

LABELS: SLIPPERY AS AN EEL, WATCH THE WATCH, SPEAK MEMORY

VIEW COMMENTS (145)

BlueBaby NOV. 26, 2011 AT 10:21 AM

It finally all comes down to this moment. If he is found guilty, will the punishment fit the crime?

Miser NOV. 26, 2011 AT 10:32 AM

I may be in the minority here, but this reeks of Kangaroo Courtism.

Anonymous NOV. 26, 2011 AT 10:40 AM

Saul Bellow often portrayed the Good and The Great in his novels. The Great characters often thought of themselves as above Right and Wrong. Ergo Prime Mover.

JohnsBrain NOV. 26, 2011 AT 10:46 AM

Idea: How about letting the readers vote on PM's fate?

SHOW MORE COMMENTS

○ ○ ○   **THINKS OUT LOUD**   ✕

WHIMSY WITHOUT REGRET

Left and right

Entry No. 654 - POSTED: NOV. 26, 2011

Thinks Out Loud: As if I were a boulder in a river's current, people slid past me on their way to my right or left shore. Choosing to not influence their decision, I stared forward with Prime Mover slouched on a chair just out of my reach. tallboy stood beside him. "I'll vote when everyone is in place," he said to me, even though I had not asked him to wait.

"Hey, that didn't take long. Everyone *is* in place," tallboy said. "My turn." He hopped past me. I took a couple of steps toward Prime Mover, who ignored my proximity. I could now turn to see the results and still have him beside me.

"You have made your decisions," I said to the group. "Prime Mover, stand and regard the Judgment." As defiant as ever, he turned and rose at the same time. On one side stood two Sensates, the Connector and Jeannie.

Everyone else had taken up positions on the other half of the room.

"Let me guess which group is which," scoffed Prime Mover. "Not that you have any right to judge me."

I ignored his comments. My arm indicated the larger body. I could not help noticing tallboy and Angela were holding hands (though not looking at each other). The group was serious, silent. "You find Prime Mover guilty?"

"Yes," they chorused.

"And, you," I turned to the smaller group, "you find Prime Mover innocent?"

"Sort of," said the Connector. The two Sensates simply nodded.

"Not exactly innocent," Jeannie chimed in. "Technically, he is guilty, but I don't feel comfortable in large groups."

"Very well," I said as I turned directly to Prime Mover. He stared back at me with empty, uncaring eyes. It was like looking into a vacuum. Words floated into my mind. "Prime Mover," I intoned, "you have been found guilty of crimes against humanity, including enslavement and kidnapping."

"What are you going to do about it, execute me?" Prime Mover snarled.

I ignored him. "In addition, you were attempting to take advantage of the laws of space and time for your own selfish ends, to even assume control over humanity. It is the judgment of this tribunal that you be physically restricted and no longer able to pose a threat to society, to abjure the rights of others, or interfere with the basic operating elements of the universe."

No one cheered. Prime Mover gave us the finger. As tallboy and Teva approached, he added a mocking smirk, gave them a half salute and an eye wink, grabbed his chair and threw it at them. That gave him a second to dash toward the glass doors leading to the back deck. Teva kicked the chair away but was still ten feet behind the fleeing man. Without a backward glance, Prime Mover did a rather elegant swan dive into Lake Washington. His swimming stroke was uneven, though, as he tried to make headway in what had become choppy water from a rising wind.

The group gathered at the edge of the deck. Standing just beyond the open sliding door, I felt as if I were watching a movie.

"Teva," Vaitiare said.

"Let him drown."

"Teva, please," added Emily.

"This is the last time," Teva groused as he dove off the deck. Within seconds he was within a few feet of Prime Mover, who acted as though he was unaware of his pursuer. For a half dozen strokes Teva matched Prime Mover's pace and direction. Then he grabbed him by the collar and pulled Prime Mover back to us. tallboy and Eddie helped hoist the soggy figure onto the deck. I saw Vaitiare go over to Teva and give him a kiss on the cheek after he pulled himself out of the water.

The others in the group and I returned to the main living room where an impromptu meeting commenced. Everyone was energetically talking at once.

"So, what do we do with him?" Chen asked in a voice louder than the others. "Turn him over to the police?"

"Not recommended," Angela said. "He's wily. You've seen how he can turn things around. He'd make us the guilty ones."

"Actually," I said to the group, some sitting, some standing, "there is an option."

LABELS: JUSTICE, HIGH-TECH SUSPENSE, SWIM SWAM SWUM

VIEW COMMENTS (156)

JoeCurr NOV. 26, 2011 AT 11:19 AM
I was going to be a lawyer but it required too long of a courtship.

WinDough NOV. 26, 2011 AT 11:39 AM
Ya gotta give that Prime Mover some points for perseverance. Hey, it's not too late to visit $howUp and win big!

Toddler NOV. 26, 2011 AT 11:52 AM

Actually, the team is at a moral crossroads.

SHOW MORE COMMENTS

WHIMSY WITHOUT REGRET

Candy time?

Entry No. 655 - POSTED: NOV. 26, 2011

Eddie: We all turned toward Thinks Out Loud to hear his plan. Before he could begin to explain, tallboy and Teva escorted a now defiant Prime Mover back into the living room.

"You are all a bunch of fools," PM said. I searched for Emily and saw her standing beside Kohia, the pair too far away for me to be able to eavesdrop on their conversation.

Jeannie made her way to the front of the room. "Got a short-term solution to keep this guy under control," she said as she held up a bag.

"Now wait a damn minute," Prime Mover practically shrieked when he realized her intent.

Chen shook his head. "I don't think we have the right to administer that kind of treatment." Prime Mover nodded his agreement.

"Why not?" tallboy asked. "It's what he did to us and would again if he had the chance."

Jeannie advanced until she was face-to-face with her adversary, his arms pinned back by Teva. "At least until we figure out what to do with him," she said, looking over to Thinks Out Loud for approval. He gave a subtle nod.

It took tallboy and me to hold Prime Mover's head in position so Jeannie could place the candy in his mouth. I didn't like constraining him, but someone had to. "Time for your medicine, my dear," Jeannie teased.

"Stop!" Emily strode to the center of the room, Kohia backing her up. Jeannie still held the candy at Prime Mover's tightly shut lips. "What are we doing? Aren't we becoming just like him?"

"Do you have another suggestion, Emily?" Angela asked as she came forward.

331

"Drugging him is not the answer. For one thing, he'll never have to deal with his crimes, come to terms with them."

I spoke. I don't know where the words came from, yet I said them. "Ordinarily I would agree, but these are not ordinary circumstances. This man is dangerous, highly dangerous. And tricky. He has never shown anyone else mercy, so why would we expect him to change?" Emily was glaring at me. tallboy and I had released Prime Mover's head, which now hung down like an unsupported stuffed doll's. "It is the only way we can keep Prime Mover from fighting us until we decide how to handle him."

"Do the rest of you agree?" Emily asked. She was near tears. People nodded or said low yeses. Chen remained quiet. "Could you at least give him just half a dose so he doesn't drift totally into oblivion?"

Thinks Out Loud gave another nod, Jeannie snapped the candy apart, and Emily walked out of the room. Even though I didn't agree with her, I felt so much admiration for that woman.

This time Prime Mover didn't resist and took the candy into his mouth without our having to restrain him. "Sweet dreams," he said to himself.

Isaac, Thinks Out Loud, recommended we all take a break and added he wanted to give some thought to a developing idea.

For the remainder of the afternoon, the group mulled around; some people even took naps. Feeling restless, I went for a walk. When I got back, I noticed Emily alone on the deck, her back to the house. My insides turned into a great big knot.

I joined her. "Emily." She didn't respond. "Emily, what you said was right in a way, but the guy is so conniving, he would take advantage of any kindness we show him. That's why we have to do this."

Still gazing out at the lake, she said, "Are we becoming like him?"

"Perhaps we have to become a little like him to keep him under control. He's evil, you know."

Emily said she always thought people, even evil people, could be redeemed in some way. I didn't answer because I didn't know the answer. Finally, I offered, "Maybe someday he could be reached."

She turned her head toward me, and I sank into that melting feeling, my reaction whenever I sensed her combination of softness and firmness.

"Emily," I began.

"Not now," she interrupted.

"But how do you know what I'm going to say?"

"This isn't the time."

I tried to touch her, but she pulled back. "Emily, we've been through so much. Shouldn't that count for something?"

"It does, though it doesn't count for everything. I need to get my life back in order. I may have to drop classes. I've been reprimanded at work, and I don't know if they'll let me come back. Couldn't tell my manager what was going on. She thinks I'm flaky." She kept her eyes on the water. "I need some time."

I didn't like the way this was heading. "Time?"

"Eddie, I think you are fantastic. You know that."

"Are you saying we aren't a couple?"

She almost laughed. "Were we ever a couple? We got thrown into a dangerous situation, and, yes, we helped each other."

I couldn't believe I was hearing all these, all these clichés. I added my own. "So you want to be friends?"

"Yes," she said. "For now." What about James Bond getting the girl in the last scene? Well, at least she had a tear in her eye. Emily turned to go back indoors, and I was left to stare out into the lake. Clouds had moved in, and the water was a smooth sheet of metallic gray. A thought presented itself: Perhaps I wasn't the James Bond character.

I heard the sliding glass door open and turned to see Chen leaning out of the house. "Thinks Out Loud is back. He wants to tell us his idea." With a last look at the gray lake below the gray sky, I retreated inside.

LABELS: MORAL DILEMMAS, RELATIONSHIPS, COURSE OF TRUE LOVE

VIEW COMMENTS (150)

FixTure NOV. 26, 2011 AT 12:31 PM
I'm pulled in all directions. I feel for Eddie. I feel for Emily. I even feel a little something for Prime Mover.

Anonymous NOV. 26, 2011 AT 12:42 PM

Granted the guy is a sleaze ball, but what gives them the right to take the law into their own hands?

AFriend NOV. 26, 2011 AT 12:44 PM

They are not really outside the law. Rather they are dealing with a situation so unique a traditional law environment would likely not be able to parse the complexities of these issues.

SHOW MORE COMMENTS

○ ○ ○   **THINKS OUT LOUD**   ✕

WHIMSY WITHOUT REGRET

Exit plan

Entry No. 656 - POSTED: NOV. 26, 2011

tallboy: When Thinks Out Loud walked in the door, a group of us were clustered before the TV watching the news. Half of us were also working our phones. Chen had called Eddie back in from the deck. He joined, sort of, preferring to stand to the side. What was up with that? It's how he used to act if he didn't get his way when we were growing up.

Anyway, on the news there was a follow-up about the AltaSystemics fire. Standing before the darkened building, the reporter was saying that only the outsides remained, the inner floors having collapsed during the fire. Next to the reporter was a young woman, introduced as the company's Greeter. The reporter asked three questions at once. "Where were you during the fire? Did you see the company president? What did the company actually do?"

"Well," the woman began hesitantly, "there was all this smoke and some explosions. I didn't know what to do. When Prime Mover ran past me—"

"The AltaSystemics CEO?"

"Yes, he ran past me shouting 'Help! Help!' I think he was trying to find a way to help. He turned and went further inside the building like he had forgotten something. I started coughing, so I left my station and retreated out the front door. I think he was looking for employees to save. Prime Mover was that kind of boss. Oh, I'm not at liberty to say anything about the company except that AltaSystemics is your link from a bland today to a better tomorrow."

The reporter thanked her and addressed the camera. "Is the body of this Prime Mover buried deep under the rubble of the building's collapsed floors never to be exhumed or blown apart in one of the internal explosions? Investigators would like to sift through the debris in search of some answers, but the remaining outer walls are still a potential hazard. This is Eileen Cody, KOMO News at 6." Looks like I won't be blogging for AltaSystemics anymore, I thought.

Emily turned off the TV and greeted Thinks Out Loud who joined her.

"Friends," he said, "I'd like to propose a plan of action that includes what we can do with Prime Mover. I went down to the harbor and consulted with Hank, the first mate of the Bogsworth. He said we are welcome to sail with him back to Polynesia. And that we can take Prime Mover with us." Thinks Out Loud presented the information without fanfare or drama as though this was simply the best option. No one said anything, but I couldn't tell if that meant approval or rejection. "As for his punishment, I propose he be banished to Fénua, the uninhabited sacred island I landed on after the storm. It was there I began my own form of regeneration. Perhaps the experience would lead to similar results in Prime Mover." Thinks Out Loud went into more detail about providing periodic food and support shipments and keeping tabs on Prime Mover.

Jeannie blurted out, "Well, then, I'm coming too. Someone's gotta make sure Prime Mover takes his medicine during the voyage." Entertaining himself by watching his own moving fingers, the former CEO sat cross-legged near a wall, Teva poised over him.

"If you wish," Thinks Out Loud answered.

Emily looked misty eyed. "You know where I stand on this issue."

TOL acknowledged her statement with a brief nod and surveyed the rest of us. "Then for those of us departing, this is our last evening here. We leave in the morning." He went over to Emily's mom and spoke quietly with her.

LABELS: RETRIBUTION, PUNISHMENT FITS THE CRIME

VIEW COMMENTS (156)

Explica NOV. 26, 2011 AT 5:48 PM
So, in other words, Isaac, you're off for a cruise after that madman tried to take over the world. Actually, I just want to say thanks.

Hummer NOV. 26, 2011 AT 6:34 PM

As the fellow once said, "It ain't over til it's over." And even then, it may not be really over.

SHOW MORE COMMENTS

Winding down

Entry No. 657 - POSTED: NOV. 26, 2011

Emily: Is this how it ends? People packing, hanging out in small groups or by themselves, taking walks. In a sense we may have saved the world, but our celebration is a muted one. We did a rather forced toast and had pizza for dinner. Enjoyed some Washington reds from my generous mother. Maybe that's the way it should be. No one would believe us anyway.

As I drifted through the house, I encountered all these little scenes. The Sensates were huddled together, except for Patricia, the one who testified. She was actually talking to my mom. Teva and Vaitiare were in close conversation in the living room. The Morse brothers were visiting with Jeannie, who was keeping an eye on the sedated Prime Mover. I'm not sure where Eddie had gone off to.

Thinks Out Loud was writing out on the deck. He seemed the calmest, although he kept looking in the direction of Teva and Vaitiare from time to time.

Kohia found me in the kitchen eating crackers and hummus. I think she could tell I needed company. She asked some questions about life in Seattle and U-Dub. She seems to be naturally curious. I wish I could have been friendlier, but I felt so enervated.

We were all asleep by eleven.

LABELS: POST-TRIAL SYNDROME, LEST YE BE JUDGED

VIEW COMMENTS (153)

Krishnaman NOV. 26, 2011 AT 11:48 PM

Emily, your outer and inner selves are aligned.

The Good Doctor NOV. 26, 2011 AT 11:54 PM

Get some rest, all of you.

SHOW MORE COMMENTS

○ ○ ○   THINKS OUT LOUD   X

WHIMSY WITHOUT REGRET

Morning

Entry No. 658 - POSTED: NOV. 27, 2011

Thinks Out Loud: A final posting for old times' sake.

Morning of our departure day. People stirred and stretched and slowly came to life. Emily's mom had already been out and had returned with bagels, cream cheese, and coffee. She said she wanted us to get a good start on our voyage. As for the travelers, I didn't have an exact count. There were Teva, Vaitiare, Kohia, and myself. The unpredictable Jeannie also wanted to join us. Add Prime Mover and the Connector, who would be under our guard. And of course the Morse brothers.

We placed our luggage by the door. I was surprised to see Eddie put his duffel bag next to ours. "Eddie," I asked, "are you coming?" Others stopped to see what he would say.

"Yes, if you'll put up with me."

I heard a sharp intake of breath. Emily.

"And what will you do on Tiaré?" she asked.

"Not exactly Tiaré. I have a business opportunity on Tahiti. A new way to do deep sea salvage."

Emily shook her head. "What about college? You can't stop midway."

"I'll finish up via independent study and online courses."

"Right," she said, her tone unsupportive. Eddie took an aggressive bite of his bagel. Out of the corner of my eye, I saw Teva and Vaitiare practically nuzzling each other. When she kissed him on the cheek, I looked away.

In another surprise move that wasn't such a surprise move, the Sensates came forward and began saying goodbye. Robed in white with hoods, they looked the part of monks. So it made sense when they said they were headed for the Bodhiheart Sangha Center. One of them displayed a phone showing the Center's home page. I found a certain appeal in the idea of mindfulness meditation. Interestingly, it had been two days since they had stopped taking the drug candy, but I couldn't really see any change in their ethereal demeanor.

One Sensate separated from her group. "I'd like to come with you," said Patricia, as she lowered her hood. Her direct eye contact and the way she centered herself reminded me of Teva. "I feel the call of Tiaré."

"Are you certain you wish to live on the island? It's a very different way of life," I said.

She paused as if for effect and said, "Exactly."

Emily offered to drive the Sensates to the Center on Capitol Hill. They bowed, said thank you, and explained that they would rather walk. "A chance to breathe through movement," one said. With another bow to Patricia, they moved single file up the driveway and into the morning, a wedge of blue sky breaking through the gray.

"Want to go with them?" Angela asked as she walked up to me.

"There are many ways to meditate," I snapped and immediately regretted the tone of my reply. That was not like me, and Angela certainly didn't deserve that kind of response.

I was about to call a taxi, a van, to take us to the port, when a yellow Prius pulled up.

"This is the moment," Teva said, although I didn't know how we would fit all of us into the compact car. Then he added, "I must be on my way," and for the first time since I had known him, this master of control and rootedness, lowered his eyes as he passed me and picked up his travel case.

"Teva, now where are you going?" I actually stammered.

"A private mission," he said almost under his breath. I felt Vaitiare brush up against me. Her mood was lighter, her face relaxed. I told Teva I did not understand. Would he meet us at the boat? He answered no, that he would next be with us on Tiaré. "Thinks Out Loud, *hoa*, my friend, may you swim like the dolphin, fly like the gull, and be as fertile as the coconut tree," Teva said quickly, and with that he jumped into the cab and was gone.

At the door, Vaitiare gave him a warm wave. I had followed her. "You know where he is going, don't you?"

She ran a finger down my cheek. "I am pledged not to say." She went back into the house. Remaining at the threshold of the door, I wondered who else had plans contrary to my expectations.

LABELS:

VIEW COMMENTS (158)

Gobbler NOV. 27, 2011 AT 8:06 AM
They really weren't a team for very long. I don't get all this hard-to-say goodbye stuff. Go over to my blog, CatchingUp, for real nostalgia and looking back to TVs with cathode tubes, dial phones, and transistor radios.

VincentFrederick NOV. 27, 2011 AT 8:39 AM
Length of time does not necessarily indicate depth of connection. These people have been through a lot together and that's what counts.

SpecMan NOV. 27, 2011 AT 8:39 AM
That Teva, always full of surprises.

SHOW MORE COMMENTS

○ ○ ○   **THINKS OUT LOUD**   ✕

WHIMSY WITHOUT REGRET

Goodbye time

Entry No. 659 - POSTED: NOV. 27, 2011

tallboy: Angela and I also decided we would drive over to campus. She keeps asking me to tell her my real name, and I keep saying it's tallboy. I think she likes me. I mean she even laughs at my jokes.

All through the house, the remaining folk were readying for departure. It was quiet, like we were involved in some kind of ritual.

Before leaving, I found Eddie at the back deck. "So, looks like you're going," I said.

"Don't try and talk me out of it." He stared out at the lake.

"Wouldn't think of it. Should I tell the parents?"

"Already did. Sent them a text. They texted back they're on the Love

Boat cruise to Puerta Vallarta."

That didn't surprise me. "Eddie," I said, "I know we haven't seen as much of each other these past several years or the past ten years."

"You're nine years older," he answered.

"Right, but what I'm trying to say is that all this Prime Mover business brought us closer together, didn't it?"

He cracked a smile. "Well, I did help you to break your candy habit."

There was one more item I wanted to mention. "Are you and Emily okay?"

At first he didn't answer. "Sure, we're okay."

I didn't say anything, but I kept my gaze constant on him.

His words came slowly. "It seems Emily and I have broken up. At least she did."

Not having any worthwhile brotherly advice, I let the topic drop. "Eddie, stay in touch, no matter where you end up." He asked me what I was going to do now that I was unemployed again.

"Not sure. I'm thinking about game development. Got an idea for a high-tech suspense video game with some sci-fi flourishes."

"Plus getting to know Angela."

We gave each other a brotherly hug, then a stronger hug, and I added a slap on the back. Angela was waiting for me at the glass sliding door. She had tears in her eyes. I took her hand, and we walked through the living room and said goodbyes. There were hugs all around.

Hey, I guess this is my last posting in Thinks Out Loud.

Angela, if you read this one…it's Stephen.

LABELS:

VIEW COMMENTS (165)

Dolfan NOV. 27, 2011 AT 9:22 AM
Well, I don't know about you, but I am getting misty! (And I'm not acting.) Plus, I got the supporting role of Cléante in Taproot's upcoming Tartuffe!

JourneyMan NOV. 27, 2011 AT 9:39 AM
In my humble opinion, they each have their own paths to follow, their own destinies. . .some with a bit of overlap.

SHOW MORE COMMENTS

○ ○ ○ **THINKS OUT LOUD** ✕

WHIMSY WITHOUT REGRET

Land's end

Entry No. 660 - POSTED: NOV. 27, 2011

Emily: I did a quick head count of our travelers—Thinks Out Loud, Vaitiare, a very quiet Kohia, the two Morse brothers, Jeannie, Prime Mover, the Sensate, and an equally quiet Eddie. Plus, we still had the Connector, who because of limited prospects, had agreed to join the crew of the freighter. Definitely more people than could fit in the Range Rover, so I had asked my mother to call another taxi, preferably a van. We were moving in all directions. People were thanking my mom for everything she'd done. Dressed designer casual including a colorful bracelet from Guatemala, she led us outdoors to the car. With me came TOL, Vaitiare, Prime Mover, and Jeannie. That left the others for the taxi. Chen was also coming along to say goodbye. Faster than I expected, the taxi in the form of a van showed up while we were putting bags in the Rover. With my mother standing at her front door and waving, we backed out of the driveway, our next stop the Bogsworth.

"I don't have a passport," Jeannie said leaning forward from the back seat. "I mean I have one somewhere but not with me." Next to her, Prime Mover watched the passing scenery as though he were already on his way.

"Just tell the consulate in Tahiti that you lost it," I suggested.

"Emily," she answered sitting back, "I didn't know you could be so crafty."

"Our country is less concerned with our leaving and more with our arrival," Thinks Out Loud said.

We worked our way over to commercial Aurora and then headed south toward the downtown waterfront. The industrial feeling shipping area was just beyond the matching football and baseball stadiums in SoDo.

"I just got a text message from Chen in the taxi," Jeannie interrupted. "He thinks we're being followed."

I glanced in the rearview mirror and saw the van behind a car behind us and a line of cars behind the taxi. "Hard to tell," I said. "It's mostly a lot of traffic headed to the Bainbridge Island ferry."

At Alaska Way, we made our left toward the port. So did the taxi. All the other cars went right, except for a dark limo, which came our way. That didn't prove they were following us, but I did feel my stomach tighten.

"Take the next exit, right, and follow the signs to Container Terminal, Pier 34," said Thinks Out Loud. I turned and the taxi followed. The limo kept going. Good.

Before us stood gigantic giraffe-like cranes. We passed rows of storage containers the size of tractor trailers. And we reached a gated entrance.

The guard motioned for me to drive up to his window. "If you're booked for the cruise lines, they're due north at Magnolia Bluffs."

I thanked him but said we were actually looking for the steamer Bogsworth. Some of us were sailing on the ship.

"Let me check the cargo manifest," he said. He was burly and thick necked and spoke as if he had a cigar in his mouth. "I don't see you listed."

"Excuse me, sir," Thinks Out Loud said as he leaned toward my side of the car, "we are not actually cargo. We are traveling on the Bogsworth as part of an ecology team. They are providing us passage to islands cruise lines don't visit. Check with the captain to confirm."

He called a number and asked about us. "Uh huh. I see. Yes." Hanging up, he closed his registry, looked us over one last time, and waved us through. "Ecology team," he said smoking his invisible cigar.

"I didn't actually lie," Thinks Out Loud said as if he had read our thoughts. "It is the essence of what we are doing."

After passing more rows of huge metal containers atop containers, we received an open view of the Emerald City downtown paralleling the waterfront to our right. Rising before us, the Bogsworth. It wasn't the newest of ships. And only a third the size of the cruise boats. It had a dark reddish hull and a single smokestack. Men both onshore and on the ship were moving equipment and crates around. They glanced at us as we approached and stopped at the wharf's edge.

"Mates!" It was Hank who chugged down the loose looking gangplank to meet us.

We exited the car and Thinks Out Loud shook his hand. "We're here," he said, "and we've brought a friend." He indicated Prime Mover. "Oh, the other car has another ex-employee looking for work at sea."

"The more the merrier," said Hank. "Jackson, Bert, Felix, come help with their gear." Three muscled men jogged down the gangplank and began to pick up the luggage.

The taxi had stopped right behind me. Eddie and the others joined us.

"Are all of you coming?" Hank asked. I said Chen and I were here to see everyone else off. Down the gangplank walked a bearded man dressed in the whitest, best pressed uniform I'd ever seen. Hank introduced him as the captain. I didn't catch the name.

But Eddie went from a wide-eyed look to a broad smile. "Edward," said the captain, "we meet again."

"Captain Kuborn," Eddie managed to say. He clasped the man's hand and spoke to the rest of us. "Captain Kuborn is, I mean, was the captain of the boat that travels between the islands." He turned back to the captain who looked at him with mild amusement.

"The Bogsworth's captain took ill as the freighter approached Hawaii, so here I am. The company flew me to Honolulu. Welcome aboard everyone." More of the crew were looking down from the deck. How many of them were former Connectors?

My friends and our guests were about to walk up the gangplank when the squeal of tires and screech of brakes caused us to turn toward the noise. Zooming up next to my car was the limo and before it stopped, men in dark suits were flinging open doors and jumping out. They were armed and shouting for no one to move. My group froze. Captain Kuborn made a slight nod to his crew, some of whom eased back into the shadows of the ship. This wasn't their fight. The invaders were focused on our party.

"We want Prime Mover!" shouted one of the men. I couldn't place the accent. "Now."

"Of course," said Thinks Out Loud with a tone of authority that surprised me. "Mind if I ask why?" How could he maintain such composure?

"We represent a group of investors in AltaSystemics. We want to discuss certain downturns in the portfolio."

Without waiting for his fare, the taxi driver sped off.

Thinks Out Loud nodded as though the information was significant and worth thinking about. "That's the problem with start-ups," he said shifting to a more conversational tone. "Most don't return on investment." He had assumed an entirely different persona. Did he have some improv in his past?

"Shut up," said a second man in a voice heavy with raw meanness. "Give him to us." With his gun, he pointed toward Prime Mover.

Thinks Out Loud nodded again and came forward a half step.

"Don't move!" the first man shouted. Thinks Out Loud stopped.

"Teva would take them out," Jeannie whispered.

"So, you want Prime Mover. Thing is, he's just a shell of his former self. Look." Thinks Out Loud pointed to a limp PM, who was being supported by Chen. The dark-suited men showed no sympathy.

From the deck, a dozen crew, tactically in two groups, rose up, assault rifles in hand.

Thinks Out Loud indicated their presence. "You gentlemen really should think this through."

In answer they pointed their weapons first at the crew then at us and then back at the deck.

"Shoot us and they shoot you. Try to shoot them and some of them will still shoot you. Drop your guns," said Thinks Out Loud.

No one on either side moved. Seagulls hovered above the scene. A lone buoy's bell tolled with the rise and fall of the water. With a reluctant sign from their leader, the men in suits dropped their weapons. I hadn't realized I'd been holding my breath the entire time. Captain Kuborn motioned for some of his crew to retrieve the guns and surround them.

"Please leave," said Thinks Out Loud. "I'm sorry for your losses. Use it as a tax write off."

The crew members backed the men into the limo and stood near the car like guards until it rolled away from the wharf.

"Did you get the license?" Captain Kuborn asked.

"Yes, sir," said one of the crew.

"Good. You know what to do."

"Aye, sir." He ran up the gangplank.

"Very clever," I thought.

LABELS:

VIEW COMMENTS (166)

FisherKing NOV. 27, 2011 AT 12:22 PM
Wow.

Ringside NOV. 27, 2011 AT 1:09 PM
Hey, they actually protected Prime Mover.

SHOW MORE COMMENTS

○ ○ ○   **THINKS OUT LOUD**   ✕

WHIMSY WITHOUT REGRET

Farewells

Entry No. 661 - POSTED: NOV. 27, 2011

Eddie: As we gathered near the gangplank, Jeannie leaned over to me. "All of us: grace under pressure," she said.

"Sort of," I answered. "More like how to sweat off five pounds in five minutes. Now the Morse brothers, they don't scare easy." The two elders were chatting with the captain and looking as if they'd just spent the past hour strolling the beach.

Gazing past Jeannie, I noted Kohia stood close to the car. I walked over to her. She was dressed in Western clothes now—a blouse and jeans, and she looked like she could be a student.

"Big trip ahead for us," I said.

She didn't answer. Instead, her mouth began to quiver, and then she regained her composure and brought her dark eyes up to mine. "I've decided to stay," she said simply.

Kohia read the confusion in my expression. "Eddie, the thought of not returning to Tiaré pains me. My heart and head have been twisting around each other, but I have decided. I am staying. And I plan to attend the University. Remember when we were pretending I was a student? I do not want to pretend. I really am interested in understanding the role of women in today's Polynesia, in Women's Studies."

She gave me a light kiss on the cheek. "Thank you for saving the brothers Morse and spending time with me." I almost felt like her brother.

We parted. Retreating, I ran my hand along the rusty metal rail at the edge of the pier. I'd miss her presence.

All the more reason to lose myself in that salvaging job.

Chen was nodding his head and waving to the ship when I went over and gave him a quick self-conscious hug. "Good work," I said.

A deep blast of the Bogsworth's horn signaled it was time to sail. Those of us departing continued hugging those who were staying. One more goodbye remained. When I got to Emily, she pressed herself against me, I inhaled her body's scent a last time, and I whispered, "Bye. For now."

"Take care of yourself," she said more evenly than I would have expected. But she did reward me with a smile, and her trademark teeth biting of her lower lip. "Bye. For now."

Jeannie was already on board with the half-awake Prime Mover. Two crew members were welcoming the Connector to "his new job." The Sensate was taking slow, deep breaths. On the wharf, Kohia and Vaitiare were speaking in Tahitian and holding hands. I could almost feel emotional waves rising from them before Vaitiare pulled away and came on board. For once she didn't look regal, more like she was parting from a sister.

Only Thinks Out Loud remained ashore. Was he having second thoughts? Vaitiare noticed his position and gave him an eagle's stare. Unaware of us, TOL was thanking Emily, wishing Chen well and saying something to Kohia about "many paths, one journey."

Following a second blast of the ship's horn, Thinks Out Loud strode up the gangplank and joined us on the deck. Unlike passengers on a cruise ship with its festive goodbye ceremonies, ours was a downplayed departure. We heard Captain Kuborn issue the orders for "Cast off main lines," and the engines in the bowels of the ship went from a low hum to a livelier churn. Ever so slowly the Bogsworth eased away from the pier. Standing beside the car, Emily, Chen, and Kohia continued to wave as we pulled back from shore and into the deeper waters of Elliot Bay.

Hank appeared and asked if anyone wanted a tour. Jeannie and the Morse brothers enthusiastically said "yes!" The remainder of us continued to watch from the deck.

Thinks Out Loud caught me staring down into the mesmerizing deep green water. Did he think I was considering diving in and swimming back to her? I returned his look and shook my head to indicate it was just a passing thought. Our friends had gotten back in their car, which slowly moved away as well. The Bogsworth made a sweeping turn that gave us a glorious view of the Seattle emerald skyline tinted by the afternoon's remarkably bright sun. I had moved a few rungs up an outside ladder for a better view when I noticed Vaitiare approach Thinks Out Loud as he stood by the rail. Against his shoulder, she rested her head.

LABELS:

COMMENTS SECTION CLOSED

○ ○ ○   **THINKS OUT LOUD**   ✕

WHIMSY WITHOUT REGRET

Entry No. 662 - POSTED: NOV. 27, 2011

Thinks Out Loud:

Loyal Readers,

I asked them, the brothers, if they would send a message back one last time for a first time. I had to cajole and wheedle and offer a box of the finest dark chocolates (with absolutely no hard candy shell), and finally they agreed to one last/first time.

This gives me the chance to speak to you directly and to offer not exactly a warning but at least a cautionary note as you venture deeper into this blog: Keep all your senses on alert, maintain a healthy skepticism mixed with a touch of faith, and be willing to open your mind and your heart to what may seem like unrealities beyond our common world.

That's more than enough for now, or as Teva would say, "The fish do not wait."

Thinks Out Loud:

Dear Readers,

The sea voyage from Seattle to Tiaré was relatively calm. Thankfully, no typhoon induced a repeat of my previous experience on the ship. Twice, we found Prime Mover sleepwalking in precarious locations by the ship's railing. We increased his candy dosage before bedtime. Even in his daze, he actually led the crew in some improv practice every other day. Three Word, Freeze Tag, Props (in this case mostly steamer items).

Teva was there to meet us when our ship anchored just offshore. With him stood a blonde woman, tall and watchful. His fiancé. Teva had returned to Pennsylvania to the Amish village where he'd lived a few years ago. There he rekindled a romance with Ruth. Love breaks boundaries. Although her dancing is more restrained than that of the islanders, she is adapting to life in the South Seas and has become like a sister to Vaitiare.

Eddie went to work for the diving company in Tahiti only to get laid off when they were bought out by a Korean subsidiary of Samsung. He's been invited to stay on Tiaré and is still making up his mind whether to join us. He also talks about getting his degree online from a New Zealand university.

He is aware Emily and her mother are coming for a visit next month. Kohia remains in school at the University of Washington and is vice president of the Pacific Islanders Student Association.

Patricia, the Sensate who came with us, lives in the village on the other side of the island and is something of a tribal mystic.

Vaea, my friend, has also been my teacher in the ways and customs of his people. In turn, I taught him (and his two sons) how to throw a Frisbee, which they do with great skill and accuracy.

I am now the island's storyteller. (I'm learning more Tahitian each day. *Ia orana i te matahiti api.* Happy New Year.)

Prime Mover has been isolated on Fénua, as had been our plan. During that time, he has lived a simple life, minus the candies, and, we hoped, has been looking inward and outward. We check on him monthly to make sure he was surviving. Last week we convened and discussed whether to have him transition over to Tiaré. We bring him here next week for a trial run, so to speak. Interestingly, he said he would like to teach improv to the islanders. And he wants to go by his given name—Art. Is he still the wily and treacherous character we knew? We'll find out.

Jeannie said she would keep a watchful eye on him. She has also been getting to know some of the local boys. Plus, taking drumming lessons. Claims she is doing research for her master's sociology thesis.

Now living in a location I cannot disclose, the Morse brothers have said no to more time travel. They did apply their knowledge by helping to organize the last batch of postings during the final confrontation with Prime Mover including, just for fun and to mix things up a bit, adding in an early posting about the new restaurant on the space station, originally Jeannie's idea. Recently, they've said something about doing casual research into gravitational vortexes. Hmmm.

The people of Tiaré from both villages held meetings to discuss how much contact they should have with off-islanders. They still say no to cruise lines, Hollywood execs and bottled water entrepreneurs lusting after the island's springs. They did approve the visit of eco-tourists in small numbers and for limited amounts of time. I'm helping with the marketing materials. *Come to Tiaré; leave your smart phone at home. Tiaré, the Real World.* Also helping to organize the eco-tourism program are tallboy and Angela, still an item, who came to the island last month.

Chen, who supplied us with candies for Prime Mover during his first weeks here, says he has a boyfriend: It's the History of High-tech professor, who wanted to wait until the class was finished before showing an interest. (Prof. Stevens also gave the team members in his class extra credit for what he called 'imaginative technological extrapolations.')

Vaitiare. On a wide bluff overlooking the Pacific, the princess and I married in a traditional Polynesian ceremony three months after we returned to Tiaré. (We did add the Jewish custom of the breaking of the wine glass.) She remains as proud as ever, although I suspect upcoming motherhood might soften her a bit. And I mean that in a good way. Kind of a warmer regalness. (Am I being patriarchal?)

Eddie has told me readers of Thinks Out Loud have been asking about the posting that never got sent because the Morse brothers were kidnapped. Chief Keoni was about to announce the results of the judgment, remember?

Here is that lost posting:

Losing the vote?

With a nod toward me, the Chief repeated the vote had been taken, the islanders had spoken, and (he paused, perhaps for dramatic effect) the "leave-the-island" votes had attained a majority of one. I wanted to ask if I got a vote but held back. To my surprise Teva stood with the "stay" group massed away from the beach, and to my disappointment, Vaitiare stood among the "leave" group near the water.

"Chief, don't you get a vote?" I asked.

"Yes, I do." He moved inland.

A tie.

Much lively discussion ensued among the islanders, and I began to feel a bit uncomfortable. Look at the tumult I was causing. With a loud handclap it was Vaitiare who gained the people's attention, and once there was silence she walked to a midpoint between the two groups and spoke in a calm yet determined manner. Appearing at my side, Kohia translated. Vaitiare said perhaps there was a middle way. Rather than immediately being sent off the island (or being fully accepted), she proposed I go on a vision quest to discover my purpose. The Chief, Vaea, Teva, and all the islanders turned towards me. All were silent. A vision quest. What did I know about vision quests? Maybe if I approached it like I was playing a video game. That could be fun! Except video games don't *really* matter. I had a feeling that a vision quest mattered quite a lot.

"I'll do it," I said. The islanders' response was not a shout nor a cheer but more a group grunt, neither affirmative nor negative. More a "let's see what happens" murmer.

Kohia filled me in on the process: I would be given provisions, including some special vision-aid potions, and led by Vaea to the cave where I would sit alone for however long it would take to have my vision.

"What kind of vision?" I asked. "This is new territory for me."

"Look inward," said Kohia. "The gull knows when it is time to soar."

There you have it.

The other day I mentioned to tallboy about when he was first blogging on Thinks Out Loud how great it was the way he had stepped in to block Jeannie's meandering postings.

"Me?" tallboy answered as he savored a bite of fresh coconut. "I thought you were the one who kicked her off."

I denied having anything to do with such editorial decisions. "Didn't even know it was happening at the time," I said. "I was busy with other matters."

"If you didn't cut her off, and I didn't either, then who did?" asked tallboy.

Good question, I thought. Good question.

Martin Perlman

ABOUT THE AUTHOR

Born and raised in Atlanta, Georgia, Martin Perlman has spent his adult life out West in California, Colorado, and Washington. Influences on his psyche include repeated viewings of *Rocky and Bullwinkle*, repeated listenings to Tom Lehrer and Firesign Theatre, and repeated readings of the collected works of James Thurber, J. G. Ballard, and Flann O'Brien (Brian O'Nolan).

In an age of specialists, he considers himself to be one of the last of the generalists.

Along the Way, he has been a pipe and tobacco salesclerk, a ski lift operator, a dishwasher at an Italian vegetarian restaurant, a bay leaf harvester, bookstore clerk, freshman English instructor, proofreader and stock boy for an independent publisher, harmonica player for a rock band, the only dues-paying member of an improv group, freelance writer, staffer for a weekly news and entertainment magazine, short story and humor writer, a director of communications at a health foundation, and a communications specialist at a university. (And, until funding ran out, a web content writer for a high-tech start-up that floundered during the dot com-collapse.)

He lives in Seattle, Washington, with his wife, Lane, and daughter, Lila.

Thinks Out Loud is his debut novel.

CPSIA information can be obtained
at www.ICGtesting.com
Printed in the USA
LVHW01s0209030818
585752LV00005B/1091/P

9 780997 503906